POMME DE TERRE

By the same author:

ABERCROMBIE TRAIL

POMME DE TERRE

Candace Simar

NORTH STAR PRESS OF ST. CLOUD, INC.
St. Cloud, Minnesota

Dedicated to the memory of
Clyde Jensen
Thanks Dad
for teaching me to love history

First Edition, June 1, 2010

Printed in the United States of America

Published by
North Star Press of St. Cloud, Inc.
P.O. Box 451
St. Cloud, Minnesota 56302

www.northstarpress.com

Acknowledgements

Assistance from the Minnesota Family History Center in St. Paul, the Otter Tail County Historical Museum, the Grant County Historical Museum, Fort Abercrombie Historic Site and Museum, Fort Snelling Historic Site, and a Five Wings Art Grant made this book possible.

The headlines at the beginning of each chapter were found in archived Minnesota newspapers from various towns around the state. In an effort to provide a cohesive story line, they are attributed to *The St. Cloud Democrat*, a fictional newspaper.

I gratefully acknowledge the generous help, insight and critique received from Diana Ossana and Larry McMurtry. Workshops with Sands Hall, Robert Olen Butler, Josh Kendall, Diana Ossana, Bret Anthony Johnston, and Lisa Tucker were invaluable in the creation and revision of *Pomme de Terre*. Many thanks to early readers and editors: Angela Foster, Charmaine and Jim Donovan, and North Star Press. Most of all, thanks to my husband, Keith, for ongoing help and support.

Foreword

THE YEAR 1862 WAS A TUMULTUOUS ONE in Minnesota history. The youngest state in the Union, Minnesota was one of the first to send men to fight in the Civil War. With the men gone, women and children were left to fend for themselves. The Civil War drained soldiers formerly stationed in Minnesota military outposts leaving the state undermanned and unprotected. Budget woes related to war expenses caused payments promised to the Sioux by treaty to be very late. Indian Agents at the Lower Sioux Agency refused to hand out needed supplies until the gold arrived. The Sioux were starving.

The result was the Sioux Uprising of 1862, the largest Indian war in United States' history. Because it happened between the bloody battles of Shiloh and Antietam, the uprising went mostly unremarked. However, its effects on Minnesota and the Sioux Nation still reverberate today.

My historical novel, *Abercrombie Trail*, tells the story of Scandinavian immigrants caught up in culture clash and broken treaties that led to the uprising. Although the government declared the uprising over in the fall of 1862, *Pomme de Terre* tells the story of settlers living in the western part of the state where raids continued through the following year.

Thank you for taking the time to read this important story. I hope you enjoy it.

Candace Simar

Dakota Territory

Wisconsin

Iowa

Crow Wing River

Mississippi River

Minnesota River

Fort Abercrombie
Foxhome
Dayton
Alexandria
Woods
Pomme
de Terre
Sauk
Centre
St. Cloud
Pig's
Eye
Hutchinson
Upper Agency
Birch Coulee
Fort Snelling
Lower Agency
Fort Ridgely
New Ulm
Mankato
Burr Landing

Rick Jaskowiak

1

"Union Forces Routed by Rebs at Bull Run"
St. Cloud Democrat, July 22, 1861

IT WAS ONLY A PIECE OF STRING.

At first glance Serena Brandvold thought her mother was joking. One look at her face proved she was serious, indeed deadly serious. Mor, Mother, pressed the length of string into Serena's hands—about two feet long, stout and ordinary.

"When a baby is born," Mor said, "use clean string to tie the cord in two places. Not too far apart, mind you. Knot it as tight as you can." She leaned over and plucked a thread off Serena's *bunad,* the traditional Norwegian dress worn only on special occasions. "Don't worry, it won't hurt. There's no feeling in the cord."

A quick worry filled Serena's chest. Surely she wouldn't have to deliver babies in far-off Minnesota. Here in Burr Oak, Iowa, Mor and Auntie Karen were always helping women birth babies. No one would expect her to deliver babies, would they?

"Then you take a sharp knife and cut between the knots." Mor's face strained and Serena noticed the thrust of her chin, a sure sign she was fighting back tears. "Keep the baby on your chest until the cord is cut."

Serena blushed deep red to the roots of her hair. Mor was talking about babies, hers and Gust's. She would be a *kjerring,* a married woman, and needed to know such things.

Serena remembered the recent birth of Bossy's calf, the smell of blood, the tearing of flesh, and the bellowing heifer. Her voice trembled. "And the afterbirth?"

"Put the baby to breast after the cord is cut. The afterbirth comes by itself. Don't let anyone be so foolish as to pull on the cord to hurry it. It will come as the baby suckles." Mor was all business now. She poked the needle into the pincushion, the black thread hanging from its eye. "And if it happens when the ground isn't froze solid, bury the afterbirth in the garden." Her face relaxed into a smile. "Auntie Gunda always said it made the potatoes grow extra large."

"Auntie Gunda!" Serena said. "I haven't thought of her for years."

"And knead your belly." Mor's face took on that worried look again and her chin went up. "If the afterbirth doesn't come, knead your belly and keep doing it until it comes. Check the sun and keep track of the time. Don't let anyone pull on the cord unless several hours have passed and it hasn't come yet."

Serena's mind whirled. How could she remember everything? Maybe she should be writing things down.

"And keep kneading your belly every once in a while for the first few days after the birth."

"What do you mean?" Was her mother speaking in a foreign language.

"You rub deep and hard," Mor said. "Right over the lower part. It'll hurt, hurt like the blazes. But don't let that scare you." Mor had a fierce look in her eyes, a look that scared Serena, made her look away. "By that time the worst is over." Mor took the pincushion to the shelf in the corner of the small bedroom. "It staunches the blood."

"Will there be a lot of blood?" Serena's voice was very small, almost childlike. She felt like she was five years old again and caught with her finger in the honey pot. She laughed and heard how it sounded like Gust's laugh, almost too loud, forced.

"It's bleeding that kills women in childbed." Mor's face was unreadable except for the up-tilted chin. "You rub your belly deep and don't mind the hurting. It'll stop the blood."

"What else?"

"Just remember what I say. Don't forget."

"I'll keep the string safe." Serena steadied her voice and carefully placed the string into her reticule that lay on top of the ancient trunk that housed her belongings. "And I'll remember not to pull the cord."

Another hour and she would be Mrs. Gustaf Gustafson. Nothing would spoil her wedding day. She twirled around until the *dossa*, the full skirt, of the *bunad* flared around her. A rusty stain on the white blouse refused to come out but it was still beautiful. Serena donned the *hogehue* hat, and beaded belt.

"It's handsome," Serena said as her mother adjusted the belt. "The *hjerterose* embroidery is exquisite, every stitch to perfection."

"Ja," said her mother. "It's been in the family for generations. Today I give it to you as my mor gave it to me on my wedding day. My father was only a cotter. They had nothing to give except their love and this *bunad*."

"Mor!" Serena gasped a quick inward breath. It was her mother's prize possession. She always knew she would wear it on her wedding day but never thought she might keep it. Serena visualized the map showing the great distance to Norway, east across the wide ocean to the country shaped like a ragged teardrop. "It's too much. It's all you have of your family."

"Nei," Mor said. "You will take it with you to Minnesota and wear it in honor of all those who wore it before you. You'll wear it at the baptisms of your children and on feast days. It brings good luck and a blessing." Mor straightened up and rubbed the kink out of her back. "It will do."

"*Tussen takk!* A thousand thanks! I'll take good care of it." Serena smoothed the wrinkles in the skirt for the last time before leaving for the church. "It will be like taking a bit of you with me."

"Someday your daughter will wear it." Her mother reached up and wiped her eyes with the back of her hand. "I'm sorry, Serena. I promised myself there would be no tears on this happy day."

"I'll name my first daughter after you." Serena grabbed her mother around the neck and hugged her hard. "Lena Christine will be her name."

"I hope I'll live to see her." Mor stepped back a full step, away from Serena. "You'll be so far away."

Serena thought of the map showing Iowa, the long journey north to Hutchinson, Minnesota, where Gust had rented a farm.

"It doesn't have to be forever, you know." Mor picked up her knitting and eased down on the chair. Serena had never known her to be idle, and she watched the calloused, rough hands as they knitted and purled. "Come back if it doesn't work out." Mor set the needles in her lap and looked up at Serena. "You and Gust could build a cabin on the back forty and work this place with your far." Mor picked up the needles again and purled in earnest.

"We'll do that," Serena said. "I'll make Gust promise to come back if things go sour."

"Your far isn't getting any younger. He could use the help."

"I'll write every month." Serena pulled a handkerchief from her pocket and blew her nose. "I'll never miss. I promise before God."

"You needn't be so dramatic," Mor said. "Just write me, and I'll write you. Nothing short of death will stop the letters from me."

2

"Reason for Union defeat is poor generalship;
North delayed Attack too Long."
St. Cloud Democrat, July 22, 1861

GUST STRUGGLED INTO HIS GOOD SHIRT and prayed the sweat rolling down his back would not cause a stink to ruin his wedding day. His mother had toiled all morning ironing out the wrinkles with flatirons heated on the stove. If only she had been as successful in ironing out the problems between Gust and his father.

His father was impossible to please. The chores were never done well enough. His friends weren't good enough. Even Serena wasn't enough in Father's eyes. Heaven forbid a Swede should marry a Norwegian. You'd think she was Catholic to hear him worry the issue to death.

A crippled leg kept Gust stuck at home drudging farm chores while his brothers went off to war. It seemed to him the situation with his father grew even worse with his brothers gone. Mother said it was because Father worried about the boys. Whenever Gust ventured to a barn dance or husking bee, Father was sure to wake him an hour or two earlier the next morning just out of spite. Even after Gust turned twenty-one, Father never paid him a dollar in wages.

It was his mother who forced the loan that made his wedding to Serena Brandvold possible. Almost a month ago, Gust had been in the barn stripping Brunhilda, a fresh heifer. The young cow was nervous and jumpy. When his parents opened the barn door, Brunhilda startled and kicked the bucket against Gust's sore leg, sending him into an agony of cursing.

5

"Watch your language!" Mother said with a hard crimp in her mouth. She nudged Gust's father closer and nodded for him to speak. "Your father has something to say."

Gust had never known anyone to force his father to do anything. He rubbed his leg and pulled away from the heifer, guarding the half-filled bucket with his other hand while balancing on the three-legged milking stool.

"I've changed my mind about the loan." Father looked down at his scuffed work boots and toed a lump of dried manure on the earthen barn floor.

Gust stood, knocking over the stool in the process but managing to spare the fresh milk. His mother rescued the bucket from his hands.

"But you're making a mistake." Father looked up. Gust saw his set jaw and anger-sparked eyes. "You'll never make it on your own."

"It's good land." Gust's voice cracked. He clenched his fists. "I'll pay you back after my first harvest."

"Marry that Norwegian girl if you must," Father said, "but stay here in Burr Oak. There's plenty of room."

"I want to be on my own," Gust said.

"Who knows how long your brothers will be gone," he said. "You could live here rent free."

"I won't be a cotter." Gust gritted his teeth. What kind of life would Serena have in his father's house, knowing how he felt about Norwegians? "Minnesota is the land of opportunity, a place where someone just starting out can get a place of his own."

"Opportunity is *this* farm."

"*Your* farm." Gust's voice took on a hard edge.

"Yours. And your brothers." Father's voice tightened. "Why do you think I've worked so hard all these years?"

"Enough," Mother said. "It's settled."

"You'll come back begging for another handout," Father had said. "You'll never make it on your own."

GUST SIGHED AND PUSHED THE LAST BUTTON through the matching hole. It was over. The loan was in his pocket ready to pay the rent on the Hutchinson farm. Soon he and Serena would be married. He tucked his shirt into his good pants. Just the thought of Serena made his knees wobble and his voice turn to dust. She was the most beautiful girl in Burr Oak. He still could not believe that she had agreed to marry him.

All things work out in the end. Because of his leg, he had been home to court the lovely Serena. Serena with her long blonde braids and eyes the color of sky. Serena with her gentle touch and sweet soprano voice. He had loved her as long as he could remember—had loved her since he first heard her sing the "Star Spangled Banner" in the one-room schoolhouse they both attended.

Another hour and she would be his wife.

They would say their vows before the Swedish Lutheran minister and eat dinner with Serena's parents. Their wedding journey would begin after the noon meal. The wagon was packed and ready to hitch to Brownie, an ancient horse given reluctantly by his father as a wedding gift. Gust knew a perfect camping spot for their first night together, a wooded knoll along the Mississippi River about ten miles north of Burr Oak. His face reddened at the thought and he breathed a little faster.

When he knocked on the door, Serena greeted him shyly from beneath her pointed hat. It wouldn't be long. For now, he had to be content with letting his love speak through his eyes. He took her by both hands.

"You're beautiful," he said at last.

Jerdis and Jensina, her twin sisters, peeked around the doorway, giggling and laughing. "Are you going to kiss her?" Jensina said.

"Gust, I have something to talk to you about." Serena glared a warning glance at her little sisters. "In private."

"Of course." The wedding band rested safely in his pocket. It was time to leave for the minister's house.

They stepped outside and walked to the shade of an ancient elm tree. Gust leaned forward and tried to plant a kiss on her lips but she turned away.

"Gust!" She stepped back against the tree trunk and cast an anxious glance towards the house. "My parents will see."

"Let them look." Gust felt his love for Serena filling his chest until it ached. "You'll soon be my wife. Then I can kiss you all I want." He pressed up against her and kissed her lips hard. It was all he could do to keep his hands off her.

"Gust! This is serious."

"Kissing, yes serious."

"I mean it," she said.

The tone of her voice caught him off guard. "What's wrong?"

"Before I marry you," she said. "I have something important to ask you."

"What could be more important than kisses?"

"I need something." Serena looked him in the eye. "I need your promise that if things go badly in Minnesota, you'll bring me home again."

"Serena-girl!" He laughed too loudly. "What could go wrong? The farm has rich soil and the army needs wheat."

"Even so," she said. "My parents say that if things don't go as we hope, we can come back and live with them. Build a cabin on the south forty and work the farm together."

"You're being silly."

"Promise me," Serena said. "Promise and I'll marry you."

Gust hesitated. He would rather die than return to Burr Oak. It might be tolerable if he had success under his belt, but even so, Gust would rather live as far away from his father as possible.

"Otherwise I won't." Serena's voice was firm.

"You're fooling." When she didn't answer, he realized she meant it. The buttons on her *bunad* pulled tight across her bosom. His eyes fixed on the top button. He could almost see the tops of her breasts. "I promise." His voice melted to a near-whisper. "If things don't go well in Minnesota, we'll come home again."

Serena heaved a sigh. "Then let's get married."

3

"Lincoln Calls for More Men. Now Is the Time to Enlist."
St. Cloud Democrat, August 18, 1862

GUST GUSTAFSON LEANED ON THE BOTTOM HALF of the barn door, easing the weight off his sore ankle. He scanned the morning skies, worrying about the wheat and chewing a handful of grain plucked from the field. A wispy cloud resembling horsetails drifted overhead. His father always said a mare's tail cloud meant rain. Rust already threatened the southeastern field. Rain might destroy the whole crop.

His cousin Luther Madsen had found the rental farm in Hutchinson. The fifty-six dollar loan from his father put in his first crop and rented the farm but it weighed on Gust's back. If only the weather held, Gust could expect to repay the loan and plant another crop in the spring.

His old man couldn't say a word against him if he repaid the money on time.

The ripe wheat chewed into a sticky gum, nutty and sweet. The army needed flour to feed the men fighting in the South. Because of that the price was good.

He limped back to the cabin with new resolve.

"Serena," he called in the door. "I'm going to Sorenson's to borrow a cradle to start harvesting the wheat. Rain's moving in."

"How long will you be gone?" Serena wiped her hands on a towel and met him at the cabin door. Her blonde hair hung down her back in a loose braid and made her appear younger than her eighteen years.

9

"Should be back by noon if I hurry." Their horse was lame. He faced a two-mile walk to Sorenson's and his ankle was killing him. For sure it would rain—his ankle was a most accurate barometer. "Wish I had that mule I've been talking about."

"The baby's sick," Serena said. "I don't know what to do."

"You worry too much, Serena-girl. Babies always have some complaint or the other." He pushed his hat down a little further on his dark curls and gave her a hurried kiss on the top of her head. "She'll be fine."

"Ask Mrs. Sorenson if she has any nutmeg. Mor always used it for stomach complaints."

Gust didn't answer but waved a hand over his head as he headed east toward the Sorenson farm. He lengthened his stride and winced with every step on his right ankle. If only he had that mule.

Deer flies circled his head. The air smelled of damp earth mixed with wood smoke from the kitchen stove. Pig weeds grew taller than the fenced barnyard. Brownie neighed and stomped as Gust passed by. Even with her bad leg the old horse wanted to go with him wherever he went. Maybe that explained why he didn't put her down—he couldn't bear the thought of it.

He often told Serena that Brownie was a good watchdog. Just the other night she made such a commotion that Gust had gone out and found a fox lurking around the henhouse. Ja, Brownie was still valuable. It cost nothing to feed her in the summer. He'd keep her a while longer.

Maybe after the harvest there would be enough money to buy a mule. He hoped for as much as fifteen bushels of wheat to the acre. If he could get back by early afternoon, he would cradle the first field by dark.

His thoughts turned to Serena. She was a good wife but worried too much. The baby was fine. Probably just teething. Serena needed to let loose a little and enjoy life. She had changed from the carefree young bride of last summer. She spent too much time writing letters home and rereading the flimsy pages that came at regular intervals from Iowa.

Once the wheat was harvested, things would be different. Gust would pay off his father and buy her a new dress and take her to a dance or two. She loved to dance and was a sight to see twirling with her blonde curls.

He was not much good on the dance floor, but when the wheat was sold he would have reason to dance. When the debt was paid, Gust would be a free man.

He spied Martin Kimbler with a broken-down wagon on the trail. Martin wasn't young, maybe the age of Gust's father. Martin's face was beet red and the sleeves of his wool shirt were rolled up to mid-forearm.

"Can you help me?" Martin called. "There's Indian trouble."

"Indian trouble?" Gust said. "What kind?"

"They're raising hell by New Ulm." He wiped the sweat from his face with the back of his arm. "I need to fix this wagon and fetch my missus. Folks are gathering in Hutchinson to make a stand."

"New Ulm is forty miles away," Gust said. "You can't believe every rumor."

"Indian payments are late," Martin said. "The government owes the Sioux, and they're on the warpath over it."

Gust remembered reading about the late payment in the newspaper. Some speculated that the government needed the money to fight the Rebellion in the South more than it needed to pay the Sioux as promised by the 1858 Treaty. But that newspaper was months old by the time he got it from Sorenson. Surely the payment had been made by now.

"You're worrying over nothing," Gust said. "The soldiers'll take care of it."

"Better safe than sorry," Martin said and wiped his forehead again. "You'd best get your family and ride to town with me."

Gust almost laughed. It would take more than a rumor to make him leave his wheat in the middle of harvest. Even if it were true, New Ulm was too far away to concern him. What would the Sioux want with poor farmers in Hutchinson? It was too ridiculous to consider.

"I won't leave my wheat," Gust said, "Indians or no Indians. But I'll help you with the wagon if you'll let me borrow it to market my wheat in another week."

They levered the axle with an oak branch and reinforced the broken spot with pieces of wood nailed and wrapped with ends of old rope. It took more time than expected. Gust watched the sun travel across the sky. If he didn't get home soon he would have to hold off the cradling until tomorrow.

He had wasted the whole morning.

4

"Indians Attack Lower Agency"
St. Cloud Democrat, August 19, 1862

SERENA SIGHED AND RETURNED TO THE DISHPAN. She scrubbed the dried egg yolk off the greasy plates. Lena, their month-old baby, had fussed all night with scours, but Gust thought nothing of it, worried only for the wheat. She wished again they lived closer to her family. Her mother was always helping out sick folks. Serena could remember as a young girl being sent to a neighbor's to help with the garden when there was a new baby in the house.

If only someone would send a girl to help her.

In her mind's eye, she saw the map on the schoolhouse wall, the location of Burr Oak and the trail that took them north to Hutchinson. It was a long way.

And lately, whenever she was alone, Serena thought about something her aunt had said before their wedding. She had begged Auntie Karen to tell her fortune by reading her coffee grounds. It was a lighthearted request, but when Auntie had looked into her cup, she had said nothing at all.

"What is it?" Serena said.

"It's nothing." Auntie Karen pushed the cup away with a laugh. "Lutherans don't believe in silly superstitions. It's nothing at all."

"Tell me," Serena said. "I need to know."

Serena expected her to predict a happy future with Gust, maybe how many children they would have or if they would find wealth and adventure.

12

"See this pattern." Auntie pulled the cup towards Serena. "The way grounds are scattered around the rim of the cup? Means death and war."

Serena suppressed a wave of fear and instead giggled a nervous laugh.

"It's foolishness!" Mor took the cup and refilled it from the iron pot. "Certainly it means something different here in America."

They had all laughed. But Serena noticed Auntie Karen took out her handkerchief and spat seven times into it when she thought no one was looking. Spitting would break a curse.

Now Serena wondered about it, what it had meant. So many things could happen on the frontier.

Serena felt spent. Maybe it was because of the recent birth. She rinsed the plates with water from the teakettle and dumped the dishwater over the delphiniums by the door. The blue blooms reminded her again of home. Mor had tucked the flower seeds in with the log cabin quilt the year before on their wedding day. Such a happy time. She would never forget the look on Gust's face.

Lena whimpered, and Serena stopped to nurse her. Lena clawed and grasped with her small hands, finding no comfort in her mother's milk. Serena tipped Lena over on her knee and jiggled her, trying to pacify the small baby. She sang a Norwegian lullaby. Nothing worked.

"*Stalkers Liten!*" Serena tried to nurse her again, anything to still the crying. "Poor little one!"

Serena patted Lena on the back as she gulped milk. She was a good baby. Worth all the trouble she had caused. It had been a difficult pregnancy, and Serena couldn't keep food down. She remembered Auntie Karen having morning sickness for a few weeks before Arvid was born. Serena's lasted month after month, until her bones showed on her wrists and her face reflected white in their only window.

Gust butchered a rooster hoping to fatten her up.

"You've turned into skin and bones except for the bundle you carry in front," Gust said one dreary February day when Serena thought she might die from loneliness and sickness. But when Gust had wrung the bird's neck and plucked the feathers, he laid the carcass on the table for Serena to dress.

She tried. It was a job she had always dreaded, touching the entrails with her bare hands, pulling out the organs layered in yellow fat, the smell of blood and guts. Gust became angry when she retched during the process and furious when she couldn't eat a bite at supper.

"I've killed one of our roosters, and you won't even eat it," he stormed. "I can't please you no matter what I do. You just moan around here like a mama's baby crying for the tit."

"Gust," Serena tried to pull herself together, gagging on a morsel of the stringy meat that still tasted of blood in her mouth. "Don't be silly. I'm sick, that's all. It has nothing to do with my mor."

When he left to milk the cow, Serena puked in the chamber pot and hurried to throw it behind the house before Gust came in again. No matter what he said, she couldn't eat the meat.

But that was months ago.

Lena fussed and squirmed, thrusting her legs straight out, squealing in pain. Her forehead was hot. Serena dampened a rag and wiped her face. She couldn't remember if she should add more blankets or take them off for a fever. What had Auntie Karen done?

Serena walked the floor, cooing and singing to the little one. "It was all worth it. I'd do it again for you, I would. You're worth it all."

Serena's pains had started the last day of cultivating. She thought to mention it to Gust at breakfast but hesitated, knowing he would be impatient with any disruption. She knew first babies took a long time and thought she would tell him at nooning. What if false labor disrupted Gust's work? She would tell him only when she was sure.

It was definitely labor. When Gust came in for dinner, she would have him fetch Mrs. Sorenson whether the work was done or not.

But Gust worked through the nooning. Serena walked her little cabin alone, back and forth, fearing she might die alone with the misery, almost hoping she would. Serena wished with all her might that Auntie Karen could be summoned to help her instead of crabby old Mrs. Sorenson. She remembered Auntie's advice to keep walking.

Walking was all she could do, and she staggered across the floor, stopping to clutch the bedpost during the worst of the pains, tucking the string in her apron pocket and setting the butcher knife on the table within easy reach.

She didn't know if she could continue life in Hutchinson away from her family. She pretended her mor walked beside her through that long day.

Serena spoke to her, telling her everything on her heart. In a whirlwind of pain, Serena heard her mor's voice reminding her that women birthed babies every day and survived. But when Serena spoke to her it was Gust who replied.

"Don't worry, Serena-girl," Gust said. "I've got the corn cultivated and will fetch Mrs. Sorenson. I'll be back before you know it."

He kissed her on top of her head and hurried off. Ja, his eyes were worried. She saw that. But she also saw him hurry to leave her, to get away from the suffering. She could not get away. Another pain, harder this time, gripped her belly, and she screamed and fell to the floor. No one was there to hear, she could scream if she wanted.

She was still screaming when Gust returned with Mrs. Sorenson, her voice hoarse and spent.

"Serena," Gust said. "Be quiet now. Be a good girl. Our baby is coming."

"You can leave now, Gust," Mrs. Sorenson said. She was stern faced and tight lipped. Serena had always been afraid of her. "You've done your damage already, mister."

"Gust," Serena said, "don't leave me. I'm scared."

"Don't be silly," Mrs. Sorenson said. "There's nothing he can do anyway. The baby'll be here in no time."

But Lena took her time. When the baby finally ripped out in a river of bloody water, Serena no longer asked for Gust. Her cries were only for her mother.

"Oh, Lena." Serena kissed her on her forehead and felt the hot skin touch her lips. "I'd do it again to have you in my arms. A mor and daughter should not be parted. I pray to God I'll never be parted from you."

Lena quieted, and Serena laid her on the rope bed. There was so much to do. How could she get it done with a sick baby? Lena screamed again, and Serena patted her on the back, tears sprouting from her eyes. "I'm so homesick, *stakkers liten*, that all I can think about is home. But your far will not even discuss it."

Lena had been only a day old when Serena gathered her courage and spoke to Gust.

"I'd like to move home to Burr Oak. My father says we can build a cabin on the south forty."

"Serena-girl." Gust rocked Lena in his strong arms. "You're talking foolish now. The baby's born, you'll be well again in no time, and the wheat is growing. We're doing good."

"I want to live closer to my parents. What if Lena gets sick, or if we need help with something? It's too hard away from everyone."

"We're not moving home." He put Lena on his shoulder, patting her back until she burped. "Don't mention it again."

Serena sat up in bed and penned a letter to her parents, telling them of Lena Christine's birth. She kept her promise; they named their daughter after Serena's mother, although Gust had wanted to name her Olga, after his grandmother.

"I will wear the *bunad* to her baptism, Mor and Far," she wrote. And she did wear it, although it was tight around her waist and milk soaked through the bodice. She wore it while the visiting Swedish Lutheran minister baptized Lena Christine Gustafson into the Holy Christian Church. Mr. and Mrs. Sorenson stood as godparents for their child, but homesickness marred Serena's joy.

Lena screamed as her loose bowels moved again, and Serena lifted her from the bed. Brownie made a commotion in the yard. She hoped it wasn't another fox in the henhouse. She peeked out the window but saw nothing. It would have to wait, whatever the problem. Lena was sick. Maybe teething or colic but a million things could happen to a baby. Serena thought of the dreaded summer complaint that took her baby brother years ago. Lena might be feverish but maybe she had too many blankets swaddled around her. How could Serena know what to do?

She paced back and forth across the small cabin floor. What could be wrong? She had enough milk. Her dress dripped the sticky liquid. Maybe the fresh tomatoes from the garden had tainted her milk. Some folks said "love apples" were poisonous, but Serena's family had been eating them for years without harm. Maybe it was the cucumbers and green onions she had eaten yesterday. They had tasted so fresh and good that she had made a pig of herself. It must be the cucumbers and onions. She would have to be more careful.

She carefully laid Lena on the rope bed and changed her, placing the soiled rags in a bucket under the log table already filled with the putrid mess. She was almost out of clean rags. Sometime that day she would have to fetch another pail of water from the stream behind the barn, build enough fire to heat the water and wash them.

Tears welled up again, but she quickly blinked them away. She was fully grown, a married woman with a child. She had to forget about herself and think of her family. That's what Mor would do. Brownie continued to neigh and stomp. A rooster crowed, and a hen clucked around the doorway. Serena prayed she would find the strength to do everything. It was too much.

The washing would have to wait. String beans and tomatoes needed picking. Cucumbers were the right size for pickling, and the dill was headed. Preserving her garden produce was a necessity for their survival and must take priority. She would take Lena with her to the garden and hope for the best. She wrapped her in a blanket and started toward the door.

A nagging worry cut through her thoughts. Something was amiss. Brownie was suddenly quiet. No rooster crowed. Other than Lena's fussing it was quiet. Too quiet. Serena glanced out the small window.

Her heart jolted to a complete stop.

Three Indians, naked and painted, stood beside the barn. One had his face painted half black and half green and gestured toward the trail where Gust had gone for the scythe.

Serena drew back from the window and pressed her back against the cabin wall. They might see her. Serena prayed that Gust was safely down the trail, safe from the painted men. Then she prayed Gust would come running to the house and rescue her and Lena from the savages.

What could she do? She must protect Lena.

Indians had been to their farm once before when they first moved to Hutchinson—but they weren't painted. They had carried a deer across their backs to trade for bread, had walked up to the cabin with their barter. Serena remembered the odor of their oiled bodies, the nakedness of their dress, and how their eyes glittered when they looked at her blonde hair. She had cowered behind Gust, trembling with fear. Gust teased her about it for weeks, reminding her that the treaties had solved the Indian problems in Minnesota.

Serena slowly edged up to the window and saw Brownie on the ground with an arrow in her side. Why would they kill old Brownie? She made too much noise.

The Indians wanted their presence kept secret.

She inched away from the window. Her eyes searched for a place of safety but found none. They would see her if she left the cabin by its only door. The single pane of glass was on the same side of the house as the door. Their trunks and supplies were tightly packed under the rope bed. If she barred the door, they would know someone was in the cabin. She needed to leave the door open and hide. Maybe they would think no one was home.

Serena pulled up the trapdoor to the root cellar under the cabin floor and huddled in the darkness, Lena clutched in her arms. It was a small place, just a hole in the ground topped with a wooden cover in front of the fireplace. Gust called it their "fraidy hole." Said they could hide there if a cyclone threatened. Thank God, it wasn't filled with potatoes yet. The air smelled thick and earthy, almost choking in its heaviness. Rays of light streamed down through the cracks in the floor. Spider webs wrapped around her face, and she slapped them away.

She put Lena to her breast in an effort to quiet her. The baby gulped great swallows of air and milk, twisting and contorting her small legs and arms. Serena could feel Lena's bowels churning as she held her close, and it frightened her almost as much as the Indians outside. Oh, God, what could she do?

The floor groaned above her, and the door slammed. Next she heard a grunt and a harsh laugh as a white cloud sifted down through the cracks, their precious sack of flour scattered and ruined.

The cracks in the floor. Oh God, they could look down and see her through the cracks in the floor. She froze.

Serena felt an uncontrollable urge to sneeze. She pushed her face into the baby's blanket and stifled it with all her might. Lena squirmed and fussed, and it seemed to Serena her kicks grew weaker. Serena put her hand over the baby's mouth and held her closer. The scours exploded from the wee one onto Serena's dress and apron, and Lena made a sharp cry just as dishes crashed onto the floor above her, the breaking glass contrasted with the heavy thud of cooking pots. Serena froze and covered Lena's mouth even more tightly. Lena's eyes bulged, and she kicked in feeble protest.

The Indians laughed again and spoke in their guttural language. Thank God, they hadn't heard. The sound of breaking dishes covered Lena's cry.

Time stopped. Every breath lasted an hour, every movement slowed. Serena's heart pounded in her ears, each beat an eternity. She heard the sound of trunks pulled from underneath the bed and the voices of the Indians as they pilfered through their possessions. Serena felt faint, and she willed herself to breathe, to keep her baby alive.

Thank God she had looked out the window before leaving the cabin. Thank God.

What if they fired the house? She and Lena would burn to death. Or smother from smoke. What if they found the trapdoor? They would be scalped and butchered, or worse. Serena knew the stories. The Indians were savages, heathen not to be trusted. What if Gust didn't return? What if Gust was already dead? She prayed over and over that Lena wouldn't cry out and kept her hand clamped over her mouth.

Serena held her face in Lena's blanket, knowing the whiteness of her skin might attract the attention of the Sioux, fearing it might show through the cracks in the floor. She didn't move a muscle. Lena stirred, and she pressed tighter, forcing her squirming to cease. Finally the door slammed.

She smelled smoke but was too terrified to leave her refuge. She lessened the grip on Lena's mouth. They would be killed by fire. Lena would never walk or say her first words. Gust wouldn't know what happened to them. Mor would never see her first grandchild.

"*Stalkers liten*, this is the end." Serena kissed Lena's forehead. She burned with fever. No longer did she hear footsteps above her. Lena screamed as her bowels moved again.

Serena clamped her hand over Lena's mouth. "Be quiet," Serena hissed through clenched teeth. "Be quiet or they'll find us."

5

"Almost 500 Whites killed; 2,000 Indians Around Fort Ridgely;
All the Sioux Bands United."
St. Cloud Democrat, August 27, 1862

A gleam of light caught Drumbeater's eye as he set rabbit snares along a deer trail. He dropped to his belly and peeked through a hazelnut bush, holding his breath to catch every sound, pulling his knife from its sheath. It might be *toka ahe do*, an enemy attack.

Earlier that day a flock of sand hill cranes flew in a chain of circles, a sure sign that many spirits were leaving the earth. This evil omen left him wary and suspicious. He feared something bad would happen but he didn't know what it might be.

Drumbeater heard childish cries, crackling leaves, and a man's guttural command to keep quiet. An enemy of the People would not bring a child on a raiding party. He strained his neck to see without exposing himself, holding still in spite of a pesky deerfly biting his forehead. He relaxed when he recognized his uncle and slapped the fly.

Crooked Lightning carried a sleeping *washechu* child in one arm and dragged another by the hand. Sunlight bounced off the white-haired one in Uncle's arms. Drumbeater shivered in spite of the late afternoon heat, his eyes riveted on the child. Its hair was as white as the head of an eagle.

Face paint indicated that Crooked Lightning traveled with a war party— yet he came alone. What could be his reason to bring the *washechus*?

Drumbeater forced himself to use wisdom, to scan the surrounding area. Perhaps Ojibwa braves followed in secret. But the *shechoka* sang in the poplar trees and *oopehanska* warbled in the oaks. The bird tribes were most reliable in reporting trouble. Nothing unusual—he fastened his eyes again on the *washechu*.

His heart pounded so he could hardly speak. "*O'mita koda*." His voice sounded barely above a whisper. "Welcome." Tradition required that he greet his esteemed relative, but his eyes stuck on the small one like *winawizidan* fastened to its strange garment and tiny footwear.

She was a girl-child with white hair that curled as the shavings off a birch twig. Her garment, torn and dirty, was covered with cockleburs. Blue veins showed through closed eyelids. Her skin was as white as the deepest snow in the Moon of Difficulty.

Drumbeater held back his hands from reaching out. His fingers ached to touch her white hair. Ice on the Water, a warrior from the Spirit Lake Band, boasted a lance with such a scalp, white locks with curls as tight as the buffalo. Ice on the Water claimed the strong medicine of the *washechu* scalp made him indestructible in battle.

The sleeping girl opened her eyes, and Drumbeater stepped a full step backwards. Her eyes were blue—startlingly blue. As blue as the wing of a jay. As blue as the river on a cloudless day or the eggs of *shechuka*. Their beauty cut through him, staggered him.

He peered at the older child, another girl-child, but only brown eyes stared back from beneath tangled, brown hair. She clutched angry fists at her sides. Her eyes were red and swollen from crying and a streak of red skin showed on her back where the cloth had been torn away. Otherwise her skin was as white as the small one's. He wanted to lift the *heyake* draped in rags around her body and see the rest of her whiteness. But such behavior would undoubtedly shock his uncle with its rudeness. She sobbed in great gulping swallows, a gap in her mouth where one bottom tooth was missing.

"Ho!" Uncle spoke, slightly out of breath, his back straight as an arrow. Sweat beaded on his temples, dripped down over thick eyebrows. Deerflies buzzed around his head but he ignored them as befitted a warrior. "I have traveled far to see your face."

"There is food." Drumbeater forced his eyes away from the white hair, irritated with the older child's sobs. A daughter of the People would never disgrace herself with such behavior, even one of so few years. "We are honored to share our fire with our esteemed relative."

Crooked Lightning stood tall, broad shouldered and proud in stature. He wore two eagle feathers hanging downward, signifying wounds received as he counted coup in battle, and three other feathers painted red and cut to indicate scalps taken. Green and black face paint accentuated high cheekbones and a hawkish nose.

"These are *hakadah*, the pitiful last of their people." Crooked Lightning thrust his chin towards the girl-children and shifted the one in his arms. "The responsibility of my life-and-death friend."

Drumbeater nodded solemnly as understanding enlightened him. A man's character was most deeply tested by the responsibility of friendship. Among the People, a great warrior kept obligations to life-and-death friends no matter how inconvenient. Uncle's friend most likely wanted the *washechu* for medicine, or maybe to adopt and marry into the tribe when they were old enough for the Feast of Virgins.

He yearned to take the small one into his arms. But Uncle was neither tired nor weak. To offer help might offend. Instead, Drumbeater led the way back towards camp, hoping everything was in order as it should be, wishing that Uncle brought the small one as a gift for him.

Drumbeater carefully scanned the surrounding area for enemy signs before pushing back a plum bush that shielded the camp from view. In Leaf Country, Ojibwas lurked to do damage to the People, and every precaution must be taken. Although the camp was built along a river, it was also close to a lake filled with rice ripe for harvest. The village hid behind a covering of heavy brush, not easily seen by someone across the water.

Dangerous, the way the young one's hair reflected sunlight. He should blacken it with mud. But perhaps darkening would hinder its strong medicine.

At the start of the Moon of Wild Cherries, Drumbeater and Willow Song had moved their teepee from the Sisseton planting camp to this stretch of river along the edge of Leaf Country. Willow Song worked like a muskrat, drying and storing a supply of *psinchinchah* dug from the riverbed. Already she boasted stores of *manak-cahkcah*, root of the wild lily, and maple sugar tightly wrapped in birch bark and secured with vines. Slabs of dried fish and pouches of dried berries waited for the Moon of Difficulty when food was scarce and fierce cold tested the People's strength.

His heart swelled with pride to see Otter's cradleboard rocking gently from a wild grape vine as Willow Song fashioned reed baskets in preparation for the rice harvest. The dogs ran forward and sniffed at their feet, wagging their tails in welcome. It was good Uncle would rest his eyes on his industrious wife and future warrior.

During Drumbeater's boyhood, Crooked Lightning had been held up as an example of model behavior. His father's brother, Uncle was an elder of great respect among the Wahpekute, the Lower Sioux. Since his marriage to a daughter of the Sisseton, Drumbeater had moved west to live with her people as was practical and proper. But Crooked Lightning's exploits were sung and celebrated even among the Sisseton for his daring bravery and the many times he had counted coup on the enemy.

Most astonishing, Uncle knew the tracks of the *washechu* imprinted on paper birch. When his woman, Many Beavers, pitched her teepee near the *imnejah-ska*, at the very mouth of the great fort called Snelling, Crooked Lightning learned the white man's tracks from a Black Coat.

Someday Drumbeater hoped to learn the strong medicine of the *washechu* tracks.

Willow Song rose to greet them, wide eyes fastened on the child sleeping in Crooked Lightning's arms, too well-mannered to ask the question spoken by her astonished eyes.

"Is my woman in camp?"

"No, Uncle," Willow Song said in her quiet voice. The others would arrive soon, the women and old men harvesting rice while the men traveled west to hunt buffalo. Drumbeater was one of a handful of braves left behind to guard rice camp. It had always been the way of the People. "Many Beavers comes tomorrow or maybe the day after."

Crooked Lightning hesitated. Without a word, Willow Song reached for the girl-child and carried her into the teepee. The girl-child's pale face contrasted sharply against Willow Song's brown skin.

"Birdie!" The older child lunged wildly on the heels of Willow Song, screaming as if stung by the bee tribe, pounding on Willow Song's legs with both fists.

"What does the *washechu* say?" Drumbeater said, shocked at such uncivilized behavior. Among the People, children knew to be silent before their elders. Even Otter no longer cried out at night when enemies might be listening.

"She calls for Little Bird, her sister." Crooked Lightning lowered himself beside the fire pit, sitting with crossed legs, flipping his long hair behind his shoulders. "I think that one is from badger tribe, fierce in defense of family."

Tradition demanded that Drumbeater smoke with his uncle. He chafed against this obligation, wanting only to touch the *washechu*. He slapped at a mosquito and added a branch into the dying embers of the fire. The grass lay green beneath his feet although he had seen a red leaf among the sumac during morning prayers, a sure sign that summer was almost over.

Drumbeater fetched the red pipe from the teepee where it hung beside the sacred drum from the lodge pole. As keeper of the drum, Drumbeater must watch over the drum as if it were a family member. He had trained himself to know its whereabouts and safety at all times. To lose the drum would bring great disgrace upon him and his family.

Assured that the drum was in its proper place and with pipe in hand, Drumbeater knew he should return to his uncle at the fire. But he couldn't resist stepping towards the buffalo robes where Little Bird already slept. He stroked her white hair as soft as the skins of the rabbit tribe. Her hair tightened even more in the warmth of the teepee and framed her pale face with rings of curls like the buffalo tribe. Perhaps it was a bad omen, like the sand hill cranes flying in circles. Or a good omen. Strong medicine.

He wished she would open her eyes so he could swim in their blueness. The thought of such *wakon* sent thrills through his body. "Little Bird," he said quietly. "Wake up."

Badger pushed between them and glared up at him with blazing eyes, raised fist and pouted lip.

Willow Song chuckled. "Be careful! Badger will fight you." She reached out to Badger with a soothing cluck and handed her a gourd filled with fresh water.

Drumbeater stepped back in disgust and tapped *kinnikinick* into the ceremonial pipe, keeping a watchful eye on Badger. She was a disagreeable child with disgusting manners, truly bad medicine.

But perhaps Wakantanka, the Great Mystery, sent Badger to guard her sister, the little bird of *wakon*. It was something to consider.

"Did she eat?" How could Little Bird sleep through all the noise? "Maybe she is sick."

"*Honkita*," Willow Song said. "Too tired for food. First sleep."

Drumbeater pushed past the older sister and returned to the fire. He stirred a pine bough into the coals for its shielding smoke against the mosquito tribe. Crooked Lightning shifted away from the smokiest place, choosing a spot where the smoke wafted past him instead of choking him.

Drumbeater sat across from him and touched a burning stick to the bowl of the red stone pipe. He puffed until the tobacco smoked, then passed it respectfully to his uncle. Crooked Lightning accepted the *chan du' hu pah zu za pee* with great dignity, lifting it first to the Great Mystery and then to the four winds with shaking hands. He released the smoke slowly through his nose, taking several slow puffs before passing the pipe to his nephew.

Drumbeater wondered at the shaking hands. Uncle had always seemed the strongest of the strong, never showing any signs of weakness. For the first time Drumbeater noticed the white streaks in his long hair, the lines around his eyes, the cording of his neck beneath the war paint.

Drumbeater sat impatiently, trying to appear at ease, waiting for his uncle to speak. Hurrying an elder was out of the question, but something was wrong. The bad omen. The *washechu* girl-children. He had thought it odd when Crooked Lightning sent Many Beavers to stay with relatives in the Sisseton Band. Tradition prevented direct questions, and if she knew the reason, Many Beavers kept it to herself. Perhaps Uncle would explain.

Willow Song placed boiled muskrat spiced with wild onions before the men, murmuring an almost inaudible prayer to Wakantanka as she lowered the dish, "Spirit, partake."

Crooked Lightning nodded, picked a choice morsel from his dish and threw it into the fire. Drumbeater watched with great respect, knowing Uncle offered the best meat to Wakantanka. Perhaps his hands shook from hunger. Then Crooked Lightning ate sparingly from his bowl with an appreciative grunt, restraining himself as was proper for a man of his reputation, patient enough to let the food cool before eating as was necessary for good health.

"Do the White Eyes sleep?" Crooked Lightning said.

"Yes, Uncle," Willow Song said. "Like bear in winter dens."

Crooked Lightning returned to his food. Drumbeater wished for an excuse to go to the teepee and again touch the *wakon* child. Even a single lock of the curly hair might bring great *pay jee hoo tah* to his medicine bag.

"The Mdewakanton and Wahpekute bands make war against the White Eyes." Crooked Lightning's voice startled Drumbeater. "The Rice Creek band brings this trouble upon us."

"How did this happen?" The Rice Creek band had frequented his mother's village when he was a boy.

"The Rice Creek band has always been quarrelsome," Crooked Lightning said with a frown and kicked a dried branch into the flames. "Always in trouble somewhere, unable to get along with the rest." He looked up into the trees for a long moment as if he sought the squirrel tribe, or listened for the approach of enemies.

"I knew Brown Wing from the Rice Creek Band."

"He was one who started the trouble," Crooked Lightning said. "Shot a *washechu* man and his family over a nest of hen's eggs."

Loons warbled over the water, and Drumbeater felt his pulse quicken. "But surely the actions of a few young braves cannot cause a war with the Long Knives."

"Once *washechu* blood has been shed," Crooked Lightning said, "there is no turning back."

"What do the chiefs say?"

"Big Eagle urges restraint," Crooked Lightning said. "As do Traveling Hail and Wabasha, but the young men are anxious to prove themselves and will not listen to the elders."

It was the way of the People. Until he showed bravery in battle, a young man was denied a wife, the use of *kinnikinick*, and eagle feathers.

"Surely the Ojibwas are more worthy enemies." Drumbeater said at last.

"It is well known that the *washechu* fight only when compelled," Uncle dipped his fingers into the meat, "and are unworthy of counting coup." He licked his fingers. "Even the Big Knives force their warriors to the front like antelopes instead of leading them into battle like a great chief. They are cowardly, an uncivilized race." Crooked Lightning reached for a gourd of water. "They have stolen the hunting lands of the People."

"But surely the Great Chief will keep his word."

"The Great Chief turns his eyes far to the *itokaga* where his children war against each other," Crooked Lightning said. "The Great Chief has forgotten his starving Dakota children."

Dusk fell upon them and the *mdoza* tribe warbled its haunting cry over the river, flying low over the waters, searching for fish. Although the embers died down, Drumbeater made no move to stoke the fire. A fire might attract a lurking Ojibwa.

"Little Crow leads the warriors, but even he admits there is little hope for success against the Long Knives." Crooked Lightning slapped a mosquito from his ankle. "We fight and die for nothing."

Suddenly a blood-curdling scream ripped through the air and raised the hair on the Drumbeater's neck. He reached for his knife and sprang to his feet before hearing Willow Song's soothing words. It was only Badger, crying out in her sleep.

"What are her words?" Drumbeater felt a quiver of fear go through him, and he struggled to maintain his composure. There were too many omens, too much medicine—good and bad.

"Badger calls for her mother." Crooked Lightning's eyes glittered. "Her mother is dead. Father and brother also."

"You killed them?"

"I failed to protect them." Crooked Lightning's voice was humble, true sign of a great warrior. "These were the relatives of my life-and-death friend, the *hoksiyokopa* named for him and destined for greatness in the *washechu* tribe. That one would have been a chief, I think, had he lived to be a warrior."

"What is the name of this life-and-death friend?" A life-and-death friend to his uncle meant he was friend also to Drumbeater, almost a relative.

"Evan Jacobson. He comes from a far tribe beyond the great waters and drives the coach-with-wooden-wheels. Though a White Eyes, he is a real human being." He sighed. "I failed to protect his people from Blue Bottle's tomahawk."

"Evan Jacobson." The strange name tingled on Drumbeater's lips, the harsh syllables of the White Eyes. "What does it mean?"

"It means nothing." Crooked Lightning moved to the left, finding a more comfortable position away from the shifting smoke. "Only civilized people have names with meaning."

That his uncle was life-and-death friend to a *washechu* astonished him. Drumbeater practiced the name again, memorizing it.

Then a thought stabbed through his mind like a warrior's knife. "Will not Blue Bottle be angry?"

"I must honor my friend." Crooked Lightning shrugged.

"Will not Blue Bottle follow and take the *wicapaha* of Little Bird?"

"I leave the girl-children here with you while I fight with Little Crow. When the trouble is over, I will send Evan Jacobson to come for them."

Drumbeater's heart swelled with pride. He would make a new song about Crooked Lightning, how he saved the *washechu* girl-children because of his bond with his life-and-death friend. The song would echo forever in the lodges of the People. Crooked Lightning, true warrior, man of highest integrity, one who follows the *washechu* tracks.

"And if I am killed, Many Beavers will hide the girl-children in the Turtle Mountains until the trouble is over."

"If you are killed," Drumbeater said with deep feeling, "I will avenge your death."

"Yes," Crooked Lightning said matter-of-factly. "Your duty. But first return the girl-children to Evan Jacobson."

Inside the teepee Badger whimpered. The faint odor of the skunk tribe permeated the air, and a coyote howled in the distance. It could be an Ojibwa making the cry of the coyote tribe.

"The White Eyes want to own the whole world." Crooked Lightning's voice settled into the singsong tone used at council fires. "Even each other. They have painted some men black and force them to be slaves." Uncle's face blended into the shadows pressing in against the glowing embers. "Now the paint will not wash off, and these men are slaves forever. The *washechu* are jealous and war against each other because the Great Chief does not allow all men to have slaves."

A *hinakaya* hooted in the bushes, and Drumbeater listened again for signs of the enemy. An owl call was an evil omen, often heard before attacks.

"I think the *washechu* wants to paint the People black to have more slaves." Crooked Lightning brushed a lock of graying hair from his eyes. "I will not be a slave."

Drumbeater sat as silent as a stone. He would not be a slave either. Even the thought of living on the reservation was repulsive, the reason he had moved west with his wife's people.

"The children of the People hunger. Yet the traders guard the food-payments from the Great Chief in storehouses with iron doors." Crooked Lightning's lower lip curled. "The food belongs to us and yet they lock it away."

"The trader Myrrick said the People should eat grass or their own dung if they hunger." Crooked Lightning spat into the embers, hissing like a snake. "That one is already dead with his mouth stuffed with grass."

Uncle pulled a small beaded bag from inside his tunic, reached into the bag and took out a small roll of paper birch. Drumbeater ran a finger across the squiggly marks.

"Look closely," Crooked Lightning said. "The white man's track."

A cold fear settled in Drumbeater's belly, and he cast an anxious glance at his wife suckling Otter through the doorway of the teepee. Love for them staggered Drumbeater with its intensity, weakened him. How quickly a life could be taken, lost forever.

"How strong is this medicine?"

"Strong enough to own the earth," Crooked Lightning said after long silence.

"But the earth cannot be owned," Drumbeater said. "Not like a man owns a horse or a dog."

"Strong enough to part the earth into parcels of ground, to divide the days into portions like moons."

Drumbeater shook his head and smiled, waiting for the laugh that would signal a joke. When the laughter did not come, he knew Uncle spoke earnestly. Though he spoke of the impossible, his uncle would not lie. "Straight Tongue says that the People must take on the ways of the white men."

Crooked Lightning had learned the tracks from Straight Tongue, a Black Coat called Whipple. Otter burped loudly on Willow Song's shoulder as she sang a soft lullaby, a prayer that Wakantanka would watch over them through the night. "Straight Tongue says that white men will not stop until they own it all."

"But how can a man own the earth?" Drumbeater flushed with shame at questioning someone as wise as his uncle but he couldn't help himself. His mind could not grasp it. "Can a man own the air? The bird tribe?"

"The Great Father in Washington makes tracks on paper and claims the land as his own." Crooked Lightning sighed. "His medicine is very strong."

"The People have lived on this land forever."

"Remember how Ojibwas pushed our fathers out of our northern lands, forced us to spread south and west? Long ago we moved freely to the edge of the great waters to the north and to the prairies of the south." Crooked Lightning's eyes carried the sadness of a goose whose mate has been killed, the burden of a dog pulling a travois. "Whipple said the *washechu* first pushed the Ojibwas out of their homes in the east. They in turn pushed us out of the north. Now the fat-eaters push again."

An owl swooped down with flapping wings and scooped a mouse from the grass. Another evil omen.

"The Sisseton will fight with you." Drumbeater's thoughts fluttered like young birds pushed from the nest.

"Little Crow made the mark that sold the hunting grounds to the White Eyes." Crooked Lightning brushed a buzzing fly out of his hair. "Let him fight to get it back."

"Our warriors are strong and courageous. If we help you, we can push them out forever."

"If we all die fighting them, we will never conquer the *washechu*. The Long Knives carry the mysterious iron and explosive dirt."

Willow Song laid the sleeping Otter into a nest of soft hides lined with the fluffy white down taken from cattails. Carefully, she positioned the dream catcher, a willow hoop with feathers spun into its web.

"The dream catcher snags the truth and lets the bad thoughts escape through the hole in its center," Crooked Lightning said at last. "Inktomi gave us this wisdom."

Darkness had fallen. They settled into a long silence. Listening to the loon tribe on the river, hearing in the distance the howl of a wolf, the screech of an owl. Above, the sky glowed with stars, as many as berries on a bush, as many as the stones along the shore of the big water to the north.

"Inktomi said both good and bad forces steer the People. You must listen to the good." Crooked Lightning pushed his long hair behind his shoulders with a toss of his head and a flick of his thick hand. "Or else you will be led down the path of destruction."

"What is the good force?"

"To heed Straight Tongue's message and move west, away from the Long Knives—or else cut your hair and become a farmer like the *washechu*."

Drumbeater looked at the trees surrounding them. On the prairies were no sheltering trees. Just open land and tall grass. He didn't want to be painted black and made a *wayaka* for the White Eyes. He didn't want to scar the earth with iron tools and plant crops like a woman.

"Tomorrow we will fast and enter the *eneepee*, vapor bath," Crooked Lightning slapped a thirsty *caponka* on his cheek. He stood. "We will make medicine. Ready your drum, Nephew."

A choking sadness fell suddenly upon Drumbeater. He wished only to raise Otter in Leaf Country in the ways of the People. Away from the White Eyes.

"Tears for women and war whoops for men to drown sorrow." Crooked Lightning's voice carried a hard edge.

Drumbeater kicked a glowing ember towards the middle of the charred heap of ashes. The dogs whined and curled up into furry balls near the mouth of the tent. The dampness of night filled the air and cooled the earth. It was past time for sleep.

"Tomorrow we make medicine," Crooked Lightning said and his eyes glittered again with the light of the stars overhead. "And then I go to my death."

6

"Little Crow Leads Bloody Uprising in Minnesota Valley"
St. Cloud Democrat, August 26, 1862

G UST RETURNED HOURS LATER AND FOUND Serena and the baby still hiding in the cellar.

Serena's relief was so great that she could do nothing but sob. Her legs were wooden, her mind blocked. They had survived after all. Or had they?

The savages had burned the wheat and destroyed their small garden. The stores of food so painstakingly gathered were ruined. Dead chickens littered the yard. The delphiniums had been pulled up by the roots, blue petals crushed in the grass. Dishes lay smashed against the wall of the cabin, and the wedding quilt had been taken. Serena found their precious cache of pennies from the egg money scattered across the yard.

"We need to get out of here," Gust said while he shaded his eyes with his forearm and looked toward town. "It looks like they're coming from the west. We need to travel east without delay. They might come back."

Serena numbly watched him wrap a few of their remaining possessions in an old sheet. She knelt and gathered the pennies from the dirt while Lena slept in her other arm. Lena must be getting better. She gathered a blue petal from the delphiniums and tucked it in her apron pocket.

Dark smoke billowed over the trees to the west and the smell of it permeated every breath.

"Looks like they hit the town," Gust said as they stumbled out of the yard, "God help us."

Serena carried the sleeping Lena wrapped in a small blanket woven by her mother. Gust limped beside her, carrying a bundle of extra clothes and the small Red Wing churn that had been stored in the root cellar.

They were almost out of clean swaddling cloths. What would they do if they couldn't stop to wash along the way? She refused to consider the savages behind her, the burning buildings to the west, the danger. Instead she thought of Lena, only Lena, the cloths she needed, getting her to a place of safety.

"Let me carry her," Gust said.

"Nei," Serena said in a voice more fierce than she intended. "She's more content with me."

They joined others fleeing the savages: a couple pushing two children in a wooden wheelbarrow, two maiden aunts visiting from St. Peter, a young bachelor farmer, the Sorensons. The expressions on everyone's faces were the same—disbelief and horror.

A stranger invited them to ride in his lumber wagon. It was a relief, Gust's ankle being bad and Lena sick. The man wore a blank expression and mumbled to himself.

"I don't know what happened," he said over and over. "I was just over the hill in the cornfield when I saw the smoke." He looked at Serena until their eyes locked. "Why would they kill my Lydia and our sweet babies? What had they ever done to be scalped and butchered in our own home?"

Gust fidgeted in the wagon box. Serena knew he was trying to think of something to say, something that would make the man feel better. Gust was like that, awkward in speaking his feelings. It was one of the reasons Serena loved him. But there was nothing to say to the man in such a hard place of grief. Words weren't enough.

Finally Gust said, "Do you want me to drive for you?"

"No," he answered. "I'll drive. I just wonder why it happened."

Serena looked at the man with pity but had nothing to say. There was too much to take in. Her mind could not imagine his loss. What could make the Indians do such terrible things? She and Lena might have been killed and butchered. It made no sense. Serena kissed Lena again, hugging her.

How quickly things could happen. Just that morning they were looking for a good harvest and suddenly everything changed. What would they do?

She searched Gust's face. Serena knew how he felt about the harvest, the need to repay his father. How could he endure such a blow? If only they had stayed in Burr Oak, none of this would have happened. If only they'd never married at all.

Minnesota was a terrible place.

Lena weakened with each passing hour, her little body burning with fever. The nutmeg did not help.

A stagecoach crowded with people met them on the trail. Men sat on top of the coach carrying guns or pitch forks, their long legs hanging over the side. Beside the red-headed driver, a young girl sat holding a little boy. The boy's nose bled, and the girl staunched it with her apron while holding the bridge of his nose. Through the open coach windows, Serena saw huddled women and children.

"Is there a doctor in your group?" Fear made Serena bold, helped her call out to complete strangers. "My baby is sick."

The men looked at each other but kept silent. "No doctor," said the driver in a strong Norwegian accent. "What's the matter?"

"Fever." Serena placed the fussy baby against her chest and rubbed her back. "Been sick since yesterday."

"Sounds like summer complaint." A gaunt woman with missing teeth pushed open the coach door and climbed out of the stage. Her hair was falling out of its pins, and she made no move to fix it. Her apron was almost threadbare and her shoes worn. She stepped over to the lumber wagon, hitched up her skirts, climbed up on the wheel and reached over to pull up Lena's gown. The woman frowned as she looked at her stomach. "No spots. Measles are going around."

"I ate tomatoes." Serena's words were breathless and ran together. "Maybe it's my milk."

"I doubt it," the woman said. "My Jacob never sickened, and I ate 'em near every day. It's the summer complaint."

"Nutmeg didn't help."

The woman's eyes were kind. "A wet rag on her forehead might bring down the fever." The woman patted Lena on the head and stepped down from the wagon wheel.

"Who are you and where are you headed?" Gust asked the driver.

The woman crawled back into the stage, and Serena tried putting Lena to her breast again, half listening to the men's conversation. The baby was lethargic, sleepy. A cool compress would help. Surely there would be water along the way.

"I'm Evan Jacobson, heading west to warn Fort Abercrombie. These folks will ride to the first town." The driver hesitated a little. "Want to follow along? There might be a doctor."

"No," Gust said. "We're going to Fort Snelling."

"Then get a message to the commander. Tell him Evan Jacobson goes to warn Fort Abercrombie."

The stage lurched forward and raised a cloud of dust as it made its way down the trail. Serena's mind whirled. What would Mor do? What would Auntie Karen recommend for summer complaint?

"Mister, I need to stop and wet a rag."

They came to a slough by the side of the trail. Gust dipped part of the sheet into the mucky green water and handed it to Serena. It smelled stale and swampy, but Serena placed the rag on Lena's head. Maybe it helped a little.

She shielded Lena from the hot afternoon sun by draping the blanket over their heads. Humidity pressed in, and the cicadas buzzed by as they traveled in the wagon. She nursed Lena, but it brought no relief. Serena's mouth dried to parchment, and she worried her milk would dry up. She needed water, but they had to keep moving. Indians were behind them. They didn't dare stop.

Finally after hours of fussing, Lena slept. Serena held her close and prayed. There might be a doctor in the next town. Maybe the worst was over.

"I'll take her for a while," Gust said, reaching for the baby and pulling back the blanket.

"Don't," Serena said. "She just went to sleep."

Gust let out a gasp and put his hand on Lena's head.

"You'll wake her."

"Serena-girl," he said as big tears sprouted from his eyes, "she's gone."

"Nei! She's better, see how she sleeps." Serena pulled Lena closer to her chest, clutching the blanket around her, stroking Lena's face. Lena's face felt cold and her lips were blue. "Her fever is down!"

"She's gone home with Jesus." Gust's voice was soft and sorrowful. He reached for the baby. "Give her to me, dear Serena. Our baby's gone."

"Nei!" Serena screamed and pushed him away.

"There's nothing we can do," Gust said and when she saw his face drip tears, she knew it was true. "Sweet Lena is gone."

Serena let Gust take Lena out of her arms and she sat in silence, gripping the gray blanket that had been Lena's since her birth, wishing she were dead also. How could she live without her baby?

They buried Lena beside the road half way to Fort Snelling. There were no boards to build a coffin. Gust, with tears flowing, found a hollow log and chopped it down to size with a borrowed axe from Sorenson. They tucked the sheet around Lena when Serena refused to let go of her blanket. Serena clutched the blanket to her face, inhaling Lena's fragrance. With a stab of grief, Serena realized her mor would never see her first grandchild.

There was no preacher to read over the grave but one of the women from the tattered group sang a Norwegian hymn, "I Know of a Sleep in Jesus' Name." The woman knew most of the words, and when she didn't, she hummed the melody.

"I know of a sleep in Jesus' name, a rest from all toil and sorrow;
Earth folds in her arms my weary frame, and shelters it till the morrow;
My soul is at home with God in heaven; her sorrows are past and over."

Serena could not sing although the words echoed in her mind. She knelt by the small grave and sobbed. It could not be, their precious Lena gone. It was too hard to bear. She felt as if the ground had been pulled from beneath her feet and she reached out to Gust to steady herself.

The man with the wagon tried to recite the Twenty-third Psalm but his voice trailed away in the middle.

"I left my Lydia back at the farm, buried her in the garden with the babies." He sniffed loudly and dissolved into tears. "I didn't pray over their graves. I was afraid and just left them."

"You did the right thing," Mr. Sorenson said. "We'll go back and have a decent burial later."

Then Mrs. Sorenson led them in the Lord's Prayer, and the service ended quickly.

"I'm sorry to rush you." Mr. Sorenson wiped his face with a ragged red handkerchief pulled from his pocket. "But we daren't tarry in this place with the savages on the loose. We must get to the fort."

Serena thought to herself that there needed to be something more. Her daughter was worth more than a mere pause alongside the road. She was worthy of real prayers, a genuine minister. But, she reasoned, if tears were prayers, enough prayers were said to send her off to heaven anyway, preacher or no preacher.

As the lumber wagon pulled away from the grave, Gust held Serena and tried to comfort her. Serena would not be comforted. She struggled out of his arms and looked back as long as she could, visualizing the map showing the road to Fort Snelling, trying to mark the spot, planning someday to return.

It was the end of the world, the end of her world.

Serena's milk flowed for days, the pain nothing compared to the grief in her heart that numbed her to everyone and everything.

7

"Refugees Flee Sioux Cruelty"
St. Cloud Democrat, September 2, 1862

I WANT TO GO HOME," SERENA SAID after they finally arrived in Fort Snelling. Her face was impassive. She had barely spoken during the long days on the trail. "I want my mor."

"Serena-girl," Gust tried to make a fire in the cold drizzle. They were impoverished, not even a kettle to fix their meals. They had nothing except the Red Wing churn and Lena's blanket. "I'll take care of you, you'll see."

"I want my mor," she repeated. "I want to go home."

"We can't." Gust wondered how they would survive. They had only sixteen cents left from the egg money. "We can't go back to Hutchinson because we have no money for another year's rent and the crops are ruined. There's no money to go back to Iowa either." He scraped a clod of mud from his boot with his pocketknife. The weather had been rainy on the trail. His father was right; mare's tail clouds meant rain. "I'll find work. When the trouble is over, we'll try again."

Serena gave him a silent look that unnerved him. How could he explain that they couldn't go back because of the money owed to his father? No matter if they starved, going home was out of the question until he had fifty-six dollars in hand. He had been so close. Another week and the harvest would have been gathered. Damn Sioux! Damn them to hell! He would never give his father the satisfaction of seeing him fail.

"You promised," Serena said. "You said we'd go home if things didn't work out."

"Don't worry." He drew her closer. "We'll have more babies. It'll be all right."

He had thought her lost forever when he came home that terrible day. It was the smoke that alerted him, smoke rising in billowing clouds beyond the trees where his wheat waited for the cradle. Dear God. His leg throbbed and sweat dripped down his back, but he had broken into a run when he saw the smoke. Not Serena. Not the baby. Running with the borrowed scythe thrown across his back.

I'll be a better person. Only spare Serena. Prayers sprang from a deep place, leaping unbidden to his lips. *I'll go to church.* Gust ran in spite of his leg, lurching across the pasture towards the house. Brownie lay dead on her side. *I'll be a better husband.* Weakness threatened his bones. Not Serena. Not the baby. Tears burned his eyes. *I'll take her back to Iowa like she wants. I'll keep my promise.* Sobs filled his chest when he saw the house standing. He burst through the door, seeing the scattered possessions, the broken dishes as if in a dream. Where were they? Flour covered the floor and there were scuffled tracks where the Indians had walked. He glanced out the window, expecting to see Serena and Lena dead on the ground. He barely noticed the burning wheat, though choking smoke made breathing difficult. He flung open the cellar door and looked down into Serena's terrified face. *Thank God.*

It didn't matter what happened as long as Serena was still with him.

Ja, it was hard to lose their little one. His heart ached when he thought of her, but it would have been unbearable to lose Serena. He couldn't live without her. There would be other babies, but Serena was all he had in the world. So what if they didn't return to Burr Oak? He would take care of her. She would see. It would be all right.

But Serena was not all right.

Gust thought she looked ill during that first long night camped out by Fort Snelling. Soldiers from the fort brought soup for each family. Gust spooned broth into her mouth from a tin cup but she turned away. By morning she was out of her head with fever, calling Lena's name over and over again, calling for her mother.

He had to find help for her or she might die as well. He would be left alone. In desperation, Gust sought Bishop Henry Whipple, a missionary by the fort.

The mission house was packed with refugees, some wounded, many ill. They found room only for Serena. Gust settled her as best he could on a pallet near the fireplace and then wandered outside and climbed on top of the woodpile. A few stars shone through scattered clouds. At least the rain had ended and he was off the damp ground.

Millions of mosquitoes kept him awake. When he finally dozed off, he dreamed of running to the cabin and finding Serena and Lena lying in a puddle of blood. Gust awakened in a cold sweat just as the bishop came outside for kitchen wood. It was almost dawn and Bishop Whipple looked like he hadn't slept either. Gust rolled down from the woodpile to help. The movement caused him great pain when his full weight landed on his bad leg, and he bit back a curse. He was unsure how to address a reverend, unsure how to converse with a man of the cloth.

"How's my wife?" Gust knelt by the chopping block and gathered oak chips into a gunnysack the bishop handed him for that purpose. Oak chips made good kindling, and a hot fire was needed for the cook stove in his kitchen.

"She's sleeping." Bishop Whipple straightened up, a hand to his lower back. He wasn't a young man, but his hair grayed only around his ears. Gust decided he was about his father's age. "Not many Minnesotans can say that."

"Have you heard anything?"

"The Santee Sioux are warring across the state, killing and destroying everything in their path." The bishop slumped on an oak stump and rested the armful of kitchen wood on his knee. "The western half of the state is almost empty. Folks left everything, fleeing for their lives. You should hear the stories they tell."

"Where's the army?"

"Governor Ramsey's sending Colonel Sibley to put down the insurrection." Bishop Whipple turned a sad face to Gust. "And calling home troops from the south."

"Thank God." Gust spit in the dirt by his feet.

"Only the Eastern bands are involved."

"Like hell," Gust said and was immediately ashamed of his language in front of a clergyman. "Look at what they've done."

Bile rose in Gust's throat. He picked more chips and threw them into the sack. They were the ones who had burned his crops and ruined his chances of repaying his father. The Sioux were to blame for killing Lydia and her children. Even Lena's death could be laid at their feet.

"The whites aren't blameless." Bishop Whipple leaned over and placed the armload of sticks on the ground. He reached in his pocket for a pipe and bit the stem between his teeth. "The Indian payment was late last year because of the war. This year it still hasn't come, and the Indians are starving."

"But what made them turn on us?" Gust said. "I've never treated them badly. I don't even know one Indian from another."

"The Indian agents at the reservation," Bishop Whipple took the cold pipe out of his mouth, "told the Sioux to eat grass if they were hungry."

"What?"

"While the storehouses were filled with food that belonged to them. The food was there but not the money."

"I don't understand," Gust said.

"The treaty promises both gold and supplies. The agent decided it was too much work to make separate distributions and insisted the food stores be handed out at the same time as the money." Bishop Whipple placed the cold pipe between his teeth again. "Which never came."

"That doesn't make sense." The bag bulged with oak chips. Gust handed it to Whipple. A rooster crowed in the distance. The air filled with the sound of bird songs and barking dogs. A baby cried inside the mission.

"No sense at all." Bishop Whipple gathered his armful of wood and stood to go back into the mission. "The men are fighting in the South. The Sioux see it as an opportune time to chase the white men out once and for all."

"Can they do that?" Gust had thought they would be safe at Fort Snelling. Sudden terror gripped him.

"The army is spread too thin," Bishop Whipple said and walked toward the house. "We are defenseless against them."

8

"40,000 Refugees, 10 Counties Emptied"
St. Cloud Democrat, September 4, 1862

A FEW GOOD MEALS AND HOT CHAMOMILE TEA mixed with wild honey relieved Serena's fever. Only a hoarse cough lingered but her spirits were low.

Bishop Whipple loaned her paper and ink to write a letter to her parents. With great care, Serena told of Lena's death and their survival of the Indian uprising. She wrote as small as she could to force as much information as possible on the single sheet, writing her love in the margins, filling every inch with the sorrowful news.

Serena knew the anguish her mother would feel when she read the letter, but she wrote without tears. Maybe they were used up, emptied out. Maybe she was already dead and didn't know it.

Serena and Gust remained at the mission after Serena's fever left, helping out where they could. They had nowhere to go. Serena cooked for the refugees gathered around the fort for protection. Gust chopped firewood. The work never stopped. As soon as breakfast was over, Serena started cooking dinner. As soon as dinner was over, she cooked supper. Mountains of dishes, three times a day. The work a blessing—it kept her from thinking.

"I'm afraid for the Sioux," Bishop Whipple said one afternoon as Serena stood wiping the cups and spoons. "This may be the end of them. If not now, surely after the war is over in the South."

Serena felt like a dead person, washing the dishes or sweeping the floors without thought or emotion. At his words, she looked at the reverend and noticed how tired he looked. Did he even sleep? He cared for the sick and wounded, fed the refugees, never resting.

"What do you mean?" Serena tried to focus her brain on his words, pushing back the fog that clouded her mind.

"They've named the soldiers sent home to quell the uprising," Bishop Whipple said. "They're calling them the Exterminators."

Although she had lived in America most of her life, she had trouble with some English words. "What does that mean?"

"It means they are sent to wipe them out."

"Good," Serena said and picked up another cup for drying. "Look what they've done to us."

"I've spent my whole life working with the Sioux," Bishop Whipple said. "They're backed in a corner with nothing to do but fight. Minnesota is big enough for all of us to live in peace together."

Serena disagreed but did not reply. If the bishop had been with her in the cellar, he would think differently. He would know better if he had seen Lydia and her babies. But she could not focus her thoughts. She felt more dead than alive. If only she were buried beside Lena along the road to Hutchinson.

Donated supplies stood heaped around the mission, and more donations arrived every day. Bishop Whipple said that even more people would be helping Minnesota except for the horrible news from the war in the South. Headlines shrieked Union losses in the Shenandoah Valley. The uprising was mentioned only in smaller print on the inside pages, although hundreds had been murdered and the state was in despair.

Gust found an abandoned shack in Pig's Eye where they could live until they decided what to do. The rent was cheap, but Serena dreaded leaving the safety and security of the mission. When Gust told her they were leaving, she could not reply. Bishop Whipple gave them a cooking pot, cloth ticking, and a sack of corn.

Serena sewed the ticking into a mattress with a borrowed needle and stuffed it with balsam boughs. It was lumpy but smelled fresh and kept them off the dirt floor. Gust traded two days' work for an axe and began cutting firewood. He could sell split oak for $4.50 a cord. There were downed trees in Pig's Eye from a July cyclone, free for the taking. Lena's blanket was too small to cover them and Gust paid a few of their precious pennies for an old buffalo robe to keep them warm.

Everywhere there were others like them, folks trying to start over, afraid of more attacks.

Serena's arms ached. She wondered if it was because she had clasped Lena so tightly to her chest while they were fleeing the savages. They ached so badly she couldn't sleep. For the first time in her life, she stopped singing as she did her work. It was as if the melodies had died with Lena. The words from the songs still floated in her mind but the tunes were missing. She wandered the house, gazing out the window at the flowing water.

Trying to remember, trying to forget.

9

"The Miscreants Deserve a Measure of Vengeance as
They Have Never Yet Received."
St. *Cloud Democrat*, August 28, 1863

DRUMBEATER AWAKENED BEFORE THE DAWN, his heart pounding, his hands reaching toward his knife. What had awakened him? The hooting *hinakayga* from the night before had been a warning. Perhaps even now Ojibwas surrounded their teepee. He heard Otter's heavy breathing from the cradleboard. Little Bird, the *wakon* girl-child, whimpered and called out.

"She's hungry," Willow Song whispered groggily at his side.

As she rustled in the packs for something to eat, Drumbeater held his knife and crept out of the teepee. He scanned the horizon for signs of the enemy. In spite of the girl-child's warning, the bird tribe twittered their predawn songs. Dogs wagged their tails and licked his outstretched hands. All was quiet, although yesterday's strange feeling of doom lingered.

He returned to the teepee. Although too dark to see clearly, Drumbeater saw the sleeping forms of Otter and Badger, silent in the dampness of morning. He smiled to think how Badger had fought Willow Song. She was courageous. In spite of her poor manners, she deserved her rest.

Little Bird turned away from the meat and called out strange words.

"What does she want?" Drumbeater whispered. "Is she sick?"

"She asks for *aguyape tachangu*," Crooked Lightning chuckled out of the darkness. Drumbeater had not known he was awake. "She asks for the spongy-lung bread of the *washechu*."

45

"I have no *aguyape tachangu.*" Willow Song sighed. "But I have good meat and maple sugar."

She held a bit of hard sugar to Little Bird's mouth. At first she pushed it away but then sucked eagerly as she tasted the sweetness. Willow Song placed a small bit of muskrat between her lips. Little Bird chewed and swallowed, reached for more.

Drumbeater's stomach growled, but it was a day of fasting, a day to make medicine. He pulled on his moccasins and walked to the river's edge, stripped and dove into the frigid water to bathe as was his habit. The sun purpled the world's eastern lip as he stood silently before the dawn, a cool wind blowing across his wet skin. He had always loved the smell of early morning, that moment before the sun appears on the horizon, the way the bird tribes chattered in the trees. Geese glided on the rippling river. Across the water a moose drank cautiously, lifting his nose to sniff the air with weeds hanging from his mouth, watching Drumbeater with distrust for a long moment before dipping his nose into the water again.

Silently Drumbeater gave homage to the Great Mystery, the creator of the sun, sky, and earth. Wakatanka wrapped himself in light, stretched out the heavens like a teepee overhead, and made the clouds his pony, riding on the wings of the wind. In wordless adoration, Drumbeater lifted up his people: Otter, Willow Song, Uncle, and the *wakon* child. He prayed the White Eyes would leave them to live in peace as they had always lived, free men on the earth.

The sun inched above the horizon. Drumbeater soaked in the vivid color and light, watched the outline of aspen against the morning. When he walked back to the teepee, his mind drifted. Did the White Eyes pray to the Great Mystery? Were they civilized enough to pray for peace?

Drumbeater had already counted coup, touching his enemy in battle. He had stolen horses and earned status as drum-keeper for the tribe. He wanted only to care for his family and live in peace. He had no quarrel with the *washechu*—he wanted only to be left alone.

When Drumbeater entered the teepee, Little Bird skipped across the doorway like a grasshopper learning to hop. He reached out and laid his hands on her head, rubbing his fingers on the twists of her golden hair that felt like a fisher's tail, soft and swirling. Little Bird looked up at him without fear, her blue eyes piercing into his heart. He felt a strange sensation in his head, a turning motion as if he traveled in a squaw boat on a turbulent river.

Badger pushed boldly between them and spoke angry words in her tongue, scolding like a red squirrel.

"She threatens your life if you touch the little bird," Uncle said with a laugh. His hair glistened wet from his morning bath, and he tied it away from his face with a cord of weasel skin. "Little Crow will not succeed if all *washechu* fight like Badger."

Drumbeat steadied himself and gathered the drum and beater stick with great respect, draping the carrying thong over his shoulder. The drum was crafted from a hollow pine log and a painted beaver skin laced with rawhide strips. The beater stick was of red willow with a leather head.

"Ho," Uncle said with an approving nod. "First we enter the *eneepee*, then we make medicine."

It was a perfect end-of-summer morning, the dew heavy on their feet, the forest laden with acorns and hazelnuts, the squirrel tribe gathering nuts for winter. In a secluded meadow, Willow Song had erected a small tent with a hot fire burning nearby. Stones heated around the edges of the fire, the sacred *tunkan*. Inside the *eneepee*, waited a leather skin filled with water.

All was ready. Drumbeater flushed with pride at his capable and beautiful wife. He had chosen well.

They moved the hot *tunkans* to the center of the tent using forked sticks to protect their hands, and then sprinkled them with water from the flask. A heavy steam hissed and filled the *eneepee*. The men sprinkled more water on the *tunkans*, praying the Great Mystery would cleanse them from all imbalances, and then sat in silence as the cleansing steam performed its task.

Crooked Lightning retrieved another rock from the outside fire. Drumbeater felt a stab of guilt knowing he should be the one fetching the *tunkans*, but his stomach roiled and the strange turning continued in his head. He sat as still as he could, hoping it would go away, that he would not disgrace himself with weakness. Fasting was practiced often among the People and though it was not unusual for him to be hungry, Drumbeater had never felt this way before. Perhaps he was ill.

Maybe it was the sense of doom that refused to leave his mind.

"Falling Mountain, your Grandfather, told me his dream before he died." Sweat rolled down Crooked Lightning's face, and he wiped it with the back of his hand. "It was after he was gored by the white *tatanka* but before his spirit passed into the mists of the Great Beyond."

Drumbeater gave Crooked Lightning his full attention. Every Dakota youth sought the Great Mystery for a vision to guide him through life but only on rare occasions did anyone share this dream.

"Wakantanka gave Falling Mountain a vision so startling that his breath was sucked out of his mouth and the light drained from his eyes." Crooked Lightning sat perfectly erect, as at ease in the cramped lodge as if he sat before a tribal council. "Falling Man said that he lay as a dead man for more than a day while Wakantanka showed him the end of the world."

Drumbeater held his breath lest he miss a single word and willed his head to cease spinning. This was strong medicine, a message from his ancestor, almost as if from the Great Beyond. He gripped the grass beneath him with both hands, struggling to sit upright as if nothing bothered him.

"I was young when he told me," Crooked Lightning said. "I carried the dream with me through the years." He smiled a wry smile and brushed a grasshopper off his lap. "Even the fawns skip and play though wolves peep out at them from behind the hills, ready to devour them."

"How old were you when he told you this dream?"

"Eighteen summers," he spoke a reproof with his eyes and Drumbeater realized he had interrupted. "Before the Black Coats, before the treaties robbed us of our hunting grounds. You were still a *hoksiyopakiya* at breast." Crooked Lightning squared his jaw. "I share it with you now in case I am killed and cannot tell you later."

Drumbeater lowered his head slightly, seeking cooler air below the oppressive upper layer of steam. Since his father's death so long ago, Crooked Lightning had been more of a father than an uncle. He hoped Crooked Lightning's death dwelt far in the future.

"Falling Mountain dreamed an *icamnatanka* rolled in over the prairies, coming from the east instead of the west. The blizzard destroyed everything in its path. *Wogan* piled so high that the mountains crumbled under the weight."

Outside he heard the welcoming calls of the rest of the People joining camp. Barking dogs, a child's laugh, and voices familiar and welcome.

"Falling Mountain found his name in the dream but he did not understand its meaning." Crooked Lightning spoke quietly, hurriedly as if he feared the others might interrupt. The words fell from his lips like the warning cry of a hawk. "Falling Mountain said that he did not understand until he was gored by the white buffalo. When the sacred horn pierced his body, revelation came to him."

Drumbeater's heart thudded wildly in his chest. He was in the presence of great medicine. Perhaps as strong as *washechu* tracks on paper birch.

"The white buffalo charged from the east without warning. Falling Mountain stood in an open prairie and the *tatanka* rushed in from the east and delivered its fatal blow."

He looked at Drumbeater as if expecting him to understand. Drumbeater sat in a stupor. He saw little connection between a blizzard and the horn of a white buffalo and the death of his grandfather so long ago.

"White men will come from the east and destroy the People, as many as *wasukaza* in a storm. As Falling Mountain did not provoke the white buffalo, and yet it killed him, so will the White Eyes roar in from the east and destroy the People. In his dream, the mountains crumbled. When the white men come, even the land itself is changed forever."

Drumbeater weakened and a sharp pain pierced his forehead. Maybe the air was being sucked from his lips as well. Maybe he, too, would lie as dead under the power of the sacred vision.

Otter. Willow Song. The People. All he loved. Fiercer than a blizzard. As deadly as the horn of the white buffalo. An unprovoked attack from the east. *Wakon* as great as the *washechu* tracks, strong enough to divide the earth.

They sat in silence as the steam settled. Children laughed, and a dog sniffed the tent flap.

"Enough," Crooked Lightning's voice sounded relieved, almost happy. "We dip in the river and then dance the Medicine Dance. We seek Wakan-tanka's help. You will beat the drum."

Fresh air cooled him as he left the eneepee, and icy water robbed Drumbeater of his breath for a brief moment when he first dove into the river. Maybe the pain in his head lessened—but the strange twirling continued along with the feeling of doom.

Before any spiritual crisis or possible danger, a true human entered the eneepee and made steam on the sacred tunkan.

Whatever happened, Drumbeater hoped to meet it as a warrior.

10

"Col. Sibley Slow to Quell Indian War"
St. Cloud Democrat, September 9, 1862

IN PIG'S EYE, GUST PLOTTED HIS NEXT MOVE with every swing of the axe.

It was a setback. Sure, he must pay off his debt to his father, but even if he scrimped and saved every penny, he would never be able to gather such a large sum.

His only hope was to wait until things settled down and try again. If the war continued and prices stayed high, one good wheat crop would yield money for his debt and enough to start over. He would build a stout cabin for Serena, and they would have more babies.

His eyes teared to remember his sweet daughter cold at Serena's breast, buried on that God-forsaken trail.

He swung the axe as hard as he could and heard the "pop" of splitting oak, sniffed the earthy fragrance of the wood. Damn Indians! He would have made it if the Sioux had left them alone. Lena would have lived if they had been able to care for her in peace. Serena wouldn't be moping around like a crazy woman. Damn the Sioux to hell, every one of them.

Gust forced himself to think of other things, to guide his anger into resolve.

He would make it. Nothing would stop him. He would have his own farm. By God, he wouldn't be a cotter like relatives in the Old Country. He'd be a landowner if it killed him.

Luther Madsen mailed a clipping from the *St. Paul Journal* saying the $71,000 in gold promised by treaty to the Sioux Indians would be given instead to Minnesota survivors of the uprising.

"Just think, Serena." Gust read the article out loud after supper while Serena churned. "The government is paying the victims of the uprising though the real victims are dead."

Serena looked at him with that silent look he had grown to hate, letting the churn rest on her patched apron.

"A thousand dead, Serena," he said. "The Sioux massacred a thousand settlers. The paper says it's the worst Indian uprising in the history of the United States. President Lincoln himself says so. Says the report to Lincoln lists no less than 882 people killed. And they're still finding bodies in the frontier—found seventeen more today in some slough down by New Ulm."

Serena picked up the churn and pushed the dasher up and down. She cradled the crock in her arms like she had once held Lena, and the sight of it unsettled him somehow. She wouldn't look at him.

"Listen! 'Governor Ramsey says the Sioux Indians of Minnesota must be exterminated or driven forever beyond the borders of the State. He calls for abrogating all Sioux Treaties and using the annuity money to reimburse white victims of the war.'"

Serena continued to churn.

"We're victims." His brain calculated dollars and cents, thought of a plan. "We're victims as much as anyone else. We've lost everything."

Gust limped to the capitol the very next day. The money wouldn't last with all the people affected by the uprising. The paper said more money would be issued the following spring, but Gust couldn't wait. He filed papers stating he had lost a crop of wheat (no matter if he exaggerated on the size of the field and made no mention of the rust that threatened the crop), a field of turnips (there were turnips in the garden but only one row), a cabin (it wasn't fit for living even if the Indians hadn't burned it and they were only renters) and their food stores (he didn't mention it was only one sack of flour).

After perjuring himself to this degree, he took a deep breath and wrote one more sentence. Lena was dead, after all, and Gust was not one to quibble over details. Claiming her death as caused by the Sioux increased his payment by one hundred dollars. It was almost true, but it pained him nonetheless.

Luther Madsen swore before a judge as to the truth of the written statement, and Gust walked away with two hundred and fifty dollars in his pocket. On the way home, he stopped for a celebratory beer at the Pig's Eye Saloon.

IT WAS THE CHANCE OF A LIFETIME, and Gust Gustafson knew it. To buy a farm under tillage meant a leg up, as his father used to say, a head start.

"It's good land." Andrew Salmon stood before him in the Pig's Eye Saloon and twisted his hat in his bony hands. "Eighty acres of tillable soil, forty acres of lowland good for hay."

Salmon's eyes rimmed red. His hands, rough and work worn, trembled as he folded and refolded the brim of his hat. The man reeked of sweat and old tobacco. The piano, slightly out of tune and missing a few keys altogether, played a raucous rendition of "She'll Be Coming Round the Mountain" while a tired-looking woman sang without smiling. Salmon stared at the glass of beer in Gust's hands, his Adam's apple bobbing twice.

Gust remained silent, as if uninterested. He didn't offer the man a beer or invite him to join him at the table. *Let him sweat*, he thought as he took another swallow. His ankle pained him, and he propped it up on the chair across from him. The place stank of stale beer. A feeling of power surged through him, sitting at the table with money in his pocket, drinking beer while Andrew Salmon groveled before him.

"Forty acres of woods and the Pomme de Terre River," Salmon continued. "You'll never lack for fuel or water."

Gust sipped his beer, pushed down the guilt in his mind. It was almost too easy, like taking advantage of this bumbling fool.

"And the best neighbors you'll ever find in Anton and Dagmar Estvold." He reached a trembling hand to his chin and wiped a thread of spittle. "I have to sell," he continued. "Every cent I own is tied up in that farm."

Gust tried to keep his face expressionless, his hands calm around the glass. If he kept his wits about him he would have enough money to buy a cow and a team of oxen.

"We're leaving Pig's Eye right away." Salmon twisted his hat. "Going back to Decorah to work with my brother. His sons are in the army and he's short of help."

"Where did you say it was?" Gust asked, more to make conversation than gather information. His mind calculated the money in his pocket. There was enough to repay his father, rent the Hutchinson farm for another year, and start over. But if he played his cards right, he might be able to buy Salmon's farm outright. Here was his chance.

If he bought Salmon's farm, he couldn't repay his father until after the first harvest. He needed a team of oxen and a cow or two, maybe some chickens. They wouldn't come cheap and he'd need seed to plant a crop and buy a plow. It was a gamble. Quickly he made up his mind. After all, his father didn't need the money and he did.

"Pomme de Terre," Salmon said. "Halfway between Alexandria Wood and Fort Abercrombie. Stages stop by regular, and oxcarts from Georgetown go right by the farm. It's easy to get supplies. It's a good farm, a small cabin."

"That's Indian country." Gust's words probed like a knife. "Not safe from what I've heard."

"Exaggerated," Salmon said, and Gust smelled the fear in his words. "They've arrested the bad ones and will hang the lot of 'em. There's soldiers now at the fort." Salmon swallowed again, looking at the beer in Gust's hands, bobbing his Adam's apple once more. "Indians are gone."

"But you're leaving." Gust almost laughed out loud, knowing he was going to get the farm for a song.

"All my tools was there," Salmon said. "I can't promise the cabin, but the land will be there. Prettiest farm I ever saw."

In the end, Gust carried a deed for a one-hundred-sixty-acre farm in Pomme de Terre, and Andrew Salmon walked away with barely enough money to get his family back to Iowa.

"Now the hard part." Gust spoke to Salmon's retreating back as he finished his beer. "To convince Serena."

IT WAS HARD TO EXPLAIN, THOUGHT GUST as he stumbled back to their small rented shack on the Mississippi River, but he dreaded telling Serena their good news. He felt a little tipsy from the beer and his ankle was unreliable on the uneven ground. Gust took care not to lose his footing, the deed in his pocket, or the remaining gold eagles.

Of course, they couldn't expect to move to the farm until the Indian scare was settled. They would winter at Pig's Eye and move to the frontier in the spring. But even so, he dreaded telling Serena. All she thought about was going home.

His mother would have understood. He could remember her reading the story of Joseph and the colored coat.

"Someday you'll be like Joseph," his mother would whisper to him. "You'll flourish in all you do, and your father and brothers will look up to you with respect."

He wished he were on his way to tell his mother about the reparation payment and the new farm in Pomme de Terre—instead of Serena.

It wasn't that Serena spoke back to him or complained about his decisions. It was her lack of speaking that troubled him. She didn't sing around the house anymore. She spent all her time churning or looking out the windows. Losing a baby was hard on a woman. She needed to have another one to make her forget about Lena.

Serena was passive, submissive as a good wife should be. But he wondered, always wondered, her true feelings.

Though he was too afraid to ask.

11

"ABERCROMBIE SAFE! Indians Gone! They Fought Bravely."
St. Cloud Democrat, September 23, 1862

S HE COULDN'T BELIEVE HER EARS.

Gust must be crazy to think it safe to move to a deserted farm in the wilderness. The papers were filled with the siege of Fort Abercrombie, and yet Gust bought a farm close to that western outpost. But Serena knew Gust better than anyone else. He was ambitious but not crazy. When he set his mind on something, there was no changing it. Her father had warned her about the stubbornness of Swedes. She should have listened.

After what they had been through, maybe it didn't matter. She picked up the small Red Wing churn and pushed the dasher up and down. Churning was a comfort. It gave her a chance to sit and rest and filled her empty arms as well. Somehow her arms didn't ache as much when she held the churn in her lap. It was almost as if she were holding Lena again.

Lena's eyes, gray as all infants' were but undoubtedly destined to be blue like her own, could see nothing but blackness from her narrow grave on that forgotten trail. Serena thought of the map showing the place of Lena's grave. In her mind's eye it was marked with a small x east of Hutchinson. So far away and such a lonely spot for her little one to sleep the long sleep of death. Serena remembered her dainty lips, the way Lena had patted her breast when she nursed, her perfect sweetness.

She wanted to curse Gust for dragging her so far away from her parents but stopped herself. After all, she went willingly, and Gust had wept as he chopped the hollow log for Lena's coffin. She could not damn Gust, but at the same time her feelings had changed for him.

Growing up, Serena had always admired Gust. He was the smartest boy in his class. And when his bad leg kept him out of rougher games with the older boys, Gust read books and drew pictures on his slate. Three years older than Serena, he always treated her like an equal. It was Gust who understood her love of maps. He was the one who clipped maps printed in the Burr Oak Review for her. Her parents couldn't afford to take the city's only newspaper, and Serena treasured these bits of newsprint more than she would ever admit and hid them in an old cigar box under her bed.

Once Gust gave her a kitten. She remembered how he smiled when she won the spelling bee. She was glad when he couldn't go off to war when the others signed up, glad that he wouldn't have to kill or be killed.

Though both Lutheran, Gust attended the Swedish Church in town while the Brandvolds attended the Norwegian Church out in the country. She had argued to marry Gust, begged and pleaded until her parents allowed it. They were reluctant because of the religious difference, but in the end they couldn't deny her. She couldn't wait to be on her own and away from them.

Now Serena wanted only to return to her parents. She would try it Gust's way in Pomme de Terre, though, wherever that was. But if it didn't work out in a year, she would go home with or without him. She missed the gentle wit of Far, the steady wisdom of Mor. If she were home, Serena could tell them about Lena's illness and death. They would know the words to make it better, to take the pain away. Gust had tried in his awkward way. Serena knew he had tried. He worked day and night trying to get ahead.

He wanted to go traipsing off to the wilderness. It didn't matter. If the Indians killed them all, at least they would be reunited with Lena in heaven. But if she were still alive in a year, she'd return to Iowa. The dasher slowed, the butter had turned.

The days slowly dragged into weeks. Serena put off writing her mother and father as long as possible. When she finally penned the letter, she said they would be moving home in another year if things didn't work out. It was the truth after all—she would give Gust a year.

A few tears splattered on the page as she signed her name, blurring the ink. She noticed how odd "Serena Gustafson" sprawled on the paper.

Serena Brandvold looked much better. She had made a big mistake. She might never see her family again. The twins were almost finished with school, soon old enough to marry. Serena hoped they wouldn't travel away from Mor and Far. It wasn't good for a daughter to be separated from her parents.

She tucked the letter in the windowsill for Gust to mail.

12

"Captain Freeman Afraid to go to Abercrombie—
Even with 60 Armed Men"
St. Cloud Democrat, September 21, 1862

DAGMAR ESTVOLD GLANCED OUT THE WINDOW as she finished the last of the supper dishes. Soldiers stood guard around the barricades of Fort Pomme de Terre. She felt a smug feeling of safety in spite of herself now that the stockade was nearing completion. The walls couldn't go up soon enough.

Dagmar's thoughts went to Andrew and Melinda Salmon. They had talked about going to a brother's farm in Iowa. With the Indian unrest, it was doubtful they would make it to Iowa this year. Unless, of course, they sold their Pomme De Terre farm and used the money for steamer passage.

They had all thought Salmon was jumping the gun when he up and left with the army. But maybe he had done the right thing. He left Pomme de Terre when he had the chance. Dagmar swished the rag around the inside of the frying pan, scraped a burned spot with the back of her thumbnail. After the Red Men killed Andrew's son, the fight went out of him. Of course, you couldn't blame him. But Andrew wasn't much younger than Anton—too old to start over.

And only a fool would buy a farm in Pomme de Terre with the Sioux still on the warpath. Dagmar slammed the cast iron kettle on top of the cook stove and slumped into a chair by the table. Andrew would be lucky if he got anything for the farm, in spite of years of backbreaking work. And with the price of Iowa land, he'd end up a cotter for the rest of his life.

She sighed and reached a rough hand to secure the hairpins holding gray braids in a tight crown around her head. Age had caught up to her. She thought of the droop in her chin and the swelling in her feet.

"Any coffee?" Anton walked over to the stove and jiggled the pot.

"We're not young anymore," she said. "We've lost our ox, our cow—those damn *skraelings* even took our ewe."

"Now then." Anton poured water from a wooden bucket into the coffee pot and pulled it to the hottest part of the stove. "It's a good thing our boys aren't home to hear such language." He flipped open the firebox and poked another branch into the embers, stirring until the dried leaves caught fire. He dropped the lid with a clatter.

"It's not fair." Dagmar reached for the coffee tin and grinder, pouring a careful handful of beans and turning the crank. "Our situation should be settled. Instead we're back at the bottom." The heady fragrance of fresh coffee filled the room. In spite of herself, her shoulders relaxed. Nothing calmed nerves and tempers like real coffee.

"Not exactly the bottom. We own this inn free and clear," Anton said in a measured voice. "And the fields."

"But the ox-carters won't be traveling for months!" Dagmar stood abruptly and carefully poured the ground coffee into the pot of boiling water. "Who knows if they'll ever come back?"

"We've got a roof over our heads and fish in the river." Anton pulled two metal cups from behind a curtained shelf and set them on the table. "And the army's building walls around us."

"Fort Pomme de Terre sounds better than it looks." Dagmar snorted. "The Sioux might still murder us in our beds."

Anton pulled the coffee pot away from the hottest burner as the water bubbled over the edge of the spout, hissing on the hot stove. "All these nice young soldiers will protect us. We've not a care in the world, Mother."

"And not a cow or ewe."

"So, we drink our coffee black." Anton stoked the fire with another stick of oak. "We still have our hog. And a few hens and a rooster. All that matters is that we're alive and the boys are well."

Of course, he was right. Against their wishes, Ole and Emil had enlisted and were off fighting in the South. Their letters said they were doing fine. That's what mattered. And maybe it was the Good Lord who kept them away from Minnesota when the Sioux came screaming in like Vikings. Lord only knew why they attacked—no one could understand the savage mind. What could be gained by murdering innocent people?

Dagmar wrapped a rag around her hand and lifted the hot coffee pot to pour the dark brew through a piece of cheesecloth to drain the grounds to save for re-use. They were low on everything. She didn't know how they would make it through the winter with nothing but hay harvested this year. Usually the ox-carters kept a supply of goods flowing into the fort and a steady stream of business for the inn—sleeping in the loft and buying meals at their table. Dagmar and Anton had made a good living until the uprising.

"Remember the Old Country?" Anton said after a loud slurp of scalding coffee. "You slaved for that rich noble for only room and board."

"That bastard." Dagmar bit back the words but it was too late. "Don't forget the new dress every year—and a day off at Jul." Anton often complained that she was too plain spoken, and getting more so with each passing year. Well, so be it. She had a mind and a tongue and the right to speak as well as any man.

"We're better off now." Anton fished a lump of sugar from the almost empty dish and soaked it in coffee before popping it in his mouth. "*Naar enden er god er allting godt.*" His patronizing tone made Dagmar wish she could whack the frying pan over his head. "All's well that ends well."

"Maybe Olaus Reierson will stay with us." Dagmar tried to change the subject to a more optimistic topic. "Captain McLarty says civilians in the area must winter at the fort."

"Olaus's not exactly in the fort's jurisdiction." Anton drained the last swallow of coffee from the bottom of the cup. "I doubt we'll see the Icelander."

"How will we make it with the boys gone and no hope of company?" She picked up the dishrag and wiped the table. "What if the Indians fort us up next year, too, and you can't plant a crop?"

"*En dare kan spore mer en ti vise kan svare.*" Anton's voice was indeed patronizing. "One fool may ask more questions than ten wise men can answer."

Dagmar threw the wet rag at him.

13

*"Lincoln's Emancipation Proclamation Published in
Northern Newspapers"*
St. Cloud Democrat, September 9, 1862

GUST KNEW SOMETHING WAS WRONG as soon as he saw his cousin's face.

A flock of geese honked above him. In spite of the calendar, the weather held bright and summer-like with sumac blazing scarlet midst the gnarled pile of downed trees.

"Luther," he said in a jovial tone to hide his anxiety. "What are you doing in Pig's Eye?"

"Don't forget I did this for you." Luther sat on a stump, pulled off his boots, and rubbed first one foot and then the other, slapping a pesky deer fly buzzing around his sweaty brow. "My corns are killing me, and I've wasted a day from work to bring you word."

"What's wrong?" Gust swung the axe one more time and left the blade deep in the log he was working on. A dull axe would help no one and wedging it in wood prevented rust.

"There is to be an inquiry," Luther said.

"What about?"

"Some do-gooder from Washington is coming to oversee the reparation claims." He rubbed his feet again before pulling on his boots. "Somehow they got word about fraudulent claims."

A smothery feeling engulfed Gust, just like he had felt in Burr Oak under his father's scrutiny. He felt closed in, pressed down. He heard his voice as if from a great distance. "Thanks for telling me."

"Fix it," Luther said. "My job is at stake."

"What can I do?"

"Pay it back, of course," he said. "Tell them it was a mistake."

Gust thought of the money spent on the farm in Pomme de Terre. There was no going back. It was safer to tell no one about it. Gust shifted the weight off his bad leg.

"I've been planning on moving out of this cold country, maybe going to Missouri. That country might be a little easier for my bum leg."

"There's trouble with the Rebs in Missouri," Luther said. "It might not be such a good place with the war and all."

"I'm thinking northern Missouri, away from the fighting. It's good apple country. I've always wanted an orchard."

"Well be quick about it. Either pay it back or move out. The sooner you go, the better I'll sleep."

Gust picked up the axe and split wood as fast as he could after Luther left. It was late to travel to Pomme de Terre, he knew that much. Although the Sioux surrendered at Wood Lake on September 23, they had since scattered across the plains. The army feared no large scale attacks but isolated raids continued across the western half of the state. Papers said Captain Samuel McLarty had been transferred from Fort Ripley to Pomme de Terre.

Surely it would soon be safe with soldiers building a stockade and patrolling the region. The smothery feeling pressed in, and Gust knew he had to leave at once, Indians or no Indians. If he stayed in Pig's Eye, his crime would be discovered. He could end up in jail. What would happen to Serena? He had no choice but to leave. It was the only way.

At least he had money. They'd take the steamboat to St. Cloud and stay there for the winter if the weather turned. Some years it was nice into November and an old trapper at Fort Snelling predicted a Squaw Autumn, long and warm. Maybe they'd be lucky. Salmon said there was a cabin waiting unless the Sioux burned it down. His mind was made up by the time Serena called him for supper.

"It's no use wasting money on rent when we can be on our own place," Gust said when Serena questioned the hurry of the move. "I want to get my crop in as soon as possible in the spring."

He wrote a letter to his father telling how they were burned out by the savages and were moving to Missouri. He would repay the loan after his first harvest. It was better if they thought they were in Missouri in case the government made inquiries.

Gust folded the letter to his father in thirds and sealed it with a blob of melted wax. He set it aside to cool. When Serena left the cabin to visit the outhouse, he took her letter from the windowsill and threw it into the stove. It pained him to deceive Serena, but he knew what she would say, how she would look at him. She would be disappointed, and he couldn't afford to disappoint her—not after all she'd been through.

Things would be better when they were on their own place. He'd repay his father in a year and everything would be fine. He poked a stick into the fire, pushed her fine script into the flames and watched it singe and burn. She would have another baby, a boy this time, and they would be landowners, safe and happy on their own farm. Surely the end result was worth keeping a secret for a few months.

It would all pay off in the end if he kept his wits about him. He picked up the letter and tucked it in his pocket, whistling as he left for the fort to mail it. The fort kept a newspaper posted in the sutler's window for anyone to read. Maybe there was something more about the investigations.

14

"The People Here Intend to Kill Any Blanket-Wearing and Arms-Bearing Indian Who Steps into Brown County . . . Unless the Whole Band Is Delivered to Us for Punishment."
St. Cloud Democrat, August 29, 1862

THE RHYTHM DROWNED EVERYTHING from Drumbeater's mind. Surely the medicine of the drum would ease the pain in his head.

"Hi-yi-yi!"

At the sound, old men and the handful of warriors kept back from the hunt joined them in the meadow blanketed with purple-tinged grass. Standing Tall, great chief of the Sisseton, had unexpectedly returned from the hunt. His presence caused a stir of excitement, like the ripples caused by a pebble thrown into the water.

"Hi-yi-yi!"

One by one the men joined Drumbeater around the sacred drum, each adding his drumstick to the cadence, pounding as one man.

"Hi-yi-yi!"

Loud wailing cries blended together in a haunting song that filled the clearing as a roaring wind fills a gorge, as mournful as a loon calling out to its mate.

"Hi-yi-yi!"

Although women and children were forbidden from the Medicine Dance, small boys peeked from behind the hazelnut bushes, peered out from the branches of a nearby maple. Drumbeater saw their wide eyes, knew they hungered to be warriors. He hoped they would live to be warriors, that the White Eyes would stay away.

"Hi-yi-yi!"

Drumbeater forgot his hunger, forgot his thirst, forgot the *washechu* children, and forgot his fears for the People in the mesmerizing beat of the drum. But he could not forget the pain in his head, the swirling motion that threatened to topple him.

"Hi-yi-yi!"

Crooked Lightning stepped away from the drum, bowing and dancing the story of enemy scalps, famous hunts, and counting coup. His steps flattened the tall grass beneath him, pressing out a sweet fragrance with his feet. Crooked Lightning danced the story of Falling Mountain gored by the white *tatanka* from the east. Drumbeater shivered, feeling the blizzard of his grandfather's dream, thinking how the *washechu* were as cold blooded and heartless as the storm. Uncle lifted first his right foot and then his left in the way of the People, always facing forward, always in the blessing of the Great Mystery.

Drumbeater memorized the songs and steps of his uncle. Perhaps he would not see Crooked Lightning again in this life.

The small band sang and danced their prayers to the Great Mystery throughout the morning.

"Hi-yi-yi!"

The meadow twirled. Drumbeater willed himself to stay on his feet lest he be disgraced. For a panicked minute he feared he'd fall as his grandfather fell beneath the weight of the strong medicine, his breath sucked from his mouth.

When the sun was directly overhead, understanding came. Just as Falling Mountain understood the meaning of his dream when the white *tatanka* gored him, Drumbeater realized his sickness was caused by the strong medicine of Little Bird. Touching her had been a mistake. He breathed a silent prayer to the Great Mystery, giving thanks that Badger had pushed him away in time to save his life.

Surely Badger was sent by Wakantanka to both guard Little Bird and protect others from touching her strong medicine.

They danced into the afternoon, drums echoing through the forest, singing as one voice. Drumbeater kept the cadence as steady as his pounding head. He closed his mind to the thought of a cool drink from the river. He refused to recognize the roiling in his belly, the ache in his hand and arm. He drummed until the sun dipped towards the western horizon.

Standing Tall laid his hand on Drumbeater's arm as a signal to stop. Silence echoed through the clearing. Drumbeater was almost overcome by weakness, his right hand so cramped he could not release the drumstick.

Standing Tall pointed with his chin and someone passed the red pipe of *kinnikinick*. They sat around the *eneepee* fire, and Standing Tall touched a burning coal to the bowl of the pipe, puffed a few long puffs and then passed it to the warrior next to him.

When all had smoked, Standing Tall stood. He said nothing. Just stood before them, silent as the sacred *tunkan*.

It was as if the world waited for his words.

"Little Crow makes war with the *washechu*." Standing Tall's words raised the hair on Drumbeater's neck like the strong medicine before zig-zag fire strikes the earth. "Those on the reservation hunger, though Long Knives hoard like squirrels the food belonging to the People. The traders steal. The animals flee from the scarred earth, gouged by the iron tools of the White Eyes. There are no elk or deer left on the reservation, no buffalo. There is great suffering among the eastern bands."

Someone murmured to his left, but Drumbeater didn't look his way lest the elders think he joined in the man's disrespect.

"The Great Chief sent his Long Knives to the far country. Little Crow thinks it is the time for all bands to unite and push the White Eyes out of this land of sky-blue water." Standing Tall searched the faces around the fire. "A messenger came to me while on the hunt, asking for Sisseton warriors to join the fight against the White Eyes." A murmur of surprise rippled around the circle. "I told the messenger we need our warriors in Leaf Country to guard our women and old ones during the rice harvest."

Grumbling sounded again to his left, and Drumbeater chanced a quick glance. It was Star Fist, a young troublemaker and complainer, always quick to protest any decision made by the elders.

"I return to make sure the Sisseton stay clear of this trouble. This matter concerns only the Mdewakantons and Wahpekutes." He looked directly at Star Fist. "We give the Long Knives no excuse to bring the exploding powder against our women and children."

"Little Crow is right," Star Fist said loudly. "We must fight now before our brothers die from hunger."

"I have spoken," Standing Tall said. "This does not concern us."

Crooked Lightning said, "May I speak?"

Standing Tall nodded and sat down and Crooked Lightning stood, his strong face framed against the backdrop of the green forest.

"The Great Chief in Washington forgets his Dakota children and does not hear their cries of hunger." Drumbeater fastened his eyes on Crooked Lightning and for a moment two uncles stood before his eyes speaking with one voice. "He has put Chief Ramsey, the one they call governor, over us." Crooked Lightning spat on the ground. "That one tricked our fathers to make the track of the *washechu* that gave our hunting grounds to the White Eyes."

Dogs barked from the camp, and Drumbeater remembered how the sun bounced off the hair of the wakon girl-child. He should have been more careful. The Great Mystery sent omens, but he had been too proud or stupid to heed the warning. He hoped Willow Song kept Otter away from the Little Bird. Who knew if such a young one could survive the strong medicine if it sickened a strong warrior?

"Chief Ramsey calls Sibley to bring war to the People, and we can expect no mercy at the hands of such evil men."

"But only the eastern bands are involved," Standing Tall said.

"The Long Knives will fight all of us." Crooked Lightning tightened the red blanket around his shoulder. "They care little for actual facts."

When he spoke no more, Standing Tall addressed him respectfully. "How do you know the *washechu* men, Ramsey and Sibley?"

"Straight Tongue, the Black Coat named Whipple, is friend to the Dakota." A murmur of approval blew through the circle like wind through autumn leaves. "Straight Tongue sent tracks to the Great Chief and complained that thieves and robbers were placed over us." Crooked Lightning stood erect and calm before them, poised and dignified. "I followed these tracks in the *wotaninwowapi* of the White Eyes. The newspaper told about it, how the Great Chief did nothing."

"White Eyes cannot speak the truth," Star Fist said. "This Black Coat is no different."

"Straight Tongue says the *washechu* want to own the whole world."

Crooked Lightning sat down, and Star Fist leapt to his feet without asking permission.

"I will not be among the Cut-Hairs," Star Fist said. "It's better to die as a warrior with Little Crow than live the life of a dog on the reservation."

A commotion stirred the camp, and the dog tribe barked warning of visitors. A painted brave rode his spotted pony to the clearing. Blue Bottle leapt down and swaggered up to the fire, brandishing a lance with fresh scalps. Dried blood covered his upper body and leather leggings. Blood splattered eagle feathers framed his hawkish face.

"Standing Tall," Blue Bottle said. "Little Crow waits for your warriors at the camp of Red Iron. Why do you waste time?"

"The Sissetons are not at war," Standing Tall said evenly. "What brings you here?"

"All tribes must rise up with one voice and drive the White Eyes away forever," Blue Bottle said and brandished his lance. "This is our chance to take back what has been stolen."

Drumbeater's heart pounded faster. Did he follow Crooked Lightning to take the scalps of the *washechu* girl-children?

"Messengers traveled as far as the Tetons to seek help from our Dakota brothers." Blue Bottle scanned the small circle, his eyes resting briefly on Crooked Lightning before returning to Standing Tall. "There is talk of an alliance with Chief Hole-in-the-Day of the Ojibwas." A gasp was heard. Never had the Ojibwas and the People united for any purpose. "Only a *tuwe canwanka* allows his enemies to fight for him."

Drumbeater's blood chilled and sweat poured down his face. Although Standing Tall's expression had not changed, a strange glint in his eyes warned of his anger.

"And you, Blue Bottle," Standing Tall said. "Are you a warrior or only a messenger for Little Crow?"

Several of the men placed hands on their weapons as they waited to see what might happen next. Though the People were loosely united in the Dakota alliance, each band stood alone with its own chiefs. An insult to Standing Tall would not be ignored.

"Or are you now a messenger for Hole-in-the-Day," Standing Tall spat at his feet, "to lull the People so our enemy can betray us?"

"See these?" Blue Bottle waved his lance where scalps hung like the tails of a deer. One scalp was the golden hair of a small child, the other blood-smeared braids of a *washechu* woman. "Is this the work of a messenger?"

"Did you count coup on such noble enemies?" Crooked Lightning said. "When does a warrior fight women and children?"

"And you, will you make songs about the scalps you robbed from me?" Blue Bottle pulled a knife, his eyes locked with those of Crooked Lightning, feet positioned to leap into action.

"Blue Bottle has traveled far." Standing Tall's voice was icy as the river in the Moon of Difficulty. "He must have food and return to Little Crow."

Blue Bottle slowly uncoiled his stance and replaced the knife in his sheath. Drumbeater let out the breath he had been holding. If Blue Bottle killed his uncle, it would be Drumbeater's duty to kill Blue Bottle. He wasn't sure he could do it. What was he but a mere keeper of the drum? He had no taste for blood. He had no eagle feathers.

"Tell Little Crow that since he is the one who made the *washechu* tracks that gave the land of the People to the White Eyes," Standing Tall spoke with authority, "it is only right that he fights to get it back."

"You won't join us?" Blue Bottle said.

"You started the fight in your country. You can finish it there as well."

Blue Bottle turned away from the fire and leapt unto his pony. "Death to all *washechu!*" He whooped a loud war cry as he galloped out of the village.

After a long moment of silence, the council breathed a collective sigh of relief. Only Star Fist looked longingly after Blue Bottle.

"Straight Tongue advises the People to take up the ways of the *washechu* or move to the west," Crooked Lightning said after a long silence. It was as if Blue Bottle had never interrupted the council. "Those are his words."

"Tell me, Crooked Lightning," Standing Tall said. "Will you cut your hair and become a farmer like Straight Tongue says?"

"I have seen the *washechu* and learned their tracks. I have lived with the Long Knives at the fort called Snelling. I have a life-and-death friend among them." His eyes flashed, and his jaw set firm as hard rock. "But I will die as a warrior rather than live on a reservation like a dog."

"At last you make sense," Star Fist cried but was ignored by the chief.

"Should the Sisseton join Little Crow?" Standing Tall said.

"The Wahpekutes and the Mdewakantons fight—and I join their fight—but I am not so foolish as to believe the White Eyes can be driven out." At this Star Fist muttered again until Standing Tall flashed a warning look that silenced the younger brave.

"The *washechu* are like snowflakes of an *icamnatanka*." Crooked Lightning's eyes glittered. "The Sisseston should move west, maybe as far as the Mountains of the Turtle and hope the *washechu* do not follow. It is too late for the Mdewakanton and the Wahpekute, maybe for the Whapetons, too."

"I will fight with you, my brother." Star Fist jumped to his feet. "I will die a warrior's death."

"A foolish death." Standing Tall's voice rang with authority like a tree cracking from cold in the Moon of Great Difficulty. "You hear Crooked Lightning tell how the Long Knives fight in the south. There is no honor in fighting women."

"We should kill all of them," Star Fist said with an angry scowl. "Warriors, future warriors, and the women who birth more warriors. Fight them now before they grow up and kill us."

Standing Tall tilted his head as if listening for the voice of Wakantanka. "The *washechu* are uncivilized and unfamiliar with the truth. But Straight Tongue is right. It is either bow to their ways or leave Leaf Country."

"Or fight!" Star Fist said. "Kill them all."

"Can a man push back a storm?" Standing Tall said firmly. "If we join Little Crow, the Long Knives will use it as an excuse to come here and kill our women and children."

Drumbeater felt his strength melt away. He had no desire to leave Leaf Country, homeland of the People, and travel to the Mountains of the Turtle across the plains.

"But think of the plunder," Star Fist said. "If we drive the White Eyes away, it will belong to us."

"Since when do warriors care for plunder?" Standing Tall said. "Are we women that we should seek pots and blankets?"

Heads nodded around the campfire.

"We wait until the warriors return from the hunt." Standing Tall's voice spoke with authority. "We need *wawitonpapi*, extra caution, until this trouble is over."

Drumbeater felt both relief and regret. Maybe it was possible to push the fat-eaters away if all the bands united, even the Ojibwas. Who could stand against such warriors if the Ojibwas and the People fought as one?

"When the others return from the hunt," Standing Tall's voice left no room for argument, "we will decide what to do."

Just when Drumbeater thought the council was over, Crooked Lightning stood again. He tossed his hair back over his shoulder, standing tall and proud before them. Drumbeater's heart swelled with pride.

"I bring *washechu* captives here for safety," Crooked Lightning said. "The relatives of my life-and-death friend."

Time stopped. Standing Tall's face dropped all expression. Drumbeater understood his hesitation. If *washechu* captives were in camp, the Long Knives already had reason to attack.

"Many captives have been taken, many killed." Crooked Lightning's voice sounded measured and rational. "When the fighting is over, the captives will be traded for peace—if they are unharmed."

"I'll kill them!" Start Fist unsheathed his knife. "Their scalps will drip blood from my lance."

"The *washechu* belong to my life-and-death friend," Crooked Lightning's voice edged sharp.

"Where are these captives?" Standing Tall asked.

"With Willow Song," Drumbeater said, his voice cracked. "They are *wakon*." Tongues clicked. "I touched them and felt the strong medicine."

"Bring them." Standing Tall sat with arms folded in front of him.

Drumbeater left the drum in the care of an elder and hurried to fetch the girl-children from the bustling village. The women readied for tomorrow's harvest. Star Fist's mother fashioned a canoe from birch bark with help from Standing Tall's woman. Willow Song sat outside the tent, finishing the reed baskets needed for tomorrow's rice.

"Badger makes war cries when I go near Little Bird." Her face showed relief to see Drumbeater. "If I take Otter out of the tent, even to suckle, they cry out in their strange tongues. I think they cry for their mother."

Drumbeater thought of the hair on Blue Bottle's lance. He sighed and edged into the tent, cautious of the *wakon* child, taking pains to avoid touching the small one. He motioned for Badger to bring Little Bird and follow him. To his relief, she understood him and followed him back to the council fire, dragging Little Bird by the hand, dogs following at their heels. Other children gathered and reached out to touch the *washechu* girl-children. A pair of spotted dogs snarled and snapped.

"Ah!" Star Fist's eyes glittered as if he looked on a beautiful maiden, as if he saw his chance to count coup. "*Wakon!*"

The others clucked and stretched hands toward Little Bird's hair.

"Her touch sickened me," Drumbeater said. "*Wakon!* Strong enough to kill a healthy man."

"Safe to touch if on my lance," Star Fist said. "Watch."

He lunged towards the child, but Crooked Lightning stepped before him. "These belong to my life-and-death friend."

"Enough," Standing Tall said. "What do you want done with these captives?"

"I want them returned to my friend after the trouble is over."

Several old men whispered between themselves. "How can this be done without bringing blame to our people?"

"I will be responsible," Drumbeater said. As he spoke, the pain left his head and the dizziness stopped.

"Kill them now!" Scarlet Fist shouted.

"Drumbeater takes responsibility," Standing Tall said. "They will not be harmed."

Overhead a *wanmdi* flew a sweeping circle above the council fire. A blessing of the Great Mystery, a good omen. Sunlight glanced off its white head and tail as on Little Bird's hair the day before. The men stood in awe as the eagle looped again over the clearing. A single feather floated down, settling in the grass at Little Bird's feet.

"Ahhh." Voices murmured and twittered like birds scattering before a gun. An omen. A sure sign of Wakantanka approval.

Drumbeater reached in his medicine bag and laid a strand of tobacco on the grass for the eagle, his heart pounding in his ears. He was doing the right thing. This proved it.

Star Fist stomped his feet, stormed away from the council and jumped on his pony. "I will fight the White Eyes." He glared at the elders. "Someday you'll sing songs about the bravery of Star Fist."

"Or his foolish death," Standing Tall said.

As the council disbanded, the grandfathers remained around the fire and sang strong-heart songs for the ones leaving to fight the *washechu*. Grandmothers, wives, and mothers joined the older men in singing the songs that brought courage to the hearts of their warriors and allowed them to triumph over their enemies. They sang for Star Fist and Crooked Lightning, their voices lifted to the skies imploring the Great Mystery to guide these warriors of the People.

Crooked Lightning slowly rode out of camp on a borrowed pony, his face painted half green and half black according to his medicine. Crooked Lightning didn't look back or acknowledge Drumbeater as his pony passed by. Star Fist's *uncheedah*, Turtle Woman, rushed out and clutched Crooked Lightning's leg.

"Take care of my grandson," Turtle Woman said. "Star Fist is young. He needs the wisdom of an elder to guide him."

Crooked Lightning nodded but said nothing, pulling the halter to slow the horse but not completely stopping. Turtle Woman picked up a rattle and shook it towards the skies, singing songs imploring for courage against the enemy. Crooked Lightning rode out of the village in silent dignity, pushing through the hazel bushes and out of sight.

Drumbeater prayed a desperate prayer that he would see his uncle again. He should be the one riding out to battle instead of Star Fist.

Strong-heart songs grew louder once Crooked Lightning was out of sight. The grandfathers and women sang into the night for Blue Bottle and Little Crow, for the Mdewakanton braves and Wahpekute warriors who killed the fat-eaters.

The People were a loose alliance—but still an alliance.

15

"Indians at Sauk Center. Reported Murders.
Great Destruction of Property."
St. Cloud Democrat, October 3, 1862

GUST PRESSED DOWN A NAGGING WORRY about the investigations. Surely it would all blow over by next year. With the war in the South and the trouble with the Sioux, there should be other things more newsworthy. He would get a newspaper subscription to keep up with the news as best he could. And he would wait to contact Burr Oak until the investigations were over. At least if he had a good wheat crop, there would be enough money left over to repay the government—if it came to that.

Gust scanned the newspapers for any word of the inquiry, any mention of Indian problems west of St. Cloud. The papers reported the end of Fort Abercrombie's siege, the deaths of station keepers by Foxhome and Dayton, the murder of two men on the road past Chippewa Station. Would it never cease?

Gust and Serena packed their few possessions. They memorized a borrowed map, traced the Pomme de Terre River with their fingers, and touched the dot on the map that was their farm.

They rode *The Time and Tide* up the Mississippi River as far as St. Cloud. They traveled deck passage to save money. Any other time, Gust would have fretted about the limited baggage allowed, but they had little to bring with them. Serena napped on the deck, and Gust watched the shore drift by, dreaming of his own place, trying to forget the investigations.

Soldiers stood guard, a reminder of the lingering danger. Gust approached a young private holding a Sharps rifle and chewing a mouthful of tobacco.

"Have you been fighting in the South?" Gust felt guilty about his bad leg, and he missed his brothers. Maybe the soldier knew them.

"Yep." The young man spit a stream of brown tobacco juice over the side into the swirling waters of the Mississippi River. "I was captured at Shiloh. Held prisoner in Georgia before they let me loose to fight the Sioux."

"So how was it?" Gust leaned on the deck rail and stared into the churning water behind the great paddle.

The soldier did not take his eyes off the shores, looking intently for signs of attack. He snorted and spit another perfect stream of brown juice into the river. "They lined us up on one side of a field and lined the Rebs up on the other side of the field and had us shoot at each other until most of us died. Then they threw us in a pen without enough to eat or drink, left us to rot and die. How do you think it was?"

"Did you fight with Iowa boys?" Gust felt ashamed, as if his gimpy leg wasn't quite bad enough to keep him out of the fray. But the soldier needn't be so patronizing. For God's sake, he had been under attack by the Sioux and knew what death and killing looked like.

"There were Iowa boys at Shiloh and at the prison camp."

"Did you meet Sigurd Gustafson?" Gust asked. "Or Severt or Tosten? From Burr Oak?"

"Nah," said the soldier and glanced hard at a narrowed place in the river where bushes pressed in from both sides. He didn't speak until the boat passed that vulnerable spot. "Never knew anyone from Burr Oak. Spent time in prison with a Jon Anderson from Iowa City."

They watched the shores, the soldier never relaxing his stance. He was good, Gust had to admit. They were safer with the private standing watch.

"Did you fight the Sioux?"

"I was with the Exterminators," the soldier said. "We marched all the way out to Fort Abercrombie. It was hotter 'n hell and dangerous to boot. A lot of us were still weak from the poor food in the Reb prison."

"You marched all the way out to Dakota Territory?" No wonder they hadn't let him join up. His leg would never have made it.

"And fought the Sioux when we got there. The fort was under siege."

"Did you see the fort at Pomme de Terre?"

He huffed a laugh. "It's not much of a fort. Just earthen defenses on a hill by the river."

"I bought a farm at Pomme de Terre."

"You're crazy in the head." The soldier spat again. "It's Indian Country."

"But the paper says the uprising is over," Gust said.

"Sure," the soldier said. "That's why people are still getting killed."

16

"Communities Unite for Purpose of Self Defense"
                    St. Cloud Democrat, October 14, 1862

W HEN THEY LANDED IN ST. CLOUD, Serena watched Gust haggle for a team of oxen and a rickety wagon from settlers going south on the same steamboat. The people stood stony faced and silent.

The oxen, named Buddy and Bets, had ferocious horns and gentle brown eyes. "Aren't they beautiful?" Serena tried to avert her thoughts from those getting on the boat, fleeing the very country they were seeking. She rubbed their sides and fed them grass pulled from the side of the road.

"Hope they make it to Pomme de Terre," Gust said, "they're skinny but maybe we can fatten them up. We'll need them for spring planting."

There was money for a crate of chickens and one rooster. Gust brought them to the wagon, waiting for Serena to notice.

"Chickens!" Serena said.

"We'll need eggs and meat in Pomme de Terre." He spoke calmly though Serena noticed the happiness in his eyes. "We'll sell eggs to the soldiers at Pomme de Terre."

They left Buddy and Bets by a water trough on the corner of Washington Avenue and Germain Street and entered Tobey & Co. Mercantile. The sign above the door boasted provisions, dry goods, boots, shoes, ready-made clothing, crockery, hardware, woodenware, paper hangings, and Yankee notions. While Gus haggled with the owner about the price of flour, Serena wandered to the back of the store to examine a shelf of calico.

A woman sat on a crate in the corner, silently without expression. A baby about a year old sat on her feet and played with the buttons on her shoes. The child looked up at Serena and smiled through a dirty face. Her heart lurched. If Lena had lived, she would be sitting up, smiling with new teeth.

"Hello." Serena returned the baby's smile.

The woman did not answer, just looked at the floor.

"You're baby is beautiful," Serena said. "Is it a boy or a girl?"

The woman stared down in silence.

"Are you all right?"

The woman did not answer, but Serena noticed a quiver in her chin. The woman leaned over and picked up the child and set him to nurse. Serena felt her own milk drop at the sight. The woman did not make eye contact. It was as if Serena was not there. The infant slurped loudly from his mother's breast, twisting and turning to look at Serena. Tears dripped from the woman's eyes.

Serena returned to the counter where Gust bargained with the storekeeper.

"Who is the woman in the back?" Serena asked.

The storekeeper looked at her and hesitated. Then he whispered, "She was freed at Camp Release. Was kept by the Injuns for weeks." He put his index finger up to the side of his head and made a twirling motion.

Serena's strength drained away, and she grabbed Gust's arm to keep standing.

"At least she has her baby," she heard herself say. "They didn't hurt the baby."

"Ja, but killed her husband with an axe right before her eyes." His face clouded. "And they murdered four other children."

Gust drew in his breath and reached out to place his arm around her.

"They sawed her little girl's leg off at the hip with a hunting knife. Made the poor woman watch."

"They cut off the little girl's leg?" Gust shook his head in disbelief. "Why?"

"Who knows why those damned savages do anything?" the storekeeper said in a loud voice. "Excuse my language, missus." He lowered the volume to a whisper. "They're inhuman. Made the woman watch her daughter bleed to death, wouldn't let her tend to her. When she fought them, they killed her other children before her eyes. Bashed their heads in with a club until she stopped resisting."

"My God."

"General Sibley made a deal with Little Crow," the storekeeper said. "Said the army would treat the Indians fair if they returned the prisoners and turned themselves in."

"How many prisoners did they have?" Serena thought how easily she and Lena could have been numbered with them. The fear of it settled hard in her belly.

"They released over a hundred whites, mostly women and children." He paused to wrap a string around a brown paper wrapped bundle. "And a hundred and sixty half-breeds at the same time. Seems they didn't limit the attacks to whites alone."

"What did they do with the prisoners?" It didn't make any sense to Serena. Why would they kill some and kidnap others? The pieces of the puzzle didn't fit.

"They dragged them all over the prairies. If they couldn't keep up or tried to escape, they killed them. They violated the women and abused the children, starving them and bashing them around like pups." He slammed his hand down on the counter, and their receipt fluttered to the floor. "It's untelling what this poor woman went through. No wonder she's gone lunatic."

"Does she have someplace to go?" Serena wondered if there would be room at Pomme de Terre for the woman and her baby. They could take her with them and help her get well again.

"The army brought a group of women and children from Camp Release to St. Cloud a while back, hoping someone might know them," the storekeeper said. "Jane Swisshelm, from the *St. Cloud Democrat*, took this woman in for a few weeks and coaxed her story out of her." He pointed to a newspaper on the counter. "It's in this week's paper."

The banner across the front of the page said, "SPEAK UNTO THE CHILDREN OF ISRAEL THAT THEY GO FORWARD. EXODUS CHAP XIV VERSE 16." Serena wondered why someone would choose that particular verse to represent his newspaper. Surely there was a more appropriate Bible verse if a person needed one.

"Miss Swisshelm contacted her people to come for her." The man set a pound of saleratus and a sack of flour on the counter. "They're coming from Meeker County. Won't be here for a week or two."

"What is she doing until then?" Serena said.

"The Methodist preacher said he'd take her in until her family comes." He wiped a smudge of flour off the counter with the edge of his hand and brushed it onto the floor.

"He'll be here in a little while. Had a funeral to preach."

"By God, Lincoln better do something," Gust said. "Honest folks won't put up with it much longer."

"The military trials are going on right now." The storekeeper spat in the spittoon with a ringing sound.

"They don't deserve a trial." Gust counted out the correct number of coins. "They burned me out and ruined my crops. We lost everything."

Not everything. Serena thought how little they had lost in comparison to the woman in the store. She listened as Gust told their story to the store-keeper. He didn't mention Lena's death or say anything about the reparation payments. Something was wrong, but she couldn't put her finger on it.

"I agree," the storekeeper said. "They should be wiped out like ver-min." He gathered the rest of the order. "Where you headed?"

"I bought a farm at Pomme de Terre," Gust said. Serena watched him shift the weight off his bad leg. It was something he did when he was nerv-ous or unsettled, the first indication that he felt unsure about his decision to move to the farm.

"You're not dumb enough to move west with the Indians stirred up." The storekeeper wrapped several smaller items and tied them securely with string. "We've a strong fortification right here. There's no need for you to risk it on the frontier. We could use another man taking turn at guard duty."

"Thank you, but my plans are firm." Gust gathered the packages off the counter and headed toward the door, guiding Serena along with him.

"The army says no travel west of here."

"There's a fort going up at Pomme de Terre," Gust said. "We'll be safe enough."

"It's late in the season," the storekeeper said. "I wouldn't advise travel this time of year, Indians or no Indians. Winter could commence any time."

"An old trapper predicts a Squaw Autumn," Gust said. "Another two or three weeks of nice weather before cold settles in."

The storekeeper shook his head. "You'd best not depend on fables when your lives are at stake. A lot can happen in the frontier."

"We'll stick with the main road and get to Pomme de Terre in plenty of time."

"As long as you're going to the fort." The storekeeper rubbed the back of his head. "Don't say I didn't warn you."

Gust did not reply. Serena thought how nothing short of death would stop him from having his own farm. The bull-headed Swede didn't listen to anyone.

Gust loaded a side of bacon, a barrel of salt pork, a sack of flour, saleratus, salt, a gallon of molasses, a sack of cornmeal and one of navy beans, a bag of sugar, and two ten-pound tins of coffee beans. He tucked away an ancient Danzig muzzle-loader, a small bag of powder and another of percussion caps. Serena's quick eyes noticed the purchase.

On their way out of town, Gust stopped at the newspaper office and signed up for a year of *The St. Cloud Democrat*. A sign propped in the window said, "We will receive wheat, oats, corn flour, wood, good butter, eggs, or anything else we can use, in payment of subscriptions to the *Democrat* or debts due the establishment. Now is the time to subscribe or settle old bills."

To buy a subscription to the newspaper! Such extravagance! They stopped for the night at a small farm, and Gust offered to buy both a cow named Dolly and Rosebud, a bred heifer. In the morning he tied the two cows to the back of the wagon. Surely it was risky to buy stock so late in the fall when they had no fodder gathered for the winter.

"How can we afford all this?" she asked. "There couldn't be this much value from our small garden and few crops in Hutchinson."

"How were they to know what we lost?" Gust said calmly. "It was my word alone—so what if I claimed we lost more than we did."

Serena sat stunned. God would never bless falsehood. She knew that much from confirmation. She remained silent for miles, lost in thought, thinking of the little girl whose leg was sawed off by the Sioux, thinking of Lena.

Most farms were deserted. That night they slept in an empty farmhouse. Rats had chewed great holes in the mattress on the bed. Pots and pans hung from pegs on the wall unharmed. A tintype of a boy in a military uniform stared back from the wall. A jug of perfectly good vinegar sat on the floor. The place smelled of dust and mice. Serena wondered how the little cabin in Hutchinson fared, if travelers also lodged there and gazed at the remains of their belongings, if they wondered who had lived there and why they left.

How comforting it would be to have a tintype of Lena to look at whenever she wanted. Sometimes Lena's features dimmed in her mind's eye. Serena feared she would forget her face entirely.

"We may as well take what we want." Gust casually surveyed the items. "No one will be back to claim them."

"I am not a thief!" Serena said. "I won't take what belongs to another human being whether they come back or not."

Gust's face reddened, and he stormed out of the cabin, slamming the door behind him. Perhaps she had been too outspoken. He was the head of the house, after all, and she had promised to obey him. But right was right, and she would not forsake the Ten Commandments. God help her, it was all she had left to cling to.

Serena calmed by the time he returned with a foaming pail of fresh milk. He made no mention of the harsh words, nor did she.

"I'll make cottage cheese with the extra milk," she said. "We'll feast tomorrow."

Before Serena climbed into the rat-chewed bed that night, she stood at the single window and searched the surrounding fields and trees. Nothing. Finally she lay down by Gust and prayed no rats would find their bed, no living creature would approach the cabin. Gust chased a swooping bat out the door.

It was a long time before she slept.

THEY FOLLOWED THE ABERCROMBIE TRAIL. Serena reviewed the map from memory and knew they were headed in the right direction. They bounced and bumped over dried sloughs and poor roads. The first frost killed the mosquitoes, but Serena wrapped her face and hair in layers of gauze, trying to protect herself from the hordes of deer flies and gnats that followed them across country.

It seemed they had been on the trail forever, their routine established into near normalcy. Wake up before dawn and milk the cow. Let the chickens out of the crate long enough to scratch for their food, take care they get back into the crate lest they become food for some wild critter. Lead Buddy and Bets to water, then Dolly and Rosebud. Make breakfast plus enough to take along to eat on the trail for dinner. Travel until noon and take a rest during the hottest hour of the day letting the animals eat and drink. Continue traveling until dusk. Fight flies every inch of the way. Look for clean water. Find a deserted cabin to sleep in. Make enough fire to brew a pot of coffee. Try to ignore the desolation of the country and refuse to consider what may have happened to the original builders of the places where they slept. Keep going west in spite of weather or tempers.

17

*"Let Our Present Legislature Offer a Bounty
of Ten Dollars for every Sioux Scalp"*
St. Cloud Democrat, October 21, 1862

OLAUS REIERSON, A BACHELOR WHO SURVIVED the uprising, lived near a place called Chippewa Station. Gust had driven into a cold northwest wind most of the day and was ready for a hot cup of coffee when they stopped at the dwelling. Olaus boasted a snug soddy and a fancy grindstone. Gust fairly drooled over the grindstone, wishing he could afford one of his own.

"Come and use it any time you wish," Olaus said. "I'd enjoy company."

Even better, Olaus knew Andrew Salmon and had visited the farm on the Pomme de Terre River. He gave them directions to their new home.

"You could be there by dark if you hurry." Olaus scanned the sky. "But there's a feel of weather in the air. You'd best stay the night and leave in the morning."

Gust noticed the gray clouds gathering in the western horizon, had been eyeing them all morning. Surely there was time to get to the farm by night.

"Thank you," Gust said. "But I think we'll head to our own place."

The fact that other people still lived in the area encouraged Gust more than he would admit. It wasn't impossible after all. Surely the reports of the Sioux were exaggerated. Ja, he had seen their deviltry, but even President Lincoln said it was over. The headlines in *The St. Cloud Democrat* spoke of other matters, the uprising news relegated to the back pages. They would live on their own land in peace and prove the naysayer wrong.

The road passed along the south and west shores of Pelican Lake. They kept to the high ground to avoid the sloughs but even so, the corduroy road nearly rattled the hens from their cage and the teeth from his mouth. When the trail veered west, he turned on the ox cart trail. Olaus said the farm was on the Red River Trail.

The wind shifted to the northwest. Dark clouds gathered overhead like thick layers of cotton batting. Gust watched Serena pull her shawl around her and tuck her skirts around her legs. His nose dripped from the cold wind. If they didn't find the farm soon they might get caught in a storm. Snow was possible any time in Minnesota. He scanned the horizon and pushed down a gnawing worry.

A strange noise alerted them. Gust pulled the oxen to a stop and listened. It seemed painfully quiet without the screech of the wagon wheels.

"What is it Gust?" asked Serena. "Is it a Sioux war cry?"

"Shhh!" His voice was sharper than he intended. "I'm trying to hear."

Peering ahead, they saw a stage coming down the trail behind four horses. The driver was a young man, wearing a crumpled straw hat, singing in a voice not entirely on pitch. A soldier dressed in blue cradled a shotgun and dozed at his side.

". . . . My Sally am a spunky gal, singing Polly wolly doodle all the day."

Gust let out his breath. Not a Sioux war cry, only the bad singing of a stagecoach driver. Gust recalled how Serena sang on their wedding journey to Hutchinson. Mile after mile her clear voice sang Norwegian songs. She taught him the words, laughing as he tried to sing along. She hadn't sung a single note the whole trip from St. Cloud. In fact, he hadn't heard her sing since Lena's death. A lump formed in his throat and moisture clouded his vision.

"Whoa!" The stage driver pulled up, facing Buddy and Bets nose to nose on the narrow trail. The soldier roused and pulled his gun into a shooting position.

"What in God's name are you doing out here?" The young man tipped his hat toward Serena as if in apology for his language.

"We're on our way to Pomme de Terre." Gust sat a little straighter on his seat behind the oxen. The heifer bawled. "We own a farm near the fort."

The soldier relaxed his grip on his gun and tipped his hat. "You'll have to excuse the driver," he said. "He's new to the route and antsy to boot."

"I never met anybody traveling west," explained the young man. "Even the die-hards are leaving."

"Why?" Serena pulled her shawl tighter around her shoulders. "The Indian scare is over."

"Yes, ma'am," the young man said. "The Indian war is over according to General Pope and the U.S. Government. It's just they forgot to tell the Sioux."

He laughed heartily at his own joke with a wheezy, silent laugh and stopped only when he noticed the stern look on the soldier's face.

"Like I said," the soldier said, "this one has a lot to learn. Now his predecessor was a true hero—fought in the Abercrombie siege."

"Where is he now?" Serena said. Maybe she had read about this man in the newspapers. "What's his name?"

"Evan Jacobson," the soldier said. "He went back to Fort Snelling after the siege. Had family business to tend to."

"We met him during the uprising," Gust said. "Red hair?"

"I heard he's getting married," the driver nodded. "Imagine leaving the glorious life of a stagecoach driver to get hitched." He laughed his wheezy laugh again.

"He'll be back in the spring," the soldier said. "Unless he joins the army."

"Are we soon there?" asked Gust. "To Pomme de Terre?"

"Yes, sir," the driver said. "Through this length of swamp and you'll come to the Pomme de Terre River."

"Our farm is situated on the Pomme de Terre River," Gust said.

"Then you're almost home." The driver tipped his hat once more. "And a good thing. We have bad weather following us."

"Snow?"

"It was freezing rain we passed through about ten miles west of here," the soldier said. "I expect you'll run into it."

"Thanks for the warning," Gust said.

"Good luck then." The driver maneuvered his team around the ox team and wagon. "We need to get to Chippewa Station before the storm catches up with us."

As they watched them leave, Serena said, "We forgot to ask their names."

The icy drops soon pelted their faces. Gust cursed under his breath. Serena pulled her shawl around her and made a tent to shield her face. Buddy and Bets bawled in protest and would have veered off the trail if Gust had allowed it. He forced them into the face of the storm, rubbing his bad leg now and then, cursing the oxen for their slowness. Gray clouds thickened overhead and pressed down upon them. Prairie stretched between scattered hills. They slogged through a frozen slough. At least the bugs had disappeared.

Gust wiped blood off his face.

"Damn ice cuts right into my flesh," he said. "If I shield my face I can't see the trail to keep the oxen going in the right direction."

"Should we pull over and make camp?" Serena said.

"Don't be silly," Gust said. "We'll sleep in our own cabin tonight."

What if the cabin had been burned down? Salmon made no promise that the cabin would be standing. Gust kept his worries to himself.

They pushed forward into the face of the bitter wind, fighting the ice shards as best they could. Finally the storm passed over. The trail frosted with the glint of ice, and Gust watched carefully lest the milk cows slip as they trudged behind the rickety wagon. Gust almost wept with relief when the little cabin came into sight but tried to put on a brave front for Serena.

Salmon had not exaggerated.

The rolling hills and the wooded forty by the river were just as he said. Gust knelt down and sniffed a handful of black dirt, rich and loamy, perfect for corn and wheat. His mouth almost salivated with the knowledge that it belonged to him. His eyes feasted on his farm. No one could take it from him. It belonged to him. He couldn't see it fast enough, couldn't absorb the meaning.

He explored the little barn on the edge of the pasture. The tools lay unmolested along one wall, even a one-man plow. The shares needed sharpening before planting but otherwise it was sturdy and useable. A thatched roof snugged the barn. Plenty of room for chickens and cattle. Eventually they might raise a few hogs.

Fields surrounded the buildings and woodlots by the river sat just as Salmon described. A few ears of corn hung on dried stalks in the field closest to the house.

By God, it was a goldmine!

Fairly bursting with enthusiasm, Gust stomped into the cabin. A pervasive odor of skunk met him at the doorway and no door hung on the leather hinges. It was a single room, long and narrow, with a slanted roof and dirt floor. A small rusty stove sat in the middle with a crooked pipe going up through the thatch. A log table and stump chairs were the only furniture except a rope bed in the corner. Dirty, with dust and cobwebs everywhere, it held possibilities. He looked under the bed. No skunks in the cabin but they had been there—he could smell them.

Gust searched for Serena and found her standing in the cold, her arms around Rosebud's neck, her face buried in her side.

"Serena-girl," he said. "Look at the sunset." Pinks and purples painted a stripe low in the western horizon where the weather had cleared. When she didn't respond, he picked her up and carried her over the threshold into the cabin. "Welcome to your new home. It's yours forever. No one can take it from you."

Serena straightened her skirts and looked around the room. She pressed a handkerchief to her nose without a word.

Another time her lack of enthusiasm might have angered him, but nothing could discourage him that day. He was a landowner. He would repay his father and become a free man. Serena had been through a lot. Soon she would be back to her old self. He remembered her smile, the way she sang in the kitchen while she worked.

Gust hardly knew what to do first. First he needed to make a door for the cabin and find fodder for the animals. How odd that there was no door on the cabin. He brushed it out of his mind. Who cared as long as he was able to replace it? Wood needed cutting, and if the weather held, fall plowing could be done. Serena would pick the corn left in the field.

The sky was the limit. A landowner! For the first time since the uprising, Gust believed they would make it. They had survived, in spite of the damn Sioux.

18

"When New Ulm Was Evacuated, All the Strychnine in Town was Put into Some Whiskey and Left There for Indian Consumption."
St. Cloud Democrat, August 31, 1862

THAT NIGHT WHEN LITTLE BIRD CRIED out in her sleep, there was no one to interpret the strange tongue. Little Bird refused meat, refused even the maple sugar. She awakened Badger with her war whoops—as well as the dogs barking outside the teepee. Badger gathered her sister in her arms, kissed her face, and stroked her hair until she quieted. After the dogs returned to their rest, the girl-children fell asleep holding each other.

"That one is a true person," Willow Song said of Badger. "See how she cares for her sister."

Drumbeater thought how Badger protected him by keeping him away from the strong medicine of Little Bird's hair. He could have been killed. Perhaps Badger carried the stronger medicine. Maybe the strength of the heart was more important than hair color.

The next morning the camp bustled with the thrill of harvest. Willow Song left at daylight to harvest the rice on a nearby lake while Turtle Woman watched over Otter and the *washechu* girl-children. Turtle Woman cackled about the firm grains in each husk and, bragged that this season would yield more rice than the last *waniyetuyamini*. Drumbeater prepared to hunt the moose he had seen again at morning prayers.

A moose provided *waconica* for the coming winter and its antlers were useful as paddles or carving material, the hides for clothing or teepees.

Drumbeater must remain close to rice camp, but if he were lucky, he might still surprise the *ta* near the river bend.

Drumbeater was searching the riverbank for moose tracks when he heard a loud scream. At first he thought it might be the cry of the *inmutanka* but when it sounded again, he knew it was from the village. He raced back towards camp, tearing through the brush and leaping over a dead tree in his path. Ojibwas! It must be Ojibwas.

When Drumbeater was still a young boy, an Ojibwa war party attacked while the People were busy with harvest and the warriors still on the hunt. Precious stores of dried meat, maple sugar, and roots were stolen along with several children. Two of the children were Drumbeater's cousins. The thought of Otter being stolen and raised as an Ojibwa made his heart pound, his breath come in panting gulps. He pulled his knife as he ran but when he reached the village, he found no raiding enemies.

The scream sounded again and he recognized Badger's voice.

When Drumbeater threw back the tent flap, he saw Turtle Woman pinching Little Bird's nose with strong fingers while clamping her other hand over her mouth. Little Bird kicked with feeble legs, her eyes bulging and her face as blue as her eyes. Badger sobbed at the side of the teepee, clutching her stomach with both hands.

"Stop!" Drumbeater pulled Little Bird away from the old woman's grasp and quickly placed her into Badger's arms. He dared not touch the Little Bird too long lest the swirling sickness return. Little Bird gasped with an open mouth like a fish out of water, and Badger sobbed great gulping sobs.

"What are you doing?" His voice trembled with rage until he could hardly speak.

"If she is a *wakon* child like you say," Turtle Woman said in a calm voice, "she will live without breath. I only test her medicine."

Drumbeater restrained his hands from reaching for the old woman's throat. She was an elder. He owed her respect. It was the way of the People.

"Thank you, Grandmother," Drumbeater said in a quiet voice, forcing his anger down. A warrior showed strength by controlling himself. "You may go now."

Turtle Woman shrugged her shoulders and shuffled away to her own fire in sloppy moccasins, berating the *washechu's* medicine as inferior to that of the People. Although the swirling pain had not returned when he touched Little Bird, Drumbeater was most cautious in his dealings with the *wakon* girl-child. Children, he corrected himself. Badger also carried the strong medicine.

Badger quieted but Turtle Woman had left a mark on her face when she kicked her away. Perhaps Turtle Woman would suffer ill effects from her rough handling of the girl-children. It would serve her right. The thought of how close Little Bird had been to death left Drumbeater in a cold sweat.

It was no small thing to be responsible to a life-and-death friend.

Many Beavers, Crooked Lightning's woman, entered the camp later in the morning, a dog pulling her loaded travois. Her eyes flickered disappointment when she learned Crooked Lightning had left to fight the *washechu*, but her face did not change expression. Instead she pitched her teepee while the girl-children watched Many Beavers steady the poles from the travois and drape the hides.

Drumbeater hesitated to leave camp again. He felt unsettled, as if danger lurked around them. He scanned the skies for omens but only strong sunlight in a clear sky showed above. The leaves on the sugar trees showed their first tinge of red. It was too late to surprise a moose but Wakantanka might smile upon him if he hunted again at twilight.

"Uncle brought these captives for safety." Drumbeater said as the woman secured the teepee with rawhide strips. "He sends them to you."

Many Beavers showed no hint of surprise. "Blue Bottle told me how my husband robbed him of their scalps."

"Did you see Blue Bottle?" Drumbeater said, his mouth suddenly dry, his throat raspy, remembering the fierce light in his eyes.

"He and Star Fist camp beyond the falls." She picked up a rock and pounded a stake. "Blue Bottle says he will steal the *washechu* girl-children before he leaves. He thinks their hair will protect him in battle. He doesn't want to die fighting the Long Knives."

Drumbeater drew in his breath sharply. There was no safety among the Sisseton as Crooked Lightning had hoped.

Many Beavers reached out and fingered the sun-touched hair of Little Bird. Neither Otter nor Willow Song suffered by touching her, nor Turtle Woman who tanned a rabbit hide next to her teepee. Perhaps Little Bird's medicine was bad only for warriors.

"Do they have names?"

"The small one is Little Bird and the older one is from the badger tribe," Drumbeater said. "We do not know their *washechu* names."

Drumbeater worried that he had spoken foolishly at the council fire in promising to return the girl-children. If they stayed at rice camp, Blue Bottle would kill them. "I am to bring them to Evan Jacobson after the trouble is over."

Little Bird cried out and hung onto Willow Song's legs when she returned to the teepee to suckle Otter. Little Bird and Badger pulled away from Many Beavers' kind hands, wanting only Willow Song.

They needed hides. And meat. Drumbeater carried a heavy responsibility to his family and tribe. Yet a promise to a life-and-death friend.

The words leapt from his mouth without thought. It was as if his tongue spoke words from the Great Mystery. He merely opened his mouth and the words spewed out like the call of a goose. Life-changing words. Words that might fall crushed before the eastern wind of a *washechu* blizzard. "Standing Tall leaves tomorrow for the camp of Red Iron." What if he could not find the life-and-death friend? "I will go with him and return the girl-children to their people."

Many Beavers turned and untied the leather thongs holding her teepee without another word. She was obviously going with him. It was lucky she arrived in time, that she warned of trouble with Blue Bottle. Surely Wakantanka directed his steps. Willow Song and Otter would remain in rice camp and finish the harvest.

He hoped he was doing the right thing.

19

"Orphans of Uprising to be Kept in Minnesota.
Offer from Ohio Asylum Rejected."
St. Cloud Democrat, October 28, 1862

THE WEATHER DIDN'T HOLD.

The next morning Serena and Gust woke to a skiff of new snow across the ground. Their breath puffed small clouds of vapor in the cabin, and a thick layer of ice froze across the top of the water bucket. She built a fire with fingers clumsy from the cold while Gust milked the cow.

Serena shuddered to think they might have been on the trail if the weather had changed a day earlier. Thank God they were here. What would they have done? It was bad enough to be at the farm with its deserted buildings and standing corn, in a terrible cabin without even a door to close behind them. How could they have survived without shelter? The wind howled in from the west, a mournful, lonely sound.

She had hoped to meet their neighbors before winter imprisoned them in the cabin, but there was too much work to do before winter settled hard. Supposedly folks still lived in Pomme de Terre, and soldiers were quartered there, only down the trail, maybe closer than she thought.

Serena picked the remaining ears of corn dangling from dried stalks. She filled one old gunnysack and dragged it into the cabin to protect it from rats and mice, then filled another. While she worked, she focused her mind on pleasantries, remembering Christmas celebrations from her girlhood, recalling the summer she and Gust courted.

Anything but the Indian uprising, anything except Lena's grave.

She felt eyes upon her from the surrounding trees, worried that any minute she would take a bullet or a hatchet in the back.

The Sioux had been there. Serena knew it though Gust said nothing. The table bore gouges and the foundation on the west corner of the house was scorched black. And where was the door? No one built a house without a door. Nei, the savages had been there and would most likely come again to finish their deviltry.

Auntie Karen's coffee grounds had been right.

Would she ever forget the crashing dishes and flour sifting through the cracks in the floor? Serena had tried to remain totally still in the fraidy hole, pressed against Lena, hoping to remain hidden, scared to move a muscle.

More trouble loomed ahead. They were not safe at Pomme de Terre, no matter what Gust said. She picked faster, eyeing the clouds in the northwest, wishing with all her strength they were in Burr Oak and not this terrible place.

But maybe it didn't matter. Her life had ended with Lena's death. She filled her apron with the last cobs of dried corn and returned to the cabin where she stuffed it into the sack hanging from a nail on the wall. Gust would be in for dinner soon.

She picked up the bucket of milk from the floor and poured it into a kettle on the stove. Something gray floated in the creamy whiteness. Serena screamed and dropped the bucket. Milk spilled over the stove and dripped down, pooling on the earth-packed floor. A drowned mouse.

How could she live in such a place?

The cabin was no better than her father's chicken coop. She hated the skunky smell still lingering in spite of her attempts to remove it with water and vinegar. Their small stores might be enough to get them through the winter. Fresh eggs would help if they could keep the hens producing. She was thankful for the potatoes and corn but longed for the pork and poultry from her father's farm. It would be years before they could afford to slaughter a large animal for table use and at least next summer before they could spare a hen.

At home there was plenty. Jensina and Jerdis laughed as they washed the dishes. Auntie Karen lived down the road, always near to help in times of trouble. They lived without fear of Indians. Her father kept his promises. Her mother never feared having too little to eat or that she would see her children butchered by savages.

Gust had promised they could return home if things went bad in Minnesota. It was hard to believe they could get any worse.

He hadn't kept his promise.

Serena lugged a pail of water from the river, took a jug from the shelf and splashed vinegar into the bucket. Carefully she dipped a brush into the water and scrubbed the inside logs of the cabin. The wood soaked up the water. She was careful to stay away from the chinking. It might loosen up and make a worse mess. No matter how many times she scrubbed the walls, the odor lingered.

Mice and rats overran the place, spoiled their food supply and dirtied the cupboards. At night they scurried along the log walls and across the bed. One night a mouse tangled in Serena's hair, waking her when it tried to pull away. How could they survive in such a place?

The chinking pulled away from the logs in places, and the wind blew in through the gaps. That was the trouble with a log cabin; the logs shifted and were drafty. A soddy would have been warmer and certainly no dirtier. But a cabin wasn't as dark as a soddy, and for that Serena was thankful. Dark days depressed her and every day was a dark day in a soddy.

At least she had found a patch of pie plant growing behind the house. And the water from the river was clear and good. Maybe if her family were closer she wouldn't mind living at Pomme de Terre. After all, it was the people she missed, not Iowa.

She missed Lena most of all. The mere thought of Lena caused her milk to drop. Serena found herself listening for her cry during the strangest times, when she went to the little outhouse out back or while she was fetching water from the river. Her ears strained to hear what would never come.

She bent and dipped the brush once more into the almost empty pail of water and then poured the few drops remaining over the pie plant behind the house. The cold west wind sent a chill through her, and she could feel her wet hands chapping. At least Dolly gave plenty of cream and she would rub some on her hands before bed.

Clothes hung stiff and dry on the line outside the cabin. She carefully folded the clean rags as she took them down. Once during the trip, she had dared hope she might be expecting again. She was mistaken. With a sigh she stacked the rags in an old bucket in the corner. Maybe it was for the best. There were no schools, no churches, nothing out here. There was nothing to offer a young child, no opportunities.

Sometimes she saw plumes of smoke coming from the direction of the fort. Maybe there were churches and schools there. Maybe it was not such a wilderness after all. Maybe the Indians were all gone and they could live in peace.

Maybe.

20

"Bishop Whipple Asks: What Shall We Do with the Indians?"
St. Cloud Democrat, November 4, 1862

GUST SCYTHED SWAMP GRASS ALONG THE RIVER. Though dried and of poor quality, it was the best he could do for winter fodder. It wasn't enough. He would have to think of something. Maybe other farmers in the area had extra hay to sell.

He hooked up the team and dragged several downed oak trees beside the cabin. He could chop and split this during the cold spells, right by the cabin where it would be convenient.

Dead trees alongside the house were not pretty but practical. A nagging thought came to him that it would be a good cover for attacking Indians. They might fire the trees and burn them out. It took only a spark to ignite a thatched roof. He pushed the worry out of his mind. The uprising was over.

At least he was far enough away from St. Paul where the do-gooders wasted time on the reparation investigation. They'd never find him in Pomme de Terre even if they could prove his perjury. Luther would be the last person to report him. For God's sake, Luther was as guilty as he, declaring Gust's perjury. He found a spade in the barn and concentrated on digging potatoes. They needed every one if they were to survive the coming winter.

"Serena!" he called from the potato patch. "Come and help!"

He was almost to the end of the first row when she came, pushing her hair behind her ears and tying a scarf around her head. She carried a gunnysack.

"Good girl!" he said. "You think of everything. Look at these potatoes! How large and firm they are. Wait until you see the ones I grow next year."

Without a word Serena knelt in the dirt and began the tedious job of picking up each potato, clearing as much soil as possible from each one before throwing it into the sack. She sorted the ones damaged by gophers into a separate pile lying on the dirt. They wouldn't keep through the coming months and needed to be used first. Gust looked at her with pride. He had chosen wisely. She was a smart girl, always doing the right thing when it came to farming or gardening, never shirking a difficult task.

He attacked the potato patch with new vigor, turned the hard soil of each hill and taking a pitchfork to lift the potatoes from the dirt. It would not do to pierce a potato with the tines of the fork. His father had whipped him once for doing that very thing. His father would approve of his work today.

Gust wasn't discouraged. In fact he was almost euphoric in spite of his aching leg. The sky was the limit as to how successful he might be now that he was a landowner. Like Joseph, crowned and triumphant before his brothers, he longed to write home of his good fortune, to tell his father the payment would come with the next harvest. Then he realized he could not contact them.

Surely the inquiry about the reparation payments would blow over soon.

Darkness settled by the time the potatoes were dug. Gust dragged the potato sack into the cabin and lit the lamp. Serena straggled after him with her apron overflowing with potatoes.

"Tonight I'll make *krub*, potato dumplings," Serena said in a calm voice. "And tomorrow I'll bake *lefse*."

"God bless you, wife!" Gust hung the sack of potatoes on the wall alongside the corn and turned to Serena with enthusiasm. His arms cradled her waist as she placed the potatoes on the table.

"I'm busy."

"Serena-girl," he said. "You are so beautiful. How can you expect me to keep my hands away?"

"There are more potatoes," she said. "We need to bring them in tonight in case it freezes."

Gust kissed the back of her neck. "You smell so good. Always smell so good."

He reached up and pulled a pin from her braids and watched her blonde hair come undone. His voice fell to a murmur, and he pulled out another pin and undid her braids until her hair flowed out in blonde waves. He buried his face in it.

His hands fingered the buttons on the front of her dress. "Come to bed." They opened clumsily with his heavy fingers.

GUST FELT GIDDY WITH THE DELIGHT of being a landowner. His dreams rested within easy reach. Serena would realize he had known what was best for them. She may not be too excited about the farm on the Pomme de Terre River now, but she would think differently after the harvest.

Gust decided to drive the wagon into the fort and inquire about hay. Perhaps the army had extra they might sell. If only he had another month to chop wood to barter for supplies. He'd rather save his cash for emergencies. It was going like water. At this rate, they would soon be penniless again.

He carefully opened the wooden box he'd taken from an abandoned cabin along the way. Serena had not said a word about it at the time, but her crimped mouth had shouted disapproval.

Inside the box were his baptism and confirmation certificates as well as those of Serena and Lena. His stomach lurched when he thought of Lena's baptism. They had been so hopeful then, so close to success.

The deed to the farm lay securely next to them. He reached into the box and took out a small leather pouch. Carefully he removed coins and placed them in his pocket. As he put the pouch back into the box, he changed his mind and put it into his pocket instead.

Losing his animals over the winter would set him back for years. There was no alternative but to buy hay at whatever price it cost. It was all or nothing.

21

"303 Sioux Condemned by Army"
St. Cloud Democrat, November 18, 1862

O NE DAY THE SUN SHOWED BRIGHT in blue skies overhead. Snow dripped from the edges of the barn roof and dripped through the thatch on the house, splashing on the stove with a satisfying hiss. Serena filled the mattress ticking with fresh cornhusks, gathered after the ears of corn were harvested. Gust limped into the cabin. "You'll stay home with the stock," he said. "I'm going into the fort to buy hay."

Serena gulped and struggled to hold back the tears. Perhaps mail awaited them. Didn't she have just as much right as he to meet their neighbors and get acquainted?

"Ja, ja," Serena answered in a forced voice. "But bring a letter from my mor when you come back."

The hours dragged, and Serena willed herself to keep busy. She felt Indians looking at her so she did not return to the fields. Instead she carried ashes from the stove and dumped them behind the outhouse. Out of the corner of her eye she spied a piece of wood propped against a tree. It was the cabin door, hacked and ruined. Holes pierced the surface and blotchy dark stains dripped across the wood. Her fingers touched the holes, felt the splinters and the rough texture. A chill went through her.

She had planned to strain the ashes to make lye soap. Instead she entered the cabin and barred the door and finished stitching the tick given to them by the missionaries in Pig's Eye. She had emptied it before they began traveling, and it still carried the scent of pine boughs. She inhaled the clean fragrance. If only she had balsam to fill it again, but there were few pines at Pomme de Terre. Someday she would have goose feathers for a feather tick. Until then they would sleep on dried cornhusks. She finished the stitching and spread the mattress on the bed. It would be noisy, the dried leaves crackling with every movement, but it would be more comfortable than the bare ropes stretched across the bed frame. Gust would be pleased.

Serena stood looking out the window. The filmy glass distorted the view. Dolly bellowed to be milked. Poor girl—Serena knew from experience how it hurt to have too much milk. She scanned the surrounding trees. Nothing moved. Nothing at all. She ran to the barn as fast as she could.

Her cheek rested on Dolly's warm flank, and she pulled the teats in rhythmic motion, hearing the streams of milk splash in the bucket, smelling the combination of fresh milk and cow manure that reminded her of home. Serena and her mother always did the milking together. Her mother would milk Bertine while Serena milked Hildegard. They talked and laughed as the milk buckets filled and their fingers stripped the teats.

The barn felt empty without Buddy and Bets, and she refused to consider what might have happened to Gust on his journey, or why he was so late coming home. She closed her mind to the thought of Indians attacking along the trail or sneaking up behind the cabin. She decided to forget the hacked door entirely. Whatever had happened was over.

Serena stood with the full bucket of milk by the barn door, watching through the cracks, examining the space between the house and barn. Chickens pecked around her feet. Still nothing, nothing at all moved in the yard. She gathered her courage and dashed out of the barn and ran as fast as she could to the house, her heart pounding and her breath coming in great gulps that turned to sobs. Milk slopped onto her dress. She slammed and barred the door behind her. She stood at the window, examining every place an Indian might hide. The tree beside the house offered many hiding places. One branch resembled the silhouette of a crouching Indian draped in a blanket. It was only sticks and leaves. Nothing to fear. Nothing at all.

A deer strode across the yard, beautiful with his rack of antlers. She sat down at the table and started a letter to her mother. Gust had one in his pocket to be mailed in Pomme de Terre. It was time to write another.

It was almost dark when Serena heard the squeak of the wagon wheels over the hill. She lit the lamp and moved it closer to the window, relieved beyond description to see Gus and the wagonload of hay. She ran out to meet him.

"Any mail?" Serena's heart beat in her throat. Weeks had passed since hearing from home. There must be something.

"Nei, just the *Democrats.*"

"Nothing from your parents, either?" Serena said in disbelief. "What if something happened to one of your brothers? Surely they'd write and tell us."

"There were casualty lists posted in the paper," Gust said. "Maybe there will be something about the Iowa soldiers."

Headlines described battles in the south and listed unbelievable numbers of dead and wounded. But of course there was nothing about Iowa casualties.

"I need to unload the hay," he said as he stood to leave. "Supper will have to wait until I'm done. I need the wagon ready for picking stones in the far field tomorrow."

"But what about Pomme de Terre?" Serena pulled at her apron. "Surely there are things to tell me about our new neighbors."

"I bought hay from Anton Estvold," he said. "They're older, have sons off to war, and are as nice as can be. They are door neighbors, only about a mile as the crow flies, though it's farther by taking the trail. Their land adjoins ours though they make their living as innkeepers for the ox-carters."

"Norskies?"

"Ja," said Gust. "Norwegians. Good folk. They said to greet you."

"What did you find in Pomme de Terre?" Serena stoked the fire, adding small wood to make the coffee cook faster.

"The Estvolds."

"Did you see soldiers?" She slammed the stove door shut and pulled the coffee pot to the hottest burner.

"Ja," he said. "The soldiers are building fortifications around the buildings, in case of more Indian troubles." He took a deep breath and leaned over to rub his aching leg. "It's just a precaution, you know."

His words sounded hollow, but Serena didn't say anything, didn't allow herself the luxury of being alarmed. If it were dangerous, surely the authorities would demand that they move into the fort for the winter. Gust didn't say anything so it must be all right. Even a *skraeling* wouldn't be so foolish as to go raiding in the dead of winter.

The next day it snowed again and the dreaded winter settled in for good.

22

"Let the Sioux Race be Annihilated."
St. Cloud Democrat, September 4, 1862

They had already left camp when Drumbeater heard someone calling out to him. He and Standing Tall pulled back their ponies. Many Beavers spoke softly to the dog pulling the travois. The dog pulled off the trail, and Many Beavers took hold of the two girl-children lest they be thrown from the travois.

"Husband!" Willow Song ran through the underbrush, breathless and panting. The first hint of coolness tinged the air, and a tribe of geese honked overhead on their southward journey. "Wait!"

Drumbeater turned in surprise. Willow Song was known for her modest and chaste behavior. It was most unusual for her to make a loud noise. He had taken the sacred drum and his pipe. What else had he forgotten?

"I must go with you." Her eyes flickered fear, and her lip quivered. Her breath came in heavy puffs and her face was dusky from running. "Please take me along."

Little Bird reached out and grabbed her around the neck and clung tightly. Badger jumped off the travois, startling the dogs so they ran off the trail with the travois banging behind them. Many Beavers scolded and chased after.

"What is wrong?" Drumbeater reached over and placed his hand on her arm. Her body trembled as if afraid. "Is Otter all right?"

She pointed mutely at a small looking glass in her hand. Drumbeater's heart thudded in his chest. It was a bad omen for a woman to look into an *ihdiyomdasin*.

"I'm afraid." Willow Song's voice trembled. "Looking into the glass means certain death. *Uncheedah* left it in the teepee, said Blue Bottle left it when he was in camp, and she thought to test its medicine on Little Bird. I looked before I knew what it was."

"There's nothing for you to fear," Drumbeater said, hoping he spoke the truth but wondering at the bad medicine of the *ihdiyomdasin*. Many dangers lurked in Leaf Country. Ojibwas were quick to take advantage of an unprotected village. Willow Song might drown from a tipped canoe or bleed to death from a slipped hatchet. Her teepee might catch fire in the night. A sickness could overtake her.

The bird tribe warbled in the trees, and a lumbering porcupine waddled through the brush.

Many Beavers dragged the dog back to the trail, the travois unattached and falling apart. She knelt to retie the binding ropes. The dog cowered in her presence, whining his apology.

"We must come with you," Willow Song said again.

Achhh! What was a man to do? To bring them along meant risking contact with the White Eyes.

Standing Tall stood silently waiting for the decision to be made.

"Pack quickly and come along." He could not ignore the omen. "Is this agreeable to you?" Maybe he should have consulted the chief before speaking. It was bad enough that he left the rice camp when the women and children needed protection. If Willow Song came along, it meant one less woman to harvest rice. The tribe would suffer.

"The omen is bad," Standing Tall said. "But whether or not the omen pertains to her staying or coming, I cannot say."

That was what troubled Drumbeater. Maybe taking her along meant she would meet her death. There was no way of knowing.

"It is good they come along," Standing Tall said at last. His eyes flickered over the trail, followed a scampering chipmunk seeking acorns beneath a giant oak. "The White Eyes will know that we mean no evil if we bring our women and children with us."

After a short delay, when Many Beavers and Willow Song dismantled the teepee and packed the small stores of food and cooking pots, the little group passed slowly southward, towards the land of the *washechu*, towards war.

Badger laughed as Many Beavers showed her how to both fasten and unfasten Otter's cradleboard to the travois. Such learning was part of every child's education and Many Beavers smiled as Badger held Otter's cradleboard with one hand and put her other arm around her sister.

The trees showed orange and yellow along the river. A dry smell filled Drumbeater's nostrils, the smell of autumn, the Moon of Picking Cherries. He gnawed a worrisome thought like a beaver gnaws a sapling, a worry about the lack of rice, and the loss of meat. The Moon of Great Difficulty would come, *washechu* or no *washechu*, and they would hunger.

A few years before, grasshoppers had taken the rice crop. He shuddered to remember the hardships of that winter, the old ones and children who perished. The men worked through the winter hunting and fishing through the ice, but the omens were against them. They had only survived by boiling animal hides into a thick soup.

They would survive again.

Once as a small boy, Crooked Lightning had taken him on the fall hunt, a rare privilege for a young one. They had traveled to the far country where herds of buffalo darkened the hillsides. The open spaces of the prairies had terrified Drumbeater. He had longed for the sheltering trees to hide him from lurking enemies.

A choking feeling made him swallow hard. The *washechu* might chase them out of Leaf Country and force them to live on the open prairies. His father once said that living in Leaf Country provided a better education. Dakota brothers living on the prairie did not understand the mysteries of the animals and plants in Leaf Country. "Their wisdom is limited," he had said. "How can they learn what they do not see?"

And so, like all the young boys in the tribe, Drumbeater learned both the lessons of the prairie and the lessons of Leaf Country. "It makes the heart of the Leaf dwellers more balanced," his father had said. "A great blessing of Wakantanka."

It was bad enough the Ojibwa claimed most of Leaf Country but terrible that the tracks of the *washechu* on paper birch might push them out of Leaf Country forever. He wanted Otter to have the better education, that knowledge of Leaf Country and all its animals and plants. He yearned only to raise his son in peace.

Drumbeater tried to be *tuwe taku*, an optimist. Maybe Wakantanka sent the *washechu* girl-children to purchase the freedom to live where their spirits belonged. He would bring the girl-children to the man-of-the-wooden-wheels and maybe the medicine of Little Bird would be strong enough to trade for peace in Leaf Country.

But if the medicine wasn't strong enough, Drumbeater vowed to make a song about Leaf Country, a song so powerful that the very leaves of the trees would live forever in its words and melody.

A song of such strong medicine that it would echo through the generations.

The song would sing about the woodland creatures, the birds and animals of Leaf Country, all that was good and beautiful.

Drumbeater's heart quickened to think of the great song but he hoped it would be unnecessary. He hoped with all his might that the Mdewakanton and the Wahpekute would fight the *washechu* in their own land, and leave the Sisseton alone.

On their second day on the trail, Drumbeater pondered the lesson of the *kanketanka*, the way it pounded on fallen trees and rotting wood. Surely Wakantanka hid a lesson in the woodpecker tribe. The girl-children dozed on the travois next to Otter's cradleboard. Willow Song gathered blackberries into a small basket, picking as she walked along the faint path of the deer tribe.

Suddenly the dog pulling Many Beaver's travois snarled and bristled. Before Many Beavers could reach for the cradleboard, a black bear ambled out from behind a chokecherry bush and batted out a long paw, swiping the dog's head. It howled a terrible war cry and ran off the trail, charging through the brush. The travois bounced hard against a fallen tree and Little Bird flew into the air and landed in a hazel bush.

"Birdie!" Badger clung to Otter's cradleboard frame as the dog disappeared into the woods, dragging them away.

"Wokagi!" Willow Song's voice shrilled. "Come back!"

The women streaked after the travois, Willow Song's berries dropped to the ground. Little Bird scrambled to her feet. When she saw the bear, she screamed in her strange tongue. The bear turned slowly to the sound of her screams. Drumbeater prayed a desperate prayer to Wakantanka that he would have the courage to kill the bear before it could harm Little Bird. He reached for his knife. It was his duty.

The bear rose up on hind feet and stared at the *washechu* girl-child with bright eyes, a fleck of foam dripping from its mouth. Drumbeater grasped his knife tighter. He must protect the child of Uncle's life-and-death friend. Drumbeater must protect her for the honor of his uncle even if it meant his death. He would aim for the bear's heart. Drumbeater's death song rose up in his throat, and he made ready to leap at the bear.

But before Drumbeater could make his move, Standing Tall's arrow zinged through the air into the bear's left eye. The bear hesitated a moment, batted a huge paw at the arrow stuck in his eye, and then slowly crumpled to the earth, like a leaf floating to the ground.

Wakantanka had sent the omens. Drumbeater should have been watching, guarding his family instead of daydreaming. Standing Tall must watch over him as if he were a child. Would he never learn?

His strength returned to his legs and he bolted after the travois as Standing Tall picked up the screaming Little Bird. The brush tore at Drumbeater's clothing, slapped his face. He ran towards the voices of the women, the barking of the dog, and the smell of the river.

He had forgotten the river. If the dog dragged the travois into the water, Otter and Badger would surely drown. His son was strapped to his cradleboard. Who knew if the girl-child could swim? Many among the People lost children that way. The dog tribe was unreliable, always quick to run after rabbits or small animals.

When he pushed through the underbrush, he spied the river. Drumbeater's heart melted in his chest. The dog already floundered in the water, pulled down by the weight of the travois. Badger splashed beside the dog. Willow Song and Many Beavers swam toward them.

Badger's white face flashed in the sun as she pulled the cradleboard out of the water. Willow Song grabbed it from her hands and untied Otter, pounding his back until he let out a strong war cry.

Badger clutched Willow Song's neck with both arms, pouted her lower lip and glared hatred at the struggling dog in the river. Many Beavers swam out to rescue the dog and the travois.

Drumbeater breathed a prayer of thanks that the sacred drum was tied securely to his pony and that the future warrior had been spared. He scrambled over to them, stepping into the icy water, feeling his feet sink into the muddy river bottom. With shaking hands he took Otter from Willow Song's uplifted arms.

"She saved our son." Willow Song smoothed Badger's hair and held her close. "Badger pulled the straps tying Otter's cradleboard to the travois before the dog could drag him away into deeper water."

Drumbeater pressed Otter to his chest, sniffed the scent of wood smoke from his wet black hair, felt his heart beat like a fluttering bird.

"We were too far behind." Willow Song pulled Badger to her side, patting her back and wiping water from her eyes. "We would have never made it in time."

Overhead an eagle flew out from around the river's bend and skimmed over the water, dipping into the waves with a loud shriek. It pulled a fish from the water and looped overhead before flying away again.

A good omen. Truly the medicine of Badger's heart was stronger than Little Bird's hair. He had been slow to see the truth. He saw it now.

"You will be rewarded," Willow Song dug in her packs until she brought out lumps of maple sugar. "May you grow up to be a mother of many warriors."

Drumbeater thought of Star Fist's words, that all *washechu* should be killed: warriors, future warriors, and women who would bear more warriors.

"We must blacken Little Bird's hair with mud from the river." Drumbeater's breath slowed to normal. "The sun might glint off her hair and attract our enemies."

He would make a song about Badger, how she rescued Otter from drowning, how she kept him from touching the strong medicine of her sister's hair. How the calling eagle proved once and for all that the medicine of the heart was stronger than the power of sun-glazed hair.

23

"Mr. Lincoln Pardons All but 39 Sioux. Minnesota Outraged."
St. Cloud Democrat, November 25, 1862

SERENA SCRAPED THE FROSTY WINDOW with her fingernail, breathed on the glass and scraped again. Finally, the moon glowed through the scrape. Gust watched as she fitted her eyes to the scraped spot and looked outdoors.

"What do you see?" he said at last.

"Nothing," her voice sounded small. "Only the moon's reflection on snow."

"It's a full moon," he said. "The fields are as bright as day."

"Brighter." Serena blew and scratched again. "Nothing is brighter than light on new snow."

"What are you looking for?"

"Just wondering about Indians," Serena said.

"The Indian danger is over," Gust said. "They'll be hanged at Mankato." He laughed too loudly. He quickly lowered his voice. "You've read the papers. There's nothing to worry about."

Gust knew Serena wasn't sleeping well, but blamed it on Lena's death. Babies died. There was always some sickness afflicting small ones, and it was unreasonable to expect every child to live. Little Lena might have died anyway, Indians or no Indians. Most families lost children. The thought of Lena brought a thickness to his throat. He never voiced his grief. It was hard for him to speak her name aloud, and he missed her more than he would admit. Missed her innocent smile and small hands reaching for his beard.

110

"Serena," he said, "come to bed. It's too cold for you to be up."

"Ja," she answered in a flat voice. "I'm just admiring the moon."

He needed to be the strong one, to care for Serena. She looked thin and ghostlike in her white gown and cap, so silent and mournful. He missed the old Serena, the one filled with music. He hoped he hadn't made a mistake in refusing to return to Burr Oak. He could have written home and asked his father for money to return to Iowa. If he had wanted, he could have found the money to go home.

And he hoped he hadn't made a mistake by refusing to winter at Fort Pomme de Terre, as Captain McLarty had demanded.

"I'll have you brought in in chains," McLarty said. "There's Indian trouble all around us. It's not safe out there alone."

"I'm free, white, and twenty-one." Gust clenched his teeth and felt his face turning red. "I'll do what I want and no one can stop me."

No Indian in his right mind would go looking for trouble with a fort full of soldiers nearby and the weather too cold for man or beast. No, there were no Indian worries this time of the year. Even a fool could figure that much out for himself.

THE ROOSTER'S CROW AWAKENED them the next morning. Gust was out of bed, dressed and headed towards the barn before it quit crowing. His sharp mind mapped out the day before him, first the milking, then a quick mucking of the barn before breakfast. After breakfast there was kitchen wood to split and plowshares to sharpen before spring planting rolled around again.

His grindstone was too small to do a good job. Olaus Reierson's foot-powered grindstone sharpened iron plowshares in minutes. Of course, Reierson had been in Minnesota for years and it was to be expected he would be better situated. A bachelor from Iceland, he survived the Indian Uprising by forting at Pomme De Terre where he fought off the Indians alongside the Estvold family. By God, that Reierson was a man to stand by, a genuine hero.

The more Gust thought about it, the more he was convinced he needed to visit Olaus and use his grindstone. He could catch up on the news about the reparation investigations. Olaus was on the stage line between Fort Snelling and Fort Abercrombie and heard the news every week. Maybe they could play a little cards after supper. It would be good to have some male company.

Gust's heart beat faster as he planned the trip. He would put the sleigh runners on the wagon box after breakfast. The oxen were slow, and he wouldn't get there until dusk. Serena could milk the cows until he got back.

Serena would be fine left alone for a day or two.

24

"Condemned Sioux Abused by Outraged Citizens of Henderson"
St. Cloud Democrat, November 25, 1862

SERENA FELT A HAND SQUEEZE HER HEART and the blood drain from her cheeks. She gripped the table edge for support. "You're going where?"

"To Chippewa Station." He lifted and drained his coffee cup. "Olaus has the best grindstone. Our plowshares will be ready in no time at all."

"But it's winter," she stammered. "Bad weather might come up."

"You worry too much, Serena girl." He shoveled eggs and bacon with vigor, wiping his plate with a heel of bread. "I'll put the runners on the wagon box and be there before dark."

"When will you be back?" Her voice sounded far away. She noticed the quick way Gust pushed the food into his mouth. It was easy to see his mind was made up.

"Tomorrow night." Gust wiped his greasy mouth on his shirtsleeve. "Or maybe the day after, depending on how the trip goes."

Serena watched him leave with the stumbling oxen and the rickety wagon. Only a man would make such a trip in the middle of winter, leaving his woman alone and defenseless. It was all she had come to expect from Gust, and that saddened her even more.

The silence pressed in from all sides. She went to the woodpile and filled her apron with kitchen wood. The smell of freshly split oak tickled her nose. Oak was a comforting wood—slow to burn, giving off a steady heat in the coldest of weather. One piece of firewood was the size of a sturdy club, too big to fit in the stove.

Serena dumped the apron load of wood into the box by the stove and tossed the club onto the floor. Then she hurried to the window and scanned the clearing. Nothing.

She needed water. She took a wooden bucket from behind the door and started for the river, thought better of it and instead scooped clean snow from the drift nearest the cabin, setting it next to the warm stove in the kitchen. Many buckets of snow would be needed for the animals, but at least she would be spared a trip to the river.

It was far too early to milk the cows but Serena milked them anyway. She carried the melted snow to the barn and carefully gave a part to each animal. It wasn't much but it would tide them over until Gust returned home. The cow was due to freshen in a few months and gave only a small measure of milk. Serena scattered a little grain to the hens and was rewarded with a single egg among the hay. Carefully she placed the egg in her apron pocket. Eggs were a rare treat in the cold of winter and usually saved for Gust, but tonight it would be her supper.

She would eat when she felt like it and milk the cows when she wanted. No one would tell her what to do. It was a defiant thought, braver than she felt.

Before leaving the barn, she found a crack in the boards and stared out onto the fields and woods around their house and barns. The branches squeaked in the wind, and a pair of pileated woodpeckers pounded at the woodpile, an incessant drumming sound on the stacked wood.

There were a million places to hide.

A bitter chill made Serena tremble with cold and by sheer act of will she hurried toward the house, pulling her shawl around her head and arms, carrying the bucket half filled with milk. She ran to the door and slammed it behind her, dropped the bar, then quickly shoved the wooden table in front of the door. Her heart pounded until it roared in her ears, drowning out the drumming birds and the branch rubbing against the window.

There was no place to hide in winter. Anyone could see smoke from her chimney or the light from the single pane of glass. She would freeze without a fire. Only a small fire then, just enough to keep her alive—and a small light. She took Lena's baby blanket from the trunk and pressed it to her face, trying to smell Lena's sweet scent, remembering the hope interwoven with the threads.

She touched a small piece of straw to the glowing embers in the stove and watched it flame. Then she lit the oily wick in a saucer of fat that served as their lamp. With great determination, Serena covered the small windowpane with Lena's blanket, shutting out the light.

The lamp, a tiny glow on the rough-hewn table, spread shadows to the corners of the room. She thought to take Lena's blanket down and let the daylight in but she dared not. Instead, she pulled the wood box over to the door, stacked the kindling on top of the trunk, and then pulled a block of wood used for butchering there as well.

She would hear anyone trying to get into the cabin.

A sudden exhaustion overcame Serena. She dipped milk from the bucket and placed the egg on the table. She lay on the bed, fully dressed down to her shoes, and pulled the blankets over her. Just as she fell asleep, she bolted upright and stumbled to the cupboard where she felt for the butcher knife. She took it to bed with her, tucking it safely under her pillow within easy reach.

Perhaps she wouldn't be able to stab an Indian, but she could slit her own throat if they came. She knew too many stories of uprising survivors to be taken alive.

Serena dreamed of Lena's soft hands and gentle smile. Her hands reached for her but something separated them. As fast as she ran, Serena could not catch Lena, always just out of reach. Her pounding heart awakened her. It was freezing cold in the room and the lamp had fizzled out.

With a start, she remembered her grandmother's *bunad*. Serena had packed it safely in her trunk after the baptism. Vaguely she recalled their belongings scattered across the grass. Had the Indians taken her *bunad*? Perhaps they admired the embroidery. Lena had been sick and demanded all her attention.

What kind of person had she become to be so careless? She had squandered the precious link to Norway, her only family heirloom. She pictured the map showing the ocean voyage to the country shaped like a milkweed pod bursting with seed. Her mother had kept the bunad safe during her long journey to America but Serena had failed though her journey was much shorter. Sobs of regret wet her cheeks.

Clutching the knife in her hand, Serena felt her way to the window and pulled back the heavy cloth. Frost covered the windows, and she scraped until she could look out onto the clearing. Nothing moved. Nothing at all.

It was a mistake to go to bed early, to sleep during the day. Hours of darkness stretched before her. A mouse chewed on a piece of firewood. The gnawing sounds were her only companion. She pushed a stick of wood into the stove, blew a quiet stream of air across the embers, and huddled close to the feeble blaze. The stovepipe crackled as the metal warmed and melting frost dripped onto the floor, splashing on Serena's feet.

Everything was wrong: Lena's death, the move to Pomme de Terre, the Red Men. What were the Indians thinking to kill and butcher the good people of Minnesota? Uncivilized savages who could not be understood. She wondered if they believed in God, if they were capable of praying for peace. She wanted only to be left alone. That's all.

Why didn't the Indians understand this? Why didn't they leave them alone?

25

"Army Forced to Protect Sioux from Angry Citizens"
St. Cloud Democrat, November 25, 1862

OLAUS REIERSON WELCOMED GUST with open arms, lonely for another human voice. They sharpened the plowshares, and Olaus pulled out a bottle of aquavit and a tattered deck of cards. They played thirty-one until after midnight, according to Olaus's pocket watch.

"Tell me about the Indian raids," Gust said. "Were they as bad as people say?"

"Ja, they were bad. Indians hate white people, settlers most of all."

"Why?"

"The settlers plow the land and cut the trees. They have little argument with the army." He took a swig from the bottle, wiped it with his sleeve and handed it to Gust. "First they came through and stole every horse in the damned country. I lost a good chestnut, best horse I ever had."

"You get it back?"

"Nei," said Olaus. "Savages probably ate it. They have no appreciation for good horseflesh." He wiped a drop of liquor from the tabletop with his forearm. "I'll never find a horse that good again—especially with the Rebellion in the South."

"Did they attack your place?" Gust rubbed his bad leg. Damn cold made it pain all the worse. He'd be lucky if he got any sleep with the way it hurt.

"Nei." Olaus took another swig of aquavit. "The stage stopped with a warning, and I went with the driver as far as Pomme de Terre. He had

117

some notion of warning Fort Abercrombie. I figured I could just as easy fight Indians close to home."

"I met the stage on our way to the farm."

"A different driver." He got up and pushed another piece of dry oak into the firebox of the cook stove in the corner of the soddy. It was dark as night and little enough light glowed from the oil-dipped rag that was his only light. Olaus brought back a tin plate, shined it on his sleeve and propped it behind the lamp to reflect the light. "That any better? Damn it gets dark early these winter days."

"The Indians—did you fight them?"

"Ja," said Olaus. "They attacked twice. Came swooping in like locusts, naked and painted, screeching like demons. Scared us more than hurt us— our guns held them off. You should have seen it."

"Were there many *skraelings*?" Gust's mouth went dry and he swallowed hard.

"About fifty, but there were five rifles to meet them and a stout barricade." Olaus swirled the liquid in his bottle. "We kept our scalps, but they kept us forted up during the prime of harvest. I lost my entire corn crop to bears and raccoons." He took another swig, and Gust watched his face color red in contrast to his white hair. Olaus looked like an ancient Viking. "Damn savages robbed me of the best corn crop I ever had."

"Other attacks around here?"

"Stole every horse along the Abercrombie Trail. Damn Indians are unpredictable. They hit where they think they can get away with it."

"I read about the siege of Fort Abercrombie and the men found dead by Dayton." Gust felt his skin crawl. He glanced toward the door, relieved to see it securely barred.

"It was worse in the Minnesota River Valley but even around here whole families were caught flat footed, butchered and burned." Olaus paused to take another drink, each swig loosening his tongue. "It was carnage, believe you me. Women violated, babies hacked to death, and people beheaded and with their limbs cut off. Made no sense."

"Most people left for the settlements," Gust said. "Why didn't you?"

"I've nothing except this place. No wife, no family. Every dime I have is sunk into this place, and no damn *skraeling* will scare me out of it." He scratched his white head with both hands and stretched. "Polar bears chased me out of Iceland—kept eating my stock and killing my dogs. I won't be chased out again by man or beast."

"The danger is over, isn't it?" asked Gust, a small tremble in his voice.

"Over? You bet your life it's not! There's danger!" Olaus' face darkened to a deep purple. "You think the army solved the problem?" He laughed and pounded the table with his fist, causing the aquavit bottle to tip over. Not that there was any left to spill.

"The bad ones will hang."

"You think they caught every hot-headed renegade in the state?" Olaus' voice thickened and slurred. "Do you think they'd leave soldiers at Pomme de Terre if the danger was over? Especially with men needed so bad in the South?"

"Have you seen any Red Men?" Gust glanced through toward the single window covered with a ragged burlap sack.

"They're always around," Olaus said. "Skulking in the shadows, waiting to find a defenseless woman or child."

"I moved here thinking it was safe."

"Why did Salmon sell if it was so safe?" Olaus said. "He poured his heart into that farm, worked like a dog. Why would he leave years of work?"

Gust couldn't answer. Surely whatever danger might lurk in Pomme de Terre, owning a farm made the risk worth it.

"They can't burn me out of this soddy," Olaus said. "They can wait and skulk and try to catch me unawares, but they can't burn me out." The rag sputtered and smoldered causing a burnt smell to permeate the air. "You wouldn't catch me living in a log cabin with Indians around."

Gust thought of Serena alone in their cabin. A sudden pang of worry pierced his mind. Then he thought of his carefree trip, ten miles through the wilderness. A savage could have easily picked him off as he dozed on the sleigh. He had been lucky. The oxen were too slow to escape from anyone.

For the first time he wondered if the fifty dollars he paid for the farm by Pomme de Terre was worth it.

26

"Were the information contained in the report of the Sioux investigation placed before the people of this state, they would never trust Governor Ramsey with any official position, whatever."

St. Cloud Democrat, November 25, 1862

W E'RE ALMOST THERE," DAGMAR ESTVOLD said. "We'll warm up inside."

"You're the one who said there was no smoke from their chimney this morning," Anton Estvold said. "I doubt we'll warm by their fire."

Since that arrogant young man with the limp had been to the fort, Dagmar had watched for smoke from the old Salmon place. She knew how it was to be alone, far from family, and she wouldn't rest until Anton agreed to go with her to check on their new neighbors. His missus couldn't be very old. Gust was still wet behind the ears himself, no older than her boys.

"There's no smoke," Anton said when they came into the farmyard. His fur cap was pulled down over his forehead and a wool scarf was wrapped around his neck and face leaving only his eyes uncovered. He carried an ancient firearm in the crook of his right arm.

"Expect the worst," Dagmar said and bundled her shawl tighter around her arms. She was glad she had worn her extra wool petticoat. "No one in their right mind would let the fire go out on such a morning."

"Is anyone home?" Anton pounded on the door, the sound muffled by his woolen mittens. He called out again and banged with the sides of his fist.

The wind whipped the ends of Dagmar's muffler, and she wrapped the ends around her neck and tucked them into her shawl. It was freezing cold, and her cheeks ached. A face peeked through the window. It must be the missus, but she looked like a child, so small and white.

"I'll be right there," a voice called from inside. They heard the sounds of something heavy being dragged away from the door.

The door opened, and the girl lifted her arm across her eyes and squinted against the light.

"*God dag*, Missus," Anton said. "We're Anton and Dagmar Estvold. Your man bought hay from us at Fort Pomme de Terre."

"We noticed you had no smoke from your chimney this morning," Dagmar said, "and worried you might be sick or in trouble."

"Come in," the girl croaked. "It's freezing outside."

They entered the cabin but found it barely warmer than outside, the fire completely out. Bedclothes tangled on the floor and a butcher knife lay on the pillow, a wooden club close by. An egg on the table was frozen and cracked. The pungent odor of skunk lingered in the room.

"I'll fetch wood and start the fire." Anton pulled his collar up around his neck and left the cabin. Cold whirled in through the open door.

"I'm sorry," the girl said. She looked like she was about to burst into tears. "I'm not prepared for company."

"We're not company." Dagmar rubbed her hands together. "We're your neighbors and here to help you if you need it."

The young woman's eyes were puffy and swollen. She looked like an American flag with her eyes red and blue and her face so white. And not much more flesh on her than a flagpole. Her nightcap covered her head, and she was wearing mittens and fully dressed. She had bed slippers pulled over her shoes and a shawl wrapped around her shoulders.

"What can I call you?" Dagmar said, biting back her blunt words too late. Damn, she wanted to make a good impression and here she was already sounding bossy.

"Serena Brandvold," she answered and flushed bright red. "Excuse me, please. You've surprised me. My name is Serena Gustafson."

Cows bawled from the barn.

"The chores!" Serena said with wild eyes. "I've overslept myself."

"Where's your man?" He must be in the barn, obviously, since he wasn't in the small cabin. But why had he let the fire go out?

"Yesterday he went to Chippewa Station to sharpen his plowshares," Serena said, "in preparation for spring planting."

"Hmmm," Dagmar said. She picked at a piece of lint on her shawl and tried to hold back the angry words. "He picked a hell of a time to leave you alone."

Serena turned her head sharply.

"He must be out of his mind," said Dagmar. "The Red Men are unsettled."

Anton stumbled through the door with a stack of kitchen wood, stomping snow off his feet.

"Only a man would be foolish enough to leave a woman alone in the wilderness," Dagmar continued. "He must be . . ."

"Dagmar." Anton gave her a quick look. Dagmar met his gaze and looked down, studying her shoes. Why couldn't she say what she wanted? Women had ideas, too. It's not as if the men were any smarter.

"Don't mind my missus," he said. "She speaks her mind too freely sometimes."

Anton dropped the wood on the floor with a clatter and fed small pieces to the stove until the fire roared and the metal pipe expanded with a *thump.* The sweet smell of burning oak replaced the odor of skunk, at least for the time being. Dagmar stretched out her aching hands over the stove, gathering the first comforting rays of heat.

"The cows need milking," Dagmar said, and Anton left for the barn.

"I can't let you do the chores," Serena said. "You've done enough already. I'll do the milking while you wait in here where it's warm."

"Nonsense!" Dagmar's voice was jovial. "Anton will have the chores done in no time, and we can visit a little. I see we caught you in the middle of your morning."

"I'll fix something to eat," Serena said.

"Why don't you ready yourself while I fix breakfast?" Dagmar said. "I'd be glad to help."

Serena set out the food, turned her back to Dagmar and hurriedly changed her apron. Dagmar watched her pull a wooden comb through her unruly locks before she twisted them into a demure bun at the back of her neck, poking wooden hairpins to anchor it in place. Serena took a clean rag from the corner, tried to dampen it from the water bucket but found it frozen solid. She shook the tea kettle and managed to pour a few drops of water on the corner of the rag and scrubbed her face.

Dagmar hefted the cast iron skillet on the stove. She retrieved the butcher knife from the pillow and sliced bacon, dropping it into the pan where it sizzled and spattered. The wonderful fragrance of fresh coffee and frying bacon soon tickled her nose.

Bacon! How long had it been since they had eaten bacon? It seemed like forever, certainly before the uprising. Her mouth watered, and she restrained herself from eating a piece right from the pan.

"Mrs. Estvold," Serena said. "I'll be right with you."

"Just call me Dagmar." She wiped a spatter of grease off her face. "Although I'm old enough to be your mother, I need a friend more than a fancy name."

"Dagmar," Serena stammered, and her chin quivered as fat tears welled in her eyes, "I, too, have needed a friend."

"There, there." Dagmar pulled the skillet off to the side of the stove and turned to Serena, taking her in her arms. "*Stakkers liten.*"

She dissolved into Dagmar's arms, clinging to her. Forgotten emotions flooded Dagmar, choking out any words of comfort for the young woman. Serena was young, maybe the age of Rebecca had she lived, with eyes blue as Norwegian fjords and like Rebecca, golden hair. Of course, Rebecca had lived only a few days and her hair might have darkened with the years, but it was easy to imagine that her Rebecca might have looked very much like Serena Gustafson.

If only her children had lived. If even one of the girls were alive, she wouldn't be so lonely with Emil and Ole off to war. Or if Bjorn were alive to help with the farm. It wasn't right that a mother should lose her children. Dagmar indulged in the weakness of tears for only a minute and then wiped her eyes with her apron. She had cried gallons of tears through the years and still her children were dead.

This poor girl belonged home with her mother. Gust, so cocky and arrogant. Damn Swede! When Captain McLarty warned of the dangers of living outside the fort, he laughed it off and said that no Indian in his right mind would attack so close to the soldiers.

That showed how little he knew.

And to leave his missus alone overnight. Inexcusable! A Red Indian could have crept up to the house and murdered her—or worse.

"Gust went to visit Mr. Reierson," Serena said with a small hiccough. "I was afraid to be here by myself."

"Hmmmm." Dagmar patted her on the back before pulling a chair closer to the stove and sitting down. The first heat radiated out from the iron stove, barely penetrating the deep cold that filled the little cabin. Thank God they had wooden floors at the inn. She had forgotten how cold a dirt floor felt in winter. "Any woman would be afeared in these times. I know I would."

"Really?" Serena huddled next to the stove, reaching hands over the warmest part. "Gust thinks I'm silly."

"A woman has reason to fear," Dagmar said, "after what we've been through in this state."

"I didn't sleep all night," Serena said.

"I wouldn't have slept a wink either," Dagmar said. "There are too many savages around for a Christian woman to sleep in an unprotected place."

Dagmar poured Serena a cup of hot coffee and one for herself. "Do you have any cream?"

Serena reached over to the windowsill for a small gourd. "It's frozen solid," Serena said. "Maybe you could scrape a little into your coffee."

"That I will do and gladly," Dagmar said. "We've missed our cows."

"What happened to them?"

"The damn Sioux murdered our Bossy," Dagmar said and gouged a spoon of frozen cream and stirred it into her coffee. "And her calf. We saw them bloating in the field outside of the fortifications but didn't dare risk bringing them in for meat. A foolish waste." Dagmar sniffled and wiped her nose on her sleeve. "I raised Bossy from a calf. She was like family."

"They killed our cow, too." Serena cradled both hands around her cup and stood as close to the stove as she could. "We lost everything."

"But you have cattle and your man bought this farm off Salmon," Dagmar said. "How did you do it?"

"The reparation payments."

"Reparations, you say?"

"Ja." Serena took a sip of coffee. "Governor Ramsey divided the Indian Annuity amongst the victims."

"Never heard of it."

"Paper says there's more next year," Serena said. "Maybe you can get in on it."

Dagmar took another sip of coffee. She doubted there would be any reparation money for people out on the western edge of Minnesota. No one had ever given her anything and she wasn't about to start expecting something now.

"So you were hit by the *skraelings*?"

"Ja," Serena said as she grasped her cup with two hands, warming them. "The Sioux burned us out."

Anton came in holding three eggs in his mittened hands. His face and beard were frosted, and snot hung like icicles from his nose.

"By God," he said as he set the eggs on the table and wiped his nose on his sleeve, "it feels like a storm stirring up."

Dagmar cast an anxious glance out the window toward the darkening western sky.

"Bacon!" he said. "Mother, how long has it been since we've had bacon?"

"Far too long, I'm afraid," Dagmar said with a laugh. "We live mostly on fish."

"Morning, noon and night, we eat fish." Anton pulled off his great coat and hung it on a peg by the door. "You'll find nice pickerel in the river."

"I'll be sure to tell Gust," Serena said. "We could use some fresh fish."

Serena washed the eggs in a dish of clean water while Dagmar peeled the frozen egg on the table and put it in the hot bacon grease. Dagmar cracked the other eggs into the pan and stirred them all together with a fork, saving the shells for the coffee pot.

Dagmar knew they should be leaving, but they could hardly leave the young missus alone. Especially with a storm moving in. Maybe that foolish man of hers would freeze to death and she'd be rid of him.

"Fresh eggs are a real treat," Dagmar said. "Our hens haven't been laying."

"We harvested our potatoes and some of our corn," Anton said. He didn't remove his coat or mittens but cast her a disappointed look.

Dagmar wondered if her face was blotchy. Anton disapproved of crying women, and he was already upset with her. She hated when he was angry.

"We didn't do too bad with the Indian raids and all," he continued. "At least we have potatoes along with the fish and enough corn to get through most of the winter. And we kept our scalps. Others weren't so lucky."

Only a man would talk about Indian atrocities to a woman stuck alone on a farm. Dagmar gave her husband a sharp look, and he turned quiet. Anton pulled up a wooden bench, and Dagmar poured coffee all around while Serena put the eggs and bacon on two plates and set them before her guests, standing to one side as was good manners.

"Sit down, Missus!" Anton said firmly. "We don't hold with manners out here in the frontier. Sit and eat."

Serena pulled up the old stump and sat down. She looked down at her empty plate, and Dagmar realized that the girl had saved nothing back for herself, had given all the food to them.

"This is too much for me." Dagmar divided her portion in half.

"I don't like the look of this weather," said Anton. "We'll stay with you until your man gets back."

Dagmar gave him a look of appreciation. He was good to think of it. Of course, the young girl couldn't stay alone in a storm. Who knew when that cocky Swede would get back?

"We'd take you home with us but you've stock to tend and the soldiers at the fort will care for ours, what little we have," Anton said between bites of food. "We've no reason to hurry home."

"They're nice boys," Dagmar said.

"Boys?" Serena asked.

"Well, they're boys to me," Dagmar laughed. "About the age of our sons. And so polite. I don't know what we'd do without them, especially Tommy Harris. He's almost like family."

"But it may be a day or two before Gust gets back," Serena said. "I couldn't impose."

"We're your friends and neighbors," Dagmar said firmly. "You are not imposing. We're offering. It will be a good time to get to know each other."

"I think I'll make myself useful." Anton bundled up in his buffalo skin coat and wool mittens. He pulled a fur cap over his ears and went outside. An icy blast of wind ruffled the rags hanging to dry by the table. Then came comforting sound of splitting wood.

"It's cold out!" Dagmar said. "I hope your man is dressed warm enough for the trip."

"The wind is bad here," Serena said. "Not like back home. We were more sheltered, with woods around us."

"It comes howling out of the west," Dagmar said. "The hills break it a little but not enough."

They drank more coffee. The conversation lagged.

"I can't stand just sitting here," Dagmar said at last. "Don't you have any work I can help you with?"

"Ja, there's work." Serena dragged out a sack of corn and together they pulled the outer husks, carefully saving them for the outhouse, and then began the tedious job of shelling each kernel from the dried cobs. The cobs would be used in the outhouse as well. Nothing was wasted.

"I've known work all my life," Dagmar said. "It keeps my hands busy and my mind off my troubles."

"That's what my mor says."

"In Norway I worked as a servant to a rich man." Dagmar attacked a cob with vigor, kernels popped off the cob and flew over the table. "I worked from early morning to late night without letup. Sometimes my head ached so I could hardly stand it, but there was no rest from my duties."

"Do you have sick headaches?"

"Ja," Dagmar said. "The sick headaches were hard on me when I was younger. Haven't bothered me lately."

"My Auntie Karen has sick headaches." Serena added husks to the growing pile. "She closes all the curtains and lies in a dark room until they pass. I went over and helped with her children before I married, especially when she had the headaches."

"I've heard corn cob ashes can be used as a substitute for baking powder," Dagmar said as she shelled corn onto her apron. Her legs were slightly parted making a deep well. "Are you short of baking powder?"

"Nei," Serena said. "We bought *saleratus* in St. Cloud."

The two women worked in silence for a bit. "Are you in need?" asked Serena. "You're welcome to cobs if you need them."

"Nei." Dagmar struggled with a stubborn row of kernels. She popped her thumb in her mouth to cool the blister already forming. "The Sioux left the cobs hanging on the stalks, at least the ones within firing range of the fort."

"You said you have boys?"

"Ja, I have two grown sons in the war and another who died years ago, but none of our girls lived." Her voice quivered, and she hastily reached for another cob of dried corn. "Bjorn lived a year before taken with the cholera. He was named after my far back in Norway, born after Emil and Ole, but before the three girls."

"How terrible to lose so many." Serena's eyes looked like black holes in the snow, her face small and white.

"It was a dark time."

"And your sons off to war?" Serena shelled a row of corn so forcefully that several kernels flew into her hair. She pulled them out with her fingers.

"Emil and Ole are in the South," she said. "The things they have seen and endured." She tossed an empty cob into the pile and chose another ear out of the sack. "Maybe God spared Bjorn worse tortures by taking him young."

They shucked in silence. The wind rustled the thatch overhead.

"How can it be God's will?" Serena said. "Why would He take your son? Why would He take our baby? She never hurt a single soul, was baptized like the minister said."

Dagmar scooped corn kernels into the sack at her feet, the kernels cold and hard as tiny stones. It was hell to lose a child. How could she answer the poor girl when there was no answer?

"Your heart bleeds with grief," Dagmar said. The wind howled around the corner of the cabin and a downdraft puffed smoke around the stove door. "It never goes away but gets better over time."

She slid her thumbnail down a row of corn kernels, removing the entire row in one easy motion.

"How did you lose your baby?" Dagmar asked in a quiet voice.

Serena rested the cob on her lap. Corn silk draped from her hair and hung on the front of her dress. Dagmar felt a throb of pity for the young woman. Serena seemed to struggle for words, and Dagmar waited patiently. She remembered how hard it had been to speak of her own children's deaths.

"A man in Hutchinson came home and found his Lydia murdered by the Sioux, his young daughters, also. He was in the cornfield and never knew a thing until he came home for dinner and found them dead." Serena's voice took on a flat edge and her words gushed out in a torrent.

"That's terrible."

"And they burned our wheat and corn. It was ready to harvest. Gust had gone to the neighbors to borrow a scythe," Serena said, and her eyes almost frightened Dagmar the way they sparked and gleamed. If she were mad, who could blame her? "The baby was sick, and I was trying to get the garden work done when they came."

"You were out in the garden, then?"

"Nei, I hid in the cellar," Serena said. "The flour came down through the cracks in the floor, and I needed to sneeze."

"Did they find you?" Dagmar's stomach clenched, and she prepared herself for the worst. She'd heard the stories of what the *skraelings* did to white women.

"Nei, they didn't find me."

"Good." Thank God she hadn't been murdered like Evan's friends at Alexandria Woods. It was the mercy of God she was spared. Thank God.

"Lena died on the way to Fort Snelling." Serena looked toward the window with a vacant stare as another downdraft filled the room with choking smoke. She walked to the stove and adjusted the damper, reciting her story with a blank expression, like a confirmand reciting his catechism. "Lena had the scours, and nutmeg didn't help." She returned to the stump chair, pulling her shawl tighter around her shoulders. "I had plenty of milk but I ate tomatoes."

Serena broke into sobs, covering her face with her apron, crying as if she would never stop. "She died." Dagmar strained to make out the muffled words. "We buried her along the trail."

"You poor dear." Dagmar reached over and pulled the girl into her arms. It was easy to think she might be Rebecca, that this wee one lost along the trail might have been her own granddaughter. "It's hard to lose a small one. That I know from bitter experience."

"I didn't know what to do." Serena sniffed and pulled away from Dagmar's bosom.

"There was nothing to do." Dagmar squared her jaw and pulled another cob from the sack. "It was God's will. Nothing would have prevented it."

"Do you think so?" Serena's face was as white as the snowflakes falling outside the window, her blue eyes puffy, and her nose red from crying.

"Ja." The wind howled around the northwest corner of the cabin. Anton was rarely wrong when it came to weather. "It's always God's will when something happens, good or bad."

"How can it be God's will?" Serena said. "It was terrible, awful."

"I didn't understand it at the time, but over the years I've learned to bow to the will of God. Or maybe I'm still learning. What other choice do we have?"

Dagmar bit back angry words. She parroted the words of her mother, not her true feelings. She attacked a new cob with vengeance. God had let her down. She had prayed for the lives of her children, and yet God had taken four of them, leaving her angry and alone. She had her questions for God, that's for sure, but she would not burden Serena with them.

Anton came in with an armful of wood while the wind roared in around him through the open door.

"I hope Gust has a sense enough to stay put." Anton dropped the wood into the corner wood box. "It's too dangerous to travel in this weather."

Dagmar doubted the cocky young man had any sense at all.

27

"The Chicago Tribune *calls on the Government to turn the Negroes of the South against the Indians of Minnesota...may we not utilize Sambo for military purposes...and let the white men of Minnesota be relieved to do their duty against the other savages—the white men—our deluded brethren—of the South?"*

St. Cloud Democrat, *November 28, 1862*

"You're a fool to chance it." Olaus shifted from one foot to the other, hands stuffed into his coat pockets, beard stained with chewing tobacco. Gus hitched up Buddy and Bets and secured the sharpened plowshares into the back of the wagon bed. Every breath puffed into clouds of vapor. "The storms are fierce in this country. They blind and freeze a man."

"Thanks again for the use of your grindstone."

"Bring your missus along next time."

"I'll do that."

"If we could find another player, we might play whist." Olaus fingered his white beard, twirling the bottom with his fingers into a troll-like spike. "I'm most fond of whist, but out on the frontier it's hard to gather four people in one place."

"Come to our cabin," Gust said with an eye on the dark clouds in the west. "We'll fetch another player from the fort to join us."

"That I will." Olaus hunched his shoulders against the cold and tucked his beard inside his coat. "Maybe at Jul."

131

"Christmas!" Gust forced his voice to be jovial and he drove the reluctant beasts into the face of the wind toward Pomme de Terre. "We'd be glad for the company."

Within a mile of Olaus's place, Gust almost turned back. He shuddered to think of the long journey, but he had to get back to Serena in spite of the frigid wind that robbed his lungs of breath and burned his face. Thank God for the horsehide blanket that kept him from freezing solid.

He had been foolish to venture out this time of year.

His head ached from the night of aquavit, and his bad leg throbbed. Iowa had its share of bad weather, but Gust had never faced such wind.

"I'm in over my head," he told the oxen but the wind whipped his words away before they were out of his mouth. "Maybe I won't make it."

Gust reached for the empty aquavit bottle Olaus had sent with him, now filled with cold coffee. He took a swallow and tucked the bottle between his legs to keep it from freezing. It was handy having an extra bottle around, and he knew Serena would find many uses for it. He would watch out that he didn't break or lose it.

Yes, dangers lurked at Pomme de Terre. But Gust feared his father's debt more than he feared the Sioux. At least with the savages he could fight back; he felt helpless before his father's sarcasm and criticism.

Cleng Gustafson, his father, viewed his injury as weakness.

"He could work harder if he wanted," Gust heard him complain to his mother after the boys were supposed to be asleep. "He's lazy and doesn't try."

"He's not lazy," his mother said. "He's smarter, that's all. He'll be successful in life, wait and see."

His brothers answered Abe Lincoln's call to arms, and Gust was left alone on the farm with his father. His father acted like he hated Gust. Every straw had to be swept off the barn floor before breakfast. Every gutter cleaned before supper. Pail after pail of fresh water hauled from the well for the stock as well as the house. Wheat hauled to the gristmill for flour. Enough wood cut and chopped to keep them warm through the winters and stove wood for his mother. Work started at sunup and lasted until the sun was long set in the west. Nothing he did was good enough.

His mother said his father worried about his brothers, but Gust knew the truth. His father hated him for his weakness, for his stupidity in getting hurt in the first place. He treated him as a Negro slave, drudging without benefit of wages.

Gust shivered and pulled the horsehide blanket over his face, peeking out enough to keep the team on the trail. Success was the only weapon to defeat his father.

He would take care of Serena, he had no doubt of that. She was the girl of his dreams. He had loved her since childhood, loved her blonde curls and brooding blue eyes, the way she loved maps. Once when his brother Tosten teased him because of his sharp nose, Serena told him that she liked his nose, that it reminded her of the sharp point where Minnesota stuck out into Lake Superior. Not being sure exactly where Lake Superior was, Gust felt both comforted and accepted. Serena treated him like a normal person instead of a cripple.

But what if a dirty savage found her alone in the cabin? Olaus said they waited for a chance to kill and rape. The thought of his darling at the mercy of savages almost took his breath away. Her long blonde braids would tempt any man—a savage would yearn for them as well. He had lost Lena. He couldn't bear to lose Serena too.

It was a miracle she had escaped harm during the uprising. He would never forget how small she had looked, hunkered down in the cellar with Lena sick unto death and the Sioux raising hell. He thought he had lost her then.

Gust hurried the oxen but their pace did not change. He wouldn't leave her alone again. The wind howled in through holes in the blanket where the rats had chewed.

His arms ached from driving the oxen, and he could feel his strength drain away in the wind. He couldn't feel his feet or hands. A wave of frozen sleet pounded into him, stinging and burning. The sleet caused a sensation of vertigo, the swirling drops confused him, made him think he was going in the wrong direction.

He huddled down under the horsehide blanket and decided to let the animals find their own way. They wanted food and water and would find it by themselves. He pulled the horsehide blanket up over his head and prayed he would find Serena safely at home with the coffee pot on and maybe some cornbread in the oven. He prayed the oxen would stay on the trail. That he wouldn't freeze to death—not yet. He had too much to do.

After what seemed an eternity of shivering, the team stopped. Gust looked out, thinking he'd have to get out and lead them if they refused to travel into the face of the storm. A barn stood before him in the swirling snow. Thank God!

Gust threw the horsehide blanket back but stumbled as he climbed off the wagon. Damn leg! It refused to bear his weight, and Gust crumbled to the frozen ground as the oxen pawed and bawled to get into the barn.

A man slipped out through the barn door. It was Anton Estvold, the man who sold him the hay. Gust could see him mouthing words, but the sounds were lost in the howling wind. Sudden terror gripped Gust's chest. What tragedy had happened to bring him to their home?

"Are you all right?" Anton leaned down, grabbed him by the arm and pulled him to his feet.

"Serena!" Gust's throat ached with cold and his leg felt like fire. "Is Serena all right?"

"Ja," Anton spoke, but the wind whipped the words away, and Gust could hardly hear him. "But you're a damn fool to leave her alone."

Anton pulled open the barn door and the team lunged into the warmth of the log enclosure, jerking the wagon until the plowshare tipped over in the wagon bed. Gust limped into the barn after them and collapsed on a pile of hay, rubbing his leg and cursing under his breath. Had Estvold really called him a damn fool or had the wind twisted the words?

The team bellowed while Anton unhitched them and led them to the wooden water trough next to their stalls. Their eyelids frozen, Anton wiped their faces with his mittened hand, crooning to them in Norwegian. Frost melted on their backs and Anton wiped them down with handfuls of straw.

"Did you hear what I said?" Buddy stomped, and Anton stepped out of the way to avoid being kicked by the animal. "This is Indian country."

"The uprising is over." Gust's words sounded feeble and heat rose in his cheeks.

"Like hell." Anton forked hay to the oxen. "Don't leave her alone again. The savages like nothing better than to find a white woman alone."

Gust swallowed angry words. Anton was right—but it wasn't his business. He'd take care of his wife without help, thank you very much. She belonged to him.

"Bring her to the fort if you have to be gone," Anton said. "She can stay with us anytime."

"I needed her home to watch the stock."

Anton looked at him hard and long. Gust watched the muscles of his jaw work up and down, causing his beard to bob. He felt ashamed that this older man knew of his foolishness.

"I'll finish up here," Anton said. "Go in and warm up. You'll be lucky if you don't have frostbite."

"Wait, I need the bottle from the wagon."

Anton reached over the wagon bed, handed the bottle to Gust, and mumbled something under his breath. Clutching the bottle, Gust staggered into the cabin.

28

"Popular Outbreak at Mankato. Intense Excitement. Grand Fizzle."
St. Cloud Democrat, December 9, 1862

Serena took one look at Gust and screamed. His eyelashes and beard were frosted white beneath his frozen hat and muffler.

"I'll put the coffee on," Dagmar said.

Serena pulled him over to the stove and unwound his muffler, hung his wet mittens over the clothesline draped in the corner, and removed his frosty coat. "Are you drunk?" She spoke quietly so Dagmar couldn't hear, eyeing the empty bottle in his pocket.

"Nei." Gust shivered. "It was Olaus's bottle, too good to waste."

"Are you hurt?" Serena put her arm around him and helped him toward the bed. Cold weather always made his leg pain. They should have gone to Missouri. Even the insides walls of the cabin frosted in such weather.

"Nei." Gust staggered and clutched Serena to keep upright, leaning his full weight upon her. "Just cold."

Gust slumped down on the bed with a loud groan. Serena knelt and removed his shoes and stockings, chafing his feet with her hands. The touch of his skin reminded her of Lena's body before they buried her.

"You're freezing."

"Careful of my leg." Gust swore under his breath. "Damn cold! Not fit for man or beast!"

"Are his feet frozen?" Dagmar asked. "Should you rub them with snow?"

"Nei." Serena carefully examined his toes and feet. "They don't look frozen, but maybe we should use the snow just in case."

Dagmar fetched a pail of snow, the wind whirling in when she opened the door. Anton had been right about the weather. Serena dipped her hands into the bucket and rubbed a small handful over Gust's bare flesh.

"Damn! That hurts!" Gust pulled away. "Enough of that! It's worse than chilblains any day!"

"Lie down then and cover up." Serena pulled the ancient buffalo hide over him, wishing for the double log cabin quilt lost in the uprising. She hoped some poor Indian used it to keep warm on this cold day. Mor would be surprised to know a *skraeling* benefited from her labors. "I hope you don't catch pneumonia."

"Serena, do you have more blankets?" Dagmar poured the bucket of snow into the iron kettle and set it on the stove.

"Nei," she answered, "Except for the baby blanket."

"Wrap his feet in it, and I'll bring the coffee."

Dagmar warmed the small blanket by the stove and handed it to Serena, who wrapped Gust's feet in the precious cloth. Serena hoped the baby smell of Lena would not be replaced by the odor of Gust's feet. The blanket was all she had left of Lena, and it pained her to risk it, but she must care for her husband. She tucked the ends of the small blanket under Gust's feet and covered him again with the buffalo hide. After his coat dried, she would cover him with that as well.

"Are you sick?" Serena felt his forehead with the back of her hand.

"Nei," Gust whispered. "Just chilled. Why are they here?"

"They came to check on me." Serena ducked her head and felt her cheeks flame. "I'm ashamed of myself. I let the fire go out."

"No harm done that I can see," Gust said gruffly, and great relief flooded Serena. His eyes glowed as they looked at her, and Serena felt the need to look away, to change the subject. It would not do for Gust to say anything personal in front of company. That would have to wait, but she felt his eyes upon her, felt his desire for her.

"Why don't you lay down by your man and warm him," Dagmar said. "Rest yourself. I'll fix supper. If you have flour, I'll make soup and dumplings."

"Ja, there is flour in the sack and *saleratus*," Serena said. "But I can't lie abed while my company works."

"Nonsense!" Dagmar bustled over to the flour sack and gathered the ingredients. "Lie down and take your rest."

It was a relief to crawl under the old buffalo robe, even though fully dressed. She cuddled up close to Gust, and let him place his icy feet against her. With Dagmar in charge, Serena felt like a child again, loved and protected. With Dagmar watching over them, she could sleep without worry.

The poor sleep the night before, the extra guests, and then the fear of chilblains had exhausted her. The fire roared full blast in the stove, and she fell asleep listening to the sounds of Dagmar working in the kitchen.

When Serena awoke, Dagmar and Anton sat at the table shelling corn. A homey fragrance of fried onions filled the air. The stove glowed red. A quick stab of homesickness clutched her chest, and she bit her lip to keep back the tears. She was a grown woman, married, too old to cry for her mother.

"Are you awake?" whispered Gust in her ear.

"Ja," Serena answered. "Are you all right? Can you move your feet and hands?"

A slight movement under the bedclothes reassured her.

"Are you two ready for supper?" Dagmar said. "Looks like we'll be here until the storm blows over."

"It's early for a storm this bad." Anton opened the stove door and threw a few corncobs into the fire. A downdraft whirled smoke into the room. "Usually it's Christmas before we see anything like this."

Gust swung his legs out of bed with an audible groan.

"Got any willow bark?" Dagmar gathered the cornhusks and stuffed them back into the empty sack. "Its tea soothes pain of any kind."

"Willow bark tea, you say?" Serena said. "I've not heard of that."

"You strip bark off a willow and brew it up into a nasty tea that eases pains or fever," Anton said. "It's an old Indian remedy—we learned about it when we first came to this country. It might help that bum leg."

Dagmar placed bowls and spoons around the table. The men pulled stumps closer. Serena worried at the lack of chairs but no one seemed to mind.

At first the men were polite and formal with each other, but the tension lifted as they spooned hot soup with thick dumplings.

"Delicious!" Serena said. "I'd like the recipe before you leave."

They talked of home remedies and known cures, the price of beef and news from the fort. After they finished eating, Anton whittled a spoon from a piece of basswood while the women cleared the dishes. The talk changed to the many hazards of life—men gored by bulls or struck by lightening.

"I'll put more coffee on," Serena said. "See the frost on the walls!"

"It'll feel warmer once snow covers the cabin." Anton held up the half-made spoon to the light and ran the side of his finger along the edge of the wood. "It's natural insulation."

"Then let it snow." Gust reached for a sliver of wood from Anton's carving for a toothpick. "We need the moisture for spring planting."

It was good to be with other folks, thought Serena. Gust became more animated, joking and talking. Dagmar laughed until tears squeezed out of her eyes, and she wiped them on her apron. As the darkness settled and the winds howled, the talk turned serious.

"Tell us about the Indian war," Gust said as he shoved another log into the wood stove. Smoke spiraled out until the metal door banged shut with a clang. "What happened in this country?"

"We hardly made it," Anton said and let the whittling rest in his lap. "The stage driver, Evan Jacobson, warned us. Probably saved our lives."

Serena pictured the route on the map. "We met Mr. Jacobson—didn't we Gust? Wasn't Evan Jacobson driving that stage we met?"

"He got word at Cold Spring," Anton looked at Dagmar. "Or was it Sauk Center?"

"I think it was Cold Spring," Dagmar said.

"A priest from New Ulm warned of the massacre. Terrible things happened." Anton shook his head and made a clucking sound with his tongue. "But you know."

"How did you manage?"

"We gathered at the old fortifications on the hill," Anton said. "Damn Sioux had already killed our cow and stolen our horses."

"Don't forget our calf." Dagmar's voice rose to a shrillness almost painful to her ears. "And our ewe."

"They killed the damn ewe, and I was glad to see her go," Anton said. "She was ornerier than all our other dumb animals put together."

"You liked the stockings!" Dagmar screeched. "You don't shy away from wool stockings!"

"Ja, the stockings are good," Anton said and picked up the whittling.

"I could almost taste the *faari kaal*, the lamb and cabbage stew," Dagmar said. "We'd have had a lamb to slaughter had the *skraelings* left us alone."

"They killed the ewe, and the deer ate the cabbages," Anton laughed. "It was not in the coffee grounds for us to eat *faari kaal* this Jul!"

Serena smiled at the thought of coffee grounds predicting whether or not the ewe would live or if the deer would eat the cabbages. Surely Lutherans knew better than to put stock in superstitions, as Auntie Karen said.

"But we gathered a few hens and a suckling pig we'd been babying," Anton said and shaved a long spiral of wood from the handle of the spoon. "Kept them with us behind the fortifications."

"How many men did you have?" Gust propped his feet up on a piece of oak in front of the stove and held his hands toward the heat. Serena fetched Lena's blanket and wrapped it around his shoulders. He must still feel chilled.

"Only a handful," Anton said. "We expected the attack after the warning, were ready for them when they came."

Serena wished someone had warned them of the Indian raids. If only she could have had time to gather the *bunad* and the quilt. She and Lena could have hidden in the grove beyond the garden. She pulled her shawl closer around her shoulders and pulled the coffee pot to the side before it boiled over, using the corner of her shawl as a potholder.

"I can shoot," Dagmar said. "I wore Anton's hat, and they thought I was another man."

"She's as good as any man." Anton could not hide the pride in his voice. Serena refilled his coffee cup.

"But here we sit without cattle or horses and we've been here for eight years. Damn *skraelings* set us back," Dagmar said. "We're worse off than when we came."

Gust held out his cup for Serena to refill. He poured the scalding coffee onto his saucer, blew on it and slurped it down. "What brought you to Pomme de Terre?"

"My brother heard about the inn," Dagmar said and held out her cup. "We do a brisk business in summer, and our boys help us put in a few crops."

"The oxcarts come by right steady all spring and summer, bringing trade goods from the Red River settlements."

"You must have a big place," Serena said and returned the pot to the top of the stove. "To sleep a bunch of men."

"Ja," Dagmar said with a laugh cradling the warm cup with both hands. "We've slept as many as twenty if they sleep head to toe. They keep me busy at the cook stove."

"It's as drafty as an old barn when the wind blows from the west," Anton said.

"Which it does every damned day," Dagmar said.

"We get by, but we're not fancy. A visiting preacher complained that he couldn't find a shadow of meat at our inn," Anton said. "And he was right."

"We live on fish," Dagmar said. "It doesn't matter to us. We've never been able to afford much more."

They talked about the foods available for the taking if a person was willing to hunt for them: fish, geese, ducks, and muskrats.

"In the spring we collect goose and duck eggs along the river's edge," Anton said. "They're a real treat for the ox-carters."

"No ox-carters at all since the uprising." Dagmar wiped her eyes with the hem of her apron. "We're set back, and too old to start over."

"Now, Mother," Anton said. "We've got our health. Our boys will be home soon. We'll start over like we've always done."

"Why don't I read the damn coffee grounds and see if we'll get by or not," Dagmar said with a sly grin. "We'll find out our future."

Dagmar took Gust's empty cup and placed it upside down on his saucer. She twirled it around three times with her work-worn hands. Dagmar grasped the cup with callused fingers and turned it right side up.

"Hmmm." She examined the pattern of grounds. "It says that your heifer will birth a bull calf and bring you great fortune."

"I'd rather it was a heifer," Gust said with a snort. "That would bring better fortune."

"Read mine, you old troll," Anton said with a laugh.

"It says," Dagmar said. "That you will be the next president and put all this country's politics in order."

"I knew that already," Anton howled. "Tell me something I don't know."

Dagmar looked intently in the cup. "Look here," she pointed at a row of grounds clinging to the inside of the cup. "You'll hear news from far away."

"Good," Anton said. "We'll hear from our boys or maybe there'll be a letter from Norway. Now that's the kind of prediction I'd like to see come true."

"And you'll buy a nice ewe from the ox-carters when they start again," continued Dagmar with a twinkle. "For your wife."

"Wait a minute!" Anton said.

"I watched mine lie in the sun, bloating up and stinking," Dagmar said. "When it was over, I went out and sheared what I could from the carcass."

"She wouldn't let the Sioux rob her of her knitting," Anton said. "Women do the craziest things!"

"Women!" Dagmar snorted. "It's the men that cause all the trouble in the first place."

"Read mine," interrupted Serena. It had been a year and a half since Auntie Karen had read the coffee grounds for her. "What's my future?"

Dagmar studied the grounds for a long while and finally said, "There will be another baby—a girl to replace your loss." She pointed out the trail of grounds from the rim of the cup to the bottom.

An uncomfortable silence settled in, and Serena took a deep breath. No one, not even another daughter, could replace Lena.

"Serena says you received reparation money for your losses," Dagmar said, putting down the cup.

"Ja," Gust said. "Sounds like more money is coming next year."

"How come you didn't see that in my cup?" Anton poked Dagmar's shoulder with his forefinger.

"There's a piece in the paper about it," Gust said chewing on his toothpick and reaching for the small stack of newspapers on the shelf.

Serena looked up in surprise. Usually Gust boasted about his success with anyone who would listen. Maybe he felt guilty about lying to the government in order to get more money. That was unlike him also. She scrutinized his face, his sharp nose. There was something more—she just couldn't figure it out.

"What do you hear from your sons in the South?" Gust said.

Clearly he was changing the subject.

29

"Where Is Little Crow?"

St. Cloud Democrat, December 11, 1862

The blizzard howled out of the northwest for three days.

There was no question about it; the Estvolds would stay until it blew over. Dagmar and Serena shared the bed, and the men dragged in the horsehide blanket and slept on the cold floor, covered with their coats. Serena, worried about Gust's sore leg in the cold, would have gladly traded places with him on the floor, but it would have been improper for the female company to sleep on the floor.

The men kept the stove red hot around the clock. Together they strung a rope so they could feel their way to the barn. Anton told of a neighbor who died in a storm a few years back.

"They found him frozen in a snowdrift not thirty feet from the barn," said Anton in a grim voice. "Couldn't see the barn for the whiteness."

Serena wondered what kind of godforsaken place they had found, where a man couldn't see his own barn from thirty feet away. A shiver went through her, and she wished again for her mother. What would have happened to her if Gust had delayed another day, if the Estvolds hadn't noticed her fire out and come to check on her? How could she have managed in the storm?

The men struggled to melt enough snow to water the stock, haul hay into the barn, and keep ahead of the hungry stove. They toiled all day, never getting ahead of the chores.

And when they came in, they were hungry.

Dagmar and Serena cooked breakfasts of pancakes or Johnnycake, morning coffee with bread and molasses, dinner with great helpings of potatoes and parched corn, afternoon coffee with more bread and molasses, and soup suppers. Serena cooked liberally, not holding back their small supply of stores. If they ran out of food, they would eat fish like the folks at the fort. Or even muskrats. She had seen their houses along the riverbanks. She only wished she had enough eggs to make egg coffee.

"My mother always served company coffee made with eggs," Serena said as she and Dagmar washed the dinner dishes on the third day of the storm.

"Ja," Dagmar said. "As mine did."

"There's nothing like the smell of fresh egg coffee," Serena said. "I can smell it just thinking about it."

"It reminds me of home," Dagmar said. "The *rommegrot* suppers, the *lutefisk* and *lefse*."

"Don't talk about it!" Serena said. "You're making me homesick!"

"You have cream and flour," Dagmar said. "Let's make *rommegrot* and surprise the men."

"We could."

"Do you have a whisk?"

"Nei," Serena said. "Maybe Gust could whittle one for us this afternoon."

They carefully skimmed the cream off the top of the milk pail and placed it in a pan to settle again. Only the thickest cream would do. Gust was happy to whittle a whisk for the creation of such a delicacy, and they each took a turn rolling the whisk between their hands while the cream and flour slowly cooked on the stove.

"See how the butter comes around the edges," Anton said. "It's almost done."

"Just a little more," Dagmar said. "It's food fit for kings!"

They spread the *rommegrot* on plates and sprinkled the white, buttery pudding with sugar and a little nutmeg.

"Mor always used cinnamon on hers," Serena said with an apologetic tone. "But I'm out of cinnamon."

"We always used nutmeg," Dagmar said.

"Either way is delicious." Gust dug in with a spoon. He finished off his entire plate and looked for more.

"You can tell a boy's age by the amount of *rommegrot* he eats," Dagmar said. "First we gave him a saucer full, and then a small plate. When he can eat a full pie plate, he's a man."

"We miss our boys." Anton squeaked his spoon over his plate to get every drop of *rommegrot*. "It's been a year since they left, and the North is no closer to victory."

"We're out-generaled," Gust said. "The South has all the good ones, and we're stuck with the rest."

"Emil was at Shiloh," Dagmar said. "Bloody and wasteful of those young men."

"Ole?" Gust said.

"In Kentucky with the Second Minnesota Artillery," Anton said. "He fought at the Battle of Mill Spring last January under a man called Thomas. They had the Rebs cornered, backed up against the river with no place to go, and Thomas made the decision to wait until morning to attack." Anton paused and spit tobacco juice into the stove. It sounded a satisfying hiss. "The next morning the Rebs were gone. Not a trace. Seems they took a sternwheeler across the river and saved their whole army."

"What kind of incompetents are in charge?" Gust asked.

"The next day a general asked Thomas why he hadn't attacked when he had the chance." Anton pushed back on his log seat and crossed his long legs. "Do you want to know what he said?"

"Anton!" Dagmar slapped him across the back of his head in playful banter. "Don't tease us! Finish the story!"

"Thomas looked at the general with his innocent brown eyes and answered, 'I never thought of it!' And that's the God's truth. Ole heard the answer himself!"

"I'm glad those poor boys got away." Dagmar's face turned serious. "There's been too much killing."

"But it's better to get it over with," Gust said. "Shit or get off the pot, that's what my far always said."

"It's more dangerous farther south," Dagmar said. "I'm glad Ole is safe in Kentucky."

"When did you last hear from him?"

"Just last week," Anton said with a questioning look at Dagmar.

"I have the letter," Dagmar said. "Do you want me to read it?"

Dagmar took the letter out of her apron pocket. It had been folded and refolded so many times the paper was limp and pleated. She held the letter out at arm's length and cleared her throat.

October 6, 1862

Dear Mor and Far,

Things have been slow. We skirmished with a band of Southern raiders last week. They steal from the local farmers and grab anything they can get their hands on. We recovered three fine horses and a live hog. We returned the horses to a Shaker village where they had been stolen. The Shakers are a strange sect that does not believe in marriage or war. (Sigurd Swensrud, my friend here, says that it makes sense since many marriages lead to war. We had a good laugh over that one!) The men and women are separated and dedicate their lives to prayer and good works.

The place is overrun with war orphans. When we returned their horses, the Shakers invited us to have supper with them. Sigurd says they feed any person who comes to their door, slave or free, north or south.

We ate until almost sick. They served corn bread, fried okra, pickled pig's feet and too many vegetables to count. There was fresh buttermilk and apples from their orchard. Then they brought out three kinds of pie. It was the best meal I've had since home.

The best part was they sent the leftover pie with us and we still had the hog. Sigurd carried the hog across the front of his horse all the way back to our camp and we roasted it the next day. Good food two days in a row is something to remember. We live on army beans and hardtack. Sigurd made up a song about our poor rations that he sings to the tune of "Hard Times Come Again No More" only he changed it to "Hard Crackers Come Again No More."

Sigurd keeps us all laughing. He's from Sleepy Eye, but I'm trying to convince him to come and farm in Pomme de Terre. He would be a great neighbor. Says he won't consider it unless I can find him a wife. Keep your eyes open for one.

The papers say the Sioux Uprising is over. I heard the Rebs sent 300 prisoners home to fight the Indians and that Minnesota units were sent home as well. It may be truth or just another rumor. I can't help but feel that if I had listened to you, Far, and not joined up, I would have been there to help you out when you needed it. It's good news they're building a fort at Pomme de Terre. It brings great comfort to me so far away and worried. Please write when you can.

We are encamped at Perryville, Kentucky. I saw a darky working a cotton field today. Kentucky is a union state but allows slavery. Sigurd says there's not much profit for slaving in Kentucky since the fields are small.

Cotton is beautiful to see growing in the fields. Do you think it would grow in Pomme de Terre? How about tobacco? Every farmer here has a tobacco patch. You've never seen so much chewing and spitting as here in Kentucky.

Write soon. I think of home every day and wish I were there.

Your loving son,

Ole

Dagmar sniffed loudly and honked her nose on her apron hem. Tears pooled in her eyes, and Serena remembered how Gust detested women's tears. He said the sight weakened him, made him helpless. Serena noticed he quickly changed the subject.

"I read in the paper that both Abraham Lincoln and Jefferson Davis were born in Kentucky," Gust said.

They turned to discussing the war, the coincidences that result in greatness, the fears of the future. Their conversation lagged, and they sat digesting the delicious *rommegrot*, thinking of home and family while the winds howled around the little cabin on the hill.

"I brought something home," Gust said. "A surprise."

"Besides that nice bottle?" She'd make some willow tea as soon as the weather cleared and they could gather willow branches alongside the river.

"Cards." Gust pulled out a tattered deck from his pants pocket. "Do you folks play whist?"

"Indeed we do," Anton said. "We used to play with the boys in the evening after milking."

Serena did not know the game well, and her heart sank. Gust was a competitive partner, and in the past angered easily over her mistakes.

"How about the men against the women?" Dagmar said. "We'll skunk you, for sure!"

Dagmar's voice had a tinny quality to it, almost like a rain crow. Her boisterous laughter echoed in the dim cabin when the women scored and stilled to muttered curses when they lost a hand. Serena felt no intimidation from Dagmar, who blamed the men if they lost and bragged up

Serena's abilities when they won. They played late into the night, laughing and enjoying the rare treat of company, listening to the winds outside, snug and almost warm in the little cabin.

The next morning the winds were silent. Snow covered the west side of the cabin and proved to be good insulation. The Estvolds breakfasted and left immediately afterwards, bundled against the intense cold that settled in after the storm.

"We dare not risk another storm although your hospitality has been most enjoyable," Anton said. "We'd best be getting on home."

"The boys at the fort might worry about us," Dagmar said.

"*Mange takk.*" Serena hugged Dagmar's neck. "*Mange takk.*"

"Don't make me cry!" Dagmar wiped her eyes on her apron. "It was our pleasure. Remember, I'll be watching for your smoke every morning. If something goes wrong, don't start your fire."

"We'll come right by," Anton said. "The smoke will be our signal."

"And don't wait for an emergency," Dagmar said. "If you're losing your mind with loneliness, just signal, and we'll come over. This country is hell on women. I know that from experience." She tied her scarf tighter around her head and neck. "We'd come and get you, Serena. You could stay at the fort until spring."

Gust glowered at Dagmar. Serena watched the exchange and ignored the last sentence.

"Ja," Serena said. "I'll signal if I need you."

"*Mange takk.*" Gust grasped Anton's callused ham of a hand and shook it vigorously. "Many thanks."

Serena watched them walk briskly towards the river toward home. If only she could follow the map home to Burr Oak.

"Serena," Gust said. "Are you all right?"

"Ja." Serena wished the Estvolds hadn't left. While they were there she had almost forgotten her troubles.

30

"Lincoln Postpones Executions Until December 26."
St. Cloud Democrat, December 16, 1862

THE SHORTENED DAYS SETTLED INTO A DREARY ROUTINE.
They lived like moles in near darkness, the wick lamp needed for
even the simplest tasks. The cabin never warmed in spite of the
great heaps of dried wood consumed by the stove. Gust shoveled snow
twice a day, but the wind was quick to undo his work. The wind moaned
to them as it passed their little cabin on the hill, groaning and whining in
its misery. Serena identified with the wind song, feeling the need to express
her sadness but unable to find the words.

Serena layered her few clothes in an effort to keep warm, wrapping
herself in her woolen shawl and wearing a hat and mittens. The dirt floors
were always cold. She spread the horsehide blanket on the floor between the
table and bed but her feet still ached with cold. The buffalo robe kept them
warm at night but they couldn't stay in bed all of the time.

Gust taught Serena to play thirty-one and insisted they play every
night. And by the feeble glow of the lamp, Gust demanded Serena read out
loud while he whittled a spoon or carved a new axe handle. The lamp provided poor light and sometimes Serena's eyes ached with the strain but Gust
made her read until the letters blurred and tears burned in her eyes.

Their books were limited to the Norwegian Bible and an old almanac.
It was pure luxury to get the *St. Cloud Democrat.* The newspapers, after being
read too many times to count, were sent to the outhouse for their final duties.

Serena read the banner, "Speak unto the Children of Israel That They Go Forward. Exodus Chap XIV verse 16" on every edition. Gust said that she needn't read the banner every time she picked up a paper because he knew it by heart already. He said she could skip that line. But Serena loved the words from Exodus and always read them. Perhaps she was a child of Israel, too, and would one day hear God telling her to leave this place, to go forward.

The words soothed her somehow, and she often read them aloud when Gust was outside doing chores.

They read every word of the *St. Cloud Democrat*. She clipped articles to reread or tuck in with the next letter to her mother. She read the grim reports from the Battle of Antietam, the bloody day when more than 23,000 soldiers were killed or wounded. The numbers staggered her and made her cringe in disbelief. But when the casualty lists were printed, she could not deny the bitter reality.

At least the war was far away from Minnesota, terrible though it was.

News about the Sioux Uprising was closer to home. Although the articles horrified Serena, she sought them out and read them when Gust went to the barn for chores, every detail a slap in her face. She read about the Indian trials, read testimonies given by witnesses, each more horrible than the one before. Families hacked to pieces, babies nailed to doorframes, people beheaded, and women violated and stolen.

How people had suffered! Death and destruction as Auntie Karen had predicted in the coffee grounds so long ago. It was terrible, vicious, and Serena felt sadder with each report. Sadness upon sadness. It was like a blanket of grief covered Minnesota, a layer of mourning that wouldn't end.

She never thought life would be filled with such hopelessness, dark as the long nights of winter.

Serena stared out the window while she churned. There were no signs of Indians. They would wait for warmer weather. The Indians knew they were at their mercy, going nowhere, tied to the farm by cords stronger than chains.

Gust took care of the stock in the barn. Serena feared being alone in the house, though it was almost a relief to have him gone, the way he forced her to converse. God knew there was nothing to say.

A woman's testimony was reported in the newspaper. She had been baking bread when the savages burst into her house. They thrust her baby into the hot oven, forcing the hysterical mother to listen to the screams. Serena plunged the dasher faster at the thought of such barbarity. It could happen again, probably would happen. When the weather warmed, the Indians would come and kill once again. She knew it.

Even though Abraham Lincoln and General Pope said the uprising was over, Governor Ramsey refused to let Minnesota soldiers return to the war in the South. There must be a reason for his refusal when there was such a need for soldiers to fight the Confederates.

Gust planned for a great harvest, but Serena knew otherwise. He would go through all the work and expense of planting and tending the crops, but in the end, the Indians would destroy everything and kill them.

The raid in Hutchinson had been a divine warning, but Gust refused to listen. It was useless. They were doomed to failure. Auntie Karen had read the coffee grounds. The butter turned, and Serena strained off the buttermilk.

How she dreaded another game of thirty-one.

Outside the trees swayed as the incessant wind howled in from Dakota, searching for them in Minnesota. The wind was a wicked, living being sent by God to try them, to punish them for Gust's lies and her refusal to listen to her parents.

Never ending, it would not rest until they were dead.

31

*"The Aid of All Good Citizens Is Invoked to Maintain Law
and Constitutional Authority"*
St. Cloud Democrat, December 16, 1862

UST RUBBED HIS SORE LEG AND TOOK a swig of willow tea from
the aquavit bottle. Since learning about the remedy, he was seldom
without it. He made a point of never passing a stand of willows
without gathering bark. It was almost a miracle. Never before had any remedy dulled the pain. Bitter as gall, still it helped. Maybe the Indians were
good for something, after all.

The cold weather of Pomme de Terre caused great misery. Not that
he'd admit it to Serena. She needed all the encouragement he could muster
to help her stick it out. How could she despise the good black dirt of
Pomme de Terre? It was a gold mine waiting to be tapped by his plow.

Some days she acted like a lunatic, the way she stared out the window
and acted as if she didn't hear a word he said. She talked less and less. He
made her read and play cards just to force conversation. She had never been
this way in all the years he had known her. What she really needed was
another baby to take her mind off Lena's death, but she avoided their marriage bed, feigned sickness or fatigue.

He took another sip of the bitter tea. If Serena knew his leg was
worse, she might insist on going south to Missouri as they had discussed
so long ago. Missouri made the headlines with its border raiders and
marauders. It was no place to take a woman as beautiful as Serena. Besides,

every cent rightfully or wrongfully his was tied up in the farm at Pomme de Terre. They'd made their bed and now they must lie in it. He corked the bottle securely and put it in his shirt pocket.

His only hope of repaying his father lay in a good harvest. Captain McLarty could talk all day, but he wasn't budging an inch. Anton Estvold could call him a damn fool, but it wouldn't dissuade him. He would farm this land if it killed him. To hell with the neighbors.

On December 21, a soldier on horseback rode up to their barn. He wore a knitted scarf around his neck and face and old socks pulled over his hands. One sock was holey and a hairy knuckle showed through. Frosted eyebrows framed his fiery red face and ears.

"Good morning, sir," he said when Gust came to the barn door. "Private Thomas Harris, Fort Pomme de Terre."

"Is there trouble?" Gust opened the barn door and gestured him inside. A bitter cold rushed in the open door and caused an ache in his leg that brought tears to his eyes. "Come in out of the cold."

The horse stomped and snorted as the soldier guided him inside and barred the door against the wind.

"It's freezing." The soldier grimaced. "Any chilblains on my ears?"

"None that I can see." Gust carefully examined his face and ears. "But you took a chance coming in such weather. There must be trouble."

"Another murder by Fort Abercrombie." The soldier was about the same age as Gust, although taller. He walked with the confidence of a man who had never known the pain of a crippled leg. "Someone killed as he chopped wood by the river, a man who served with me at Ripley last summer."

Gust shivered, picked up a pail on the floor and poured water into the trough for the soldier's horse. A hot pain shot through his leg, and he swore under his breath. What if the Indians crept up on him while he fetched water? Private Harris' horse buried his nuzzle into the icy liquid, snorting and stomping his feet.

"Captain McLarty orders you to move to the fort for the rest of the winter," Private Harris said and pulled the saddle off his mount. "You'll be safer."

"Thank you for your concern." Gust forked hay for the horse. "You can tell the captain that we have too much work to do to leave the farm."

"Dagmar Estvold sends word you can stay with them."

"Many thanks, but we cannot." Gust put the pail by the door where it would be handy for the next trip to the river. He would not care to winter with people who thought him a damn fool, called him one to his face.

"I have orders to bring you in." Private Harris held the reins in his hands, twisting the straps back and forth.

"It's none of your concern," Gust said in an even tone. "I'm free, white, and twenty-one. I can do what I want."

"There's a shooting war going on in the South." Private Harris shook the saddle blanket and wiped down his horse's back with a handful of clean straw. Cold weather took its toll on animals, Gust thought. It was wise to remove sweat that might freeze and chill the horse. It was easy to see the soldier was competent with his animal, Gust admitted to himself grudgingly. "The army has jurisdiction in war."

"It's no concern to me. We're minding our own business."

"The savages are sneaky. No telling when one of them might decide to come out here and murder you while you sleep. Do you have children?"

"Nei." Gust thought of Lena's little hands. "We have no children. Just me and the missus." He picked up the wooden fork and pitched the steaming horse apples into the manure pile in the corner. "We'll be fine."

"You don't understand. The captain *orders* you to come in. You don't have a choice."

"This is America." Gust squared his shoulders and set his jaw. "A man can live wherever he wants."

"You are in the jurisdiction of the fort, and we are at war both with the Sioux and the Rebs." Private Harris fumbled with the reins in his hand but his voice was firm. "The captain orders you to the fort, and it is my duty to take you there."

"What will happen if I don't come?"

"I'll be in trouble with the captain. And he'll send someone else out here to do the job, even if it means dragging you in, in irons." He looked at Gust with pleading eyes. "It'd be a lot simpler if you'd just come to the fort."

Gust felt that smothery feeling closing in. He hated being backed in a corner, being told what to do by someone else. "Sounds like I have no choice." Gust's words were like ice. "But I won't come in until I'm finished husking the corn. I'd lose it all to rodents if left in the cabin."

"How long will it take you?" Private Harris shifted his weight from one foot to another. Gust enjoyed his discomfort. They could make him come into the fort, but by God, he'd come when he was ready and not a day before.

"Another few days." Gust mentally calculated the work left to do and the days on the calendar. Serena might perk up if they were there in time for Christmas. "Tell your captain we'll be there on December 24th."

"There's going to be a dance at the fort on Christmas Day." Private Harris' face relaxed. "Everyone in the valley will be there."

"That's what I'll tell my missus," Gust said. "I don't want her worried about Abercrombie killings or captain's orders. I'll just tell her we're going to the fort for Christmas."

At least he would save face. By God, they treated him like a two-year-old. Gust felt there had to be more to it. Captain McLarty wouldn't be thinking about them at all unless Anton reported him for leaving Serena alone. Damn him! Sure Anton shook his hand when he left and laughed over cards, but then he went and tattled to the captain.

"Will you have coffee before you leave?" Gust's said over his anger.

"Yes, coffee'd hit the spot," Private Harris said. "And I brought mail."

"Don't mention the killing to the missus." Gust rubbed his bad leg and buttoned his coat. "You know how it is."

The men stomped snow off their boots before they entered the little cabin. Wash hung on a line stretched across the room and a damp soapy smell mixed with the fragrance of freshly ground coffee.

Private Harris handed a small stack of *St. Cloud Democrats* to Gust.

"Is there anything from Iowa?" asked Serena in a small voice.

"Nothing this time." Gust saw her face crumple. It was his fault she received no word from her parents. But what was a man to do? For God's sake, it was their future at stake.

The closed-in feeling threatened him with the thought of being forted up. Gust forced himself to think about Serena, how she needed company. He could protect her from the Red Indians, but he couldn't be a female companion to her. He couldn't be her mother.

The men pulled chairs up to the table and talked weather and politics. Gradually Gust warmed to the soldier and felt his anger draining away. Serena poured the steaming brew and treated them to fresh biscuits still warm from the oven. Private Harris' smile lightened the room.

"Thank you, ma'am," he said. "I haven't had hot biscuits since leaving home last summer."

"And where's your home, Mister Harris?" Serena pressed the plate of biscuits toward the soldier again.

"Preston, Minnesota." Private Harris slathered butter on the biscuit. "It's near Winona."

"I've heard of Preston," Gust said. "We're from Burr Oak, Iowa, farmed for a short time in Hutchinson." He took another sip of his coffee. "Till the Indians burned us out."

"I'm sorry to hear it." Private Harris's eyes showed concern, and Gust decided he was a good man after all, forced to do things against his will.

"Ja," Gust reached for the loaf sugar and popped a sweet cube into his mouth. "But we made it."

"I thank the Good Lord I'm here in Minnesota rather than bleeding and dying in the South," Private Harris said. "I'd rather fight Indians and freeze to death than fight Rebs. 'Tis gory news from Antietam."

"Ja," Gust said. "The Union won't have any men left if this keeps on."

"That's why I'm glad to be in Minnesota. Even if we survive on fish! I've had enough fish to last me the rest of my life."

"Any other news from the war?" Gust said and sipped his coffee.

"Another stalemate from what I've heard." Private Harris poured a sip of coffee onto his saucer, twirling it to cool before drinking it down with a loud slurp. "The Union can't seem to outsmart the Reb generals."

"Where are they fighting now?" Gust wondered if his brothers were at Antietam, if they were even alive.

"Still around Washington," Private Harris said. "Captain McLarty got word there was a big battle in Kentucky."

"Where in Kentucky?" Gust thought of the Estvold boy.

"Perryville," Private Harris said. "I haven't heard much except the Union fought back a Reb invasion at Perryville."

"I'll have to read the papers and catch up." Gust had a sick feeling knowing Ole Estvold fought at Perryville. "A man starts to feel cut off when he's snowbound out in this wilderness."

Private Harris set his empty cup on the table, and Serena hurried to refill it. "Do you like to dance, Mrs. Gustafson?"

The men waited for Serena to answer, but she went about her business as if she hadn't heard a word.

"Serena?" Gust said.

"Excuse me," Serena said, and Gust watched a deep flush rise over her cheeks, "I was off wool gathering." She laughed nervously. It ended too loud.

"I asked if you like dancing," Private Harris said.

"Why?"

"The fort's having a Christmas Ball. You and your man are invited."

"A ball?" she stammered. "When?"

"On December 25th. Come early and stay as long as you want. Mrs. Estvold sends word you can take the night with them."

"But our stock," Serena said.

"We'll take them with us." Gust's words were slow and deliberate. He weighed every detail in his mind before speaking. "We'll crate the chickens and tie the cows behind the wagon. We'll make it fine if the weather holds."

"Good," Private Harris said.

"A visit to the fort over Jul would be just the thing," Gust said. "Maybe we can forget about the Sioux and the war and have a good time."

"And with the Sioux still unsettled," said Private Harris. "It might be best to err on the side of caution and stay at Pomme de Terre for the winter."

"No need to worry about that until the time comes," Gust said. He felt his ears warm again. He got up and threw another log in the stove. A sudden downdraft blew a cloud of pungent smoke into the cabin. "But we'll come on Christmas."

"I could help you get there if you'd go today," Private Harris said. "That's why I'm here."

"I said we'll come on Christmas," Gust said with an edge to his voice. "Tell that to your captain."

32

"Fort Ridgely Relieved—Indians Gone Towards Red Wood."
St. Cloud Democrat, September 4, 1862

RED IRON'S VILLAGE SWARMED LIKE THE BEE TRIBE with barking dogs, playful children, *uncheedahs* stirring pots over the fires, and small clusters of *washechu* and mixed-blood captives digging trenches around the edge of the village. It seemed there were a hundred teepees, maybe more. And people moving in, setting up camp.

"Ho!" Red Iron said when they finally found the chief. "There is food."

Red Iron ignored the girl-children and women as was mannerly. A short warrior with sturdy wide shoulders, Red Iron pulled back his gray hair with a leather thong. Eagle feathers were his only adornment. He stank of bear grease smeared over his skin to protect against mosquitoes, and when he opened his mouth, Drumbeater saw that his front teeth were broken and stained.

While the men settled around Red Iron's fire and smoked *kinnikinick* with the chief and another elder, the women drifted towards the edge of the village to pitch their tents. Drumbeater cast an anxious glance after them, watching Otter's cradleboard bounce on the travois as the dog pulled it over rough ground. Many Beavers brandished a stick of firewood towards the village dogs, and crowds of children following after them. The children reached out to touch the hair of Little Bird and when Many Beavers chased them away, some threw stones in their direction.

Drumbeater felt even more anxious at Red Iron's village. He feared he'd followed the wrong path, like a drowning man in strong current. He focused on the *kinnikinick*, listened to the words between Standing Tall and Red Iron about the battles won and lost, the dangers of the Long Knives's treachery. He felt clumsy, like a young heron learning to fly, and kept silent in the presence of the chiefs.

"We sent runners to Sibley," Red Iron said at last. "About trading captives for peace." He pulled in a long draft of *kinnikinick* and held it for a long moment before exhaling slowly through his nose. "It's our only hope."

"Little Crow is foolish."

"Maybe, maybe not." Red Iron passed the pipe to Standing Tall. "His braves take many scalps and have pushed out the White Eyes from the settlements to the south and west."

Standing Tall lifted the pipe to the four winds and placed it to his lips. The smell of burning *kinnikinick* filled Drumbeater's nostrils.

"Perhaps the Long Knives will learn to keep the words of the treaties."

"If Little Crow kills every White Eye in the land of sky-blue waters, it will not stop the fat-eaters." Standing Tall said. "They will only come thicker next season, like the grasshoppers on the prairies."

"Like snowflakes in a blizzard," Drumbeater said. Falling Mountain's dream clung to his mind like the blood-sucking *capanka* buzzing around them.

Drumbeater wanted only to find the life-and-death friend and return to rice camp. If only Crooked Lightning had kept the girl-children and returned them himself. He mouthed again the strange name, Evan Jacobson, warrior from the tribe across the great water, driver-of-the-wooden-wheels. What would he do if he forgot his name?

As a small boy, Drumbeater beat rhythms on a hollow log using dried sticks, imitating whatever *hoyiapi* used by the warriors. Crooked Lightning had said that a great name was needed for a future drummer of the sacred *cancega*.

But a name meant nothing to uncivilized people.

A Mdewakanton warrior raised a loud war whoop and brandished a lance with five *wikipoha*, some from children. He trotted up to the fire on a pony painted yellow like his face. A swarm of village boys followed him, elbowing to get closer, reaching out dirty hands to touch the silken locks on his lance. A pack of village dogs yipped and snarled at his heels, almost drowning out the warrior's words. "Fight the enemy!"

Red Iron scowled but said nothing, it beneath his dignity to argue, and tossed the corner of his red blanket across his shoulder. He wore no paint and did not invite the brave to smoke at his fire. Drumbeater thought the warrior too bloodthirsty to notice this insult, enough for him to receive the praise of small boys.

Many Beavers pushed in front of the warrior's horse and stood beside Drumbeater, her fingers folding and unfolding her fringed garment, her lips pursed into a small circle. She would not speak in the presence of the chiefs, but Drumbeater sensed great urgency.

"What's wrong?" Drumbeater's ears heard the sound of horses' hooves and turned to see a band of warriors riding triumphantly towards the village, returned from battle with scalps and tales of counting coup. The small boys scrambled in their direction.

"Blue Bottle."

"Where?" His dry throat almost stopped his voice.

She pointed her chin towards the place where Willow Song had set up the teepee. He couldn't bring the *washechu* girls this far to have them fall into the hands of Blue Bottle. They were his responsibility. He shouldn't have let them out of his sight.

By the time Drumbeater reached the teepee, he saw Blue Bottle clutching Little Bird by her hair and dragging her towards Star Fist and their tethered ponies. Badger fought against him, pounding his legs and screaming. Her war cries blended with the turmoil of the village, hardly noticeable in the confusion of the camp, triumphant songs being sung by the villagers, and death songs sounding for the ones lost in battle.

Badger hung onto Blue Bottle's leg until he kicked her away, sprawled face down on the grass.

"We came back." Blue Bottle's face dripped fresh yellow paint. "For scalps."

Drumbeater watched in horror as Blue Bottle drew a knife from his waist and held it against the white throat of Little Bird. She stared mutely at Drumbeater as if pleading for help, stretching a white hand towards him.

Many Beavers walked firmly towards Blue Bottle and knelt down beside Little Bird, reaching for her. "Old woman!" Blue Bottle drew back his foot and kicked Many Beavers with a vicious blow to her head.

What could he do? Many Beavers, an *uncheedah*, deserved respect but instead lay unmoving on the ground, perhaps dead. He must fight Blue Bottle to avenge her death, to protect the *washechu*. It was his duty.

Willow Song would survive if he were killed, but life would be difficult for her. He pushed down the sorrow welling up in his heart, sorrow for himself, his wife, and the life his son must endure without a father. For a fleeting moment he thought of the sacred drum.

Drumbeater stepped forward with knife held in his outstretched hand, his death song on his lips. He could not win against the strength of Blue Bottle.

Blue Bottle's eyes glinted for blood. "It is right you sing your death song, Drumbeater, coward among the People." He pushed Little Bird to the side and stepped closer to Drumbeater. "First I kill you, and then I take the scalps of the girl-children. Maybe I'll scalp you, as well. And your woman."

"Enough!" Red Iron's voice cracked sharp as the ice during the Moon of Great Difficulty. Blue Bottle snarled, never taking his eyes off Drumbeater.

"The captives will be returned to their people." Red Iron's blanket draped his shoulder in a graceful red swirl. "Blue Bottle, you will leave this place."

Blue Bottle looked at Red Iron as if seeing him for the first time, disbelief showing across his painted face. He looked at Standing Tall who stood with drawn bow aimed at his chest.

"Fools!" Blue Bottle pushed his knife into his loincloth and leapt unto his pony. The pony reared back in surprise, and Drumbeater thought for a moment that Blue Bottle might kill it. Instead he cruelly kicked its flank, beat over its head with his forearm and jerked its mouth thong. "The Long Knives will never trade the captives for peace. You are being deceived. You'll see, but only after it is too late."

Many Beavers sat up and shook her head as Blue Bottle and Star Fist rode out of the camp. Blood dripped from a cut on her forehead.

"Are you all right?" Willow Song stooped beside her, pressing dried grass against Many Beavers's wound, casting anxious glances towards the weeping girl-children.

"Hide them in the teepee." Many Beavers mouthed the words, her voice barely audible in its weakness. "They must remain out of sight."

Drumbeater saw the wisdom of her words. With shaking hands he gathered Little Bird and Badger. He forgot to be afraid of Little Bird's *wakon*, instead comforted her as he would have comforted Otter.

Willow Song's face showed white as the snows of winter. "Blue Bottle threatened Otter," she said. "Said that if I didn't give him the girl-children, he would kill our son." She placed a hand on his arm. "I thought Little Bird's medicine would protect her." Willow Song's shoulders sagged. "I thought her strong medicine would be enough."

A slow anger burned deep in Drumbeater's gut. No man threatened his son and lived. He would find Blue Bottle and kill him. But first, he must return the girl-children to their people.

Wakantanka kept the *washechu* girl-children alive for a reason. Drumbeater hoped the reason was to keep the People in Leaf Country. It was a good omen. They could be traded for peace.

"I told Little Crow to make his own camp," Red Iron said. "We'll keep the captives and mixed-bloods with us, protect them from his men. We don't want the Long Knives to think we took part in the raids."

"Hiya." Standing Tall replaced the arrow in his quiver and hung his bow over his shoulder. "We cannot keep the captives safe from those with blood in their eyes."

"Little Crow wouldn't dare attack us," Red Iron said. "The captives will be safe until the Long Knives come."

"Maybe not," Standing Tall said. "Little Crow knows they cannot win." His voice had the balanced tone of reason. "And wants to kill as many as possible before it's over."

"See what comes from the Rice Creek band?" Red Iron said. "Now we fight each other instead of our enemies."

Drumbeater kept a wary eye towards their teepee where Willow Song took the *washechu* girl-children. He hoped they were not injured. To kick such a small child was bad medicine. Blue Bottle might come back.

"Captives have dug pits around camp," Red Iron said. "For protection."

"To scar the soil like the *washechu*," Standing Tall said, "is bad medicine."

"Afterwards we will return the land to its balance."

Drumbeater's heart pounded in his ears. Perhaps there would be no afterwards. Little Crow might take the captives in spite of their best efforts. Perhaps the Long Knives would not believe they helped the captives, might accuse them of the raids. Who would tell the truth about what they had done to save their lives?

"If Crooked Lightning were here," Drumbeater said, "He could make the tracks of the White Eyes telling the truth of our actions."

"Maybe one of the mixed-bloods knows the tracks," Standing Tall said. "Or a captive."

"Do *washechu* women know the tracks?" It was a strange thought, that a white woman might carry the strong medicine, that a woman would have stronger medicine than a warrior of the People.

"Even small children, sometimes." Standing Tall said.

He wondered if Badger and Little Bird knew the tracks of the *washechu*. Their medicine was strong.

In the end, it was Many Beavers who found a distant relative who knew enough of the *washechu* tongue to inquire among the captives.

"We found a woman who makes the tracks," Many Beavers said. "The one with her head wrapped in cloth."

"We must find birch," Red Iron said. "It is on the paper birch they make the tracks."

The tracks strong enough to divide the earth.

Perhaps they were also strong enough to bring peace, to allow Drumbeater and his people to stay in Leaf Country. Perhaps he asked too much— like a coyote begging for food without hunting, like a beaver expecting warmth without building his den. But he didn't know what else to do.

Red Iron placed warriors in the trenches around the camp armed with bows, arrows and the few rifles among them. Drumbeater returned to the teepee, hungrier for his family than for food.

"They're making medicine tonight," Many Beavers said. The cut on her head no longer bled but she carried a bruise around her eye. "I heard the talk."

"Will you play your drum?" Willow Song's eyes searched his face.

He knew her well enough to see that she longed for him to stay in the teepee with her. But of all times, they needed direction from Wakantanka.

"He will go," Many Beavers said proudly. "And he will beat the drum."

Badger and Little Bird seemed unhurt from their ordeal with Blue Bottle. Their giggles and laughter filled the teepee with the normal sounds of life as they played with Otter on a pile of skins, covering their faces and peeking out to surprise him.

"See how they love Otter?" Willow Song said. "If we cannot find the man-with-the-wooden-wheels, we should adopt these girl-children and raise them as our own."

It would be good to have their strong medicine. How proud they would be as their parents at the Feast of the Virgins.

"Perhaps," Drumbeater said. "If I cannot find the life-and-death friend."

"I know this man," Many Beavers said. "He learned the tracks of the *washechu* from the Black Coat along with Crooked Lightning."

"What does he look like?"

"Red," giggled Many Beavers politely holding an open palm before her lips. "Hairy face like the fox tribe." She stroked her chin. "He cannot make the talk of the *washechu* but speaks the words of a strange tongue from across the great water."

Many Beavers took the drum from the pack and placed it respectfully in Drumbeater's arms. "Make medicine."

He looked at Willow Song a long moment. How quickly he might lose her. A stray bullet, a sudden attack, an unexpected sickness or accident. The dread lingered in his mind like the smell of the striped *manka*. He prayed a wordless prayer to the Great Mystery, asking that the *wakon* of the girl-children would be strong enough to protect Willow Song from the curse of the *indiyomdasin*.

33

*"The Indian and the Slaveholder Have Been the
Aristocrats of American Society."*
St. Cloud Democrat, December 18, 1862

DECEMBER 24, 1862, DAWNED CLEAR and cold with a blaze of sundogs standing guard on either side of the sun. A good omen, Gust
thought, but frigid weather.

"We shouldn't chance it." Serena peered out a scrape in the frosted
window. "What if a storm blows up while we're on the trail?"

"Pack up the coffee and flour sack." Gust emptied containers of
shelled corn into a single sack. "And any other food store."

"But why?" Serena said. "We'll only be gone a day or two."

"I won't let the rats eat our profits." Gust twisted a piece of twine around
the mouth of the grain sack. "They'll take anything left unattended."

Gust cast an anxious glance towards Serena. Maybe they would be
better off at the fort for the winter months. Nei, he had no choice in the
matter. It was come to the fort or be dragged there in irons.

It was Christmas—and although he wouldn't admit it, Gust looked
forward to the company of others. Back home his mother would have
baked and cleaned for a week. He wondered if she still cooked the *lutefisk*
and meatballs when there were no sons to enjoy them. He hoped she was
well, that his brothers lived. For a minute he dared hope the old man had
died but then worried for his mother.

He wished he could consult with his mother—it was harder on a
woman to lose a child than a man. He would ask her what he could do to

help Serena through this black place in her life. His thoughts often went to Lena, and he was certain Serena thought of her, too. But they didn't speak of her. He didn't know if that was good or bad. His mother would know. If only he could write and ask.

But he didn't voice this thought to Serena. It would only raise more questions about the absence of letters from home.

Iᴛ ᴡᴀs ᴀ ʜᴀʟᴛɪɴɢ, ᴊᴇʀᴋɪɴɢ ᴛʀɪᴘ. Buddy and Bets broke through the crusted snow with each step. Chickens cackled in the crate wrapped in the horsehide blanket. Dolly and Rosebud, tied to the back of the wagon, bellowed as their bags rubbed against icy drifts.

Gust's leg ached so badly from the cold that he felt short-tempered. It was a mistake to make such a trip in the dead of winter and pure craziness to risk livestock for a Christmas supper, orders or no orders. The cows lowed piti-fully. What if they lost their hens or the cow's milk supply? His father would have words to say about taking such a risk with a cow about to freshen.

The fort was a scraggly affair. Rough timbers dug into the ground surrounded a few buildings, including Anton and Dagmar Estvold's inn. Three soldiers chopping wood outside the fortifications laid down their axes and waved. "Merry Christmas," they called as Gust and Serena plod-ded through the open gate where Private Harris, standing guard at the gate, greeted them by name with a quick look of relief.

"It's not much of a fort," Serena said mildly. Gust interpreted this as criticism.

"It'll do just fine." He had taken the risk for her, after all, and she seemed unappreciative. Gust rubbed his aching leg and bit his lips to cut off the words he knew he'd regret later. "Did you bring the willow tea?"

Serena reached inside her shawl, pulled out the corked bottle and handed it to Gust. He sipped the bitter drink, slightly warm from Serena's body.

"*God Jul!*" Anton Estvold hurried to the wagon. "Come in and warm yourselves."

Gust dredged up his grudge toward Anton and rolled it over in his mind. By God, it was Christmas after all. Peace on earth and good will to men.

"*God Jul!*" Gust said.

Anton shooed Serena into the cabin and guided the team to the barn. Captain McLarty met them at the barn door. "I'm glad to see you made it." McLarty's face was stern, and Gust chafed at his tone that reminded him of his father, disapproving even though speaking approving words.

"It's foolishness to risk animals in such weather." Gust reined in the hurrying oxen, slowing their entrance to the warmth of the barn to prevent collisions with pens or stock. "Gee Buddy. Whoa Bets."

"The weather was fine in November when I first told you to come in."

Captain McLarty dodged the heavy hoofs, and Gust couldn't help but smile. He'd like to drive the oxen right over the pissant captain.

"But at least you're here now," Captain McLarty said when they were inside the barn and the doors closed against the wind. "I won't be responsible for people so foolish as to stay in harm's way."

Gust squared his shoulders. "Who said we were your responsibility?" The words tasted acrid in his mouth and he felt his face turning red. "This is America. A man can live wherever he wants."

"Gust," Anton said, coming into the barn just then. He stepped between the two men. "Your ox's leg is bleeding. He must have slipped on the ice or rubbed up against a stone."

Gust turned to look at Buddy's hind leg. Captain McLarty hesitated a moment and stalked out of the barn toward Private Harris standing guard at the gate.

"Private," he yelled loud enough for the men to hear him in the barn. "I expect a salute when I pass by!"

34

"38 to Hang, Lincoln Pardons 39th.
Largest Mass Execution in U.S. History"
St. Cloud Democrat, December 23, 1862

I**T DIDN'T SEEM LIKE** C**HRISTMAS.** Serena stumbled towards the inn with feet frozen into leaden stumps.

Christmas was supposed to be the happiest time of the year with cares laid down for the celebration. The church service, singing "I Am So Glad Each Christmas Eve" and eating *fattigmand* and *lefse.* It started with Little Jul on December 23rd when they decorated the tree and put up the wreaths, then December 24th with the gifts and *lutefisk.* It continued throughout the twelve days of Christmas with traditional foods, family visits, and celebrating. Serena could imagine the taste of pickled herring on her tongue. She clutched her bundle closer to her chest.

But what was it without family? Last Christmas they had letters from home as they huddled around the fire and dreamed of their coming child. Lena would have been six months old now, old enough to see the lighted candles on the tree and coo along with the singing. Serena's milk dropped at the thought of Lena, causing an unexpected heaviness in her breasts.

Serena shook her head back to reality. It was hard to keep her mind focused on the present.

Dagmar welcomed her at the door with a warm embrace. She smelled of frying fish and strong soap.

"Come in, Come in! You must be frozen!"

168

Dagmar's laughter rang out, the tone of her voice unlike any other person Serena had known, almost musical but slightly off pitch.

"*God Jul*, Dagmar!"

"*God Jul* to you." Dagmar guided her nearer the cook stove to warm up.

"*Mange takk* for the kind invitation," Serena forced herself to be polite.

The heat of the room made Serena's nose run. She reached within her pocket for a clean handkerchief but found only a rag left over from wiping dishes that morning. She used it to stem the flow from her nose, blowing as politely as possible while looking around the inn.

It was a single large room with a loft for sleeping. A real glass window on the south wall let in the scant sunshine, making it appear cheery and warm. Shelves lined one corner of the kitchen, and lovely china teacups and a matching teapot proudly graced the top shelf. The cook stove glowed red, and Serena watched a mouse scamper behind the stove and climb into the kitchen wood stacked along the wall.

"You and Gust will sleep in the loft." Dagmar paused to wipe her eyes on the hem of her apron. "Thank God you made it. It's too lonely to eat Christmas dinner alone, thinking about my boys so far away in that damn war."

Dagmar's cursing always startled Serena but even greater was her realization that she had not once considered Dagmar's loneliness or suffering. Of course she would be lonely with her sons off to war. It put Serena's problems into a different light.

"With all that's happened this year, it seems wrong to celebrate." Dagmar's voice dropped and her lips quivered. "We haven't heard a thing from Ole since the Battle of Perryville. We don't know if he's alive or dead."

"No mail?"

Dagmar shook her head. "Maybe if the weather holds."

"You know what they say," Serena said. What could be wrong with her parents that they hadn't written? She suppressed the urge to look out Dagmar's window. "No news is good news."

"It's not knowing that's hard." Dagmar sniffed. "The paper says eight thousand men were killed and wounded." She turned her face and wiped tears with her apron. "Damn war! Eight thousand men! Can you believe it?"

Serena's belly roiled at the thought of eight thousand women grieving for their sons as Dagmar did, as she grieved Lena's death. She forced herself to speak, although her voice trembled and her head began to whirl. "Today we shall be family for each other, my friend. You can be my mor and we will be your children."

"*Takk skal du ha!* Thank you very much!" Dagmar reached over and kissed Serena's cheeks, holding her tightly against her bosom for a long moment. "You've cheered me already!"

When Dagmar pulled the coffee pot onto the stove, Serena reached into her bag and pulled out a bowl of eggs, each one carefully wrapped in old newspaper. "I almost forgot. I brought eggs. And butter. And there's cream in the cow if poor Dolly has any to give after such a journey."

"*Tussen takk!*" Dagmar said. "We will feast indeed!"

The men joined them for a meal of fried fish and *lefse* still warm from the griddle. They talked about news from the capitol and the never-ending war in the South. As always, the talk turned to the Indian trials, stories of the survivors.

"There was a family near Alexandria Woods wiped out," Dagmar said. "Friends of Evan Jacobson, the stagecoach driver. All murdered except two little girls who were missing, perhaps taken captive."

"How old were they?" Serena felt the color rise in her cheeks. Whenever the talk went to the uprising, she felt mesmerized by the details, like a cat watching a mouse.

"Just little girls," Dagmar said, "maybe five or six years old. Last we heard Evan was still looking for them."

"How terrible for the mother!" Serena laughed a shrill laugh that carried a note of hysteria.

"The parents are dead, Serena." Gust reached for another slice of *lefse*. "We met Mr. Jacobson east of Hutchinson after the raids."

"Their mother must be worried sick," Serena said as if Gust had never spoken.

"The parents were killed," Anton said, now staring at Serena.

Serena picked up a piece of *lefse*, carefully buttered it and sprinkled a few precious grains of sugar across it, folding it into neat triangles and eating it slowly. She looked toward the window. "Mothers shouldn't be separated from their daughters."

Everyone grew silent.

"Maybe you should rest, Serena," Dagmar said. "Take an afternoon nap."

"Ja, I'm tired." Serena said slowly in a voice louder than polite company demanded. "I think I'll go upstairs and lie down."

She got up from the table and climbed into the loft without another word. She carefully removed her shoes, crept into bed and pulled a coverlet over herself. She heard muffled voices from below and stuffed her fist into her mouth to silence the sobs that suddenly overwhelmed her.

Minnesota was a terrible place.

SERENA AWAKENED IN LATE AFTERNOON to the delicious smell of frying meat. The men still worked in the barn, and Dagmar stood at the cook stove as Serena climbed down from the loft.

"We butchered our pig for Christmas." Dagmar wiped sweat off her face with her big apron. "We've reason to celebrate. We made it through the uprising with our lives. There's much to be thankful for."

"I haven't had fresh pork since we were married," Serena said. "I always enjoyed the butchering. My sisters and I would blow up the pig's bladder and use it for a ball."

"You can help me."

They fried mountains of pork chops and layered them in a huge crock. They rendered the lard until it melted into a pungent liquid and poured it over each layer of chops, sealing them from the air as it hardened back to solid fat. They continued this process until all the pork chops were cooked and the crock almost full. The men lugged the heavy crock to the coldest corner farthest away from the stove. The air was heavy with the smell of rendering.

"Pork!" Anton set the pig's head on the table." We'll feast on something other than fish, by God!"

"My mouth waters for the taste of headcheese," Gust said.

"You'll taste it sooner if you help with the scraping," Dagmar said and slapped him across the arm. "You scrape, and I'll do the rest."

Gust and Anton took sharp knives and cut the skin away from the head, scraping away all gristle and hair, carefully cutting out the teeth, eyes and snout. Then they rinsed the head in a bucket of clean water and boiled it in Dagmar's largest pot with bay leaf for flavor.

"*Mange takk*," Dagmar said. "Many hands make the work light."

The pot boiled until the meat fell from the bones. Serena and Dagmar gathered the meat scraps and pressed it into pans with the proper amount of seasoning. It set into congealed loaves of headcheese, ready for slicing.

"I heard from an oxcarter about scrapple," Dagmar said. "It's a Pennsylvania Dutch recipe using the broth from the boiled head mixed with cornmeal."

"We have cornmeal," Serena said.

Damgar salted the remaining broth and added cornmeal until it was too thick to stir. She patted it into her last loaf pan. "Now we slice and fry it."

The work agreed with Serena. By the time the lard was rendered, she felt more like her old self. In truth, it was almost like being home in Burr Oak, helping Mor with the rendering, talking and laughing while they worked.

Serena looked at Gust with new appreciation when the men returned from the barn. He was a good man to bring them to the fort for Christmas. Gust was always good to her. How could she have doubted him?

After the supper of brown crackling gravy served over mounds of mashed potatoes, fresh roasted pork and all the coffee they could drink, they settled down to a game of whist. The cards were still unturned when there was a knock on the door.

Olaus Reierson stood red faced and windblown like an ancient Viking just back from sea.

"*God Jul!*" he roared and shook hands all around with his massive hands, cold from his journey. When he got to Dagmar he gave her a bear hug and twirled her around the room. "*God Jul*, Missus!"

"Olaus!" Anton said. "I can't believe my eyes. *Welkommen!*"

"I was glad to be here last summer when the devils were on the warpath, but I'm even happier to be here today when they aren't."

"And we need to find you some supper." Dagmar went to the stove in a flurry of activity, slightly out of breath from being twirled around the room like a sack of potatoes. "You must be famished."

"More for company than for food—although it smells like my mor's kitchen," Olaus said. "I have enough aquavit for everyone to have a drop as well." He pulled the bottle from his inner pocket and set it on the table with a flourish. "After all, it's Jul!"

Gust insisted that Serena take a small drink of the liquid fire. "It's Christmas, Serena. It will do you good."

"*Skaal!*" they toasted when she lifted the cup with shaking hands and swallowed a few drops. She coughed and sputtered as everyone laughed.

"More! A few drops more!" Gust said with a look in his eyes that made Serena turn away. They were in public, after all, and even if they were married, some things were meant for private. She shook her head.

Dagmar set a heaping plate before Olaus and patted him on the shoulder. "Ah, Olaus. You knew how lonely I'd be with the boys gone."

"Ja, Missus," he answered, and his voice lost its jovial tone, "I thought how it would be for you and thought as well of my own mor in Iceland. I can't change it for her but I thought to change it for you if I could."

"God bless you!" Dagmar wiped her eyes with the corner of her apron. "You need coffee! Serena, pour him a cup."

Olaus shoveled in mounds of food in short order. He had seconds on the pork roast and scraped out the remaining mashed potatoes and gravy, smacking his lips with appreciation. The talk ebbed and flowed about crops, weather, and war.

Serena was glad to excuse herself from the table. "Let me finish the dishes, while Mr. Reierson takes my place at whist." She took the kettle of boiling water from the stove and poured a dishpan full, adding a handful of soft soap. The fat from the pork floated on the top of the pan like the white foam on the seas of Norway. She thought of the map of Norway, the many fjords and lakes.

There were lakes in Minnesota, lakes within a short drive, but she wondered if they were like the ones her parents had known in Norway. She took a rag and scrubbed in the scalding water, rinsing and stacking the dishes at the side.

"I'll wipe." Dagmar picked up a towel.

"Nei," Serena said. "You won't wipe the dishes on Christmas Eve when you have company waiting for your hand at whist. Tonight I'll do the dishes, and gladly. It's the least I can do after such a feast."

The others played cards, refreshed by the bottle of aquavit passed round the table at regular intervals. Serena finished the dishes and sat watching the others play. Finally she excused herself and climbed the loft for bed.

35

"Old Abe Must Wake up and Change his Diet; He has been Feasting too Long on Prairie Chickens and Sweet Meats. He must eat more Wild Cats and Bullpups, and less Snail soup, and that would Strengthen His Spinal Column, and that Foot would Come Down that we read so Much About, which has been up too Long." St. Cloud Democrat, December 24, 1862

GUST DEALT THE CARDS AND EYED SERENA'S DEPARTURE. If only he could join her. The aquavit had worked on him as well, and he was filled with desire. It had been too long since they had felt this way, at ease among friends, normal. The frontier life was harder than expected. His father had warned him, but he'd been too stubborn to listen. He threw the last card on the table and gathered his hand.

"I grand!" Reierson overturned his card with a slap. "Your play!"

Serena was sound asleep by the time Gust stumbled up to the dark loft. It was past midnight, and he was exhausted from the journey and his part in the butchering. Not to mention the aquavit provided by Olaus. He crawled into the bed beside Serena without undressing. She did not stir. In the blackness, Gust imagined how her blonde hair looked spread across the pillow and reached over to touch the satin ridges left from the braided crown she wore during the day.

"Serena," he whispered. "Are you awake?"

There was only silence in the loft. If only she could sleep this well at their cabin. Maybe they should stay at the fort for the rest of the winter. It might be better for everyone.

The next day was the ball.

174

"I'm not going," Serena said calmly at breakfast.

"Why not?" Gust set his coffee cup down and stared at her. Sometimes he wondered if his wife had turned into someone else while he wasn't watching. She used to love to dance.

"I just don't care to go," Serena said and took a dainty bite of scrapple. "This is delicious. I'll remember to make it next time we butcher."

"The fiddler is from Hallingdal." Anton pushed away from the table to toss another log into the stove. The stove wood was an awkward shape and Anton took an iron bar and pried it into the box. Smoke billowed into the room until he slammed the door shut. "There's a shortage of women—and few who know the Hallingkast. You'd be the belle of the ball."

"I know the Hallingkast, but the truth of the matter is I have nothing to wear." Serena looked down on her plate. "The Sioux robbed me of all my clothes except what I'm wearing. I can't go in rags."

"Not another word," Dagmar said. "I have just the thing."

Dagmar rummaged in an old trunk pushed under the bed. She pulled out a cloth-wrapped bundle and placed it in Serena's lap. "There! Now you can dance."

Serena unwrapped the bundle and pulled out a dove-gray dress with small pearl buttons. She shook it out and held it up before her. Gust saw how it brought out the blue in her eyes, making her even more beautiful.

"It's settled." Dagmar sniffed into her apron. "It is my wedding dress, but none of my girls lived to wear it."

"I couldn't," Serena said, her face a mask of emotions. "It's precious to you."

Gust thought of the lost *bunad* and wondered if she thought of it, too.

"Nonsense," Dagmar said. "I've grown too heavy to wear it. You may borrow it with my blessing."

Gust dreaded dances. His gimpy leg made him clumsy and self-conscious. But Serena was a delight to see whirling around the room. He watched her round the room with a uniformed soldier. Bars on his shoulders, he must be at least a lieutenant. His brothers would know, in the military themselves, but were too far away to ask. Gust hated to admit he didn't know things, like how to tell a captain from a lieutenant.

Whatever his rank, the officer entertained Serena with some amusing story and she laughed as the fiddler sawed out "Turkey in the Straw."

Serena twirled demurely in the lamplight, the gentleman officer holding her by the hand. The song ended, and Gust hurried to claim his wife. But he was too late. Anton Estvold lost no opportunity to request the next waltz. The fiddle started a strong three-four rhythm, and they glided away.

There were other women he might ask to dance but none would be patient with his gimpy leg like Serena. How he loved her. Gust headed instead for the doorway where a keg of beer graced the entrance.

"The paper says they hang tomorrow in Mankato," said a rough looking soldier with a pint of brew in his burly hands and sergeant stripes on his sleeves. "Thirty-eight of the red devils."

"*Skaal!*" Olaus Reierson raised his glass. "May they burn in hell."

"It galls me how old Abe Lincoln interfered," Angus Foote said. "All 338 should have gotten the noose."

"Amen!" Olaus said. "They stole my horse, ruined my crops. I kept my hair, but by God they set me back."

"We'll answer Abe in the election." Foote was a bachelor farmer known for his excellent cattle, and Gust made a mental note to talk to him about bringing Dolly out for breeding. "It'll be a cold day in hell before I vote for a man who pardons murderers."

"Lincoln overstepped himself." Olaus's voice was slurred by drink, but he held out his glass for a refill. "Folks won't stand for it."

"He's an honest man, but he's in over his head."

"He'll get no Minnesota votes unless he does something about the Sioux," Foote said. "I'm not a copperhead by any means, but he's lost my vote."

"Wanted proof, he did," Private Logan Comfort said. "Of course the Sioux were careful not to leave witnesses."

"They should be killed like rats in a corncrib," growled Olaus as he drank deeply from his glass.

"The hell you say," Foote said. "Governor Ramsey agrees. Now there's a man to hold to. He should run for president. He's done right well for us, has a family of victims living with him at the capital."

"We should send a few of Little Crow's victims back to Washington to stay with Old Abe in the White House," said a thin young man with a pimply face. "We could send that widow who was captured, the one in the paper who was rescued at Camp Release after who knows what they did to her."

"If Abe heard from her own lips what happened, he'd do things differently."

Gust agreed although he didn't speak up. Let others do the talking. But he knew that Abe Lincoln was letting Minnesota down. The army tried and condemned 338 Sioux braves. What business did he have pardoning all but thirty-eight?

Gust drank his beer but kept an eye on Serena. She was by far the prettiest girl on the dance floor, dancing with a young Halling in the leaping glory of the Hallingkast.

Gust would have been content to sit out all the dances but near the end of the festivities, Dagmar Estvold approached him as the fiddler played "Lorena," the love song of the War of Rebellion.

"Won't you dance with an old woman?" she said. "I'm too tired to dance with those young pups. By God, they drag me around like a mule on a rope."

They limped around the room at a much slower pace. Dagmar was light on her feet in spite of her extra pounds. Gust caught a smile from Serena as they rounded the corner of the room, but never did get a chance to dance with her. Every time a soldier let go of her, another hurried in to claim the next number.

Gust held Serena's arm as they walked across the parade ground on their way home.

"I didn't like seeing all those other men with you," Gust said as he loosed the bun at the base of her neck. "You're too beautiful to share. I want you all to myself."

"Nei!" Serena pulled away and pushed her hair behind her ears.

"Let it come down." He pulled the pin from her hair. "I like it down."

"Stop!" Serena quickly twisted her hair and tucked it into her collar. "We're in public."

"It's dark." He pulled her closer to him, and his voice was husky. "No one can see."

"You've been drinking!"

"Hardly a drop," Gust said. "It'd do you good to have a drop as well. Olaus, bless his soul, has given us a Christmas present."

He took a bottle from his pocket and insisted she take a nip. The ground was frozen solid and slippery in places. She stopped to sip from the bottle and almost fell over.

"I can't see what I'm doing. Let's go inside where it's warmer." He could hear her teeth chatter.

"First another sip." His hands held tightly to the bottle. "It will do you good."

That night in the loft was almost like old times, before the Sioux destroyed their world, before their baby died. They stayed awake late into the night, alone in the darkness.

36

"FATAL FRIDAY. 38 Hanged. Pardons a Slap in the Face to Victims."
St. Cloud Democrat, December 30, 1862

G UST GROANED AND TRIED TO SHAKE HIMSELF AWAKE. He had been in the middle of a perfect dream—running without a limp, almost flying across the pasture without pain, carrying Baby Lena on his shoulders. She giggled and hung onto his ears. It took him a long moment to get his bearings in the icy, black loft.

Tears sprouted in his eyes, and Gust didn't know if they were tears of joy from the dream or because of the stabbing ache in his leg that jolted him awake along with the voice calling up the loft ladder.

Gust shivered as he pulled on his pants and reached for his boots, hearing Anton rattling the stove lids until a roaring fire caused the stovepipe to *thump* as it expanded with the change in temperature. Then he reached over and pulled up the quilts snugly over Serena's shoulders.

It was almost like being home again with his father waking him early for chores. Earlier than usual because of the festivities the night before, to make sure Gust remembered that he was still a slave to his father, and that Abe Lincoln hadn't sent the army to free him.

"It's your heifer," Anton said as Gust lumbered down the ladder.

"God, no," Gust said. "Should be another month before she freshens."

Anton fed wood into the stove, but it didn't ease the freezing cold. Each breath showed vapor in front of their faces. A layer of ice topped the water bucket and coffee pot. "I can't believe I let the fire go out," Anton said. "Must've been the liquor."

179

Their morning coffee would have to wait, another irritation on a day already brewing trouble. They bundled up as best they could and trudged to the barn. The cold snatched their breath away, burned their lungs and froze their nostrils. Their feet scrunched on the frozen snow.

"God, it's cold," Gust said. Every breath seared his lungs. The fort was silent in the early morning, and Private Harris stood guard at the gate, pumping his arms and stomping his feet to keep from freezing. He waved at the men as they walked the short distance to the barn where Gust's animals were quartered.

"It's a sorry job to stand guard on such a morning," Anton said.

"Foolish, not even an Indian would attack in such weather."

Rosebud's bawling reached them before they entered the barn, a heart-rending sound that filled Gust with dread. The heifer was even more important than the calf. She needed to live or hope of building a herd was gone.

The warmth of the barn slapped him in his face with its dank odor of animals and manure. Buddy and Bets chewed their cuds and mooed low sounds of welcome. Chickens cackled in the pen and a rat scurried in the corner. Gust approached Rosebud carefully and rubbed her head, crooning softly. Her sides heaved, and her wild eyes looked in all directions as if to escape.

"Now, then," Gust said in his most gentle voice. "You'll be a mother before long."

Anton gently pressed her sides and felt around her hindquarters.

"It's stuck." Anton took off his coat and shirt.

"What can be done?"

"We'll pull that calf." Anton slapped Gust on the back. "By God, it's not the first calf to come with the help of a Norskie sailor!"

Gust held the tail up and braced his body against Rosebud as Anton felt for the birth canal and pushed his arm deep into the little cow. Anton groaned as a contraction crushed his arm against the heifer's pelvis. She bawled a pitiful bellow, and Anton pulled his arm out, rubbing it and cursing under his breath.

"Damn!" Anton said. "It about breaks a man's arm."

The calf was too far up, not even in the birth canal, but the heifer was in hard labor. Gust had pulled a calf before, but the legs had been in the canal, easy to grasp. No doubt this calf was hung up behind the pelvic bones.

"Put your coat on a while and warm up," Gust said.

"*Nei*," Anton flexed his right hand and limbered his arm. "I'll try again."

Anton wore an anguished look as he stood behind Rosebud. "We won't give up yet," he said. "If Angus Foote were here, he'd know what to do. That man is a master in husbandry."

Gust listened to him chatter about Foote and his expertise. God help us. We need a miracle.

Anton plunged his arm into the birth canal again with great straining and grunting. "I feel a hoof." Another contraction crushed his arm, almost forcing him to his knees with agony. When the contraction ended, he pulled out his arm and began the litany of rubbing and stretching. Sweat froze on his body and caused him to shiver. "I could barely tap it with my fingertip, but I felt it."

"I'd try," Gust said. "But my arms are shorter than yours." He felt he had to offer since Rosebud belonged to him.

"I'll do it." Anton's voice was firm. "I'm not one to give up."

"Then drink this first." Gust handed him the half-filled bottle of willow tea. "It might help."

"I've something better." Anton stepped over to a barrel of oats and pulled out a bottle of aquavit hidden deep within the grain. "A nip for strength."

Anton handed the brown bottle to Gust, who sipped a mouthful of the liquid fire, wiped the lip of the bottle with the back of his shirt sleeve and handed it back to Anton. Gust felt the warm buzz go through him as they waited for Rosebud's next contraction. Anton tried again.

"Any luck?" Gust said.

"Two hooves." Another contraction forced Anton's arm out. He cursed.

"I wonder how many pounds of pressure a heifer uses to give birth," Gust said.

"A hell of a lot." Anton said with a grimace. "You're a deep thinker to come up with such a question." Anton rubbed his arm while Rosebud bellowed an agonizing cry. "It's something Emil would ask."

"He's a thinking man?"

"That one would question God Almighty if he had the chance."

Gust thought about the questions he would have for Almighty God if given the chance. His crippled leg, Lena's death, the uprising.

Gust lifted the tail again and braced his body against Rosebud's heaving flank. Foamy mucus dripped from her mouth, and her eyes were bloodshot. *My God, is this what Serena went through? Is this what all women go through?*

Anton reached in again. "Both hooves free." He pulled out his arm before the next contraction and leaned back against the wall while Rosebud bellowed and stomped. An earthy musk filled his nose, and Gust dodged a kick. But at the end of the contractions, a pair of legs dangled motionless from the heifer.

"Is it alive?"

"Hard to tell," Anton said. "The rope hangs on the wall." He cradled his bloody arm with his other hand, grimacing. Sweat beaded on his forehead.

"Are you all right?"

"Ja, but she bore down on my arm, crushing it between her bones and calf." He struggled into his shirt, shivering while he buttoned the buttons.

"It isn't broken?"

"Nei."

Gust brought the rope and Anton knotted a loop around the protruding hooves.

"Together then," Anton said. "With the next pain."

They pulled with all their strength, timing it with Rosebud's contractions, until finally a calf burst forth, covered in slime. Rosebud bawled a desperate cry, as near a scream as Gust had ever heard from an animal. It unnerved him, weakened his knees, reminding him of Serena's sickbed. The smell of blood filled the stall, and the glowing eyes of rats peered from the shadows.

"It's a bull." Anton leaned against the barn wall, breathing hard, his face red from the effort. "Too bad it isn't a heifer." He picked up the bottle and drained it.

"But it's healthy." Gust took handfuls of straw from the floor and wiped the tottering calf. He set the calf to nurse, and the heifer nuzzled him, licking off the creamy coating. Rosebud stood dazed but kept standing. It was a good sign, Gust noted with great relief.

"See how he braces his legs," Anton said. "He stands like King Olaf himself."

"Then King Olaf is his name," Gust said. "We'll call him King."

"Oxen bring a good price." Anton flexed his arm. "You'd do well to train him to the yoke."

"But I'd need another to make a pair."

Gust washed his hands in the water barrel. It was the trouble of the wilderness—nothing was available, and there was never enough money. One thing led to another.

"A thousand thanks," Gust said. "You saved my heifer and calf. No doubt I would have lost both had I been alone on the farm."

Anton dismissed the thanks with a careless shrug and went back to the barrel of oats, reached deep within it and pulled out another bottle. "Now then, we'll share a drop to celebrate the birth of a king." He uncorked it ceremoniously and handed the bottle to Gust.

"Skaal to King Olaf!"

Gust drank and handed the bottle to Anton and forked the bloody straw in the heifer's stall into the manure pile, replacing it with clean bedding. The sip of liquid fire burned first, glowed, and then eased the pain in his leg.

Gust watered Rosebud and rubbed her ears. "You did a good job, mother. You delivered a fine calf."

She bawled once more as the afterbirth slipped out onto the floor. Rats, drawn by the blood, scurried in the corners. Anton threw a pitchfork at one but missed.

"Damn rats!" Anton said. "They're bold to come right out in the open. What we need around here is a cat. The rats and mice ruin us, spoiling our grain and fouling the seed saved for next year."

"I'll thin them out a little." Gust took a hoe from the wall and stunned one with the blade and stomped it with his heavy boot and threw it onto the manure pile.

"When the boys were home, they took care of the rats," Anton said. "An old man can't expect to be as quick."

"When will they be home again?" Gust replaced the hoe on the wall and fed the heifer a scoop of grain from the bin. A mouse scurried out of the grain bin, and Gust stomped it.

"When the damn war is over and not before," Anton said. "They signed up for ninety days but they won't let them out until it's over."

"Maybe they know my brothers," Anton said. "Do they ever mention Iowa troops?"

"Nei," Anton said. "But I'll ask them next time I write."

Gust plopped down on the clean straw piled in the corner and sipped again from the bottle of liquid fire. Anton sat on an overturned crate and Gust handed him the bottle.

"It's hell on Dagmar," Anton said. "Especially with the fighting in Kentucky. Of course, we don't know if Ole fought at Perryville but he's somewhere in Kentucky and it makes sense they'd keep the artillerists in the thick of it."

"It seems odd that a farm boy would man the big guns."

"You don't know Ole," chuckled Anton. "Even as a small boy, he could shoot the head off a mallard at a hundred yards. The happiest day of his life was his promotion to artillerist. I still have the letter."

"I'd enjoy reading it," Gust said. "My leg kept me out and sometimes I wonder what I'm missing."

"Don't be a fool, man." Anton spat into the straw. "War is no different than the Indian raids. It's all killing and suffering. My far in Norway told me to stay out of wars and mind my own business. It's been good advice."

Anton passed the bottle back again. It was still Christmas, after all, and no need to skimp on refreshments.

"How long have you been in America?"

"Since I was nineteen," Anton said. "Took a job in the pineries and saved enough money to send for Dagmar."

"So, what made you leave Norway?"

"My far was a cotter." Anton said. "I earned five cents a day slaving for a noble. Dagmar worked as his servant for board and room. We couldn't afford to marry under such conditions,"

"My father, too." Gust felt a sudden fondness for his father surge through his veins along with the aquavit. "He and his brother lost the home place in a bad business deal. Only five acres but it was all they had. They sold everything else they had and bought passage to America."

"What's your father doing now?"

"Farming in Iowa," Gust said. "Done real well." Tears welled in his eyes as he remembered how his father had tucked him into bed when he was a little boy. He shook his head in a futile attempt to shake off the sadness. It's the aquavit, he thought. I've had too much to drink.

"*Skaal!*" Anton said. "One more drop to celebrate the hangings. May the *skraelings* burn in hell."

"*Skaal!*" Gust thought of Lena cold in Serena's arms, the look on Serena's face when they lowered the coffin into the ground on that godforsaken trail, the utter helplessness of it all. A brief thought passed through his mind like a flying arrow, and he wondered if the Sioux also knew grief. If they mourned those hanged today. If they had suffered as much as the settlers.

They settled back against the wooden pen that housed the chickens. Anton threw a handful of grain to the hens.

"I've been meaning to ask you a question." Gust plucked a fresh straw from the stack at his feet and chewed on it. "What made Salmon leave Pomme de Terre?"

"When the Sioux raided in early September, we held them off. They kept us forted up, away from our field work while the crops spoiled in the fields or were eaten by varmints. Aggravating beyond description after all our hard work."

Gust changed positions to ease his leg.

"What about Salmon?"

"We took a stand here rather than travel on to Fort Abercrombie. Hell, what was the difference? " he paused to take a chew of snus and rolled it around in his mouth before tucking it behind his lip. "Salmon was here, of course. Olause and Angus Foote. And the Spitsberg family toward the last. They left Alexandria Woods after their neighbors were killed."

"So why did Salmon leave?"

The new calf sucked loudly at his mother's bag, rooting his feet and butting against her to make the milk flow quicker as Rosebud looked at him with dark, sad eyes. Anton rolled his snus wad around again in his mouth and wiped his chin with the back of his sleeve. He looked at Gust a long moment before answering.

"After the troops came through, Andrew was sure he could go back and harvest the corn, said they wouldn't survive the winter without it."

The liquor swirled in Gust's mind. He willed himself to concentrate on Anton's words though his face looked slightly out of focus.

"He took his boy along. We tried to warn him, but there was no stopping Andrew. That man was the stubbornest I ever knew." Anton spit a stream of brown tobacco juice into the manure pile.

The sun was just peeking over the eastern sky, sundogs bright on either side, predicting another cold day. Outside were the noises of the soldiers up and getting ready for their duties.

"It was dark when Andrew crawled back. His boy had gone to the cabin to fetch another sack for the corn. When he didn't come back, Andrew went to check on him. He found him dead."

"Nei!"

"The boy was nailed to the cabin door. All cut up. Bastards tried to fire the cabin." Anton pressed his lips together before speaking again. "Andrew put it out."

"My God." Gust spit out the straw and reached for the bottle.

"He pulled the door off its hinges and dragged it away with his boy still on it. He couldn't leave his son hanging there."

"Savages!"

"He took it hard," Anton said. "Blamed himself."

"We wondered what happened." Gust swirled the liquid in the bottle but did not take a drink. "We found the door." He wasn't used to liquor before breakfast, and it was having a debilitating effect on him. "Don't say anything to Serena"

"Don't worry," Anton said. "I wouldn't have told you except you asked." He stood, stretched out his legs and back, then stared straight into Gust's eyes. "You don't know what chance you take staying at the farm."

Gust had to look away from the hard stare. "I see," Gust said. What if he had found Serena nailed to the cabin door when he returned from the fields. Or the times he left her alone. A cold sweat chilled him.

"Is there a new baby in here?" Dagmar's voice called from the barn door.

Dagmar and Serena, bundled in shawls and mittens, lumbered into the barn, breathless and red-cheeked.

"You remember," Dagmar said with a smirk, "how I predicted a strong bull calf to bring you wealth."

"You did." Gust moved closer to Serena, close enough that their arms touched. Cold radiated from her clothing. He moved closer to warm her. Thank God she was safe and unharmed. "Maybe there's something to it after all."

"She's a troll." Anton reached over the pen to pat the little king. "We'll have her read our grounds every day so we know the news before it happens."

"She can read mine anytime." Gust rubbed Serena's arm with one finger. "I'm convinced."

"You can't take King home in such cold weather." Dagmar said. "You'll have to stay longer, at least until the calf is stronger."

Gust saw his excuse. He could stay through the winter and no one would know Captain McLarty's orders. Of course he couldn't risk the heifer's milk supply or the new calf.

"We couldn't inconvenience you."

"Nonsense!" Anton forked another mound of fresh straw in the pen with the new mother. "It's like having the boys home again."

"But we're too much trouble." Serena said.

Gust knew she was being polite. She wanted to stay on at the fort. Her face was as happy as the day of their wedding.

"Enough!" Anton said. "I'll castrate King for you. It's best to do it before fly season."

Gust hesitated only for a moment. "Many thanks. We'll stay."

Serena clapped her hands in excitement, and the look of gratitude on her face filled Gust with happiness.

"But we'll work to pay our way," Gust said. "We don't need charity."

"Then bring in the colostrum," Dagmar said. "That greedy little bastard doesn't need it all."

37

"Governor Ramsey Asks Minnesota for 1500 Pairs of Mittens"
                                    St. Cloud Democrat, January 15,1863

DAGMAR SERVED SERENA THE LARGEST HELPING.
"My mor always said new milk pudding gives women strength for childbearing." Dagmar pressed another spoonful upon Serena.

Serena colored at her words but took another small helping. It was possible, she thought. There might be another baby in the fall. She didn't dare look at Gust or Anton, just bent her head over her dish and spooned the sweet pudding. Dagmar had predicted it in the coffee grounds, after all.

Serena cradled the Red Wing churn after the dishes were done. It comforted her, took the ache away from her arms, and reminded her how she once held Lena to her breast. Lena's eyes, neither blue nor brown, glowed gray like a lake before the ice went out in spring. Her little head carried the sweet smell of all babies.

Without thinking, Serena bent her head to sniff the churn and disappointment welled up within her when she smelled only cow's milk. She plunged the dasher harder and faster. With all the fresh milk, there was butter to spare and no lack of churning, a chore Serena favored.

Since moving to the fort, Serena no longer gazed out windows. The sentry at the gate kept watch, and there were soldiers positioned to defend them if attacked. It was almost like being a girl again, unhampered by the responsibilities of adulthood. If she awakened during the night, she knew both Anton and Dagmar slept downstairs. It was like having parents again.

One afternoon she found herself humming a Norwegian folk song. The melody floated through her mind as she worked.

Dagmar gave Serena a skein of gray wool, fuzzy and warm. Serena found the end of the yarn and wrapped it twice around her fingers. Then she slipped her fingers out of the loop and wound it into a ball. How relaxing to work with wool again. It had been so long since she had done any knitting. She had knit her mother a pair of mittens as a Christmas gift the year before they married. Her mother had been so pleased. Just thinking about it made Serena ache with homesickness.

The yarn ball finished, she cast stitches on a smooth, wooden needle to fashion a pair of mittens.

"Serena," Dagmar called from the doorway as she entered the cabin, her nose red and dripping from the cold. She carried three eggs in her mittened hands. "See what your hens have given today!"

"I'm surprised they lay in this cold weather." Serena turned the needle, knitting two then purling two. She didn't look up, unwilling to risk a lost stitch. "It must be the skim milk from Rosebud."

"If you wouldn't mind," Dagmar said as she placed the eggs on the table and unwound the scarf from her head. "I'd like to make doughnuts and invite Tommy over tonight. I've that fresh lard."

"Who?"

"Tommy Harris, the private," Dagmar said. "I don't know what we would do without him. He fetches water, brings the mail after the stage comes and has been a real comfort."

"He delivered the mail to our cabin once."

"He has a wife and two small children in Preston." Dagmar huddled close to the stove and held her hands over it for warmth. "He's homesick—all the boys are."

Serena understood homesickness. That was her problem as well. She missed Burr Oak and her parents and even her pesky little sisters. How strange to be stranded with people she hardly knew and separated from loved ones she longed for. It wasn't fair. She visualized the map and the long trail homeward. Even if she started that very day, it would be many weeks before she could hope to see them again.

"Ja," Serena said. "Doughnuts for the private would be just the thing."

Private Harris gladly came for coffee and doughnuts that evening. He hooked one with his finger and dipped it into the hot coffee before taking a large bite. "Mmmm . . . delicious."

"These are good," Gust said. "What's the spice?"

"My mor's recipe." Dagmar pleated her apron with her fingers and looked down. "Just a dash of nutmeg."

"I've news," Private Harris said. "Another killing by Fort Abercrombie."

"When?" Serena noticed Gust rub his bad leg and felt a chill down her back. Fort Abercrombie was only a long day's journey from their farm by horseback. She picked up her knitting.

"Yesterday," Private Harris said. "A soldier from the fort was fishing outside the gates. When he didn't show up for guard duty, they went looking for him. Found his body by the river."

"In this kind of weather," Anton said. "I always thought they'd wait until spring for their deviltry."

"I was hoping and praying it was over," Dagmar said in a teary voice. "It must be God's will."

"How can it be God's will?" Private Harris asked and reached for another doughnut.

"All is God's will, the good and the bad," Dagmar said. "Like the deaths of my children. All God's will."

"I don't believe that," he said. "A loving God would not plan such suffering and hardship."

"Then why does it happen?" Dagmar said. "Surely He is in charge of the world He created."

"It's because we are sinners, going out of His will." Private Harris took a sip of coffee. "War and death are not His plan."

It made sense to Serena. In her heart, she knew God hadn't caused Lena's death. Her death was wrong, terribly wrong. She purled and knitted in earnest. She didn't want to look at Gust, to see what he might be thinking.

"You make it sound so easy, Tommy," Dagmar said. "I've learned there are no easy answers, only more questions."

"I'd like to ask a favor," Private Harris said. "If you can't oblige, I'll certainly understand."

Serena wondered what he wanted. He spoke in such an earnest manner. She turned her knitting and began another row.

"Would you let some of us meet in your loft for prayer meetings?"

Serena looked up and dropped a stitch. Anton set down his cup too hard and sloshed a drop of coffee over the side onto the table.

"Some of us pray together every Sunday," Private Harris said. "We started it at Fort Ripley and keep it up here as often as we can. Usually we meet out in the woods."

"But it's too cold!" Anton said. "Surely you can't keep your mind on prayers with the wind howling around your ears."

"We try to live like Christians," Private Harris said. "And we need prayer more than ever. Our families. The Sioux and the Rebs."

"Then pray in our loft whenever you wish—and pray for our boys when you do."

Dagmar wiped her eyes on her apron. "This world is a mess."

"How is your family?" Anton said.

"My wife worries about planting. My brother-in-law can't help her this year—was killed in the uprising."

"How was he killed?" Serena was ever curious about how people were affected by the Sioux raids and spoke without thinking. She looked at Gust to see if he showed disapproval at her question, but he was busy dunking another doughnut and didn't meet her eyes.

"He was with the Renville Rangers," Private Harris said. Serena saw his jaw work and then his mouth set determinedly. "Murdered one night as he stood guard outside of Mankato."

Dagmar placed a sympathetic hand on his shoulder. "Some of the men have their families coming to join them here at the fort. Could your family come?"

"It's too dangerous," Private Harris said. "And Sally couldn't travel alone with the little ones."

"If you change your mind," Dagmar said, "they could stay with us. We'd welcome the company."

"Thank you." Private Harris' voice cracked and his eyes blinked back tears. "It means a lot to me, but they'll stay in Preston for now."

"You come Sunday or any day you want to pray," Anton said. "I only hope your prayers get through without a minister."

"We'll come Sunday afternoon."

Private Harris hurried off to relieve Jon Sverdrup who stood guard at the gate in the piercing cold. Serena wondered how they could stand it. She picked up the dropped stitch and began knitting and purling again. Men having a prayer meeting on their own time without a minister. Somehow it embarrassed her, as if she had learned of a great weakness. But why should she feel that way? Her own parents might be dead, for all she knew. She would ask them to pray for her family. The yarn tangled, and she deftly pulled it back into line. If she kept working, she would finish the mitten by bedtime.

THREE SOLDIERS STOMPED SNOW OFF their boots on the rug by the kitchen door when they came on Sunday afternoon. They nodded to them as they sat at table eating dinner, unsure as to how they should proceed.

"Do you boys want coffee?" Dagmar said. "Jon, you must be frozen after standing guard all morning."

"That would hit the spot, missus," Jon said. His face showed fiery red around his beard and frost glistened on his eyelashes.

"Let me get it, Dagmar." Serena went to the black stove and reached for the heavy cast iron pot. She hurriedly pulled back her hand, took a rag from the wall and wadded it around the handle before she picked it up. She poured a scalding portion into a tin cup and used the rag to wrap around the cup handle as well before handing it to Jon Sverdrup. "Careful, it's hot."

Serena guessed Jon to be about her age, maybe eighteen or nineteen. She hoped someone would give her cousin Arvid a cup of fresh coffee that day. For all she knew, he might be with the Renville Rangers or off to war in the South. How she missed her family! Jensina and Jerdis would be twelve in February. Her mother and father would both turn forty-four in May! They were growing old without her.

"*Mange takk*, Missus," Jon Sverdrup said again. When he reached for the cup, she was surprised to see his trigger finger missing on his right hand.

He saw her eyes fix on the stubby finger and smiled. "Shot off when I was deer hunting a few years back," he said. "Lucky it wasn't my head blown off. I dropped the gun, was too excited to be careful."

"Did you shoot the deer?" Anton asked.

"Nei, the buck fever got me, and it ran away when the gun went off," Jon said with a laugh. "I'll never live it down."

He blew on the coffee, warming his hands on the sides of the cup, letting the steam warm his face. "*Mange takk,* Missus," he said.

Serena handed steaming cups of the strong brew to Private Harris and an older man introduced as Trygve Hansen. Serena recognized him from the Christmas dance. They downed their coffee quickly and climbed the ladder to the loft as Serena pulled the iron dishpan over to the hottest burner and filled it with water to heat for dishes.

"Do you think we should go to the barn?" Anton said with a worried look. "I don't want to bother them."

"There's feed to grind," Gust said.

The men pushed back from the table and pulled on hats and mittens, leaving the house in a hurry. *They act like they were afraid,* thought Serena. *Surely prayers were nothing to be afraid of.* Serena and Dagmar finished their coffee, and the sound of a hymn floated down from the loft.

. . . Still, still with Thee, when purple morning breaketh
and the dawn waketh . . .

The song, familiar to Serena from Confirmation, sent a pull of homesickness through her. Lilacs bloomed by the Norwegian Lutheran Church in Burr Oak and their fragrance had filled the air as the confirmands sang before their first communion. Tears ran down her face, and she wiped them with the backs of her hands, thinking of the faces smiling back at her from the pews. Her father always complained that his good suit was scratchy, and he squirmed during the last verse. Her mother wore a new hat with blue satin ribbons. Jensina and Jerdis fidgeted in their seats while her cousin Arvid cast furtive glances at Ingeborg Nielsen across the aisle.

"Serena," Dagmar said. "Let's wash up and pray along with them."

Serena looked up in surprise.

"Not in the loft," Dagmar said hurriedly, "but downstairs."

Quietly they washed the plates and spoons, wiping them dry and setting them on the shelf by the door. Serena picked up her knitting and sat by the stove, continuing the pattern of knit two, purl two, knit two, and purl two. The gray yarn felt soft and warm on her lap.

The men sang another hymn, one unfamiliar to Serena. She strained to catch the words.

"What song is that?" she asked in a whisper.

"Near My God to Thee," Dagmar said. "Listen."

. . . still all my song shall be, nearer my God to Thee.
Nearer my God to Thee, nearer to Thee . . .

The prayers started in a gentle hum that both soothed and frightened Serena. The men spoke openly to God, asking for His presence and protection for their families back home. Private Harris asked God to send someone to help Sally with the planting. Jon Sverdrup beseeched Him to comfort his mother and protect her from loneliness while her sons were off to war. Dagmar sniffed loudly and wept into her apron. Trygve Hansen asked God for protection from the Sioux and help for the victims of the uprising.

Private Harris asked a blessing on the Estvolds for letting the soldiers use the loft for meeting and prayed He would protect their sons. With a quick intake of breath, Serena heard him pray for her and Gust, asking for peace to dwell in their home and that God would heal them from their sorrow and loss.

Serena's tears splashed on her knitting. She didn't know why she cried, but it was a comforting, cleansing flow. She couldn't have stopped had she tried, only wept into her knitting, trying to be silent, sobs clutching her throat.

The men prayed for President Lincoln and the war, their voices muted, sincere. They sang another hymn and climbed down the ladder, leaving without conversation. It seemed they were engulfed in peace. To think people could speak to God so freely! There were no words to express the wonder of it.

Dagmar's face looked red and puffy from crying, and Serena knew hers looked the same. Dagmar acted as if she wished to say something, but no words came from her mouth. She finally blew her nose and uncovered the bowl of bread rising on the back of the stove.

"He's Methodist." Dagmar kneaded the heavy dough. "Believes a person must know God for himself, not just be a church member."

"Private Harris?"

"Wants to be a minister after the war." Dagmar folded the dough and began another round of kneading. "Feels religion should be a day-to-day matter, not just confined to the church house."

"That's strange," Serena said. "But I've often wondered why we are so reluctant to live the way we were taught in Confirmation."

"There is a gulf between what is taught and what we live."

THE DAYS PASSED SLOWLY AND SERENA mastered the many strategies of whist. One night the women skunked the men. It was a milestone, a happy carefree evening removed from the harshness of their world. They forgot the Sioux, the war, thought only of the moment.

Near the end of January a shout sounded at the gate of the fort.

"Mail! Mail call!"

A young man bundled on horseback rode in leading a packhorse carrying a bulky mail sack frosted over with glistening ice. The man fairly staggered into the barn and collapsed on a stack of hay. Serena, on her way to pick eggs, followed the crowd into the barn, eager for news from the outside, hoping there might be a letter from home. Gust and Anton walked over and stood beside her.

"Are you crazy?" Private Harris said. "Coming out alone in such weather? What were you thinking?"

"Private O'Leary, with mail for you and Fort Abercrombie," he said. He pulled his boots off and rubbed his feet. He stripped off his stockings with a grimace and kept rubbing. "I'll need some snow."

Without a word Private Harris went out and brought in a hat full of snow. He knelt before the stranger and rubbed small handfuls of snow on his feet and toes. One toe blanched white.

"Oh, my God," he said. "I've frozen a toe."

Gust pulled his bottle of willow tea from his inside coat pocket and handed it to the man. "Here's something for the pain."

"What is it?" he said, "Whiskey?"

"Nei, medicine for the pain."

He took a swig, grimacing at the bitter taste. Private Harris knelt before the man and massaged his feet then held them in his hands to warm.

"It'll be all right, only a chilblain to keep you awake tonight."

"I've got to leave for Fort Abercrombie."

"What's so important it won't wait until spring?"

"Don't know," Private O'Leary said. "I'm only carrying the message. And bringing the mail."

There were six copies of the *St. Cloud Democrat* for Gust. "Were there no letters?" Serena said in a small voice. "None at all?"

"Not for us, Serena," Gust said. "But one for you, Anton." He handed him a flat envelope, soiled and crumpled.

"It's from Emil!" Anton said. "We'll take it in to Dagmar."

Inside, Dagmar slumped to a chair and held it in her hands without opening it. "Oh, God. Oh, God." Her hands trembled.

Serena felt she might faint, as if the room pressed in upon her. Nothing from Iowa. Something was terribly wrong. She felt afraid for Dagmar to open her letter, afraid it held bad news.

"It's his writing," Anton said quietly. "Mother, don't worry. He wrote it himself."

Dagmar picked up a paring knife from the table and painstakingly slit the top of the envelope. She laid the knife down and pulled out a single page. She unfolded the letter and held it at arm's length, struggling to position it in the best light so Anton could read it with her. A stifled scream broke the silence.

Dagmar dropped the paper to the table. "Anton!" she said in a hoarse whisper. "Oh, God! Not that!"

Anton knelt beside her and gathered her into his arms and held her, rocking quietly back and forth. Harsh weeping poured out from Dagmar, shaking sobs against Anton's chest. "Shh, Mother. It'll be all right."

"What's wrong?" asked Serena. It must be something terrible. Maybe about Ole.

Anton reached over and picked up the letter and handed it to Serena. The writing, spidery and uneven, at times almost faded away in its weakness. Serena hesitated to read the letter, something so personal. It wrapped around the margins, unwilling to waste even a single inch of space. She cleared her throat and read out loud.

> December 25, 1862
> Dear Mor and Far,
> It is with great relief I write this letter from my hospital bed. I survived the Battle of Fredericksburg, Virginia, with only a bullet wound

to my left shoulder. The fighting was intense and I feared never to survive. A man to my left was struck with a Minnie ball in his ammunition belt, starting his body on fire with small explosions. I turned to help him and was fired upon by his burning cache of ammunition. I never thought to be nearly killed by a dead man, a union soldier at that, a friend.

Surely God heard your prayers that day as the surgeon says it would have been a fatal wound if only three inches closer to my heart. It had been dry here and the woods were on fire around us during the battle, set by the burning bodies of our comrades and the artillery. The trees were our only cover from sharpshooters across the field and as they burned away we were exposed to their deadly aim. We had no water to use on the flames but took off our jackets and tried to beat them down while fighting at the same time. It was like a scene from the Book of Revelations. I cannot forget the screams. When I sleep, I hear it over again, smelling the fire and the burning flesh. I thank God I survived. It is a miracle.

I have not heard from Ole. I believe he is still in Kentucky. At least he was spared the agony of Fredericksburg. May God protect him. I miss my brother and almost wish he hadn't joined the artillery so we could have stayed together. But I wouldn't wish the things I've seen upon him. I hope he has had an easier time.

The doctor says I will fight again if he can save my left arm. So far the wound has not mortified. This war is senseless. Although I have no fondness for slavery, I wonder if it is worth the carnage and hatred. My only desire is to come home.

I think of you daily and worry that the Indians may not be as quiet as the newspapers report. Have you had any more trouble? It will not be long until planting. Will you put the east field in potatoes as before? Be careful, whatever you do. I thank God the soldiers have moved to Pomme de Terre. They should keep you safe.

Please pray for me as I do for you. You were right, Far. I never should have enlisted. Please write to me at this address. The surgeon says it will be several months before I am well enough to return to my unit. God Jul! Next Christmas we will be together.

Your loving son,
Emil Estvold

"Now, Mother," Anton said. "He lives and the doctor says he'll fight again."

"Damn the war!" Dagmar said fiercely. "Damn the North and damn the South! They're good boys, too good to be shot and killed. Their enlistment was up long ago. They should be allowed to come home."

"You're right, Mother," Anton crooned. "You're right."

"Damn Abe Lincoln and damn the Rebs. Damn the United States and damn the Confederacy. We should have stayed in the Old Country. My boy deserve better than to burn to death in some godforsaken field."

"Ja, ja, Mother," Anton patted her again. "They deserve better."

Serena thought of their burning fields, ruined crops, Lena's sickness and death. Gust should have been more concerned when Lena was sick. Maybe he could have found a doctor if he hadn't been so pre-occupied with the wheat. They all deserved better.

A thick missive rested in Serena's pocket, ready to send along with the courier. She thought to give it to Gust, but something held her back. Maybe it was superstition, but Mor used to say that if you always do things the same way, you will always get the same results. Instead, she gave the letter to Private Harris when he brought firewood in from the woodshed.

"Will you mail this for me?"

"Of course, Mrs. Gustafson." He tucked the letter inside his tunic. "The courier leaves today."

38

*"Minnesota Is the Victim of the Most Astounding Calamity
That Has Ever Befallen Any State of the Union."*
St. Cloud Democrat, September 10, 1862

DRUMS POUNDED AS THE BRAVES DANCED and sought counsel from the Great Mystery.

"Hi-yi-yi."

His voice spent and his arm numb from elbow to wrist, Drumbeater pounded. His body cried out for rest, but he refused it, instead drummed through the night.

"Hi-yi-yi."

Just before dawn, Drumbeater finally left the council fire, exhausted and spent. He was almost to the river at the edge of the village when his blood ran cold. An owl hooted. Fear flooded him, the feeling that his world was falling apart, that the mountains crumbled under heavy snow from the east.

Maybe he should take Otter and Willow Song away from this place, leave the girl-children with Many Beavers and flee to the Mountains of the Turtle in the western plains. Many Beavers could return the captives. If she failed at her task, she failed. He could not fight against the omens.

Drumbeater bathed in the river. The water felt warmer than the morning air of *ptanyeiu*. He stood before the rising sun, trying to calm his anxious thoughts and forget the troubles that plagued him as he expressed adoration to the Great Mystery. Then it was as if he saw Crooked Lightning's face before him, the man who kept a promise to a life-and-death friend. Wasn't

Drumbeater also a civilized man of highest integrity? He could not disappoint his uncle. He would keep his promise in spite of the dangers.

After this decision came the blessing of Wakantanka, light resting on his face as the sun rose higher into the sky, coloring the east with vibrant colors filled with joy. An eagle winged across the sky, diving into the water for a fish. He had found his path. He would follow it.

"Ho!" Standing Tall called when Drumbeater returned to the village and was about to enter the teepee. Throughout camp, the People stirred. Dogs growled over bones. Otter babbled inside the teepee, and Little Bird squealed in delight. Drumbeater wanted only to sleep. It had been a long night but he felt the satisfaction of finding his medicine. It had been a night well spent. He shifted the sacred drum to his other arm.

"Sibley received the *washechu* tracks on birch paper." Standing Tall's face relaxed into almost a smile. "It was strong medicine to send out the tracks. The Long Knives know we seek peace."

Drumbeater felt hope flow through his veins. Peace to live in Leaf Country. Peace to raise his son as a future warrior of the People. Then he remembered how Crooked Lightning named Sibley both a thief and a liar.

"What happens next?" Drumbeater felt instantly awake. "Are they coming for the captives?"

"Yes. They come."

It was then Drumbeater saw the far camp, where the Mdewakanton and Wahpekute dismantled their teepees and packed belongings onto travois, dogs and ponies.

"Where are they going?"

"Little Crow takes his warriors to relatives in the west," Standing Tall said. "Maybe as far as the Mountains of the Turtle."

"But why?"

"They do not believe the Long Knives will let them live."

A cold hand clasped around his heart. Another urge to pack up his family and flee with them filled his mind. To run from the Long Knives, the liar named Sibley. What if the peaceful Dakotas left at camp were blamed for the uprising?

"Everyone who is friendly to the Long Knives must show a white rag," Standing Tall said. "It is the *washechu* way of peace."

"White *minihuhas*?"

"Ho." Scarlet Plume seemed unafraid. This comforted Drumbeater, reassured him. "The captives wear garments of white. We'll take what we need from them."

When Drumbeater explained what was needed, Many Beavers removed Badger's white *sanksannica* from under her garments and ripped it into long strips. Drumbeater tied one strip to his lance, another around the pony's mane, one on the dog's neck, and one on Otter's cradleboard.

"This is a strange custom," Willow Song said with suspicion. "What do *minihuhas* have to do with peace? Or returning the captives?"

"Standing Tall has spoken." Drumbeater felt irritable and anxious. Something was wrong. The hooting owl. The mirror at rice camp. He wanted the transfer of prisoners to be over and done so they could return to the harvest. There was much to do before the Moon of Great Difficulty.

Otter fussed in his cradleboard with a red face.

"Is he sick?" Drumbeater said.

"Ho." Willow Song's face showed concern. One of the captives carried the disease of red spots. Many Beavers searched among her packs for the bark of the willow that cured fevers and sicknesses of all kinds.

Only the *washechu* girl-children seemed at peace, laughing and playing on a stack of hides.

"If only we could tell them they are leaving today," Willow Song said. "They might be afraid to go with the Long Knives."

"I will travel with them until they are safely in the hands of Evan Jacobson." Many Beavers said. Her face was without expression but Drumbeater could see her anxiety in the way she fingered the leather fringe on her garment. "They won't be afraid while I am with them."

"We should take down the teepee and be ready to leave," Drumbeater said. "When Sibley takes the *washechu* girl-children, we will return to rice camp."

"I will make ready, Husband," Willow Song said with sad eyes. "But I will miss the girl-children. Otter will miss them as well."

"Evan Jacobson is a human being," Many Beavers said. "Maybe we will see them again."

39

"Send Us at Least 1,000 Men, Well Armed . . . to Drive Back These Murderers as Far as Possible. There Are Only Two Ways to Keep Our Settlements, Either to have a Strong Force to hold Them on the Reservation or Kill Them All at Once, and That Would Be Best," Sheriff of Brown County   *St. Cloud Democrat*, September 26, 1862

HAT WAS HAPPENING? Maybe the Long Knives didn't see their rags. He tied another one to his bow, another to the mane of his spotted pony. Waved still another over his head. The Long Knives with pointed guns came into the camp from all directions.

"What's wrong?" Willow Song's eyes showed alarm, and her face turned white as the cloth. "Don't they see?"

Many Beavers took the hands of the girl-children and stepped forward.

A soldier with a rifle took Little Bird's hand. She cried out and clung to Many Beavers' legs. Badger kicked the soldier and screamed at him in her strange tongue.

Everything happened at once. The soldier knelt beside Badger and asked a question in the *washechu* tongue. Badger looked at him and seemed confused, shook her head. She reached out for Little Bird and dragged her back to Willow Song.

"Evan Jacobson," Drumbeater said. The name rolled out of his mouth. Thanks to Wakantanka he remembered the strange name. "Evan Jacobson." When the soldier didn't respond, Drumbeater stepped closer and repeated the foreign name, the name of the life-and-death friend, the name that meant nothing. The soldier took the butt of his rifle and clubbed

Drumbeater to the ground, pulling Drumbeater's knife from its sheath and adding it to a pile on the ground guarded by a young soldier with a gun.

Willow Song rushed to his side while the soldier dragged away the two girl-children, screaming in protest. Another soldier armed with a gun stopped Drumbeater from following the *washechu* children.

"Evan Jacobson!" Drumbeater called out, screaming until his throat hurt. No one paid any attention. Perhaps he said the name incorrectly. He looked towards the drum, safely resting on the travois.

Many Beavers calmly picked up her pack and followed after the girl-children. The solder spoke angry words in his tongue but didn't stop her when she joined the small ones. Little Bird clung to her neck and wouldn't let go. Badger stared with vacant eyes, no longer angry.

The soldier pushed Willow Song away from Drumbeater, using the butt of his gun to nudge her away.

"What's happening?" Willow Song clutched Otter, still in his cradle-board, to her breast. Drumbeater saw his face was covered with the spotted sickness, heard his voice crack with fever. When he looked into Willow Song's face, he saw that her face, too, was covered with red spots. Would they both be lost to him? None of the People survived the spotted sickness.

All through the village of Red Iron, soldiers pushed the women away from the men, taking the weapons from the peaceful warriors.

"Where are they taking us?" Willow Song shrilled. "They are taking us someplace."

"I want to stay with my family," Drumbeater's words gasped out of his mouth, his head aching from the rifle butt.

"Sibley is not here," Red Iron said. "It is a misunderstanding. Don't fight back."

Soldiers herded the women and children to Little Crow's deserted camp.

"Why doesn't Sibley stop this?" Drumbeater said. "We sent the tracks of the *washechu*. He knows we are not the warring tribes."

Red Iron strode over to the cluster of Long Knives still on their horses, with a mixed-blood along to translate. "The white rags," he said in halting English. "Peace."

"Shut up, old man," a young soldier said. His face was very white and his hair was as red as the fox. Drumbeater wondered if he was Evan

Jacobson but Evan Jacobson was the man-with-wooden-wheels, not a Long Knife. The young soldier called out more angry words in his strange tongue.

"What did he say?" Red Iron looked to the mixed-blood.

"He says to step back or he'll shoot," the mixed-blood said. "They want the men separated from the women and children."

"But why?" Red Iron said. "What difference does it make if we stay with our families? We are at peace with the White Eyes."

The mixed-blood shrugged. "Their chief says to separate us."

"I'll fight," an elder said. "I won't be treated this way."

"It's a misunderstanding," Red Iron said. "They don't realize we are friendly."

Colonel Sibley rode into the camp, his eyes blazing. He spoke angry words to the soldiers.

"He is angry at the Long Knives," the mixed blood whispered to Drumbeater and Standing Tall. "Says that we are friendly."

Sibley barked an order to an assistant.

Long Knives scattered in all directions. Drumbeater caught a glimpse of Many Beavers and the two girl-children being loaded onto a wagon driven by a soldier dressed in blue. He pushed past the others and ran up to the wagon.

"Evan Jacobson!" The captives looked at him with blank expressions and the driver didn't look at him at all. "Evan Jacobson!" The sun glinted off Little Bird's hair, and she stared at him with blue eyes, clutching Badger's dress with a dirty hand and hanging onto Many Beavers with the other hand.

"Get back!" A soldier guarding the captives raised his gun and pointed it at Drumbeater. When Drumbeater did not step back, he cocked the rifle with a loud clicking sound and called out angry words.

Drumbeater had no choice but to step away from the wagon. As the *washechu* girl-children drove away, he felt their strong medicine leave with them. Courage drained away. He remembered to fetch his drum. What if Otter and Willow Song died from the spotted sickness?

Standing Tall sang softly, and Drumbeater recognized the cadence and melody.

"Why are you singing your death song?"

"It's good for a man to be ready to die," Standing Tall said matter-of-factly. "I'm an old man."

He should have taken Willow Song and Otter and left when he had the chance. The drum warmed his arms while his eyes searched the place where Otter and Willow Song had disappeared into the crowd of women and children. She had not taken the travois with her, did not have her precious stores of food and lodging. Surely they would not expect the People to sleep out in the cold.

Little Bird and Badger had returned to the life-and-death friend. He must believe it would happen. His wife and son were beyond reach but maybe he could get them back. He had left in his power the keeping of the drum. He must guard the drum at all cost. It was his duty.

"After dark settles, I will escape."

"Return to your wife's people." Standing Tall's song burst forth from his lips for a brief moment, quiet and low. "You have done your duty. Now you must guard the drum."

A mixed blood came by with the word that Sibley would distribute the food stores before letting the braves rejoin their families. He demanded they sit in rows of eight men in order to receive payment from the Great Chief in Washington. At last, something sensible was happening. They would collect payment and return to their families.

Drumbeater, near the back of the group of warriors, cared little for the payment from the Great Chief, wanted only to rejoin Willow Song. They sat silently through the afternoon, waiting for the payment to arrive.

But before the sun had set, soldiers clanked by with chains and leg irons. They started at the front of the group and began the slow task of chaining the warriors together at their ankles. When Drumbeater saw what was happening he pulled back, moving a few inches here and there whenever he thought the Long Knives looked elsewhere, backing away from where the Long Knives enslaved the People.

Crooked Lightning had warned that the Long Knives wanted slaves. Drumbeater remembered how the sandhill cranes had flown in a chain of circles—the Great Mystery warning him. Now the People were tethered like horses with circles of iron. He had been too stupid to understand.

Soldiers guarded the group of Dakota warriors. There were many Dakotas and few soldiers. The braves murmured that they should rise up as one and free themselves but Red Iron urged restraint.

"This is a misunderstanding. We will work this out in council. Think of our women and children."

Drumbeater squeezed backwards, away from the Long Knives and their chains. An elderly grandfather protested until he saw the drum in his hands. "Go quickly, my son," he breathed a coppery smell from his mouth. "Guard the drum for our people."

The grandfather stood and called out to the young soldier. When the Long Knife turned towards the old man's voice, Drumbeater sneaked through the lines and leapt into brush along the river. His heart fluttered in his chest like a bird caught in a snare. He gripped the drum, breathing a silent prayer of thanks to the Great Mystery.

Suddenly he heard the sound of singing, the strong heart song. They sang for him, that he would have strength to guard the sacred drum. A harsh command from the Long Knives and a gunshot stopped the songs.

He crept through the bushes until he was downstream of the camp. He tried to think of a plan to free the People from the Long Knives. They surrendered the captives willingly and yet they were being chained, treated as if they were the ones who had made war on the *washechu*. Another lie. Sibley had said only those involved with the uprising would be taken. He said the others would be free to return to their villages. Lies. All lies.

He thought of Little Bird and Badger, safe among their people with Many Beavers there to care for them. He smiled when he thought how Little Bird clung to the neck of Many Beavers like a baby loon on its mother's back. And how Badger stepped forward so fearlessly to protect her sister. What *wakon* she had. The white-haired power of the Little Bird was nothing compared to the fierce courage of Badger. He breathed a prayer of protection over that one—that Badger would find her way back to Evan Jacobson, the man whose name meant nothing.

His body trembled with the night chill. He had only his leather leggings to cover him, and the moccasins so tenderly made by Willow Song. A sorrow so painful gripped him at thought of her that he bit the side of his hand until it bled.

Be strong! He steadied his reserve and committed his way to the Great Mystery. He would follow where the Long Knives took the People. He would trust in the Great Mystery to guide him.

Drumbeater climbed a tall tree beside the river, holding the sacred drum securely under his chin until he was in a high branch. Then he cleared his throat and drummed the cadence of the strong-heart song, singing out in a high clear voice the haunting words and music. A startled loon answered from the stream. Perhaps it was unsafe to sing lest the Long Knives search and find him. He doubted they would leave the confines of the camp. They were busy guarding the peaceful Dakota while Little Crow and his warriors slipped farther and farther away.

Drumbeater sang loud and long, knowing the *wakon* of the sacred drum carried words of courage to his brothers locked in the irons of the White Eyes. Trapped like the beaver tribe in traps of iron. They had trusted the words of the Long Knives. Foolish. They could not be trusted.

He made a song about the *washechu*, how they swarmed in like a blizzard from the east until they owned the whole world. The words fell from his lips as if from the Great Mystery. He willed courage into his words, courage that would help his brothers escape. Praying that his voice was loud enough to be heard in the camp and that Otter and Willow Song would hear and be strengthened.

When he heard a voice below him, he thought his life was over. He started his death song, but instead Star Fist called to him from the darkness.

"Be quiet! You'll call the Long Knives down upon us."

Drumbeater climbed down from the tree. Star Fist and Blue Bottle awaited him.

"You were foolish to surrender," Star Fist said. "The Long Knives will kill us all. They have no concern for truth."

"If you would have joined in the beginning," Blue Bottle's eyes glowed in the waning moonlight, "it would be different now."

"You are right," Drumbeater said. All anger towards Blue Bottle dissolved in the strong truth. "I see it now after witnessing their treachery with my own eyes."

"Come with us," Star Fist said. "Little Six leads us to attack the Long Knives at the Potato River."

Drumbeater felt himself at a crossroads. It was his chance for revenge on the *washechu*, to push the White Eyes out of Leaf Country. Perhaps there was no chance of freeing Willow Song and Otter. Perhaps they were already dead. A pain pierced his heart to think of his future warrior dying away from his father.

"I must free my wife and son—if I live, I will join you."

"You will never learn!" Blue Bottle stormed away in disgust but Star Fist lingered. He reached out a hand and stroked the sacred drum. "The People received great strength from listening to your song." His face hid in the shadows and his voice was as mournful as the wolf tribe. "Standing Tall helped the captives and yet now he is chained like an animal."

"What does Little Crow say about this?"

"Little Crow says that the White Eyes are so afraid of the tracks on paper that they will do anything. He says that if Sibley turns over the peaceful Dakotas it will silence the white man's track and bring peace to the Great Father in Washington."

"The white man's track." Drumbeater cringed before the words. He had hoped the white man's track sent to Sibley would bring peace to the People. "The white man's track must be strong medicine only to the *washechu.*"

"Perhaps." Star Fist sighed. "Or perhaps the mixed-bloods who sent the white man's tracks were untrustworthy."

Drumbeater looked at Star Fist in surprise. He had never thought of him as a wise man but suddenly realized that Star Fist knew more than he. Knew enough to stay away from the *washechu* except with a war club.

"I have news of your uncle," Star Fist said. "That he was arrested by Sibley two days ago and is in irons."

"He is alive?"

"Ho," Star Fist said. "He fought with us at Wood Lake."

Drumbeater thought of his uncle, how he'd be glad to know the girl-children were returned to their people. He had fulfilled his sacred duty.

"Little Crow thinks the warriors will be *otkeya.*"

"No!" Drumbeater was aghast. Death by the rope of the *washechu* was most dishonorable.

"Forget your wife. Perhaps the *washechu* will be kind to the women and children."

Star Fist rubbed the top of the drum once again. "Come and fight the washechu at Potato River. Perhaps we can stop them at the river and keep the open prairies for the People."

"I will come . . . after I find my wife and son."

His strength left with Star Fist. He tucked the drum into the hollowed recess of a dead tree and breathed a prayer, asking the drum to forgive him for neglecting it, telling the drum how his wife and child needed him, that he would come back and get it again when he could. Then he crept back towards the camp, weary beyond description, determined to free Willow Song and Otter.

The night held many secrets. A coyote called from the woods beyond the camp. A mouse skittered across the dried grass. A striped skunk searched for food along the river.

Long ago he had played the *coyatanka* outside the tent of Willow Song during the time of their courtship. Drumbeater had blown all his longings into the wooden flute, and the song had left the *coyatanka* in sweet music, music so sweet that it won her heart.

Tonight was the same, yet different. He had poured his spirit into the music of the drum. But it was not music of love, but war. That night he made his decision. While he had played the drum and sang the strong-heart songs to the People, Drumbeater's heart turned.

If his uncle died at the rope of the Long Knives, he would avenge him. Drumbeater would try to free Willow Song and Otter, but if they lived or died, his decision was the same. He saw it clearly now. The destroyer had come. *Washechu* raged like a great blizzard from the east.

He would make a song about the end of the People. How the track of the White Eyes had stolen Leaf Country. Warriors were captured and their bows broken. The People exhausted themselves for nothing. He would continue the fight. If he were the only warrior left alive, he would fight until he had no breath.

Tonight he would find Willow Song and Otter and, if they lived, rescue them from the fat-eaters. In the morning, he would build an *eneepee* and make medicine. He would paint his face half black and half green in honor of his uncle's medicine.

Then he would go to his death.

40

L
ISTEN," GUST SAID WHILE READING THE *DEMOCRAT.* "Governor Ramsey asks Minnesotans to make mittens for the troops. Says there is great suffering for men living in tents without mittens."

Gust looked up and saw Dagmar's face working with grief. He knew she thought of her boys, fighting without proper clothing.

"We can knit mittens for the soldiers here at Pomme de Terre," Serena said. "Somewhere another mother knits for your sons, Dagmar."

Anton scrounged another bundle of wool and carded it for the spinning wheel while Gust whittled basswood sticks into velvety smooth needles.

"We have needles," Serena said. "Who will use those?"

"I will," Gust said. "Ma taught me to knit before I was old enough to know it was women's work. It kept me busy when my leg pained."

"That was smart thinking on her part," Dagmar said. "Busy hands make a body forget its pains."

"Didn't your brothers tease you?" Serena said.

"They did but never when Ma was around," Gust said. "Besides my uncle said everyone knits in Iceland, men and women alike."

"Funny to think of Olaus Reierson knitting," Dagmar said. "I wonder if he knows how."

It became their regular routine to knit after supper while Anton read aloud. He stumbled over the English words, but Gust helped him with the words he didn't know. They read about the hangings in Mankato on December 26th. They learned about Lincoln's Emancipation Proclamation that freed the slaves in rebel states. They kept up with the Battle of Murfreesboro in Tennessee. Anton's voice rose with excitement when he read about Lincoln replacing General Burnside with General Hooker as head of the Army of the Potomac. When all else was read and re-read, they read the advertisements for patent medicines and farm machinery.

Gust and Anton built a pen for King to keep him away from his mother's milk.

"You don't need it all," Gust said with a laugh, watching King butt against the fence bawling for his mother.

"Ja, he's a greedy one," Anton said.

"Aren't all kings greedy?" Gust said. "Greedy for gold, more power."

"Ja," agreed Anton. "And full of bullshit."

Gust enjoyed working with Anton. Unlike his father, Anton remained levelheaded during stressful times. Gust learned to be at ease, not fear a tirade of anger over the simplest of problems. Sometimes Gust still tensed up, waiting for the anger that never came.

Every day they shoveled manure, piled it outside the barn door to be spread on the fields in the spring, forked clean straw into the stalls for bedding, and carried water buckets filled at holes chopped in the river. The work never ended.

Gust lifted a heavy bucket and carefully poured it into the trough for Buddy and Bets. They bawled in anticipation and nuzzled into the icy water. Then he took the other bucket over to the pen where Dolly and Rosebud were kept. He petted their sides and scratched their back, whispered encouragement into their pink ears.

Gust dipped a small bucket of water from the trough and brought it to King's pen. The young bull calf butted against the pail, splashing it on Gust's leg, greedy to drink but unsure how to get the liquid into his mouth. Gust put the fingers from his right hand into King's mouth and let him suck on them, his tongue rough and strong. Slowly Gust lowered his hand and King's nuzzle into the bucket of water. King snorted and tossed his head when he tasted the water. Gust slowly withdrew his hand and King kept drinking.

"He's a smart one," Anton said. "He'll train easy to the yoke."

"I need a mate for him. It won't be easy to find one." Gust took a handful of dried straw from the pen and wiped his hands.

"Don't be so sure," Anton said. "When the spring traffic starts, you will be amazed at what the ox-carters have to sell or trade."

"If the traffic starts up again,"

"It will," Anton said. "People need land, and there's plenty of it around here."

THE SOLDIERS MET IN THE LOFT throughout winter. Each time Gust and Anton hurried to the barn to escape the prayers.

"What do they say?" Gust asked one day after the men had left. "Do they pray the same prayers we learned in Confirmation?"

"Nei, they pray from the heart." Serena fingered the hem of her apron, first twisting it, and then smoothing it out against her leg. "They speak to God alone, and with boldness."

"What would the minister say?" Gust said. "Perhaps it's heresy."

"I've heard no heresy," Serena said with cheeks aflame. "Only sincere prayers from honest men. There can be no harm in that."

"I'm not sure," Gust said.

"Don't make up your mind until you hear them for yourself," Serena said. "Don't be such a chicken."

Gust planted himself by the door the next time the men gathered for prayer. He pulled out his deck of cards, played solitaire while pretending he wasn't listening to the words from upstairs. Serena teased him, saying that he situated himself for a quick get-away if things became heretical. Maybe she was right. The prayers were foreign, so different.

When the soldiers finished, Gust had little to say. That night, after they had climbed into the loft for bed, Serena asked him what he thought about it.

"They're religious fanatics," Gust said. "Harmless."

"Why do you say such a thing?" Serena said. "They pray for us and our families—you should be grateful."

"You may be right."

He pulled her over to himself, smoothing the flatness of her belly, smelling the fragrance of fresh bread in her hair. He wondered if she was with child again. Another baby to take the place of grief in her heart, as Dagmar had read in the coffee grounds. When he repaid his father, they might return to Burr Oak for a long visit over the winter months. Maybe she would have a small one to tote with her. How pleased his mother would be for a grandchild. Gust nuzzled her throat. She smelled so good; always smelled so good. He pulled the pin from her hair and stretched the golden tresses out on the pillow. In the darkness, he imagined how it looked, silken strands for his pleasure only.

"Did you notice how the door to our cabin was chopped in two?" Serena pulled away and sat up in the dark room. "I found the door hacked almost in two behind the outhouse." Her voice cracked. "Indians did it."

"Serena-girl," he said in his most calming voice. Leave it to a woman to bring up such a thing at a time like this. "You worry too much. There's nothing to worry about."

"Gust," she said. "I know Indians tried to burn the house. They'll be back when spring comes to finish the job."

"It's over." He reached up and smoothed the hair hanging down her back. "Come."

She obeyed, of course. Serena was always a dutiful wife. But Gust lay awake, thinking of Lena, the perjury so easily committed.

So much depended on the wheat.

41

The Army of the Potomac, 1400 Killed; 8000 Wounded
The Rebel Loss 2,500

St Cloud Democrat, January 25, 1863

Y OU CANNOT GO," STAR FIST SAID in a fit of coughing, his face flushed red as *talutah*. He wiped his mouth on the corner of a ragged blanket and fell back on his bed of pine boughs. "*Wazeeyah* is too strong."

Crooked Lightning had promised Star Fist's *uncheedah* that he would care for him. Though Drumbeater's belly cramped and his feet were numb in the thin leather of his moccasins, it was his duty to carry out Uncle's promise to the old grandmother.

"I will find willow bark to ease your fever," Drumbeater said as he sorted through a stack of hides in their small shelter. "It grows where we hunt *sinkpe*, the muskrat tribe."

"Then take the best blanket." Star Fist coughed until he could not breathe and pushed a heavy blanket toward Drumbeater. Though Star Fist's skin burned like fire, his teeth chattered like the squirrel tribe. When he finally caught his breath he said, "I will stay close to the fire."

An early *icamnatanka* brought the Moon of Difficulty. The blizzard prevented them from rejoining Blue Bottle as planned. Huge drifts of *wogan* covered the earth. Rivers froze.

Drumbeater and Star Fist found shelter in this empty den of the bear tribe beneath a windblown tree. The small den smelled of earth and musk. They tore a smoke hole through the tree roots above them and kept a small fire burning. They

214

piled snow around the outside of the den and cut pine boughs to keep them off the cold ground inside. Without the heavy hides of *Tatanka*, they were never warm.

Drumbeater looked to see if spots grew on Star Fist's face. There were no spots but surely the evil medicine of the white eyes caused his fever.

Drumbeater sat on a small log and wrapped muskrat skins around his feet, turning the fur toward his skin and tying them with lengths of sinew. His throat choked with bitter memories.

He had failed to rescue Otter and Willow Song. The looking glass had predicted death. The omens were never wrong. He had found where they were being held but had to wait for a chance to get past the Long Knives. When he finally crept into the camp, he found their bodies readied for burial by Red Iron's Woman. The White Eyes robbed him even of the chance to mourn for his family in an honorable way. They had killed his wife and son as surely as the spotted sickness sprang from their medicine.

Drumbeater tossed gnawed muskrat bones into the fire along with small sticks of wood. Star Fist dozed with ragged blankets tucked around him. Out of habit, Drumbeater glanced up at the place where the sacred drum rested among the roots. The painted leather of the drum head was the only color in the dark den other than the yellow flames and green pine boughs. He wrapped himself in the blanket, gathered his resolve and stepped out into the cold.

Wazeeyah snatched his breath and threatened to steal his blanket. Drumbeater pulled it closer around him and slogged through waist-high snow into the face of the North Wind, making his way to the riverbank where the willows grew. His lungs ached from the cold, and he pulled the blanket over his face. How he longed for the shelter of *itokaga* and a good buffalo hide.

Last winter he and Willow Song were snug in their teepee, telling stories and singing songs while Otter slept beneath the dream catcher on his cradleboard. The People survived though *Wazeeyah* blew hard and long. Stores of dried berries, maple syrup, meat, and wild rice fed them throughout the Moon of Difficulty. When one tribe member lacked, there was help from another. It was the way of the People.

This year was different.

This year the People had been deceived by the white eyes, imprisoned and enslaved in irons. His uncle had been killed by the rope of the Long Knives though he was a brave warrior deserving of honor instead of disgrace. Drumbeater faced the winter without his family, without his tribe. Only Star Fist remained.

If Drumbeater thought about it too long he would lose his mind. Instead he pushed his eyes toward the good things that had happened. He had returned the *washechu* girl-children to the man-with-the-wooden-wheels. He kept the sacred drum safe through all the trouble. He at least had kept the drum.

A thick layer of frozen snow topped the drifts in open areas, and by careful maneuvering, Drumbeater walked across the top of the snow. Snowshoes would make the task easier, but they were lost to the white eyes. Perhaps he could gather enough willow branches for a new set. They had almost enough sinew from the muskrat hides.

Drumbeater reached the riverbank and plunged into a soft drift of snow, flailing to free himself. His fingers fumbled thick and clumsy as he cut willow branches. Once he thought he heard the screech of *hinakaya*—a bad omen. But perhaps it was the howling wind. Only when Drumbeater had filled his arms with willow branches, did he turn back toward their shelter.

It was easier with the strong wind behind him, and he followed his tracks back through the snow. Ahead he saw the smoke from their fire. *Wazeeyah* pushed it away from Drumbeater, so he smelled only the scent of the fresh willow. Another owl screeched. Then a sudden burst of bright flame and black plumes.

Drumbeater's heart wrenched, and he stumbled toward the den, wading as fast as he could through the drifted snow. If only he had snowshoes. He dropped the willow branches in his haste and held tighter to the gray blanket that billowed around him in the wind. His chest heaved with exertion, and sweat beaded his forehead and turned to ice. He prayed the sinews would hold the skins secure around his feet.

"No!" His voice caught and carried away in the wind. The den was on fire. He smelled the heavy smoke as he came nearer and saw Star Fist sprawled in the snow.

Drumbeater dropped to his knees next to Star Fist. His hair was singed and his clothes smoked. His cheeks blistered red, and bouts of coughing prevented him from speaking. His lips were like wild berries next to the charred blackness of his face.

"I slept too close." Star Fist whispered and broke into wails of mourning. "The blanket caught fire."

Smoke billowed from the den's entrance. Drumbeater struggled to his feet and rushed to the mouth of the den. Choking smoke pushed him back. He covered his mouth and nose with the corner of his blanket and pushed his face into the black cloud. Fire had spread until the entire tree flamed, whipped by the raging wind.

Through the dense smoke he saw the shriveled hides, the burning drum, and the twisted painted leather.

"I tried to save the drum." Star Fist's wails changed to his death song.

Drumbeater had failed the People. It was his responsibility, not Star Fist's. He removed the blanket from his shoulders and covered the burned body of his friend. He had not considered him a friend until that very moment. Star Fist, great warrior among the People.

Drumbeater collapsed beyond the smoke and sucked clean air into his lungs. The *washechu* blanket had caught fire and caused the ruin of what little they had. Their small store of hides was gone. No sinews left for snowshoes. No fur to protect their feet.

All because of the white eyes.

Star Fist had been right all along. Drumbeater thought back to that day when Star Fist had left with Crooked Lightning to fight against the Long Knives. It was impossible for the People to live in peace with the *washechu* tribe. Not even this small den was safe from their intrusion. Their medicine polluted everything in its path. A single blanket from the fat eaters was seed for disaster among the People. Everywhere their seed was planted meant a harvest of loss and humiliation. Worse than *Wazeeyah* in the Moon of Difficulty. Like the blizzard that blew in from the east in his grandfather's vision with *wogan* so heavy the mountains crumbled beneath its weight.

They would not rest until they owned the whole world.

Drumbeater's arms ached to hold his wife and son. His eyes longed to see his uncle among the People in Leaf Country. Most of all, his hands yearned to beat the sacred drum. It was the meaning of his life. It was his name. All lost to him.

Lost forever.

Without benefit of the drum, Drumbeater's voice rose in a loud wail, singing a new song. "Hi, hi, yo. Hi, hi, yo."

He sang how the fat eaters devoured everything of the People. They wanted the earth, the sky, and the bird tribes. He sang of their greed to own the whole world and the strong medicine of their track on birch paper that cut the earth into parcels of dirt. He sang of their lies and betrayal.

His voice rose higher than the mournful howl of *Wazeeyah*. "Hi, hi, yo. Hi, hi, yo." The wind carried the words to the Great Mystery, lifting them higher and higher to the mists of the Great Beyond.

He sang of his brave uncle killed by the Long Knives' rope, the warrior who was honorable to his life-and-death-friend and mighty in battle.

"Hi,hi,yo."

He sang of the wisdom of Star Fist who knew the words of the white eyes could not be trusted. He sang the strong-heart song for his friend until Star Fist grew quiet. Drumbeater forced himself to go to his side and look for signs of life.

His lungs had stopped. His heart now silent. His song was over.

Drumbeater felt the weight of solitude. Alone. No comforting tribe surrounding him. Hot tears pushed against the back of his eyelids, but he refused to weep. He was a warrior. His duty lay clear before him. He lifted the blanket from Star Fist's body and wrapped it around himself. He prayed to *Watatanka* to guide him. He needed another shelter. Food. He would rob the muskrat tribe of their stored roots and ask them to understand his desperation. With knife in hand he headed back toward the river.

Tears for women and war whoops for warriors to drown sorrow.

There was nothing left for the People in Leaf Country. Nothing except revenge.

42

"Congress Appropriates $200,000 for Victims of Uprising"
St. Cloud Democrat, April 16, 1863

BUDDY AND BETS DRAGGED WITH UNITED EFFORT and turned a strip of black richness that quickened Gust's pulse. The loamy field smelled fragrant of damp earth. The smell of money. His father always insisted on straight furrows, had once whipped him with a willow switch for leaving a snaking line across the field.

His mother had begged him to stop. "He's just a boy with a bad leg."

But his father had not wavered in his determination to produce straight furrows and obedient sons. Gust slapped a gnat on his forehead. By God, this furrow would be straight as an arrow.

It was just as he had always dreamed, his own land, rich and virgin. He had spread the rotted manure to feed the soil, another odor of money. The seeds would grow like magic, yielding a harvest big enough to pay off his father and buy a mate for King. He would train the young oxen, and next spring he would sell them to the ox-carters. Sturdy oak from the woodlot by the river would fashion a yoke. Gust would carve in the evenings after it was too dark to work outside. Too bad he hadn't thought of that earlier. He could have been working on the ox yoke instead of knitting mittens for strangers.

Buying the farm was the right thing to do even if it meant delaying payment to his father. Lord knew his father didn't need the money. He would be paid in full after the harvest and be none the wiser for it. Ja, he did the right thing.

Buddy's tail swished a bluetailed fly from his back, and the oxen bawled a piteous cry, lumbering against the traces. "Whoa, Buddy. Whoa, Bets." And by then, Serena would surely have another baby. At one point he had almost asked Private Harris to pray for another child but had stopped himself just in time. The words had almost jumped out of his mouth before he caught hold of himself. God would send another child when He was good and ready—there was no use praying about it.

He called to Buddy and Bets, sawing on the reins to finish the last furrow, the field finally ready for planting, Gust tethered the team under a shady oak in a patch of bluestem grass rich and sweet. The beasts snagged great mouthfuls with grinding jaws.

Mourning doves sang, and a pair of Canada geese flew up from the river, their wings splashing in the water, their mating calls sweet and haunting. Gust cradled his rifle in his left hand and scattered the precious wheat seed using a wide throwing motion with his right arm. The rifle's weight made him clumsy and off balance. He refused to think of the possibility of Indians hiding in the bushes along the edges of the fields, determined to finish the planting if it killed him.

Unless he planted the wheat, there would be no harvest.

He thought of the look on his father's face when he returned with money in hand. Though his brothers were off to war getting glory, he was the one planting wheat and harvesting a crop.

Wheat kernels fell in silky waves from his hand. With just the right arc in his arm he broadcast them across the black dirt. By God, it would be a harvest. And there would be another baby, a boy named Tosten after his older brother. He and Tosten would work side by side on this very land, enjoy a relationship Gust had always longed for. The dream entertained him while he planted, working all morning without sign of Indians. Dreams had kept him company every day these recent weeks while he labored over spring plowing and planting.

Gust trudged slowly home in the twilight, exhausted and dirty, his leg swollen and painful. After planting the wheat, Gust had picked a small mound of rocks from another field. As he had moved a boulder to the corner of the field, the rock slipped from his hands and fell on his bad leg leaving a deep scratch, more of a nuisance than anything else.

Gust sighed. He was surprised to discover wetness on his cheeks. He wiped his face with the back of his hands, streaking the dust in the tears. His ankle throbbed. He changed directions and headed for the river. A quick swim in the cool water would make him feel better before he headed back to the fort. Colonel Sibley should be through any day. Gust was more than ready to move his wife out to the farm where she belonged.

He scarcely noticed the frogs chirping or the flutter of ducks in the water. The river busied with animals coming to drink and the music of loons calling in the shadows. A red-winged blackbird trilled in the rushes. He spied a doe and fawn drinking across the river, just south of him.

He undressed and hung his clothes across a boulder by the shoreline and waded into the water, biting cold after the heat of the fields. Pain surged through his bad leg. Damn! After the initial shock, his leg eased. Gust lowered himself in a sandy spot, letting the cool water calm his ragged emotions and sore ankle. He laid back as the shallow water washed over him, cooling and refreshing.

He looked at his crippled leg, slightly smaller than his good leg, scarred from the original wound so many years ago. He remembered his father screaming at him to get away from the cow, how she startled at the screams and jumped to one side, crushing Gust's leg. Then it was only his own screams he remembered.

Gust drifted in the current, enjoying the coolness when suddenly the birds quit singing. The hair on his neck stood up. He was helpless to defend himself, naked in the water. He paddled back toward his clothes, trying to act like nothing was wrong. His eyes examined the bushes lining both sides of the river, his heart in his throat, as he slowly moved toward the shore. The doe and fawn stood motionless at the water's edge, heads cocked toward the bend in the river, no longer drinking. Gust trained his eyes on the river's bend about fifty yards south of where he paddled.

A white flutter caught his eye. Gust pretended he didn't notice. He hummed in an attempt to appear unconcerned and dipped his hair in the icy water. He focused on his gun lying on the bank and edged toward it.

When he was partially shielded by a clump of cattails, Gust leapt to his feet, his body heavy after the buoyancy of the water. He stubbed his toe on a stone but ran, stumbling in the water, until he was safely positioned behind the large boulder at the water's edge, his gun grasped in his hand, pain ripping through his leg.

He peeked around the boulder, eyes fastened on the spot where he had spied the white flutter. It had looked like feathers in an Indian's hair but maybe it was just another deer coming to drink. His breath came in pumping gasps. He could have been killed lying careless in the river. What was wrong with him? He was always doing foolish things. His father was right—he was so dumb he'd never amount to anything. Gust struggled into his pants, dragging the cloth over his wet legs, cursing himself for letting down his guard.

Gust scrutinized each bush and tree around him. He heard the bugler blowing chow time at the fort. His belly growled, it had been hours since breakfast. Hell, it might have been a bird or the tail of a deer. But it wasn't a deer. He had been soaking in the water and his peripheral vision caught a white flutter. Nei, it was white feathers in the black hair of a savage. Another minute floating downstream and he would have been murdered.

Gust struggled into his shirt and boots, hiding behind the boulder. Ja, a man couldn't be too careful with the Sioux. They were devilish in their trickery, like the trolls of the Old Country.

Gust waited until dusk gathered around the reeds, his gun trained on the bend in the river. He had never killed at a human being before and wondered if he could do it. God, help me.

His leg burned in the cramped position, and Gust cursed the empty willow tea bottle in the pocket of his shirt. In desperation he broke a small willow switch and chewed the bark. Perhaps it helped a little but the bitterness burned his tongue.

No one at the fort would miss him. He had made it clear to the captain that he was his own boss, not to be guarded and fretted over like a woman.

Now he would pay the price for his stubbornness. Oh, God, if the savage is really there, let him show himself.

The words were hardly in his mind when Gust saw an Indian rise from his hiding place in a clump of reeds. He wore black and green paint on his face, white feathers in his hair and carried a small axe. Gust carefully aimed his gun and slowly squeezed the trigger. The recoil of the gun pushed him backwards from the boulder and by the time he righted himself again, he saw the Indian run over the bank to the southeast, out of sight.

He had missed. Missed by a mile. Some soldier he would have made.

Gust reloaded his gun and carefully limped toward the thicket where the Indian had waited for him. Nothing left but tracks. Damn the Sioux! Damn them to hell!

When he returned to the fort, his leg paining up to his knee and the cut throbbing, he bumped into Captain McLarty by the stable.

"Good news," Captain McLarty said. "Sibley marches through tomorrow."

Gust's had planned on telling Captain McLarty about his brush with the Indian. But surely if an army marched through, the Indians would hightail for distant places. He heaved a sigh of relief.

"Then it's safe to return to the farm?"

"I think so," Captain McLarty said.

43

"Senator Wilkinson Urges Indians to be Banished from State"
St. Cloud Democrat, March 23, 1863

THE WEATHER WARMED IN LATE MARCH. After months of deep snow and bitter winds, the air freshened, smelled of damp earth. Robins sang in the pre-dawn mornings. Daylight stretched longer every day. A gentle rain took the last dirty drifts.

Gust drove the lumbering oxen to the river. Much easier than hauling water in wooden buckets that had been necessary when the snow was too deep for the animals to safely maneuver. Gust stood on the bank and sniffed loudly, pausing to rest while the animals drank.

His father always predicted three more snows after the first robin. Gust scanned the skies. It was clear blue from east to west. Good planting weather. He would return to the farm and get the crop in. No one could stop him.

He heard the screeching wheels of the stage driving into the fort. Maybe the whistling boy was driving. There would be no letters, of course, but several issues of the *St. Cloud Democrat*—maybe something about the reparation investigation. You'd think the government would have bigger fish to fry.

Gust limped back to the team. "Gee Buddy! Gee Bets!" The oxen, slow as always, made no effort to hurry. "Come on now!" He reached for a stick beside the cow path and slapped Buddy in the back. When he didn't respond, Gust goaded it in the hindquarters, cursing, He bent to pick up a small rock and was about to chuck it at Buddy's massive head when he stopped himself and threw it as hard as he could at a nearby basswood tree. His father was cruel to his animals, poking them in their snouts with the sharp tines of a pitchfork, kicking them in their genitals. By God, he was turning into his father.

The thought sobered him and helped him plod behind the beasts, entering the fort after the others were already gathered by the stage.

A uniformed armed private rode beside the whistling driver.

"I fought mud all the way from St. Cloud," the driver said. "Thought the stage would sink down to China."

"What's the latest from the front?" Jon Sverdrup called out.

"All bad," the man threw down the reins and jumped to the ground. "They're still counting the dead from Murfreesboro. No clear winner."

"How many dead?" Private Comfort asked.

"Not sure. But Abe Lincoln kicked out Burnsides. Put Hooker in charge."

"What else?"

"Abe Lincoln signed a Conscription Act. Men between twenty and forty-five are required to fight unless they pay $300 for an exemption."

The crowd turned silent.

"They're going to force a man to join up?" said Private Comfort. "You can't make someone fight."

"And they're letting the rich off?" Anton spit into the dirt at his feet. "I'm forty-six, but if I were younger, I wouldn't go. I've crops to tend."

"A decent man fights for his country without being forced," Jon Sverdrup said. "Are there that many slackers?"

Gust began preparing his wagon for the trip back to the farm while the driver passed out the mail. He climbed under the wagon box and greased the wooden wheels. Rocks waited to be picked on the south field. Too much work for one man to do.

"Where do you think you're going?" Captain McLarty stood in the barn door. "I haven't given permission for you to leave."

"I don't need your permission." Gust had hoped to leave without McLarty knowing about it. He stood. "I've got crops to put in."

"I can't guarantee your safety," Captain McLarty said. "Think about your missus."

"I am thinking about my missus." Gust felt his face turning red and heard his voice harden. "I'm thinking that unless we plant a crop, there will be no harvest. Believe me, I'm thinking of my missus."

"You can't be foolish enough to consider taking your wife out," Captain McLarty said. "You know what the Sioux do to a woman found alone. You'll be out in the fields. Think of her."

It was the stinging truth, and Gust knew it. His shoulders slumped, and he leaned against the wall of the barn. The stockade made of dry wood already gaped where the green lumber had shrunk, but Gust knew it would stand against the Indians.

Gust faced Captain McLarty. "Look," he said, this time without the smug tone. "Why can't I just go out and do my field work during the day and sleep here at night? Serena can stay here where it is safer."

Captain McLarty lowered his voice. "I've received word that Colonel Sibley plans an expedition out to Dakota Territory to put down the insurrection once and for all."

"What's that got to do with me?"

"Leave your wife here for the time being. After Sibley comes through, it'll be safe for her to move out to the farm."

"It'll be a bother, having to come back and forth to the fort every day."

"It's your only option." McLarty pulled out his pocket watch and checked the time.

"And I want your promise that, if you even smell an Indian, you'll come back to the fort."

Gust marveled at how easy the words came out. "Of course."

He limped back to the inn to tell Serena but heard loud wails before he got to the door. Inside he found Dagmar lying in a heap on the floor. Anton knelt beside her, his shoulders heaving. A piece of paper dangled from Serena's hands as Anton's tears dripped on the back of Dagmar's dress.

"It's bad news." Anton's voice quivered. "Real bad."

"What?" Gust said.

"Emil." Anton wiped his nose on his sleeve. "Mortification set in."

"Nei!" Gust felt himself pulled back to when Lena died, felt the ground shift beneath him. It was as if Lena had died again, the raw pain piercing afresh. He pulled Serena into his arms, and she sobbed against his shoulder.

"And more." Anton's face was ashen, his eyes an open maw of grief. "Ole is missing. Ever since Perryville. Maybe a prisoner."

"They don't know?" Serena pulled away from Gust, wiped her face on her apron and straightened her spine. "They must know."

"Emil dead, sweet Emil." Dagmar rocked back and forth. "And Ole missing. They're all we had left."

"We'll get the soldiers to pray. Ole can't be dead or they would've found his body. It's a sign." Serena wiped her face on her apron. "Gust, fetch Tommy Harris."

Gust wondered at her unexpected spurt of energy. Serena pulled the coffee pot over to the hottest burner. "We'll have coffee. And I'll put an egg in it."

"I'll fetch Harris." Gust looked at the position of the sun, thinking of all there was to do. There was nothing he could do to assuage such grief. He was of no help at all. "I'm thinking of going out to the farm."

Serena shot him a glance that would have withered a lesser man. Gust hurried to find the praying private.

44

"Sibley Pursues Sioux in Dakota Territory"
St. Cloud Democrat, April 18, 1863

B UDDY AND BETS JERKED AND BUMPED the wagon across the muddy trail. Chickens hunkered down in their cage, peering between the slats with sharp eyes. Gust had cackled as loud as the hens when he bragged about how many eggs they would sell to the soldiers once they got back to the farm. Had crowed almost as loud as the rooster. Serena walked beside the wagon leading King with a small rope, stroking his back and speaking softly into his ear to calm him.

"*Stalkers liten!* We'll be home soon."

There would be another baby. The clean rags lay folded in an empty bucket. She had yet to tell Gust. When Lena was conceived, Serena had told him the moment she suspected. He had picked her up and swung her around their tiny cabin. So long ago, before the pains of birth and death had touched them. They had been young and in love, sure of themselves and their future. A deep sigh escaped her lips.

If she stayed at the farm, this new little one she carried would undoubtedly meet the same fate as Lena. Coffee grounds didn't lie. The soldiers would ride over to buy eggs and find them butchered and burned out.

At least this new baby would be safe within her for five more months. The savages could kill her but her baby would be protected until the end of October. Of course, savages had ripped unborn children from their mother's womb during the uprising. She had read about it in the *St. Cloud*

228

Democrat. But surely the worst of them were hung at Mankato. The one who did such awful things must have been hung.

Maybe she should learn to fire the gun. It did little good hanging above the door unless she knew how to use it. Dagmar fought alongside the men when the Sioux attacked last summer. She could as well.

But a calmer voice reminded her that it was useless. The Sioux would come back and finish what they had started. Destroy their crops, kill them and burn their buildings. It was useless, foolish to bother with planting.

Gust wouldn't listen, cared only for the farm.

Serena had thought to ask Private Harris to pray that Indians would burn their cabin while they were gone but had hesitated, ashamed to admit how much she feared living there, feeling disloyal to Gust at the mere thought. Now she wished she had asked in spite of her shame. Surely God listened to honest prayers of good men. If He didn't, there was no hope for any of them.

A bullheaded Swede, even Gust, would understand that message. God warned them with the raid on Hutchinson but even the death of their daughter had not spoken loudly enough for Gust to hear. Her father had warned her but she hadn't listened either. Obeying one's parents was one of the Commandments. She had not exactly disobeyed them but maybe disappointing a parent was as bad.

Serena carried bundles into the house while Gust cared for the animals. The door hung on its hinges. A good sign. The faint odor of skunk touched her nostrils as she crossed the threshold. How would she ever rid the place of that smell? Something scurried in the corner, and she stifled a scream. Only a rat.

Serena hurried to light the stove. It might be late April by the calendar but still too cool without a fire. A pot of coffee would be just the thing. She looked out the single window, examining the buildings and barnyard. Nothing.

The year she had allowed Gust was almost over. Things were no better at all.

T RAGEDY STRUCK THEIR FIRST NIGHT HOME.

Serena lay awake, getting used to the unfamiliar sounds, longing for the comforting regimentation of the fort, the guards marching to and from their posts. Instead she listened to the wind howling among the rafters, like the sound of an old woman calling out for help. After restless dozing, she awakened to a commotion in the barn. Still dark, the smell of pre-dawn hung thick in the air. Chickens squawked and flapped their wings. An ox lowed.

"Gust!" Serena shook his shoulder. "Something's in the chickens."

He roused with a grogginess that alarmed her. He would be no help if Indians struck during the night, too exhausted from plowing to protect her.

"Take the gun and see what's wrong." She lifted the gun from the pegs over the door and handed it to him while he pulled on pants and boots.

She peeked out the window as Gust trudged out to the henhouse.

"Serena!" he called.

Serena wrapped a shawl around her shoulders and stealthily left the cabin.

Gust stood at the barn door, ashen. "A weasel." Three dead chickens and their only rooster hung limply from his hand. "I scared him away but he had already done the damage. I think we can still dress them out and use the meat." He sniffed the chickens in his hand. "He only sucked their blood."

Serena looked around with dismay at the blood-splattered barn. The milk bucket lay overturned and straw from the corner stack was strewn everywhere. A single hen remained, sitting on her nest and looking at Serena with fierce protective eyes.

There would be no eggs to sell to the fort. Serena pondered the meaning as she plucked feathers from the dead birds. She blew a downy strand from the tip of her nose. To think they had carried the small flock to Fort Pomme de Terre in the middle of winter without damage and the first night home they were destroyed in one swoop.

Casually she spat seven times into her handkerchief, not wishing Gust to notice but fearful of the bad luck surely turned their way. Auntie Karen read death in the coffee grounds. Had they known anything other than death in their time in Minnesota?

Downy white covered her hands and arms, and she dipped a naked bird into a bucket of cold water from the river and handed it to Gust to gut. To her relief, he took the bird from her hand and dressed it out.

She carefully glanced at him to see if he also pondered the meaning of the weasel's attack. If he did, he kept it to himself. She dipped the next hen into a pot of boiling water before beginning the tedious job of plucking. First hot water and then the cold. Like her life, troubles and calm. Over and over. She pulled a stubborn feather from the wing tip. Each time she came out of the hot water she lost something more.

Soon there would be nothing left.

It wasn't what she had planned on cooking their first full day back in the cabin, but it would have to do. The fragrance of roasted chicken filled the cabin shortly after sunup.

"At least I'm getting an early start." Gust examined the eastern sky where a growing rim of purple sprouted. "Looks like a good day to break sod for that new field."

As he left the yard behind Buddy and Bets, Serena composed a mental letter to her mother while weeding the pie plant patch behind the house, picturing the map while doing so. . . . Dear Mor and Far, I worry about you so much. Why don't you write? Have I offended you in some way? Are you ill? Have you experienced some tragedy that keeps you from writing? Please tell me what is wrong. I worry about you day and night. . . .

Surely they would answer such a letter of desperation.

If only she could write a letter to Lena. Poor Lena left alone until judgment day. She remembered her lips around her breast as she nursed, how their eyes would lock as she suckled. During the raid, Serena had pressed her hand against Lena's mouth to still her cries. *Stalker's liten!* To be handled so roughly by her mother. She hoped Lena understood—of course all things were understood in heaven. A stab of guilt made Serena change her thoughts to something else, anything else.

She broke up another clod of thick roots. The rhubarb pushed through the soil behind the house, its green and pink leaves promising pies and sauce. Her mouth puckered and watered at the thought. Her mother said rhubarb was a good spring tonic. Maybe that's what she needed to feel alive again.

She would not plant tomatoes this year. She would not risk another problem with love apples. She worked in the stillness, listening to the sound of the robins, enjoying the peacefulness of the morning.

Suddenly Serena felt her skin crawl. There were eyes upon her though Gust was in the farthest field, beyond sight or shout. The eyes burned into her back and Serena knew they belonged to the Sioux. They watched her.

So that was how it would be. She would be killed in her own garden next to the rhubarb patch. Gust would come in for dinner and find her lying scalped and butchered. She waited for the arrow to hit, the ax to fly, hoping it would soon be over, trying to imagine what it would be like to join Lena in heaven.

"Our Father who art in heaven," she prayed, and clarity came to her. "Hallowed be Thy Name." She must pretend nothing was amiss. "Thy kingdom come, Thy will be done." Carefully she stood and, in an effort to be casual, brushed off her skirt and readjusted her shawl. "Give us this day our daily bread." Her knees trembled, but she slowly sauntered towards the cabin, feeling as if she would faint from the terror that gripped her. "Forgive us our trespasses as we forgive those who trespass against us." What would they do to a woman alone in a garden with no one to defend her? "And deliver us from evil." Oh, God, I know there's a new baby coming. She's all I have left. My family is gone, and Gust is too busy. "For thine is the kingdom forever and ever." It seemed as if it took forever to get to the cabin door.

Serena grasped the latch and struggled to open it. Her heart pounded in her ears, her head whirled. She tripped over the threshold, only catching herself on the doorframe to prevent a fall. She slammed the door behind her and dropped the bar. She pulled the curtain in front of the single window and then pulled it back an inch to peek outside.

Nothing.

Her pounding heart made her chest ache. They were out there. She could feel them.

A gunshot sounded in the distance. Her heart stopped with a jolt. Had they killed Gust? Was he lying dead on the field? The fire already burned in the stove. She shut the dampers down and choking smoke filled the cabin.

It was no use. Dagmar had already seen her morning fire. The Indians knew where she hid and nothing would stop them. She opened the damper and the room slowly cleared of smoke.

Serena reached for the gun and clutched it in her arms. Gunshots were common in the frontier. It could have been someone hunting a goose or shooting a fox. A gunshot meant nothing. After all Indians shot arrows, silent and deadly. Surely Gust was safe and working. He'd come home at noon the same as usual. Everything was fine.

She huddled under the table with the buffalo robe pulled around her until Gust banged on the door for dinner. She was unable to answer when he asked why the door was barred. The words would not come, only deep sobs and weeping.

"What's the matter, Serena?" Gust gathered her into his arms. "Are you sick?"

Serena could only shake her head. The sobs shook her, garbling her thoughts as well as her words.

"Quit crying and tell me what's wrong."

She gulped her tears and willed her voice to work. Of course it was ridiculous for a grown woman to cry like a baby. She must gather her wits and be an adult. But she had never felt more like a little girl than at that moment. She only wanted to go home to her parents.

"Indians," she finally squeaked.

"Did you see an Indian?" he asked roughly. "Tell me right now."

"Nei," she answered though the words sounded more like a whispery reed than a human voice. "Didn't see one but felt them looking at me in the garden. It made my skin crawl."

"You're imagining things." His shoulders relaxed and he blew out a deep sigh of relief. "I didn't see a thing."

He laughed the same laugh he used when trying to convince someone of a lie. This time it rang hollow.

"Serena-girl, you worry too much." He sat on a chair and pulled her onto his lap. "The harvest is guaranteed. We'll have enough money to repay my father and enough left over to visit your parents. Hell, we'll stay with them the whole winter."

Serena felt her heart slow to normal rhythm. In spite of herself, Serena felt a small glimmer of hope. Maybe she had let her imagination run wild. It was easier to believe Gust than disagree. Besides, if things went well with the wheat they might go home.

But the terrors of the morning had left her exhausted.

45

"Little Crow Behind Murders in Big Woods"
St. Cloud Democrat, May 2, 1863

WHEAT GREENED THE RICH, PLOWED FIELDS as the calendar turned into May. It was an early spring. Corn curled up through the black dirt in neat rows. The farm boasted a smug air of prosperity. The hen hatched eleven yellow chicks and proudly strutted across the yard with her babies.

"Good job, Mother," Serena said. "You've done well."

Serena was careful to close the coop every evening to keep out the varmints, but in spite of her best efforts, a red-tailed hawk caught one of the chicks away from its mother and carried it off. The hen clucked around, not resting until she had the remaining ten chicks under her wingspan. Her beady eyes looked right and left, frantically searching for a safe place for her brood.

"*Stalkers liten.*" A lump pushed in her throat, and she fought back hot tears. "It's not your fault. You're a good mother."

Serena searched the skies but saw nothing of the hawk. She examined the hillsides and fields for signs of movement. She ran into the house and barred the door behind her. Carefully pulling the old rag away from the window that served as a curtain, she scanned the surrounding area for signs of Indians. Nothing.

Serena clutched the Red Wing churn to her chest and plunged the dasher up and down. She pictured the map to Burr Oak, past Auntie Karen's farm, to her old home. Serena plunged faster. The new baby deserved to be born among family, cared for and protected.

She would go home. With or without Gust. She would return to Iowa. She had no choice. The year was almost over.

The butter turned, and she felt the dasher drag. Carefully she drained the buttermilk and scooped the mound of soft butter into the wooden bowl. She rinsed it again and again with fresh water, pressing the butter with a wooden paddle. When the rinse water cleared she measured a pinch of salt and worked it into the butter, firmer after the cool washings. She patted it into a butter mold and set it in a pail of water to keep. Even if there was no flour left for bread, they could butter the fish for flavor. Serena pushed a lock of hair behind her ears and wiped out the churn, setting it upside down on a clean rag to dry.

J ON SVERDRUP RODE BY IN EARLY AFTERNOON as the sun hid behind heavy clouds and Gust picked rocks in the far field. It was hot and humid, stifling and close. Serena straightened up from gathering kitchen wood at the woodpile. Jon tipped his hat and inquired about eggs.

"No eggs," Serena said. "A weasel took our hens the first night back."

"That's bad luck," he said and mopped his face with a red bandana handkerchief, his face as florid as the cloth. "We're sick to death of fish."

"Sorry." Serena dropped the wood by the doorway. "Do you have time for a cup of coffee?"

"Not today, I need to get back to the fort before the storm."

A swirling bank of dark clouds hugged the western horizon and thunder rumbled.

"Any news?" Serena asked.

"Tommy Harris found a second cousin to plant their crop." His teeth showed white when he smiled. "An answer to prayer."

If only someone would pray for her. What would it feel like to have Almighty God intervene on her behalf?

He turned to leave the yard but twisted around sharply. "I almost forgot." He pulled a small bundle from his pouch with a grin. "Mail."

Serena accepted the newspapers from his hand but a letter fluttered to the ground. When she picked it up, she noticed her mor's handwriting. A jolt of adrenaline surged through her veins.

"*Tussen takk.*" Serena willed her voice to remain calm. "Greet Dagmar and Anton." Her legs wobbled into the cabin, and she slumped into the kitchen chair, holding the letter in her lap as thunder sounded in the west. She had heard nothing from her parents since before the uprising, not a word of sympathy for Lena's death, nothing.

Carefully Serena slit the envelope open with a table knife and pulled out several pages of finely written script. She read and then reread with such trembling the paper shook before her eyes.

"They thought we moved to Missouri," Serena croaked aloud. A fly buzzed around the drying churn. "They never received my letters."

It was impossible yet plainly stated. Gust had written a letter to his father telling of their move to Missouri. Mor had seen the letter herself. Why would he lie? And what had happened to her letters so painstakingly written?

Gust had done this to her. Serena thought of that day on the trail when he casually mentioned claiming more damages than had occurred. As shocking as that had been to Serena, she hadn't dug deeper. She should have.

She didn't know how she would do it, but this was the final straw. She would return to Burr Oak without husband, not a penny to her name, without the *bunad* or the log cabin quilt, without her daughter.

Or else the new baby would not be born at all.

The terrible thought clarified in her mind. She would either return home or end it all. Her heart throbbed with the grief of it. It was the only solution. She could not bear to see another baby die. She had married a man she didn't know, someone who could not be trusted to care for them. Surely God would understand. The letter was a sign for her to go home . . . to spare her from the other choice too terrible to consider. But Serena did consider it. *Stakkers liten,* unless she took drastic action, her baby might never draw a breath.

Serena gathered the *St. Cloud Democrats,* and her lips formed the words of the banner as she read, "Speak Unto the Children of Israel That They Go Forward. Exodus Chap XIV, Verse 16." She was a child of Israel and she would go forward. No turning back.

She searched the pages. There was something more—she just didn't know what it was. There must be something in the papers about the reparation payments, a clue that would help her figure out what Gust had done. The approaching storm darkened the cabin, and she moved closer to the window, listening as the thunder grew louder and closer.

A flicker of color near the barn caught her eye, but it was only the red breast of a robin as it gathered straw for a nest. Robins could build nests for their babies in peace, safe from the Sioux.

She would get away before the *skraelings* returned. She threw the paper down on the table and went to the other side of the small cabin. It was almost as dark as night away from the window. She knelt down and felt with her hands.

The wooden box under the bed stored their valuables. She had always left the finances strictly in Gust's realm and didn't know what was inside of it. The thought of going behind his back made her uneasy. Serena looked out the window. No sign of Gust. She had to do it.

The deed to the farm lay in the box wrapped in a piece of leather for safekeeping. Damn the day Gust bought it from Salmon. The curse boosted her resolve, and she pushed aside Gust's extra ammunition, a photo of his mother, their wedding license, and baptism certificates.

At the bottom of the box nestled a small leather bag, unexpectedly heavy. Serena summoned her courage and opened it, the smell of leather reached her nostrils and her eyes bulged. Three five-dollar gold pieces rested in the bottom of the bag. Besides the gold coins were two silver dollars, three fifty-cent pieces, a dime and a handful of pennies. Surely it was enough to buy passage home.

She carefully replaced the money in the bag and tucked it into her apron pocket. Not exactly stealing. After all, it was her money, too. But she felt like a thief, a sneaking thief. But she wasn't a liar. She would tell him to his face.

Serena reached again for the *St. Cloud Democrats*. Surely the stage company advertised fares. She opened the door and read by the feeble glow of the sun through the heavy clouds. As she read, she was drawn again to anything about the reparations. Somehow she knew the answer was in the papers.

She started with the banner and then scanned the headlines before reading every story about the reparations. Someone from St. Peter had lied about the extent of damage in his fields and was subsequently tried for perjury. Another man claimed losses of an entire field of turnips valued at $200 but later admitted it was only one row. Someone who had never lived in Minnesota claimed a loss of $83 for a crop of wheat that was never planted. It appeared most retribution payments were low, very few over two hundred dollars. Of course, most settlers had little or nothing to lose. There was no dollar amount tallied for work or grief.

She was almost ready to put the papers away when a small article caught her eye. It mentioned that one hundred dollars per child was paid to families who lost children in the uprising. She caught her breath.

Surely Gust wouldn't be so low as to lie about Lena's death in order to collect more money. The thought of it made her heart drop.

46

"1700 Sioux Exiled to Crow Creek, Dakota Territory"
St. Cloud Democrat, May 4, 1863

A STRANGE ENERGY FILLED SERENA. SHE WAS LEAVING. As far as she was concerned, the year was over.

An eerie calm settled over the house. Even the birds quieted. It was as if the world held its breath awaiting the storm. Flashes of lightning sparked the sky. Even Gust couldn't work through a thunderstorm. When he came home, she would tell him. With a shudder, Serena stepped on a fat spider scrambling across the floor.

Maybe she had time to pen an answer to her parents, telling them of her decision. Once the letter was posted, there could be no turning back. It would force her to do the right thing—prevent her from doing the other.

She reread the flimsy paper and noticed a small paragraph that she hadn't noticed in her first time through. Mor had been feeling poorly. Dear God, what if her mother was dying. She was needed at home. She retrieved the quill and inkpot from the cupboard and carefully extracted a sheet of paper from the shelf. Her mind was made up.

She pulled the table in front of the window to catch the light. How odd for such gloom in mid-afternoon. *Oh, God, help me do it. Help me to do the right thing with this baby.* In desperation she propped opened the kitchen door and pulled the table closer. By carefully situating herself so the light fell across the paper, she could see the page without lighting a lamp. Better to save the lamp for the dark days that would surely come.

Gust would need the light next winter.

Serena turned her thoughts away from Gust. For once she needed to think about herself and her baby. She needed to think about her family back in Iowa. She grasped her anger like a lifeline. He was the liar and the thief. She would not put up with it any longer.

A cool wind ruffled the paper, and she twisted her back to block the breeze. She was doing the right thing. She felt it deep in her bones.

She sat at the table for a full minute without writing a single pen stroke, groping for the words that would explain her situation without putting too much blame on Gust, striving to be fair in her account of their failed marriage. But he deserved the blame, after all. He was the deceiver, not her. She wanted her parents to understand why she could abandon her vows.

Sadness flooded her. Mor told her not to pull on the cord but to let the afterbirth come on its own. She was doing that with her marriage—cutting the cord, and letting the aftermath develop on its own. It was over.

The words splayed harshly on the page. Gust's perjury, the missing letters, and his lies—all in script small and even. She wrote how he loved his wheat fields more than his family, more than life itself.

She glanced over her shoulder and saw a fat drops of rain splatter in the dirt outside the door. She must hurry. Gust would be back any minute. She bravely listed her own sins, how she had been too stubborn to listen when they tried to guide her, how she had eaten tomatoes though many said they were poisonous, how she was too weak to live away from them. She was coming home to have this baby.

She read the words, half listening to the hen cackling in the yard and the rising wind, thinking how simple it sounded on paper. Gust was less than she expected and so she was returning home. Her baby had died and this one was at risk. It didn't begin to explain her grief, the way she felt more dead than alive, how her hopes were gone.

She did not turn her head at a sound in the doorway, dreading the thought of looking Gust in the face and telling him her plan. She could imagine the pain in his eyes, the look on his face.

Perhaps she would just hand him the letter without saying a word so he could read for himself what was written. She would give him the letter and then leave. She'd stay with Dagmar until the next stage. The sack pulled heavy in her apron pocket. There was little she needed, nothing to pack except the Red Wing churn and Lena's blanket.

She wrote another sentence, her heart clutched in her throat. She was in no hurry to kill their marriage. She steeled herself for the confrontation.

A shadow fell across the page.

Serena summoned her courage. God, give me the words. As she dotted the last i she caught a musky odor. Out of the corner of her eye she saw a Red Indian standing directly behind her. Oh, God, not now. Not after the letter is written and I've finally made my decision. The Indian crouched, short and stocky, his face painted half black and half green. White feathers drooped downward in greasy hair, some splattered with red paint—or maybe blood. He held a hatchet in his raised hand.

Oh, God. Not this way. Her heart leapt in her chest and her limbs weakened. She stifled a scream. There was no place to hide, no defense. The musket hung over the door, the knife in the cupboard. Her left hand cupped over her belly, Serena thought of the woman in St. Cloud, how they had spared her baby when she stopped resisting. She forced her mind to quit racing, her body to stay in the chair. She dipped the quill again, telling Gust of the Indian behind her who would kill her as she sat writing this letter. She scribbled her good-byes, waiting for the axe to fall.

Serena prayed he would not hurt the baby, that all the hurt would be directed at her alone. Keep Gust away. Spare him. She wrote her prayers. Send Gust to save me. Make him hurry.

She told Gust that she knew the truth, that he should bury them across the field in the pasture. She asked him to contact her parents and tell them that she loved them and had missed them, asked him to explain why the letters had not gotten through.

The Indian's breath was hot on Serena's neck, his quick eyes watching every stroke of the quill, the hatchet lowered to his side. Serena kept scribbling lest the hatchet be raised again. She wrote until the page was filled and then turned it over and filled the back of the paper. Then she wrote in the margins. When they were filled up, she wrote over the lines already written. How she wished it could have turned out differently, how she wished she could be buried beside Lena. She asked Gust to mark Lena's grave and tell her parents where Lena slept.

Finally when she thought she would go mad with the agony of waiting, the Indian stepped to the side and motioned that he wanted the quill and paper. His dark eyes glowed in contrast to the splashes of green paint on his face. She noticed a fresh cut on his right hand. One drop of blood dripped from the wound and splattered red on the paper.

With a shaking hand and a silent plea for mercy, she placed the quill in his fingers and felt the roughness of his hand against hers. It was just a normal hand, not unlike touching Gust, but his musky smell sickened her. He stood close to her, his nakedness showing through his loincloth.

She focused on the sheet of paper. She would not think. With only the roaring in her ears, Serena watched him mark the paper. He laughed like a small child, scribbling on the paper for what seemed like eternity, dropping great blobs of ink over her fine script.

Finally he picked up the paper and quill and left, not looking back, just walked out into the pouring rain.

He left the inkpot, Serena thought. *He'll be back for the inkpot.*

47

"Reports of Indian Raids Across Frontier. Citizens Demand Vengeance."
St. Cloud Democrat, May 4, 1863

GUST TRUDGED TOWARD THE BARN BEHIND the plodding team, raindrops splattering on his back and face. After the stifling heat, the rain was welcome relief. A lightning bolt crashed nearby and answering thunder roared like a cannon. Rain poured out of the heavens. He scanned the skies for signs of hail. Hail could flatten a field of new corn, kill the green rows of promise in the fields of Pomme de Terre. But surely nothing could stop him now.

If it hailed, he would replant. Once his father had replanted the corn on Independence Day and still harvested a fair crop. Yes, it took work and sacrifice but if he kept with it he would win out in the end.

Success was within his grasp.

Surely a few more months would not hurt. He would harvest his fields, and they would travel to St. Cloud and ride the *Time and Tide* to Iowa where they would winter with Serena's parents. The reparation investigations were forgotten. Nothing had been written in the papers about it for weeks.

Gust was almost to the barn when Buddy and Bets reared back and shied away from the path. At first he couldn't see anything through the sheets of falling rain but then he spied Bossy down on the ground, lying in a pool of blood, rain streaming off her carcass.

Gust dropped the reins and tore down the path to the house, ignoring the searing pains that shot up his leg, thinking only of Serena.

Oh, God. Let her be all right. Their lone hen lay with an arrow through her side, the chicks scurrying around her carcass in the rain, his heart was in his throat.

What had he done?

I'll give up the farm. I promise. I'll pay back government. Anything. He pushed against the barred door. *I'll go home to Burr Oak. Oh, God, I can't bear to lose her.* "Are you all right?" He pounded on the rough wood. *I'll do anything and never ask another favor.* "Serena! Open the door."

Her white face showed in the window. *Thank God. Thank God.* She cracked the door just wide enough for him to squeeze through before slamming it shut and dropping the bar. She shoved the gun into his arms, flitted to the window and peeked through the curtain.

"What happened?"

Serena pressed her back against the door, eyes darting around the room. Her breath came out in short puffs of air. The veins in her neck throbbed with each beat of her heart.

She worked her lips without sound. Her eyes blazed with something that frightened him more than the arrows in their cow. She nodded.

Gust's voice shook. He sounded more ferocious than he meant. He took her by both arms, forcing her to face him. "By God, tell me what happened!"

"I was writing a letter." Her voice sounded flat and distant. He concentrated on her lips. A small dot of blood dripped from where she had bitten her tongue. "To Mor and Far."

"Tell me at once," Gust insisted. "Did they hurt you?"

"Nei." Serena straightened her apron. "At first I thought it was you standing behind me, but then I smelled him."

Gust blew out a long breath. He looked to the window. Nothing in the yard but pouring rain and pounding hail.

"Only one?" Gust asked.

"Ja," Serena looked up at the rafters. The timbre of her voice set Gust's hair on end. "He watched me write. I waited for him to kill me." Gust tried to see what she looked at but saw nothing except a spider spinning a web. "I thought he would kill me and our baby."

Another baby. Gust tried to gather her in his arms, but she pulled away. How could he have been so stupid?

"I'm leaving." Her face was a mask of stone. "I'm not going to watch another baby die. I can't do it."

"Serena-girl—"

"Listen to me for once." Her voice sounded cold as the hail pelting against the window. A bolt of lightning shook the cabin and thunder clapped directly overhead. "I'm quitting you."

"You're upset." Gust tried again to touch her, but she pushed him away. "You don't know what you're saying."

"I know exactly what I'm saying." Her fists clenched, and her back was as straight as an arrow. "You promised me that if things didn't go well in Minnesota, we'd return to Iowa." Another lightning flash lit the window through the curtain. "Lena died, we lost our crop, stuck in this God-for-saken place. You lied to me. You had no intention of going home."

Gust felt his world tumbling around his ears.

She took the letter from her pocket and slammed it on the table. "You told my parents we were in Missouri. You destroyed my letters."

Gust grabbed onto the back of the chair. The room swirled around him and rain leaked through the roof onto his head. He stepped to one side but still felt the wetness falling through the thatch.

"You lied about Lena's death—said it was from the Indians." She took the leather pouch from her apron pocket and threw it at him. "You still have money left! It's the only explanation."

Time stopped and thunder sounded in the distance. "I'm going home with you or without you."

"It's not so easy," Gust finally said after a long silence. "I broke the law. I could end up in jail."

"So go to jail. I'll wait for you," she said. "But I can't live with a man I don't respect. I love you, but I won't live this way—or let my baby live this way."

He had always known in the back of his mind that he would some-day have to face up to what he had done. "I did it because I love you."

"Another lie," Serena said. "You did it because you hate your father. Nothing to do with love at all."

"I'll make it up to you."

"Just admit the truth—you hate your father more than you love me . . . or your children."

He thought of his father, how he'd gloat over Gust's failure. He'd be lucky if he escaped jail time. But according to the newspapers, most who perjured themselves were only forced to repay the money. He'd sell King and Rosebud. They'd have nothing. He could sell the team.

The money in the pouch would pay their passage home. She was right. They needed to go home. He was a grown man and could take whatever his father might measure out. Serena was more important. She was the only thing that mattered.

"Come." Gust's voice cracked, and the weight of his decision almost dropped him to his knees. He had come so close to his dream. "We're going to the fort."

"What are you saying?"

"We're going home."

She looked at him for a long time, not saying a word. She didn't smile. Didn't cry. Her face as white as could be, her body like a kernel of corn ready to pop.

"I'll pack my things."

"Nei," Gust moved the curtain and looked out across the yard. No sign of Indians. He scanned the far field, the trail toward the fort, the river. Nothing. Buddy and Bets strained toward the green grass growing alongside the path. The rain was letting up, just a drizzle. "I'll have soldiers come back with me to gather our things. You need to get to the fort."

In spite of his words, Serena pulled out her shawl and extra stockings, reached for the towel hanging on the chair.

"Come Serena."

"Hitch up the team," she said. "I want my churn."

Gust looked out the window again before leaving the cabin, his rifle loaded and held in the crook of his arm. Then he stood behind the woodpile and scanned the pastures and fields. He imagined an arrow shooting him in the back as Indians stormed the cabin to take Serena, his beautiful wife, forcing her to be a squaw, forcing her.

He spoke roughly to the team, hurrying but clumsy with the gun in one hand. The storm clouds rolled toward the east. He kept looking behind him, examining the path and the woodlot. The red devils were there, he felt it. Blackbirds called from the garden, and he remembered the stories of Red

Men imitating birdsong before attacking. The hair rose on the back of his neck, and he turned his face away from the fields he must leave, the green emeralds against the black soil.

He had been so close to making it. So close. No sign of Indians.

"Hurry!"

She came out of the cabin lugging the churn and a bundle of clothing, her hair covered with a gray shawl. She kept her eyes away from him and scurried to the wagon like a little mouse. Like a scared rabbit.

Gust lifted the gun and carefully looked again. Nothing moved except the chicks pecking around their dead mother. He scooped up the hen and threw it in the back of the wagon. He couldn't abide waste—Dagmar would cook it with dumplings. Then he saw flies crawling over poor Bossy. He'd come back with a soldier or two to salvage the meat if the critters didn't get to it first. And gather the farm equipment.

The leather pouch fell out of Serena's apron pocket when he helped her into the wagon. Good God, a woman holding the purse strings! But it wasn't time for argument. He picked up the pouch and tucked it inside the butter churn for safe keeping. It was her favorite possession and she'd be sure to keep it with her. She looked coldly at him, not explaining herself in any way, her silence screaming blame at him.

As the wagon lurched over the ruts in the trail, Gust made his plans. The stage wasn't due until the end of the week. He would leave Serena with Dagmar and return to salvage what he could from the farm. Maybe the army would buy the beef. He'd ask Captain McLarty.

He glanced over at Serena. Another baby. By God, a boy this time. A son to help with the farm. All the more reason to salvage the plow and tools before they left. He'd heard of farmers oiling their plowshares and burying them to keep them out of the hands of thieves. He'd bury them until this whole nonsense with the Indians was over. The land would keep. It might all work out in the end.

A son. His father's first grandchild. Surely he'd earn a place in his father's favor with a grandson. He could tell his father they needed to come home because of the child.

It would be better if he didn't say anything about going back to get the farm implements. He'd leave Serena with Dagmar and then make a quick trip back to the farm, pack up what he could, and hide the rest. He'd be back in plenty of time to meet the stage.

Beside him, Serena cradled the churn like a baby, covering it with the end of her shawl. She rocked back and forth, crooning and humming an old lullaby. She'd forget about this nonsense once the new baby came.

"What did he look like?" Gust wanted to hear her voice more than know about the savage. "Was he wearing paint?"

"Black," she said with a voice strained and tight. "And green. Like a mallard."

Relief washed over him. At least she was talking. He turned to speak to her and saw her cuddle the churn closer to her breast and then lean over and kiss it.

She might be talking, but by God, kissing a butter churn! He slapped the reins and hurried the plodding oxen. It was time he took her back to civilization.

When they arrived at the fort, Gust first thought to alert the soldiers to the Indian at his farm. But as he dropped Serena off at the inn, he had second thoughts. If he were to tell Captain McLarty of their ordeal, there would be no way he would sanction his return to the farm to gather their belongings or salvage the meat. He decided quickly to go out to the farm first and tell the captain later.

Tommy and Trygve were leading their horses past the inn, heading toward the gate.

"Where are you boys going on this fine day?" Gust said. "Off to fight in a real war?"

"Hungry for eggs," Tommy said. "There's geese nesting along the river."

"Maybe I'll ride along with you," Gust said. "I brought Serena in for a visit with Dagmar."

Tommy and Trygve glanced at each other and shrugged their shoulders. "You'll have to keep up."

48

"Sporadic Raids Continue. When Will the Army Intervene?"
St. Cloud Democrat, May 10, 1863

RUMBEATER CREPT INTO A BLACKBERRY THICKET, disturbing a member of the squirrel tribe, watching the *washechu* man with the short leg. Most of all, Drumbeater eyed the man's *ishtahbopopa.* Surely such a weapon carried strong wakon. Drumbeater's fingers ached to hold the rifle. He imagined what it would be like to fire upon an enemy with such power. He would be a true avenger of the People. They would write songs about him with such a weapon.

The Creator had sent a refreshing rain to cleanse the air and gladden the bird tribes. Their songs filled the air with their beauty. If it were not for the ugliness left by the white eyes, the scene would have been beautiful. But how can there be beauty when the trees are stacked on top of each other to make ugly dwellings, the ground scarred with the fields of the White Eyes? They did not know enough to respect the earth.

The *washechu* walked long steps holding the gun in one hand. He voiced a prayer to his god as he took the strange steps, unlike any dance known to the People. Drumbeater watched in fascination. The man's lips moved, and Drumbeater pressed forward a little, trying to hear the prayer. A sacred act, no doubt. Big medicine. Maybe the man would make the tracks like his woman had done.

The man with the short leg returned to the big rock and danced his strange dance again, stepping long steps until he arrived at the same place as before. Then the man did an astounding thing, something so unexpected that Drumbeater held his breath.

249

The man laid the *ishtahbopopa* against a tree and picked up a spear with a flat, iron basket on the end. He scraped against the earth until black dirt heaped into a pile. The man worked until sweat streamed off his forehead. Disgraceful for a warrior to labor like a woman. The fat-eaters knew nothing of honor. If it were not for their strong medicine, they would not survive.

Drumbeater had searched first for the *washechu* woman, but she was nowhere in sight. Such strong *wakon* that woman had! The tracks on the paper, the blueness of her eyes, and the hair like Little Bird. Drumbeater had been tempted but did not take her scalp. He was wary of crossing such strong medicine, and it was a great relief that she was gone today. Surely the Great Mystery blessed him for sparing her life. Perhaps she picked berries or searched for the bee tribe to rob its honey. Without her *wakon* he would easily triumph over this enemy, the man with the short leg, and take his weapon for himself.

The white eyes rubbed grease on his iron travois and pushed it down into the earth. Acch! Drumbeater fingered the sacred pouch around his neck, praying that the Great Mystery would not hold him responsible for turning the ground inside out, for forcing a weapon into its throat. The tracks on paper were tucked into the sacred pouch. Big medicine. The touch of the paper within the pouch strengthened him and chased the fears away from his thinking.

Drumbeater watched in horror as the man with the short leg pushed more weapons into the ground and covered them with soil. Did the man think they would grow like the corn family? Was this the secret of the *washechu's* medicine?

The white eyes flattened the ground with the iron basket and danced the strange dance back to the rock, stretching his legs into long strides that ate up the ground, his mouth working without sound. He seemed satisfied at last and wiped his sweaty face with a cloth, his face as red as the berry tribe. The ceremony was over. The *ishtahbopopa* lay against the tree by the scarred earth, away from the man, out of reach.

Without a sound, Drumbeater moved away from the brush and threaded an arrow into his bow. As he pulled it back and aimed at the fat eater's belly, Drumbeater thought of Willow Song's face and the way she had smiled at him during the Dance of the Virgins. He remembered the morning of Otter's birth and his waving fists keeping perfect time with the sacred drum. Otter would have grown up to be a great warrior, a keeper of the drum like his father.

A stab of grief knifed through Drumbeater's chest, and he lowered the bow to calm the trembling of his hands.

Drumbeater had returned the *washechu* girl-children to his uncle's life-and-death friend at too great a cost to consider. Though Crooked Lightning lived an honorable life, he was killed by the dishonorable rope of the Long Knives. The People were banned from Leaf Country forever without just cause. The sacred drum was gone. The only way to retain any dignity was to avenge his people.

Tears for women and war whoops for men to drown sorrow.

The trembling left as his duty became clear. He would never stop until his people were avenged. Only then could they rest in the spirit world. Only then could he hold up his head as a warrior.

With a triumphant yell that echoed through the meadow, Drumbeater raised his bow and pulled back the arrow. The man with the short leg looked up in surprise.

Drumbeater released the arrow and watched it fly true to its mark.

49

"Sibley Can't Find the Sioux in Dakota Territory.
So Far Nothing to Show for Expedition"
St. Cloud Democrat, June 30, 1863

M OTHER." ANTON WALKED SLOWLY into the kitchen with hat in
hand. Jon Sverdrup followed close behind him. They stopped to
wipe their shoes on the rug. "Where's Serena?"

"Taking a rest." Dagmar knew from Anton's tone of voice that something was wrong. She got up from peeling potatoes, wiping her hands on her
apron and placed the paring knife beside the kettle. "What's the matter?"

"Indians." Tears pooled in Anton's eyes, and he seemed years older
than his age. His voice cracked. "Tommy . . . and Trygve."

"Nei!" Dagmar slumped back into a chair and reached for her handkerchief. "It can't be!"

"They hunted eggs along the river." Jon's Adam's apple bobbed twice,
his voice weary, and his lips quivering. "When they didn't come back, I
went looking for them."

Anton placed a steadying hand on her shoulder. "Not half a mile
from the fort, in the bend of the river by Gust's place."

"It can't be true!" She remembered Tommy's easy smile, the prayers,
his wife and children back home.

"But that's not the worst of it—Gust."

My God!" She lifted the handkerchief to her mouth trying to grasp
the meaning of their words. "Not Gust."

Serena had been through enough. Why would God allow her to lose her husband, too? Tommy wanted to be a minister. And Trygve had such a kind heart. Damn the Sioux! Damn them.

Couldn't they just leave them alone?

"What's wrong?" Serena stood at the foot of the ladder. She looked as she had the first time they had met. Slim and pale with red rims around her blue eyes, younger than her years. Much younger. "What happened?"

Serena crumbled under the news. Dagmar and Serena held each other and wept until there were no tears left.

"You almost made it," Dagmar said at last. "You were so close to leaving."

"I don't have a black dress." Serena's eyes took on that strange light Dagmar had noticed before. "Mor gave me the *bunad* for special occasions and a string for childbirth, but she didn't think of widow's weeds. She didn't give me those."

A breeze wafted in the open door along with the pungent odors of spring. Thank God, Serena was safe at the fort. She would have been murdered along with the boys. It was an answer to prayer.

"What will I do without a black dress?"

"Shush now," Dagmar said. "Don't think about it now."

The rest of the day blurred into a nightmare. Serena sat in the rocking chair looking out the south window, towards the farm. Dagmar started and restarted a letter to Tommy's wife, working at the kitchen table.

Suddenly Serena laughed a harsh laugh. The hair prickled on Dagmar's neck.

"What is it?"

"He said we'd go home." Serena narrowed her eyes as her laughter turned into tears. "I should have known he'd die first."

Dagmar got up, dropped a hand on Serena's shoulder. "He would have kept his word," Dagmar said. "He told me himself that he'd be back in time for Friday's stage."

There was nothing to say, but the words poured out of Serena. She told the story from the very beginning. How someone in school teased Gust about his sharp nose and she told him that it reminded her of the way Minnesota looked on the map, where it jutted out into Lake Superior. She talked about his family and the *bunad* and their wedding trip and the raid in Hutchinson. Once Dagmar tried to convince her to take a nap and rest, but Serena gave her a fierce look and started over again.

From the very beginning.

Started with the nose that resembled the Minnesota map. Something told Dagmar to listen as the fountain of memories erupted from Serena like a gushing spring. Serena held nothing back, gave no thought to what she said. Some things far too personal to share with even a close friend. Other things splashed harsh and angry into the room. Serena told her about the letters and the reparations and her decision to leave him.

Then she told about the savage who had stood behind her watching her write the letter to her parents. Serena talked and wept while Dagmar listened, the letter to Tommy's wife unwritten before her.

"I once loved him." Serena wiped her eyes and nose with her apron, her words coming out in a near whisper. "But today I hate him. I hate him as much as I ever loved him. He had the last word, after all."

Dagmar had nothing to say. There were no words. She remembered this place of grief she had known only too well with the deaths of her children.

"Oh, Dagmar, what will become of me?"

Jon Sverdrup rapped on the door and hurried in, his face haggard and breathing ragged.

"More bad news." He wiped his eyes with the back of his sleeve. "Real bad." It took a long moment for him to gain his composure. "Angus Foot and Private Comfort—both dead."

"Nei!" Anton dropped an armful of kitchen wood into the box as he walked through the side door. "Where?"

"Found just past Ten Mile Lake, near the Otter Tail Crossing."

"Good God!" Dagmar said. "They're picking us off one by one."

"They were cut up." Jon's shoulders heaved with heavy sobs and he cast an apologetic glance toward Serena. "Cut bad."

Dagmar put her arms around him. He was only a boy, the age of Emil, had he lived. Tears fell for Emil as well as Joe and Angus. And more tears for Gust and Tommy and Trygve. And Serena. And for Ole whether he lived or died. And her girls.

"Angus was steady," Anton cleared his throat, but his voice quavered. "Stood by us last summer."

"I signed up with Joe," Jon pressed into Dagmar's shoulder, making no move to release from her embrace. "Served with him at Ripley."

"It's supposed to be over," Dagmar said.

"Why isn't it over?" Serena said.

"Maybe it's the end of the world, like the Book of Revelations." Anton's voice lowered to a whisper, his voice reedy and broken. "The war in the South, the Indians, people dying." He cleared his throat again and looked down at his boots.

Dagmar knew what he meant. God had abandoned Tommy and Trygve in spite of their earnest prayers, Emil died in spite of the surgeon's best efforts. Thank God, Serena was safe, going back to her people. But it was over for them. They were too old to start over.

A sudden yearning gripped her. How different life would have been had their children lived. Even one of them. If she could turn to Rebecca and reach out to her. Who knew if Ole lived? They hadn't even the comfort of knowing.

Jon clung to her with a clutch that cut off her wind, almost staggered her in its intensity. He was so young, probably scared to death that he'd be next.

Finally Dagmar pulled back and wiped her face on the hem of her apron, loosing the death grip from her neck. "Tears are useless," she said. "What's done is done."

"Where will they be buried?" Anton said.

"Outside the gates," Jon said. "Tonight. Unless the *skraelings* interfere."

"I wish I had flour for a cake." Dagmar wiped her nose again. "Damn but I'm tired of running out of everything."

"We can sing a hymn," Anton said. "Cake won't bring them back."

"Hymns won't bring them back either. It's hard to believe that God didn't hear their prayers." Dagmar sniffed. "Maybe it was heresy after all."

"You're the one who told me to bow to the will of God," Serena said and her voice was accusing. "You said everything that happens is the will of God."

"I hoped I was wrong," Dagmar said. "Wanted to believe that it was war that killed Emil, not the will of God." She fingered the hem of her damp apron and smoothed out a wrinkled spot. "It would be easier to believe that."

SOLDIERS DUG FIVE GRAVES BY THE RIVER just outside the barricade. They wrapped the bodies in wool army blankets, there being a lack of coffins on such short notice, and solemnly dropped them into the gaping holes.

Serena had some wild thought about burying Gust next to their daughter on the road between Hutchinson and St. Paul. Captain McLarty had been kind, assuring her that his grave would be marked and later on, after the savages were taken care of once and for all, she could either move her baby's body to Pomme de Terre or move Gust's grave to Hutchinson, however she wished.

Dagmar loved the man at that moment. He was a good man to speak to Serena so gently, especially after all he had been through with her man.

Jon Sverdrup snuffled while Captain McLarty read a service from a prayer book and led the Lord's Prayer. As they recited the ancient words together, Dagmar thought again of the prayers spoken in the loft, sincere and unfettered by tradition. She held onto Serena's arm and felt the poor girl tremble and nearly fall. Anton stood on the other side and between the two of them they braced her upright.

Dagmar whispered an unorthodox prayer of her own as she watched the dirt cover the bodies. "God, you see our need for a miracle here at Pomme de Terre."

Captain McLarty started "Rock of Ages," and she joined in, at first quavering and then stronger. The melody flooded her mind, and she remembered every word.

". . . These for sin could not atone, thou must save and thou alone. Rock of ages cleft for me, let me hide myself in thee . . ."

50

"The Union Conscription Act Boils over into Violence in New York."
St. Cloud Democrat, July 13, 1863

THE SUMMER PASSED QUIETLY WITHOUT FURTHER RAIDS. The papers said the bad Indians were exiled, but Dagmar thought Colonel Sibley's march scared the Indians away. At last the ox-carts were moving again. Their squealing wheels could be heard for miles.

Anton sold King to one of the ox-carters along with Buddy and Bets. Serena used the money to leave by stage in late July. She wanted to be home before the baby came.

Captain McLarty questioned the safety of her traveling alone, but Evan Jacobson, the driver, promised to deliver her to the *Time and Tide* steamboat and help her buy a ticket. He promised to leave her with friends along the Abercrombie Trail if her sickness came upon her before they got to St. Cloud. He knew everyone along the route and said that no one would turn her away.

Evan was most trustworthy, and Captain McLarty finally agreed. Serena promised to write as soon as she reached Burr Oak.

Dagmar missed her more than she was willing to admit.

Dagmar had hoarded bits of fat from the hog butchering at Christmas and from the bear Anton hunted in Gust's potato field. On a muggy August day, she melted the tallow in an iron pot over a slow fire. It was a special pot her mother had used for candle making back in the Old Country, smaller in diameter and deeper. She set the candle frame on the table and gathered the wicking, carefully measuring the desired length and

257

tying a loop on one end to hang the candles from the frame. It would take forty separate dips of each wick into the melted fat to create a candle.

But to have candles during the dark winter months!

Living in the frontier was hard on women, Dagmar thought as she worked. Poor Serena, not quite twenty and already widowed and burned out by Indians, dragged across the country by that bull-headed husband, and almost murdered in her own cabin. And worst of all, losing her baby. Now alone with another baby on the way.

She dipped the next candle, quickly dunking it into the melted fat and hanging it on the candle frame to harden.

Dagmar once heard of a baby born with a red birthmark in the shape of an axe across its forehead. Its mother had witnessed a murder while carrying the child. It would be a miracle if Serena's baby was born without a mark.

She heaved a deep sigh. What was done was done and at least God had spared Serena's life. To think an Indian would be so fascinated by penmanship that he would lay down his murdering ways. God be praised, a miracle. And another miracle that Gust brought her back to the fort before she was killed. And that she had thought to take the money purse with her.

Ja, if the truth were known, Pomme de Terre was overdue for miracles.

Dagmar glanced out the window as the stage pulled in. Usually she ran out with the others for mail call, but today she kept at her work. She wanted to finish the job while she had a chance. There might be a letter from Serena, but it was too early to expect one.

Anton burst through the door as she dipped the last of the tallow. A good morning's work.

"There's mail, Mother."

Something in his voice caused her to put down the candle she was holding. She wiped her hands on her apron and braced for the worst.

"Ole?"

He handed her a letter labeled with shaky script. Dagmar would know Ole's familiar scrawl anywhere. He never crossed the T's as he had been taught. She took the letter and pressed it to her breast, then kissed it. She lowered herself onto the chair.

"You'll have to open it. My hands shake so." Her voice trembled and she blinked her eyes, trying to focus. Ole was alive. Thank God. Thank God.

Anton, slit the letter with his knife though his hands shook as well. He handed the pages to Dagmar and sat down at the table beside her, his hand resting on her shoulder. Dagmar stretched her arm out before her as far as it would go, trying to focus the words.

"My God," Dagmar said. "It's almost three months old."

May 6, 1863
Dear Far and Mor,

I hope this letter finds you safe and well. I've had no news from you for almost six months, and I'm afraid you haven't heard from me either. What's news from Emil? I think of him daily and worry for his safety.

I am alive although barely, having survived the Battle of Perryville. I was manning artillery on the heights when a Reb cavalry charge tried to outflank us. We were outnumbered but held the high ground, firing until our ammunition was gone. Then we fought them off hand to hand as long as we could.

I never thought to survive. The Battle of Mill Springs was terrible but Perryville was worse. There was scant water and the weather dry. Hot winds sucked every bit of moisture from us, like a desert. Sigurd Swensrud saved my life at the cost of his own. He pulled me under the artillery piece after I was wounded. Then he positioned himself in front of the guns to shield me. The dead piled in great heaps around me. The Union prevailed but at the cost of too many.

When they finally collected the wounded, I was dragged to a nearby farm house set up as field hospital. The Union refused to bury the Rebs, that's how bitter the fighting, and from my bed I saw the pigs rooting until their snouts were red. It was a gory sight. Finally a farmer organized a crew of darkies to bury the dead.

The surgeon tried but mortification set in my leg. He finally took it to spare my life. I have spent the last five months recovering from my wounds. It is just now I am able to write with certainty this letter will reach you as I am sending it with a sergeant being transferred north.

There's talk of sending the wounded home by train. I am able to hobble around on a wooden leg fashioned from ironwood. I won't be much help with the chores for a while but at least I'm finished soldiering.

I am dearly sick of Kentucky and hope never to see it again. Kentucky is an unlucky place, beautiful and green like Minnesota, but not home. My thoughts turn always to home. I've watched the farmers put in their tobacco. I'll tell you more about it when I get back.

I've taken to smoking a corncob pipe—common down here. Don't worry. I'm well taken care of and in friendly hands.

I found an old paper that mentioned the hangings in Mankato. Thank God it's over. I expect to be coming home but can't depend on the promises of the army. A letter from you would mean a lot.

Your loving son,

Ole

Dagmar put the letter down in her lap, her face awash with tears. She honked her nose in a clean rag.

"Alive," she said at last. "He's alive."

"It's a miracle. An answer to Tommy's prayers."

"I'll write to him." Dagmar stood to her feet and hurriedly moved the candles to the side. "I'll have a letter ready for the stage."

"What did he say about coming home?" Anton stood before her with his jaw working and a look of disbelief on his face.

"He'll be home when the army arranges transport. God knows when that will be."

"He won't be able to climb the loft stairs." Dagmar's hands slowed to a stop. She dropped a candle to the floor. It snapped in half. "Oh, my God, he's lost a leg."

"We'll move upstairs and let him have our room."

Tears mushroomed in her eyes and Anton pulled her to his chest. "Now, then." He patted her back and kissed her forehead. "It's all right." He wiped her face with his sleeve that smelled of stale sweat and cow manure. "Our boy's alive."

Dagmar pulled away. She needed air, needed to be alone and process the news. She picked up the water bucket and left the inn without a word, not realizing she had left Anton standing alone until she had walked a few steps down the path.

When she got back to the doorway to tell him where she was going, she saw him seated at the table with his head down on his arms, sobbing. She didn't say anything, only backed away and hurried to the river.

Ole was alive.

51

"Nathan Lamson Kills Little Crow in Hutchinson. Angry Citizens Scalp and Mutilate Little Crow's Body. Bury It in Offal."

St. Cloud Democrat, July 5, 1863

BURR OAK LOOKED SMALLER THAN SHE REMEMBERED, the landing lay weed-grown and cluttered with wooden boxes and broken wagon wheels. It showed disrepair, a reminder that the merchant's sons had gone soldiering.

Serena straggled onto the landing, lugging her bundles and trying to get used to solid ground after the rolling pitch of the boat. She patted her reticule from time to time, knowing the few dollars left from selling the animals were all the cash money she had in the world. Anton had promised to harvest her wheat on shares, but a lot could happen, and she had learned to count on nothing until it was in her hand.

"Serena!" A clear voice called from a nearby buggy. Except for graying hair around the sides of her face, Auntie Karen looked exactly the same, even wearing the same black dress and shawl.

"Auntie Karen!" Serena's voice choked and tears sprouted from her eyes. She dropped her bundles onto the ground and fell into Auntie's strong arms, inhaling the lavender fragrance that Auntie always added to her homemade soap. "I've missed you!"

They kissed and hugged, cried some more and kissed again.

"How did you know I would arrive?"

"I read the coffee grounds." Karen wiped her tears and blew her nose with an embroidered handkerchief edged in fine Hardanger lace. "You know they're seldom wrong."

261

Just the mention of coffee grounds reduced Serena to gulping sobs. She clutched Auntie Karen and cried as if she'd never stop. "Oh, Auntie." Serena thought to tell her about the prediction being true, about the Indian with the black-and-green face, about Gust and Trygve and Tommy Harris.

Instead only one thing came out. "She was so beautiful." And then more tears.

"Shh . . . I know, child. I know."

After a long while Auntie Karen pulled back and patted Serena's mounding belly. "It's another girl!"

"How do you know?"

"It's always a girl when you carry high and forward," Auntie said.

"Gust wanted a boy this time." Sobs started, and Auntie Karen pulled her close again. "He wanted to name him after his brother."

"Shh . . . it's all right now," Auntie said. "You'll see. It will be all right."

Exhaustion washed over Serena. She clung to Auntie as they walked to the buggy. Auntie gathered the bundles and tucked them around Serena's feet.

"Is this everything?"

Serena nodded then noticed that Auntie was alone. Perhaps Mor was sick in bed. What if she had died? "Where are Mor and Far?" She held her breath until Auntie Karen replied. "I wasn't so sure of the coffee grounds that I dragged them along." She grinned.

Serena let out a sigh of relief. It couldn't be too bad if Auntie would joke about it.

SERENA'S EYES SWEPT OVER THE ROOM as she breathed in the memories. It was as if they thickened the air until she nearly choked. She had planned this moment for so long and now that it was here, she was too tired to even speak. She kissed her parents and sisters and then grabbed the railing for support before lowering herself to the stair.

"What is it?" Mor's brow furrowed. "Are you sick?"

Serena shook her head and swallowed hard.

"You're exhausted." Mor pulled the old gray shawl tighter around her shoulders and gave orders in quick succession. "Go right to bed. Jensina, fetch some buttermilk."

Though Serena protested, she was soon in her nightgown sipping buttermilk fetched from the cold storage cupboard suspended in the well. The cold drink was exactly what she needed after her weepy spell, but after only a few swallows, Serena set down the glass. She was too sleepy to finish it, too tired to keep her eyes open another minute.

Mor urged her under the covers and tucked her in. Serena surrendered to the luxury of being a daughter again. Through the window glass she could see the green leaves of her favorite oak and hear the cardinals singing from their nest. Serena closed her eyes and willed her body to relax.

"Rest yourself." Mor was all business. "We'll talk later."

AFTER A WHILE, SERENA OPENED HER EYES to see Mor sitting on the window seat, knitting in hand. Serena watched her mother a short while without speaking when suddenly, without warning, she imagined Lena toddling across the room, smiling with a new bottom tooth. A wave of grief pressed hard against Serena's windpipe, nearly taking her breath away.

She had thought the grief would stay behind.

"How are you?" Mor said when she noticed Serena was awake. "Do you feel any better?"

Serena nodded and reached for the buttermilk, too emotional to speak.

"I've worried about you." Mor laid down her knitting and searched her eyes. "Day and night, I worried." She worked her mouth and her voice cracked. "When the letters didn't come . . . the newspapers said all those terrible things. I knew you shouldn't marry him. I should have put my foot down."

"It wasn't your fault." The urge to defend Gust rose up in her throat, but Serena felt too weak to argue, and her feelings toward Gust were still too raw to discuss.

"It weren't tomatoes." Mor tilted her chin and squared her jaw. "I ate 'em every time."

"Really?"

"It was nothing you did." Mor picked up her knitting and purled with a vengeance, slipping the soft strands of gray yarn around the smooth wooden needles. "I lost two babies before the twins, and it were nobody's fault. Most women lose at least one."

Silence choked the room until Serena felt pressed in, almost trapped. She had forgotten how smothering home could feel. No matter what anyone said, she wouldn't be eating tomatoes this time. It wasn't worth the risk.

"Was Lena blonde like the twins?"

How good to hear Lena's name spoken aloud. "With a tinge of red, maybe. And Far's chin."

"Blue eyes?" Mor's face streamed with tears and she fished for a handkerchief in her pocket, gave up and wiped her faced on the hem of her apron.

Serena nodded and swallowed a sob. "And perfect little fingers with nails like pink shells."

They sat in silence for a long time. Serena pictured the map showing the lonely trail to Hutchinson, the unmarked grave along the road. "Someday I'll go back and put a marker on her grave."

"I'd like to have seen her." Mor knitted another row of what was growing into a baby dress.

"Sometimes I'm afraid that I'll forget how she looked." Serena's hands felt empty and she tucked them under the covers. Someday she would tell her mother about the mittens they had knitted at the fort. "On the way to Pomme de Terre we saw a tintype of a soldier, a perfect likeness."

"There'll be a tintype of this baby," Mor said. "I'll save the egg money."

"I'd like that." She feared she might forget how Gust looked, too, but she pushed the thought away. She didn't discuss Gust with her mother, not now, maybe never. Besides, this baby would look like Gust. She would see Gust every time she looked at her baby.

Serena imagined Gust limping down the road toward his father's farm. Someday soon she'd face his parents and try to explain what happened. It was like Gust to leave her with the unpleasant chore. There was no money to pay back the debt. Not unless some fool could be found to buy the farm.

She refused to think about that either. Not yet, anyway.

"I lost the *bunad*." It was easier to talk about things. "I'm sick about it. The Sioux burned it. I didn't even realize it was missing until weeks later."

"You're all that matters." Mor sniffed and turned the needles. "We're Americans now, no need to keep up with the old ways."

"And the quilt," Serena said. "Everything gone except Lena's blanket and the churn."

"It's a sturdy churn," Mor said. "Handy to have an extra when the heifers freshen."

Jensina and Jerdis argued in the kitchen about who would fetch the cows and who must wash the eggs. The pump squeaked as Far drew water for the chickens. The smell of Mor's fresh bread wafted up the stairway. The sounds and smells of home.

"Thank God you're here," Mor said. "Did you see the headlines? They finally killed Little Crow."

Serena recalled the naked Indians by their barn, the flour sifting through the cracks in the floor, the touch of the Indian who watched her write. No doubt the same one who had killed Gust and the soldiers. She shuddered.

Maybe it was best not to tell everything. At least not right away. She didn't have the strength to tell it all.

"Your far's been conscripted." Mor pulled the yarn so hard it puckered a stitch. "Abe Lincoln says every man under forty-five has to go unless he can pay $300." She pulled back the yarn, smooth the pucker. "Where are we supposed to get that kind of money?" She jerked the yarn again. It snapped in two.

"Nei!" Serena had heard the news at Fort Pomme de Terre but had never connected it with her father. "When does he have to go?"

"Late August." Mor retied the yarn and let the needles drop to her lap. "They're letting him stay until the grain is in." Tears rolled down her face. "I might as well tell you." Mor's looked around to make sure no one else was in the room. Her face looked anxious, and she lowered her voice to a whisper. "I'm with child. The baby's due early November."

A new baby! Serena was speechless. She should have guessed when Mor was poorly last spring. Most women kept bearing children until their late forties. She should have known.

"I've not said anything," Mor's voice sounded weary. She stood and cupped a hand over her rounded belly. "Your far has enough to worry about."

"Won't you tell him before he leaves?"

"Maybe," Mor sat down again and picked up her knitting. The only sound in the room was the click of needles and a chattering squirrel in the tree outside the window. Mor finished a row, turned the garment and stabbed the needle into the first stitch. "Thank God you're home. I don't know what I'd have done with both of you gone."

Her daughter kicked. Serena placed a hand on her belly and rubbed the little foot striking out again and again. "Auntie Karen says it's another girl." Tears welled in Serena's eyes and spilled over onto her cheeks. "I'll name her Lena Christine—after her sister."

"Good." Mor's chin jutted out, and she bit her lower lip. "This time things will be different."

"I was thinking how in the midst of living, everything seems wrong." Serena heard Jensina's voice calling the cows and saw her driving them with a willow switch. "When we lost our crop, when Lena got sick," Serena massaged the sore spot beneath her ribs and thought again of the grave along the trail, the shady spot by Fort Pomme de Terre where Gust and Tommy slept. "But it's in looking back I see how God was there."

How mysterious the ways of the Lord. How desperate she had been, how tempted to end it all if she couldn't leave Pomme de Terre. The soldiers' prayers were answered. She saw it clearly now. The Indian was too fascinated by the pen and ink to complete his murderous intent. She had been strong enough to put her foot down, to demand Gust do the right thing before she and the baby were killed. God had answered. At least part way.

"I've learned to believe." Serena thought about the cold winter days and Tommy Harris' prayers in the drafty attic. "At least I've learned that."

"You have to start somewhere."

Serena pictured the map of her long journey home. The bumpy stage and the endless trail. The smell of burning oak that propelled the *Time and Tide* down the Mississippi River. They had left with so many hopes and dreams. She returned without Gust. Without Lena. Without the dreams.

Auntie Karen would midwife at Serena's next childbed and stand as godmother. Far would leave with the army, but the war couldn't last forever. Her mother was carrying up front and high. Her new sister would be born with the winter. Somehow they'd make it.

"Our babies will grow up together," Mor said. "If it's a girl, I'll name her after Auntie Gunda."

For the first time in a long while, Serena's face relaxed into a smile.

THE END

Sources

Over the Earth I Come: The Great Sioux Uprising of 1862, Duane Schultz, St. Martin's Press, New York, 1992

The Sioux Uprising of 1862, Kenneth Carley, Minnesota Historical Society Press, St. Paul, Minnesota, 1976.

Dakota War Whoop: Indian Massacres and War in Minnesota, Harriet E Bishop, Edited by Dale L. Morgan, McConkey 1965.

The Great Sioux Uprising, C.M.Oehler, De Capo Press, New York, 1997.

Through Dakota Eyes, Edited by Gary Clayton Anderson and Alan R. Woolworth, Minnesota Historical Press, St. Paul, 1988.

"Fort Abercrombie 1862", Supplement of *Richland County Farmer-Globe*, Wahpeton, North Dakota, 1936.

Minnesota Days, Our Heritage in Stories, Art and Photos, Edited by Michael Dregni, Voyageur Press, Stillwater, Minnesota, 1999.

Ever the Land, A Homestead Chronicle, Ruben L. Parson, Adventure Publishing, Staples, Minnesota 1978.

It Really Happened Here, Amazing Tales of Minnesota and the Dakotas, Ethelyn Pearson, McCleary and Sons Publishing 2000.

The Peace Seekers, Dr. Elden Lawrence, Pine Hill Press, Sioux Falls, South Dakota, 2005.

Perryville, This Grand Havoc of Battle, Kenneth W. Noe, The University Press of Kentucky 2001.

The Soul of the Indian, Charles A. Eastman 1911, reprinted 1980 University of Nebraska Press 1980.

Indian Boyhood, Charles A. Eastman, McClure Phillips & Co., 1902.

Light on the Indian World, The Essential Writings of Charles Eastman, Edited by Michael O. Fitzgerald, World Wisdom, Inc. 2002.

Let Them Eat Grass Trilogy, John Koblas, North Star Press, St. Cloud, Minnesota, 2006.

Book Club Discussion Notes for *Pomme de Terre*

How are situations today similar to those in the 1860s?

    Marriages are not always successful

    Moving and starting over is always difficult

    World events and political situations impact individual lives

    Indian attacks similar to terrorist attacks of today—sudden without warning

    False reparation claims were filed after 9/11 as they were after the uprising

How have women's lives improved since the 1860s?

    Women can vote, own property, and have a say in their lives.

    Patriarchal authority is no longer the norm

    Modern medical care has decreased infant mortality and improved the lives of women

    Consider the benefit of the multiple support systems our society has in place to prevent the impact of catastrophic events such as war or natural disaster

In what ways have women's issues remained the same?

    Women still work hard for their families

    Modern stress is different but still challenging

    Illness, children, marriages, financial situations, and living away from family still cause anxiety and heartache

How might things have been different in 1862 had good communication systems existed?

It's been said that the government in 1862 wanted to free the slaves and kill the Indians. Do you think this is an accurate statement?

What can be done to right the injustices done to the Native Americans? Is it too late?

Who was your favorite character and why?

Has your opinion of the Sioux Uprising changed since reading Pomme de Terre?